We looked at each other, bashfulness striking us both at the same time. She was so exquisite my heart hurt to look at her. Her muscles were so developed that she seemed stocky despite her slight build, and yet she looked so vulnerable standing in front of me, pale skin gleaming, black hair tousled like a little boy's. If I didn't say something, I'd break apart.

"Liv," I whispered, trying to force air past the lump in my throat, "you are so beautiful, and I—"

"No." She touched my face. "Shh, you don't have talk."

Visit

Bella Books

at

BellaBooks.com

or call our toll-free number

1-800-729-4992

The Perfect Valentine

Edited by Therese Szymanski
and Barbara Johnson

Bella
BOOKS

2006

Bella Books, Inc.
P.O. Box 10543
Tallahassee, FL 32302

Printed in the United States of America on acid-free paper
First Edition

Editors: Barbara Johnson and Therese Szymanski
Cover designer: Sandy Knowles

ISBN 1-59493-061-9

To all those who love and are loved

Contents

A Valentine from Bella to You
All You Need is Love

This book is not to be read on the Beltway (one of us tried doing that while perusing submissions, and it didn't go well).

It's also not suggested reading for the doctor's office.

Ditto for at-work reading.

So, when is a good time to read this book? How about in the tub? After all, that's what it was created for. Beyond that, you should read it whenever you'd like to get turned on and wet. Preferably when you either have a partner to help you satisfy the urge or the time, talent and toys to do so yourself.

If you listen to the literary critics who tell us there are only ten plotlines in the whole of English literature, you might believe it isn't possible to create a truly original anthology. You might start to think anything written today is merely a rewrite of those ten plotlines, simply exercises in changing the protagonists and antagonists—mixing and matching and recombining. Not so. There are unique anthologies yet to be crafted and enjoyed, and we hope you will think so of the one you are currently holding. However, if you are expecting a collection of stories that try to prove how far we can delve into the realms of kink, this is not the book for you. These stories are not about how many different positions can be used, how many different twists can be thrown in, or how far we can go with literal bloodlust and still claim it's good sex.

It bothered us that so many stories, and entire anthologies, seem to exist to prove how hip humiliation and degradation can be without one iota of something as uncool as romance and love in the scene.

Frankly, we don't care what all the other kids on the block are doing. While others attempt something "new and different" by exploring extreme realms of S/M, BDSM, explicit cruelty, and whatever else they can think of, we prefer to focus on quality stories, good themes, and talented writers. We'll take our stand with stories that fall within loving, hot, and well-written parameters. We'll tell writers to surprise us—and you. We'll invest editorial energy in new writers so the future of lesbian erotica can be brighter. We'll understand that we're women and it doesn't have to hurt to be good.

We're willing to move forward by going back to basics. We're willing to stand out by giving you new dreams and fantasies to explore. We'll aim to be extraordinary by honoring the ordinary. We'll do our part by revering joy, love, hot sex, and downright good storytelling. For us, exploring this genre isn't a journey to the outer edges, but diving into the center of a lesbian's heart and mind. And, of course, her body—as often as possible.

We believe love and erotica go hand in hand. Like strawberries dipped in chocolate, you can have them separately, but together they are exquisite—especially when shared with the woman you love.

♥

We believe sex and love are not mutually exclusive—they go together like needle and thread, like red roses on Valentine's Day, like lube and a really big dildo.

We don't hold back—we believe in love, and just how fucking hot it can be. And that if you're in love, you ought to be fucking.

We believe in keeping things simple, so we have. We've found 23 stories that show what we wanted to tell you: That sex—and love—is sizzling hot.

It all comes down to the fact that sometimes you need a little ass fucking, and sometimes you don't. Sometimes you feel like some S/M or a scene with a stone butch, and sometimes you don't. But if you're the reader we're looking for, most of the time you feel like some love and hot sex between lesbians. Simple.

We hope you enjoy this book. It took a lot of time to make this happen, so it'd really suck if you didn't like it.

Happy Valentine's Day. We hope you get exactly what you want.

Barbara Johnson

Do Overs
Karin Kallmaker

She said she had something special planned. Today, the seventh anniversary of our first date, I woke to find a note on the bathroom mirror that said simply, "It's time for another first date. See you there."

All day at work I mulled over what she meant. Our first date had been, well, *uneven* was generous. We'd been introduced at a party and a flame had definitely flickered. She'd called the very next day to ask me out.

At home after work I found no further information, but it was obvious she had been there. I peeked under the covers on the neatly made bed and saw that towels were already in place. Candles waited on the bedside tables, ready to be lit, but the fire inside me was already leaping. Thinking it was hardly fair for me to be the only one squirming through dinner, I searched the back of the closet for the dress I'd worn that night, seven years ago. If she wanted another first date, she'd have to endure me wearing the crimson dress she'd sworn I would never keep on for longer than five minutes.

I was on time to Artorio's, the restaurant where we had agreed to meet seven years ago. Tonight, however, I wasn't shocked to realize it was Valentine's Day. Neither of us had had any thought of February 14 when we'd chosen the time and place to meet. Long out of the dating pool and both of us with little expectation of more than a heated fling, our date had been simply set for "Friday night."

Seven years ago she had been flustered and embarrassed that there was no way we'd get a table that night, nor at any of the other nearby restaurants we'd tried. Fog had blown in, the night had turned colder than my little crimson dress could cope with, but, for me, everything was okay when she draped her purple suede jacket over my shoulders. The scent of her cologne surrounded me with warmth.

We had our first date at Taco Town. There were no hearts or roses.

Tonight I was ushered to a table in the darkest corner Artorio's had to offer, and there she was, looking just like she had that night in black slacks, a white silk blouse and the very same suede jacket. She even wore her dark hair down around her shoulders. She rose, but didn't kiss me—instead, a nervous hug.

"You look wonderful," I said, which was true.

Her gaze flicked over my body. "So do you. That color is perfect for you." She looked me in the eye, then, a smoldering look. "Thank you for wearing the dress."

"You're welcome." I ran my hand over the jacket, loving the way the suede brushed to a deeper purple. "Are we really pretending this is our first date?"

"Yes. Except this time we're not strangers." She leaned over to whisper in my ear, "I know exactly what you like and I'm going to give it to you."

I flushed, then chilled. Her arm was quickly around me, and I instinctively tipped my head back for a kiss.

She looked at my upturned face, her eyes smoky, and said,

"That's right. You're mine and you were since the moment we met."

I nearly smiled—she had not been this assertive that first night. We'd eaten tacos, sparingly, and she'd looked morose at times. Later she admitted she was certain I would give her a brush-off hug at my door.

We ordered drinks and shared a salad. Artorio's made wonderful pastas and served them generously, but we chose just one entrée and shared that as well. Her hand constantly brushed my thigh, my hip, my arm and in a hundred little ways she made me feel that I was beautiful. Her touch told me that later she was going to take me to bed and show me, over and over, that I was the center of her passionate being.

Penne nearly consumed, her fingertips lazily stroking the back of my neck, she said conversationally, "That dress is wicked."

"I don't know what made me wear it seven years ago. I didn't usually . . . make such a statement on a first date."

She brushed her lips against my ear lobe for just a moment. "You wanted to be made love to."

"I wanted to be fucked senseless that night," I said in a low voice. "As you discovered."

Her laugh was low and knowing. "It took me a while to believe it."

I flushed and she had to have seen it. My nipples tightened against the cool lace of my bra. That night, at my door I had allowed a nervous kiss. The date hadn't been a success and yet I was wanting to take her inside. Her arms had been tight and warm. There was a look in her eye, sometimes, that said she wanted to gobble me up. Whatever it was, the very useless panties I wore were soaked.

I leaned back enough to gaze into her eyes. Though it was nothing new to her I wanted to remind her of how I had felt. "I thought it was just hormones and you were hot and sexy. It wasn't until you put your hands on me that I realized it was you making me dizzy. You still make me dizzy."

Her hand crept over my thigh and I wanted to spread myself for her. "Baby, oh baby, I didn't know you could give yourself like that—"

"Neither did I—"

"I didn't love you the way I should have."

I was amazed to see the glimmer of tears in her eyes. "It was still good."

"But not all it could be."

"Is any first date all it can be?"

"Tonight," she whispered, "is a do over. This is how I wish our first date had gone."

One fingertip brushed just high enough to flick the lace edge of my panties. She watched the shudder travel my body. "Let's skip dessert."

"Okay," she breathed. "But honey . . ."

I closed my eyes as that fingertip flicked the lace again. I wanted to feel her whole hand cupping me.

"Look at me," she said, her voice low and taut.

I managed to open my eyes and the shimmer in her gaze, even through the fog of my rising lust, sent a thrill through my stomach. "Yes, lover?"

She gave a little gasp because that word drove her crazy and I knew it. That I could use it, even as turned on as I was, also stoked her fires. She liked me sexy and beguiling but at some point during the night, she wanted me to become so utterly hers that I forgot how to tease her back. "Are you listening?"

I nodded, my heart pounding.

"I am going to love you tonight. There is nothing I won't do to you. But if you come without my permission the date is over."

I moaned. My eyes closed. I felt muscles in my abdomen shifting as I grappled to sort them out, control the ones I knew I would have to keep in check until she let me explode. I would have to stay focused on my body while she did everything in her power to lift me outside of it.

"That's right," she whispered. "I wanted you like that our first date, but I didn't know you could take it. I wouldn't let myself believe I'd found a woman who wanted what I needed to give."

Swollen with desire, I felt as if the single tie on my dress was going to pop. She touched me lightly as we left the restaurant, her hand at the small of my back. On the sidewalk, she quickly flagged a cab and we were inside the dark backseat within moments.

She cuddled me into her arms, kissed me. Lightly touched my knee, my thigh. Pulled me to her a little closer. Ran her fingers over the tie of my dress with a look that said, "Yes, I know. All I have to do is pull and you're mine."

Every kiss left me wanting. Every touch made me ache for more firm caresses.

That night, seven years ago, she had touched me like this—her hands teasing and arousing, her mouth promising intense intimacy. We'd stood at my front door for over fifteen minutes before I found the wits to say, "Would you like to come in?"

Huskily, she had answered, "Very much so."

We had made it no farther than the other side of the door for at least another fifteen minutes. Long, languid kisses, heated licks and nibbles, but her hands never strayed south of my waist. I was all but wiping my crotch on her slacks, saying Yes with my body as loud as I knew how, but she would only kiss me and hold me.

Finally, I had pushed her hand down my hips. Her moan had been earthy as she flattened me against the door. "Yes?"

"Yes," I had moaned back. I wanted her to shove her fingers into me, take me right there.

She didn't. We were writhing against each other, her breathing as hot and ragged as mine. I had wondered what more permission she needed. "Take me to bed, please."

She had kissed me deeply and possessively then, and I had thought, "Now we're getting somewhere."

"Which way is the bedroom?"

"Down the hall, past all the books, and turn right."

Her gaze turned devilish and the next thing I knew she'd scooped me up into her arms to carry me bride-over-the-threshold style.

My feet hit the hallway wall and her grip slipped slightly. Instead of being up on her waist, I started to sag and, as I discovered that night, there is nothing at all sexy about being carried in a way that makes you feel as if your butt is going to drag on the ground.

We arrived at the bedroom with me feeling like my ass was an anchor and her slightly out of breath. We fell on the bed. When I could see her face she looked morose again.

"That didn't go quite as I had hoped."

"This is where I want to be." My little crimson dress had slipped down my shoulders, revealing the matching, inadequate, lace bra. I kicked off my shoes and reached for the single tie that kept the dress around me.

"Let me," she said. She kissed me hungrily and I forgot all about how we'd gotten on the bed. My clothes were askew and she was still dressed. I liked the vulnerable feeling and I wanted to be naked for her. Something about her excited me in ways I'd nearly given up wanting.

Breathing heavily and explosively wet, I watched her pull on the tie. The bow loops moved and she pulled a little harder. Then we were both looking at a knot.

"Just tear it," I had said, desperate to be hers.

"No, the dress is beautiful and I don't want to ruin it."

"Then I'll leave it on."

"I want you naked," she'd muttered.

That first date had nearly ended there. Tonight she was leading me up the steps to the apartment we now shared and I didn't think there would be any trouble with knots.

Her arms went around me as she put the key in the lock and we kissed for several minutes before she turned it. She undid my hair clip and filled her hands with the curls she loved as we explored each others' mouths. Her touch stayed tantalizingly away from where I wanted her most and I wondered if she wanted to replay that long, long session of teasing.

Finally, she ushered me inside, and the door had barely closed behind us before she backed me up against it. Her thigh was suddenly pressing hard between my legs, hard enough to lift me onto my tiptoes.

"This is what you wanted, isn't it? You wanted it, just like this."

"Yes, baby, you know I did."

Her hand was under my dress, fingers slipping past the lace of my panties. "I can feel how wet you are through my slacks." She leaned in close and said very quietly, "Wet enough to be fucked?"

"Yes. Please."

"Wet enough for how hard you want it?"

I whimpered. I could feel myself melting into desire, safe to let myself want everything she had ever done to me, to fit seven years into one night. She would not make me feel dirty for wanting her so much, for loving sex like this, and she would not leave me wanting.

I made myself refocus on her words, but it was hard when my panties were plastered to my crotch and the tips of her fingers brushed over my pubic hair.

"I've learned that I can have you right away, make you come for me, and still enjoy all the teasing and seduction afterward, because we both know you'll want more. We both know I can't wait to give you more."

"Please," I panted, "will you . . . will you come while you fuck me?"

She growled into my neck, nipping lightly. "I might. If you can take it long enough."

I shuddered as I raised my head. My body was in flight, but I would not let the challenge go unmatched. "I will take everything you give me. I know you'll give me everything you can."

Her fingers sank into my swollen, slick folds, squeezing me possessively. "God, you're soaked."

"For you, baby." My voice gave way to a rising cry as muscles clenched and ached.

"Don't come," she said sharply. "Not yet. I haven't fucked you yet."

Through gritted teeth I answered, "You've been fucking me since the restaurant. I'm so turned on, so high, baby, *please*."

"I love you like this. And like this . . ." Her fingers slipped inside me, then her thigh pushed them deeper. "Oh, yes. You feel so fuckable tonight. This is how I wanted it that first night, to have you just like this."

She was as turned on as I was and the knowledge only aroused me further. This was what I had wanted, too. She fucked me harder and faster, pinning me to the door. My legs were nearly limp. The only muscles in my body that wanted to move were surrounding her fingers. Release . . . I needed release.

"Come now," she whispered. "I want to feel it."

I cried out as I shook against her. All the while her voice filled my head with a continuous moan of pleasure. I loved the way she made me feel, but even more I loved the way my responsive abandon turned her on.

My insides had not stopped quivering when she said, "Let's go, baby. I'm taking you to bed."

She wrapped my legs around her waist and pulled me hard against her. My engorged clit ground against her large belt buckle as her hands cupped my ass. We kissed, hot, hard, frantic, as she carried me down the hall. The light switch was pressed up by a swipe of her shoulder. Next to the bed she continued to hold me just a little while longer. "I think you are liking your legs around me."

"You know I am," I whispered. I felt slightly more composed as she let my legs slip to the ground. Only as I stepped back did I realize she was already pulling on the tie to my dress.

The bow unraveled smoothly and with another of her primal growls, she stripped the dress roughly off of me and pulled me into her arms. I kissed her dizzily, eagerly, then gasped as she pushed me onto the bed, my bra dangling from her hand. The look in her eyes stole my breath as she pulled down my panties, shrugged out of her jacket, and fell onto my naked body.

Seven years ago she had slowly worked out the knot, then gently eased the dress from my shoulders. We'd coiled into each other, kissing, stripping, hands wandering. Slow and sweet, her touch had been at times gentle enough to make me cry.

I knew, by morning, that I had sensed more to her than sweet and gentle. That she could be that way was important, yes—sometimes I need gentleness. She opened a part of me that night and yet there was a part of me that she hadn't touched, not the way I had wanted. We had made love, but we hadn't fucked. I was satisfied and frustrated all at once.

But tonight, after seven years of exploring our boundaries and pleasures, she wasn't being gentle with me. She knew she didn't have to be. We had both learned.

"This is what I wanted from you, the moment we met." She shoved my legs apart and gazed down at me, plainly desirous. "I love your cunt. I love it wet and red and full like this."

She bent to me, capturing my clit between her lips. She squeezed, tugged, pulled, then played her tongue over it. I lifted my hips to her, wanting to give her everything she might ask for, and her hands clamped onto my thighs, holding me down while she feasted on me.

My nails raked over my breasts as I writhed against her mouth. I felt opened by her tongue. My nipples ached for attention and I twisted both, knowing if she was watching she would enjoy the sight.

The delight between my legs abruptly stopped. "Leave those to me." She lifted my hands from my breasts and stretched my arms over my head. "Tonight I'll do all the touching."

Her body was stretched the length of mine and the scratch of fabric against my bare skin drew shudders from me. "Please," I whispered, though I could not have explained what it was I was pleading for.

"You're moving too much, baby. I want you right here on the bed when I get back."

"Where are you going?" The fog in my eyes cleared a little as I gazed at her in alarm.

She settled astride my hips, one hand still holding my wrists over my head. I watched as she slowly unclasped and removed her belt. "I want to get ready to love you all night. To do everything I wish I had the very first time. Don't let go."

Panting, I watched her wrap her belt around my wrists, then around the spindle in the headboard. I could free myself in a matter of moments and she knew that. The tight leather of her belt was only a reminder of the order she'd given, and I would follow it willingly, not because she forced me. "I won't. I won't let go."

She kissed me hungrily and her fingers found both of my nipples. "I'll take care of these. And you."

I hissed as she twisted them slowly, then flicked her tongue just once over each red tip. Then she was off of me. She flipped off the bedroom light as she went into the bathroom.

The dark calmed me a little, and as my breathing quieted I heard the sound of drawers opening and closing and water running. It was only a few minutes before she said softly, from the doorway, "That night you were so beautiful. I wanted to look right for you. But we both know I prefer being more comfortable when I'm fucking you."

A match flared and one of the candles blossomed into soft light. I gasped, reflexively pulled on the belt, and all the calm I'd felt fled as my body tightened in response to the sight of her. She'd pulled her hair back into a tight, low ponytail, leaving her angular face and dark eyes exposed. The white muscle tee was one of my favorites because of the way it framed her strong shoulders. Slowly, my gaze moved down to linger on the obvious swells of her breasts. I licked my lips, thinking how much I liked the texture and taste of her nipples when they were that hard.

I could hear my heart pounding inside my head. I wanted to look at what she had on below her waist, and yet, for just a moment, I resisted. I knew what I'd see and once I did I would lose control. I would be hers and unable to talk or even think. "I love that shirt, but could you take it off? I want to feel your skin."

She had one hand hooked on the waistband of familiar denim cutoffs. I didn't look lower. Not yet, I told myself. With a soft smile, she said, "Okay. But that's the last thing you ask for. After this, it's what I want to do to you."

She peeled the tee up her torso and I moaned looking at her wonderful body. She shied away from any profession I made about her beauty, but she could have been a sculptor's model for a sexual, powerful nymph with luscious breasts, broad shoulders and muscular arms. She was a beautiful, strong woman.

"Thank you," I whispered.

Then I looked down.

God, those cutoffs. They'd been washed hundreds and hundreds of times the last seven years. She had never put them on without them getting wet from one or both of us. The zipper bulged and I groaned. From the size of it, she might have chosen the biggest toy but it didn't matter. Whatever the size, shape, color, it was her cock, and she was going to take care of me with it.

My mouth was watering and I started to let go of the confining leather. I wanted to unzip those shorts and feel her cock heavy in my hand. I wanted to smear it with lube and guide it into me, and then beg. And beg.

"Don't let go," she said sharply. She leaned over me, pulling my hips down so that my arms stretched more tautly over my head. "You're mine."

"Yes, lover, yours, always." All I could think about was her cock inside me. Was there anything else I should have been worried about? A thousand distractions exist in every moment of daily life but when she laid her body on top of mine it all went away. There was only one imperative in my mind: being hers. Whatever she wanted, whatever turned her on, however she wanted to fuck me, take me, I was hers.

The kisses were wild, bruising our mouths. She rubbed the

bulge of her cutoffs into my cunt as I wrapped my legs around her waist.

"Oh, yes," she breathed as she arched her hips against mine. "Oh yes, we're going to fuck all night."

My eyes threatened to roll back into my head. She was riding my clit and I wanted to come so badly I was losing track of the room with the effort of holding it back. I was guided only by her touch and the ragged edge of her breathing, that is, until another noise intruded.

I didn't place it right away, then my entire body jerked as I recognized the sound of her zipper. "Yes, please, baby. Please fuck me. Please, I need it."

I begged. I knew she was going to fuck me until I couldn't move, until the words were all gone and I had forgotten my name, but I begged anyway. She could have no question as I arched under her, again and again, trying to find her cock with my sweating, dripping cunt.

"This was how I wanted you that very first night," she said in my ear. "I wanted to love you like this. Part of me knew this is how we'd be together, but I didn't trust it. Now I do. I love you, baby, and now I know . . . this . . . is . . . what you want."

She pushed in and didn't stop. Pulled out and pushed in again, harder.

I yelped, yanked with all my strength on her belt and tilted my hips to take her next thrust. "Do you hear it? Do you hear my cunt?"

"God, yes." She was moving faster and faster, holding me tighter and tighter. Every delicious inch of her split me open more and more until I knew we were flying. She groaned into my ear and I could feel her own climbing passion. I wanted to come, I needed to come, but if I could take it, if I could hold on, she'd reach that place inside her head where fucking me was so good that she melted. I wanted her that high, too.

So I held on. I had forgotten why I was clinging to her belt, but

I held on. I didn't come, I fought it, tightened, relaxed, screamed with the difficulty of holding it back and I gave her my cunt to fuck, to love, to enjoy.

"Oh," she panted. "Oh, you're so wet. The sound of my cock in all that wet . . . oh."

I was saying something, over and over, but the sense of it escaped me. Thoughts were trapped inside my mind while she used my body, pleasured me, pleasured herself.

She shoved into me and froze and in the candlelight her eyes would not let mine go. We strained, unblinking, mouths trembling, then she said, her voice deep in her throat, "Come. Come for me."

My body convulsed as every muscle reacted to her order. My strangled cry twined with her guttural shout as I shook under her.

"God, how do you do that? I can feel you squeezing my cock, don't stop, baby, don't stop coming, oh like that!"

She was moving again and so was I. My climax had crested and we were on to the next. Her arms were shaking as she held herself above me and our gazes were so deep into each other I could see her pupils flicker with the candlelight.

The bed rocked under us as we rose and fell together. With a little groan, she used one hand to free my wrists and I gratefully ran my hands over her sweating back, then around to her breasts as they moved against mine. I had not known seven years ago how to touch her. I had no clue how to break through that highly sexual but highly guarded top energy. It had taken me years to accept that my every moan of pleasure was hers as well. She poured her energy and power into me. Every orgasm was as much hers as mine.

But I knew this, now. My fingertips captured her nipples and squeezed, hard.

"Oh, fuck," she moaned. She let her weight fall on me and grappled for my arms. "You're not going to behave unless I hold you down, are you?"

Seven years ago, at this point, we were cuddling and softly

entwined. Tonight, even though we reached a level where we held each other and could only breathe, I knew we were just getting started.

Moving together I could feel time blurring. How long, how deep, how hard ceased to matter. I felt her love for me from the inside out. She moaned against me every time I swelled to her touch, and her hands possessed me.

With a deep sigh, after what might have been hours, she peeled herself off of me. I groaned slightly as my legs finally unwrapped from her waist. "Oh . . . cramp."

She massaged my inner thighs with a smile, making sympathetic noises as my muscles involuntarily trembled. "Relax, honey. Just relax for a bit."

"How am I supposed to relax with you between my legs wearing that wonderful toy?"

After a short forage in the bedside table drawer, she turned to me with a smug grin as she set a little gold box on my tummy. "This will help. Happy Valentine's Day."

"Oh, sweetie." I was so intent on the aroma of chocolate I didn't realize she'd found something else until a long-stemmed white rose joined the box. "How romantic. You are so good to me."

"And don't you forget it." She opened the gold box and withdrew a dark truffle in the shape of a heart.

I watched in surprise as she bit into it. "Hey, I thought those were . . . oh."

She leaned over me, offering the treat to me with her teeth. Laughing, I nibbled, then bit down. Soft caramel threatened to spill down my chin so I quickly licked my lips. Then it made sense to lick hers and we were abruptly, feverishly sharing the sweet textures with our tongues.

I shuddered as I felt her cock slip into me and still we kissed, my hands roaming her back and stroking her ass as she slowly moved inside me. The chocolate endorphins sent wonderful zings through my blood as her cock brushed over my engorged nerves and I found myself laughing.

"What?" She paused, gazing down at me.

"Oh, lover," I said quickly, fearing I'd hurt her feelings. "It feels so good. Everything feels so good."

She settled on top of me again, resuming her slow, steady movements. "Well, that's a first. I don't think I've ever fucked you until you laughed before."

"I feel wonderful."

"Good. You're supposed to."

"How about you?"

"You take my breath away, every time. What more is there—smart, beautiful, a good kisser, and hell on wheels in the sack."

"Well," I added, "and I love you, madly."

Her eyes lightened as she smiled. "Yeah. And I love you—oh fuck! That hurts!"

"What, baby?" I watched helplessly as she scrambled to her feet.

"The damn rose—thorn got me right in the boob. I knew there was something I'd forgotten to move." She brushed off the flower.

She showed me the reddened puncture mark and I kissed it tenderly as I perched on the edge of the bed. "I'm so sorry. It's a love wound."

She sighed as I wrapped one arm around her waist. I nibbled my way across her breast as I took hold of her cock. The texture of her hard nipple against my lips was wonderful to me. "This is better than chocolate."

"Sweet talker—oh, bad girl." I bit down on her nipple and she shivered. "Mmm . . . you need to stop doing that, because I'm not done with you."

"I've just started with you. That first night I didn't touch you at all, and we're having do overs, aren't we?" I gently drew her down on top of me, and, as soon as she relaxed, leveraged her over on to her back.

She laughed in my face. "Do you really think you can hold me down?"

"Yes," I said softly. I tugged hard enough on her cock for her to glance down. "I know just what will keep you on your back."

Her eyes glowed as she watched me slowly settle on her cock. "Okay, you win."

"I thought so. I love you." I closed my eyes as I took her as deep as I could, arching my back and stretching my arms over my head. When I opened my eyes she was smiling at me. "What?"

"You're beautiful."

"You're biased." She shifted her hips and I put my hands on her chest with a gasp. "Oh, like that."

Her hands gripped my shoulders, holding me firmly down on her. "You seem distracted. I thought you were going to do me."

I let out something between a laugh and a groan. "I *am* doing you."

She arched, knocking the breath out of me. "Take your time and enjoy yourself. Honey . . . what are you doing?"

I leaned down to grapple between the mattresses, finally touching the small item I'd tucked there earlier. "Getting your, oh . . . yes."

She guided me firmly down on her cock. "I don't care what it is. You need to stay right there."

"Valentine's present," I managed to finish. I handed her the small packet.

"Sex Cheques?"

"Uh-huh. You can cash them whenever you want. Thought you . . . oh." Something about the position was just right. The inside of me was loving her cock more every minute. "You might want to use one tonight."

"Hmm." She read aloud, "'Good for one bubble bath.' Well, maybe later. Oh, here we go. 'Sex until we can't move.' Let's do that."

"Okay." I closed my eyes again, savoring the feel of her inside me. Tonight it felt as if I would never get enough.

"You're still moving," she said.

"I need to."

"So I guess we're not done."

I shook my head as I lost all my words again. Her fingertip touched my clit and I quivered.

"Look at me."

It was hard to focus on her, but I managed.

"We're not done," she said, and I was surprised to see tears in her eyes. "Not tonight, not ever. You and I will never be done."

A sensation swooped through the pit of my stomach, the same one that had happened seven years ago when I'd woken up in the morning with her still in my bed. The way we fit, laughed, loved, fucked—nothing could feel more right than the way we loved each other.

We laced our fingers together as I moved more and more frantically. Gazing down at her, basking in the fierce love I saw in her eyes, I promised myself that in seven years she would wake to find a note from me asking for another first date.

I wanted do overs with her for the rest of my life.

Secrets of the Heart
Radclyffe

I must have looked suspicious because the sales clerk moved to the end of the counter nearest me, leaned his elbows on the smudged glass surface, and fixed me with a baleful stare. I suppose the fact that I'd been standing in front of the card rack for twenty minutes, unmoving, struck him as odd. If he'd known me, he wouldn't have found it strange. He might even have appreciated how impossible it was for me to choose a Valentine's Day card for this particular woman.

From the instant I'd scanned the messages scattered over the ubiquitous pink and red cards, I'd known it was hopeless.

Be Mine. Forever Yours. Your Forever Love.

Perfect sentiments, and everything I wanted to say. Except she didn't know, and I didn't dare tell her.

"Help you with something?" he grunted.

When I didn't answer, he probably thought I was crazy or just plain rude. He had no way of knowing that I wasn't seeing any of the cards and that his voice barely registered as background noise. I was replaying the conversation I'd had over breakfast that morning with the woman who had put me in such a quandary.

"So," Sheri said as she stuck her head in the refrigerator and rummaged around on *her* shelf for something I wouldn't even recognize as food, "got a date tonight?"

"Uh-uh," I replied around a mouthful of last night's pepperoni pizza. We'd agreed when we moved in together that we'd keep our food separate because she pronounced my eating habits "disgusting," and I contended that cold pizza and beer was an All-American meal. On the other hand, yogurt and granola and things that resembled the stuff that came out of a lawnmower bag struck me as being unnatural.

She turned around and leaned her back against the closed enamel door, spoon in one hand, a carton of purplish, gooey stuff in the other, wearing only a lacy white bra and very, very tiny bikini panties. In between those minuscule scraps of material masquerading as garments was an acre or so of alabaster skin that stretched and dipped over one of the nicest landscapes I'd ever seen. The rosy areola blushed beneath the snowy white silk as if embarrassed by my scrutiny, and I hastily looked out the window. I fixed on the latticework of telephone wires superimposed on the zigzag line of the fire escape that hung by a few loose bolts from the adjoining apartment building. If I squinted, the view resembled a Mondrian, which was far safer for my blood pressure than the image of a Judy Francisconi calendar model that I saw every time I looked at Sheri. Being an MFA grad student tended to make me think like that. Sheri, on the other hand, was studying modern dance. Her body was her instrument, and she thought nothing of displaying it. We were roommates. I was gay. She wasn't.

In all fairness, it wasn't that she didn't think of me as a sexual being when she walked around the apartment in less than a chin-to-ankle cloak, which is probably the only kind of garment that *wouldn't* have made my heart sing and my lower regions beat out a frantic rhythm in accompaniment. She was just comfortable in her skin and had no idea that I dreamed about using her body as my canvas to paint upon. I had decided months ago on gold body paint. Just a subtle rendering, to accent the already perfect picture—a circle around her right nipple, connected by a diagonal slash across her high arched ribs to a ring that rimmed her shallow bellybutton. I could feel her skin beneath my fingertips as I spread the wet glitter along the path my tongue longed to follow, ending in a dusting of promises in the blonde curls between her thighs. My gold-tipped fingers would guide her legs apart, and then I would lower my head to—

"Davy? Da-vi-da. Hel-lo-o."

I jumped and flushed. Or, flushed *more*, to be strictly accurate. Sheri stopped with her spoon halfway to her mouth and looked at me with an odd expression. "What's the matter with you? You look sick."

Lovesick, maybe.

"Nothing," I croaked. Then I coughed, trying to cover how tight my throat had become as I'd made my imaginary journey down her body. My hands trembled, and I shoved them between my blue jean clad thighs.

"So?" she asked.

I shook my head, totally befuddled. Had we been talking about something? My nipples were stiff beneath my T-shirt, tingling and tight, unashamedly clamoring for attention. The rest of me was on point too—hard and wet, the desire to taste her skin so intense it sucked all the blood and good sense from my brain. Jesus, it was getting so I couldn't be around her for more than five minutes without going crazy. "So, what?" I finally managed.

She cocked a hip, which tightened that little patch of silk flush across her mound, hinting at the prominence of her clitoris where the tantalizing rise gave way to the valley beyond. I brushed the back of my hand over my mouth, afraid I might be drooling.

"Do. You. Have. A. Date. Tonight?"

"It's Tuesday," I said stupidly.

"It's Valentine's Day, so that doesn't count."

Valentine's Day. *But I want you to be my Valentine.*

"Oh. No. I forgot."

I supposed I should ask her the same thing, but I just didn't want to know. It was getting harder and harder to watch her go out on dates and then spend the night pretending I wasn't thinking about what she was doing, or about what someone might be doing *to* her. I'd envision her in her sexy short skirts and tight little tops, having dinner with some guy, or dancing with him, or—uh-uh, no. I couldn't go there. In fact, I'd started spending more and more Friday and Saturday nights away from the apartment just so I wouldn't see her going out. I was getting to be a regular at the all-night movie theater around the corner on Chestnut.

"Does that mean no date?" she probed.

I nodded.

She gave me a quick little smile and dropped her spoon into the sink. Then she leaned over, opened the cabinet beneath it, and discarded her yogurt container. When she straightened up, my eyes were still leveled at the place where her breasts had been seconds before, riveted on the nipples just peeking out over the scalloped lace edges. I tore my eyes up her body to her face, and she grinned.

"Me neither," Sheri said. "Wanna have dinner with me?"

"Sure. You want to try that sushi place we read about in the *Weekender*?"

Her smile got kind of funny, as if I'd missed something.

"No, I thought we'd eat here. You buy some wine, and I'll make dinner."

"Like cook?"

She walked past me and ran her fingers through my hair. "Yes, dummy. Like cook."

Be Mine. Forever Yours. Your Forever Love.

I stared at the cards. It was impossible. She'd think I was crazy. I turned around and walked out of the drugstore empty-handed.

I did better with the wine. Sheri pronounced it, "Yum. Good."
"That looks good too."

I stood behind her as she stirred colorful things that didn't
really look like food together in a big pan on top of the stove, her
wine glass on the counter beside her. She'd pulled her thick blonde
hair up off her neck and held it in place with a tortoiseshell comb.
A few wisps had escaped, and they trailed down over her throat.
The steam, spicy and rich, rose from whatever it was she was cooking and mingled with something sweeter, something *her*. I leaned
in closer to breathe her scent, and my crotch brushed over her ass.
The touch charged through me, setting every nerve ending ablaze.
For a second I was so stunned, I didn't move. Then, before I could
jump away, she gave a little roll of her hips and pushed back into
me. That's when I knew I'd lost my mind. Because she couldn't be
doing that. Could she?

"Davy?"

"Huh?"

"Reach up to that cabinet right over my head and get me the
cumin, will you?"

"Sure."

To accomplish the task, I had to lean against her and stretch
over her shoulder. I had a choice of steadying myself on the burner
or her waist, which was bare for a good eight inches between the
bottom of her tight, black-cropped T-shirt and the top of her hip
huggers. I hesitated for a few seconds, figuring the end result
would be pretty much be the same. Whether I stuck my hand in
the fire or rested my palm against her skin, I was going to go up in
flames.

"Something wrong?"

I swear she did that thing with her hips again, and I had to lock
my knees to stay standing. What the hell, if I was going to burn, it
might as well be worth it. I curved my hand around her waist and
reached up over her head. "Not a thing."

I was right. Her skin was hot. Hot and smooth and so fucking
soft. The tips of my nipples ached as my chest brushed over her

back. My crotch was so tight up against her now that my fly nestled in the little cleft between her cheeks. My clit was so hard it felt like it was going to come bursting right out through the faded denim.

"Don't move," Sheri said in a tight little whisper as she did something in front of her to make the steam disappear. Then she leaned back against me, turned her head, and licked my neck.

I forgot about the cumin and wrapped both arms around her waist. If I turned my palms up I'd be holding her breasts, and there wouldn't be any way I could pretend *that* was an accident. I was shaking all over; I couldn't move a muscle.

She pivoted in my arms and slid hers around my neck. Her face was very close, and she had that little smile again, the one that said I was still missing the punchline.

"What?" I whispered.

"How long have we been roommates?" She kissed the tip of my chin.

"Ten months."

I edged my hand under the back of her shirt and stroked my fingers up and down her spine. She threaded her fingers into my hair and rubbed against the front of my body like a cat.

"You haven't been around much on the weekends the last couple months," she commented. She kissed the corner of my mouth, then very daintily bit the center of my lower lip.

I was still reeling from the heat of her mouth when she yanked my T-shirt from my jeans and pushed it out of the way so she could slide her bare belly over mine. She did that a few times while she kissed me for real, her tongue slicking in and out of my mouth like steam running down the windowpane, hot on cold, and wet. My thighs started shaking the way they do when I have to come really bad, and I knew I wasn't going to be able to hold us both up much longer. I walked her a couple steps to the right until her butt bumped up against the counter. I grabbed onto it, bracing my arms on either side of her hips.

"What are you doing, Sheri, huh?" I muttered while I grazed my teeth down her neck.

She arched her back and gave me her throat, and while I sucked, she gasped, "When's the last time . . . you saw me go . . . out on a date?"

"Don't know."

I bunched her T in my fist and dragged it up to get at her breasts, licking at her nipples while I shifted just enough to get her thigh between my legs. She grabbed my ass and squeezed while she pushed her breast into my mouth. My teeth were going to leave marks.

"That's because . . . it's been months, you dummy."

She took one hand off my butt and scrabbled around on the kitchen counter while I lost myself in the wild race of her heart and the piercing pleasure of her leg squeezing my clit while I rode her. She pulled my head up with a hand in my hair and waved a little white square in front of my face.

"Here," she said breathlessly, her eyes huge, her lips swollen and the color of Valentines. "This is for you."

She started opening my fly while I struggled with the little envelope. My hands were shaking so badly it took forever, but I finally fished out the simple red heart with the white letters that said, *Be My Valentine*. Underneath the words, she'd written *I Love You, Sheri*.

So easy, after all. I said yes, and then I kissed her and kept kissing her while I undressed her. She tried to do the same with me, but I brushed her hands away. I had not yet given her *her* Valentine. I knelt between her legs and followed with my mouth the secret path I had painted on her body so many times in my mind, tracing my tongue over her softness, her sweetness, her sharp tangy places, until she started making little whimpering noises, and I knew it was time to tell her all the things I'd been wanting to say to her for forever. I pressed my fingers to her thighs, teasing her clitoris with my tongue until she got impossibly hard and her fingers clenched fitfully in my hair.

"You're making me come," she whispered, a note of awe in her voice.

Be Mine.

"Oh. You are. You're making me come right now."

I love you.

"Please there. I'm coming. There, there, oh there . . ."

Forever Yours.

"There," she sobbed. "Oh now . . . now . . . now . . ."

I closed my eyes and sucked her gently until I felt her swell and burst inside my mouth.

Your Forever Love.

By Any Other Name
Heather Osborne

"Valentine's Day is a fraud," Kim said, two plastic shamrocks waving and dipping from the springs attached to her headband.

Amy wrinkled her nose at the green beer the bartender thrust in front of her. She didn't have a taste for beer, especially beer with green froth that looked like it would be better suited to a beaker in a mad scientist's lab. "It's a celebration of love," she said.

"It's an excuse for couples to brag that they aren't alone." Kim tapped the beer glass. "Are you going to drink that?"

Amy shook her head. Kim grinned and upended the stein, chugging. Her shamrocks danced madly, sproinging back and forth behind her tilted head. Foam trickled from the sides of her mouth, and she put the glass down, choking and laughing. She caught the spill with her fingers, then sucked them clean. Holding up the stein, she shouted, "Next year in Dublin!"

The crowd roared its approval, and there was a sudden surge toward the bar for pitchers and pints.

Amy hunched away from the press of bodies. "You're not Irish," she said.

"You're not in love," Kim returned, with a philosophical shrug. "I might be by February."

"Is that a promise?" Kim licked the last of the beer from her lips. "Eleven months. It could happen. Maybe I'll be Irish by then." Amy dipped her head to hide her smile, but Kim quirked an eyebrow at her and laughed. "I'm too cynical for you?"

"It's not that—"

"Sure it is. You want someone to shower you with gifts. Someone who'll do random, spontaneous, romantic things. Like a singles want ad: 'Woman seeks same for rain shower frolicking and ski lodge cuddling; long-stemmed roses and chocolates a must.'"

Amy narrowed her eyes and nodded, making a show of checking items off her personal list of clichés. "Walks on the beach at sunset, barefoot—"

Kim snickered. "We're two thousand miles from a coast in every direction."

"And . . . balloon rides." Amy had always wanted to try that.

Kim stared at her incredulously. "You mean, up in the air?" She gave a shudder and sipped at the new beer the waiter had delivered unasked. "You're a braver woman than I. God. Heights."

"It can't be that bad. Nothing around you for miles . . . the view must be amazing." That was romance—the two of you, alone, above the entire world. That was what love was—feeling like the whole world was perfect just because the two of you were. Amy sighed. The bar was smoky, and she had a sneaking suspicion that the one table in the corner singing Irish ballads was going to catch on with the rest of the patrons any time now.

Kim started to hum *When Irish Eyes Are Smiling*. Badly.

Amy stood up and reached for her purse.

Shaking her head, Kim pushed her hand down. "Let me. I'm the one who drank it, anyway."

"I'm afraid this isn't my thing," Amy said. "Bars."

"Not enough romance," Kim said, nodding with solemn understanding. Her shamrocks bounced. "Picnics on rowboats. Candlelight restaurants. Bicycles built for two!"

Amy nodded, chuckling. "That sounds lovely."

Kim touched the back of her hand, her brown eyes suddenly serious. "Then we should do that." The shamrocks swayed crazily, and Amy held back a laugh.

"I'm not sure," Amy said, glancing around the bar. The singing in the corner was escalating to drunken swaying. Kim celebrated St. Patrick's like it was going out of style, but she wouldn't touch Valentine's Day with a ten-foot pole. Amy was the opposite. She wanted the quiet dinners that Kim spoke so derisively about. Amy loved staying in and curling up with a romance novel and a mug of hot chocolate. Kim was the type to chain herself to trees on Arbor Day or dress as a werewolf on Hallowe'en and jump out at trick-or-treating kids yelling "Boo!" Amy . . . wasn't.

Kim followed her gaze. "Okay, bad choice for a first date," she said, with a wry smile. "I'm sorry. Give me another chance?"

Amy raised an eyebrow. "Will there be long-stemmed roses?"

"There could be," Kim said. "You'll just have to wait and see."

"You know, there were maybe four different saints that have been sort of squashed together to make up the guy we call Saint Valentine," Kim said, brandishing a bouquet of roses and baby's breath.

Amy accepted the flowers with a blush. She held them up, inhaling the green scent of freshly cut stems. Kim had kidded about raiding gardens for crocuses because they at least weren't stereotypical. The roses, though, were perfect—the buds just beginning to open, so they would last a week or more. "Thank you."

"It's April second," Kim noted, with a satisfied smile. "I can be spontaneous any day of the year."

"Isn't that the definition of spontaneous?" Amy asked, waving Kim in while she searched for a vase. "To happen at any time?"

Kim shrugged. "I'm just saying, why wait for February? It's cold then. So, no picnics."

Amy grabbed a vase from the top of her refrigerator and filled it with water from the sink. "There's going to be a picnic?"

Kim grinned smugly. "I was paying attention—I think picnics were on the list."

"You didn't have to," Amy said. She spread the roses evenly in the vase, arranging them, then rearranging.

"Maybe," Kim said. She reached out and touched a petal, softly. Amy could feel her standing very close behind her, and she shivered. "It's all right, though, isn't it?"

"Yes." Amy smiled, ducking her head. Her hair, long and loose, fell down in front of her face. Kim tucked it back with rose-scented fingers.

"Good," she whispered.

Amy wondered if she was about to kiss her.

Kim let out a breath of laughter and stepped away. "Then I hope it's okay that I rented a bicycle built for two."

Amy whirled around, barely noticing that Kim was only inches away. "You didn't!"

Kim's smile broke out like sunshine, her eyes dancing. "I did! You would not believe how hard it is to ride it by yourself. And with a picnic in the basket—"

Amy rushed to the screen door and stared out. There it was, a huge contraption with two seats and two sets of pedals, with a bright wicker basket attached over the back wheels. "You're going to kill us!"

"Hey, you'll be on that thing, too. If there's any dying, it's at least going to be a murder-suicide pact." Kim grabbed her by both hands and started leading her outside. "Come on!"

Amy let Kim pull her to the bike, which leaned on its kickstand. "No, Kim . . . This isn't going to work. We'll fall, we'll—"

Kim let go of her hands and circled the bike, staring at it like a general studying a potential battlefield. "I rode it over here," she said. She rubbed her hands together, a determined gleam in her eye. "Do you want the front or the back?"

Amy held her head in her hands, then peered through her fingers. The bicycle was still there. She started laughing, her shoulders shaking. If she chose the front, she'd have to decide where they were going. If she chose the back, she'd be terrified of not being able to see. "I don't know."

"It's kind of like a trial question," Kim said, with a wicked grin. "My subtle way of asking if you're a top or a bottom."

Amy felt her face go hot. "Are you?"

"What, asking? Of course not!" Kim patted the bike. "I'll just wait for you to choose. If I'm lucky, I'll find out if I'm right."

Amy blushed even more. This was worse than the bar. She couldn't make an excuse or run away—her house was right there. She could say it was impossible, that she couldn't ride. But she had a feeling that wouldn't work. Kim buckled on a helmet, and when she turned back to Amy, one look was enough to tell her that Kim knew exactly what she was thinking. She'd promised Kim another chance. She'd had no idea how ridiculous she was going to look when she did.

Really, the shamrocks should have been a clue.

Kim tossed a helmet at her. "Well?"

"Front," Amy said firmly, and pulled the helmet on. If they were going to do this, it would be on her terms as much as possible. She could keep them away from hills and potholes anyway, even if she had no say over the pace.

"All right," Kim said, with a mocking half bow and a gesture toward the bike. "Your carriage awaits."

Amy strode to the front of the bike and clenched her hands on the handlebars. "Let's go."

"Ooh, butch," Kim said. "I like it. Mount up!"

Amy threw her leg over. She felt the balance of the bike shift as Kim did the same. She got one foot on a pedal, then tensed up. "I can't do this."

"You can." Kim rolled the bike forward slightly. Amy gasped and tightened her hold on the handlebars. "Trust me," Kim said, with a laugh. "It's just like riding a bike."

"Funny," Amy gritted out between her teeth. She took a breath, squared her shoulders, and started pedaling. Miraculously, the bike didn't dump them the very first second. They wobbled precariously for a long moment, getting their pedaling rhythms synchronized.

"Whee!" Kim yelled. "This is amazing."

"What's amazing is that we aren't dead," Amy called back to her.

Kim poked her in the back. "Who cares about dying? We're riding a bicycle built for two."

"You're very fixated on that."

"Is this, or is this not, the most romantic thing you've ever done?" Kim poked her again to emphasize the question.

Amy leaned into the pedals. "If I say yes, will you promise there's no rowboat waiting for us at the park?"

"I promise nothing," Kim shouted. "It's April second. Who knows what wacky, romantic surprises await us?"

"Please tell me that's a rhetorical question," Amy said, but she was starting to catch Kim's enthusiasm. The rush of the pavement beneath the wheels and the smell of freshly mown lawns made her giddy. She realized she had a silly smile on her face, and she only grinned wider. This was way different from riding a regular bicycle. She was trusting Kim to keep the balance and not to loaf, and Kim was trusting her not to run them into curbs or brick walls. Amy guided them into the park, along the paths toward the river.

"Where are you taking us?" Kim asked.

Amy giggled. For the first time, Kim was the one who sounded uncertain. She steered off the path to the grass under the poplars. "I don't know."

"Did I mention I was a top, too?"

"Really? You hide it very well."

This time the poke caught her right under her ribs. Amy shrieked and pulled her elbows to her sides, letting go of the handlebars. The bike jackknifed abruptly and tipped over, ditching them on the grass.

"Oof," Kim commented mildly. "You okay?"

"No. I'm dead." Amy rolled onto her back and tilted her head toward the sun, red and dazzling through her eyelids. Grass itched under her T-shirt.

She felt Kim leaning over her, blocking the sun, an instant before she kissed her. Amy caught a startled breath. Her pulse fluttered in her wrists, racing, as she lifted a hand to cup Kim's cheek. She slid it higher, into Kim's hair, and pulled her closer. She smelled crushed grass and sweat, then tasted the warm mint of Kim's mouth. "Mmm—"

Kim's hands rested on either side of her shoulders, and she was leaning so close their bodies were nearly touching. Amy wanted to yank her down all the way, but Kim was kissing her with slow and insistent thoroughness. Amy felt the heat of the day like a caress, warming her body. Kim's breath was fast and ragged, and Amy lifted herself into the touch, smiling into the kiss.

Kim lifted her head at last, her lips curving. "Hey."

Amy picked dead grass out of her hair. "Necrophiliac," she said fondly.

"It was CPR," Kim protested. "As if I'd let you stay dead."

"My hero," Amy said, reaching up to kiss her again.

"Cherubs as cute naked babies with wings are a Hallmark invention," Kim offered as they walked home from the restaurant. It was raining lightly, a late summer drizzle just hard enough to patter on Kim's umbrella and hiss under the tires of passing cars. "They're from the Bible, a class of angels that really look like fire-breathing monsters."

"Why do you keep telling me this stuff?" Amy rested her head on Kim's shoulder, curving herself under Kim's arm. It had been gorgeous when they left for dinner, so she'd decided against a jacket.

"I'm worried the candles and the violinist might have convinced you I have a soft spot for holidays," Kim said.

"It's August twenty-seventh. It's not a holiday."

"That's right." Kim tapped her fingers against Amy's arm. "You've proven my point."

"No, I haven't. You had no point."

Kim opened her mouth to say, "Yes, I did," but Amy nudged her with an elbow before she could. Amy wondered if the telepathy was a sign of something—Kim's predictability, the stage of their relationship, or whether ESP was a valid theory.

Kim gave a wounded sniff at Amy denying her the fun of a senseless argument. "The point is, Valentine's Day is a marketing ploy aimed at yuppies who are struggling to define themselves by their consumerism."

"So you . . . what? Consume on every other day?" Amy swayed her hip into Kim's, a teasing shove.

"And twice on Sundays," Kim agreed. "If you're not sleeping in."

Amy snorted softly into Kim's shoulder, then turned her head and kissed her collarbone.

"Hey, I'm explaining something here," Kim said.

"And I'm distracting you," Amy replied. With her hand around Kim's waist, she slipped her fingers under the hem of her shirt and brushed them back and forth over her waist. "Is it working?"

"You're an evil woman. Utterly depraved. Totally amoral." Kim sighed and arched into Amy's touch as they turned onto her street. "Have I mentioned that those are some of my favorite qualities?"

Amy twisted around to face Kim, trying to stay under the umbrella as much as possible. She grabbed her by the hips and tugged her forward. "I aim to please."

"Oh, really?" Kim raised an eyebrow, amused, then leaned forward and kissed her. Amy let a small sound escape her when their tongues met. God, could Kim kiss. Amy relaxed into her arms, abandoning herself to Kim's warmth. She concentrated on dissolving Kim's words, kissing her hard until she moaned. Kim moved to clutch her tighter and lost her grip on the umbrella. It dipped, sending a spray of icy water down Amy's back. She sprang back.

"Sorry!"

Amy shivered. "Inside. Now."

"You know, I was just thinking that."

"That's better than thinking about holidays." Amy led the way up the steps, getting her keys out. "You have a weird thing about Valentine's Day. I mean, you know this, right?"

"I do not have a *thing*."

Amy laughed. "You're the one who brings it up." She tossed her keys on the counter.

Kim pretended to be wounded. "Pre-emptive strike."

"So you're saying I shouldn't expect anything special then?" Amy gave her best seductive smile, swinging her hips as she walked toward her. "Not a card, not a singing telegram?"

Kim's eyes widened as she watched her approach. "I'm not saying you shouldn't expect anything," she said. "I'm saying, why February fourteenth, huh? Why bow down to society's arbitrary rules?"

"Because otherwise we'd have anarchy?" Amy suggested.

"I'm a rebel," Kim said, leering.

Amy giggled and let herself be pushed toward the bedroom. "Do you have any other holiday hang-ups I should know about?" She leaped onto the bed.

"It's not a hang-up." Kim stalked across the room toward her.

"But I want to know your opinion of birthdays and anniversaries," Amy protested as innocently as she could.

Kim lunged at her across the bed. Amy yelped and scrambled backward. Kim crawled after her, getting tangled in the sheets.

Amy shied away from Kim's tantalizing grin. "What about Channukah? Labor Day? Kim?"

Kim pounced on her, pinning her to the bed, then reached past her and pulled out a bottle of Hershey's syrup. "I'd tell you," she said, "but then I couldn't lick chocolate sauce from your bellybutton."

"Oh," Amy said faintly, staring at the bottle Kim held. "Clearly you have no romantic tendencies at all."

"Exactly," Kim said, and flicked open the bottle's cap.

♥

"Valentine's Day probably had nothing to do with love when it was first celebrated," Kim said, flinging open the door of the ski lodge and lugging their gear inside. "It started as a fertility rite. There were orgies in the cornfields to convince the seeds they should grow."

"I like that plan." Amy carted luggage into the room, stopping to stare at the beamed ceiling and the huge, burnished logs of the walls. "There is a hot tub, isn't there?"

"Of course." Kim opened doors and peered into cupboards. "Nothing says après-ski like chlorine and heat stroke."

Amy reached the bedroom and shoved their bags into a corner. She glanced down the hall to where Kim was checking out the view from the balcony. While her back was turned, Amy stripped off her shirt, tossing her pants after it. The lodge was cold, and she was immediately covered with goose bumps. She lifted her arms and let her hips sway, so, so, as if Kim was already lying on those soft sheets, waiting. Amy caught her breath and realized she was getting ahead of herself. She grinned. "Perfect."

"Did you say something?" Kim called.

"The bedroom is gorgeous."

"Is that supposed to be a subtle hint—" Kim stopped dead in the doorway. "Oh."

Amy gave her the most predatory smile she knew how. She was pretty sure her heart had stopped beating entirely when Kim walked in. When she'd looked at her like *that*. "Yeah. Oh."

Kim swallowed. "This is—"

"An ambush."

Kim nodded. "Right."

Amy circled her, herding her toward the bed. The sheets were pearl-grey silk, and the bed was enormous, with down comforters and pillows everywhere. Kim sat down slowly, still staring, her mouth hanging open. Amy bent over her, placing her hands on either side of Kim's hips. "You're not the only romantic here," she said.

Kim blinked, then leaned sideways to look past Amy's shoulder. "There's someone else in the lodge?" she whispered.

Amy burst into giggles. She pushed Kim back, laughing, and straddled her, with Kim's legs hanging off the bed behind her. "Shut up."

As Kim started to protest, Amy kissed her, smothering her reply. Amy had never known that kisses could be like this, that she could feel so much while wrapped up in someone else's arms. Her tongue glided against Kim's, and she closed her eyes at the sweetness of it. Anticipation surged through her. She felt like a hummingbird, thrumming and darting, and she licked her way deeper into Kim's mouth. She wondered if Kim felt joy the way she did, filling her and spilling over.

Kim moved back on the bed. Amy, kneeling over her, followed. She raised her hand to cup Kim's cheek, holding her still.

Kim lifted her hands to cup Amy's breasts, making Amy moan. The feel of Kim's hands, warm and still, the soft movements of her lips, melted away anything Amy might have been thinking. Amy let her eyes drift closed, bracing herself against the headboard, the better to enjoy what was happening. Her nipples were already hard from the room's chill, and when Kim rolled them between her fingers, pleasure arrowed straight to her clit. Amy lifted her head and gasped.

"This isn't fair," Kim mumbled from beneath her. She raised her head and closed her teeth on the point of Amy's shoulder, far too gently. She tasted Amy's skin, slowly, considering. Her hands swept down Amy's back, over her ass, then down the backs of her thighs.

The sudden, flaring desire spread so fast that Amy gasped. "What . . . isn't fair?" she asked, her breath hitching.

She felt Kim smile, then the slick warmth of her tongue. Amy kissed her back hungrily, tilting her head to get closer. Kim moved her hands to Amy's shoulders until Amy got the hint and shifted on the bed. Kim pressed upward, seeking contact, and it was her turn to moan. She stroked one finger back up Amy's thighs, so lightly that Amy could barely feel it, yet it filled her whole world. She spread her knees farther apart. Eyes squeezed shut, she released an open-mouthed sigh.

"I'm overdressed," Kim said softly. "God, you're beautiful when you do that."

"Seduce you?"

Kim chuckled. "That too."

Amy smiled and kissed her way along Kim's jaw, mouthing the warm space behind her earlobe. Kim hummed, low in her throat, a sound of satisfaction and longing.

"It's not Valentine's," Kim said in a puff of air somewhere near her ear.

"I can be romantic in November." Amy busied her fingers on the buttons of Kim's shirt, spreading it open and moving her kisses downward, sucking at the hollow of Kim's throat.

"Yeah . . ." Kim arched upward. "Oh, yeah . . . you can . . ."

Kim linked her hands loosely behind Amy's back, urging her to sit down completely. Amy tightened her hands on Kim's shoulders, shivering, concentrating on the feel of Kim's body against hers. Her hair fell in loose waves around her face as she dipped her head and breathed slowly. She worked her hips gently against Kim's. The deep thrill of the contact spread like lava through her veins. As Kim's hands wandered over her back, Amy twitched at the almost-ticklish feel. She was wet and hot, and she could tell Kim felt the same way. There were still too many clothes between them.

Amy whimpered and wriggled closer. They both groaned as contact increased, and Kim bent forward to catch Amy's nipple in her mouth. She circled it with her tongue, then finally sucked it hard. Amy reached for Kim's top and pulled it over her head, quickly. Kim's nipples were dark and erect; her breasts looked so soft that Amy just wanted to rest on them forever, taste them, take them. Amy tossed the slightly-worse-for-wear shirt aside without a second thought.

"Hey!" Kim said. "That was . . . yours. Okay. Never mind . . ."

Amy moved lower, drawing tiny patterns with her tongue. She loved Kim's skin, smooth and tender beneath her lips as she kissed her way over the curve of Kim's breast, pausing to suck.

Kim lifted off the bed, pushing into the touch. "Amy—right there, yeah—"

Amy wanted to explore every single inch of Kim's body and find all the tiny places that made her shiver and moan. She moved her mouth over Kim's neck to her chest, then down her arm, purposefully avoiding all the places Kim wanted her to touch. Amy found the crease inside Kim's elbow, flicked her tongue over the pulse there, smiling when it jumped under her mouth. She moved lower and drifted her fingertips across Kim's tanned, taut stomach, loving the way the muscles jumped. She swept her hands back and forth, now with fingernails, now palms, then dipped her tongue into Kim's bellybutton. Kim gasped and thrust upward, moaning. Amy licked her way over Kim's stomach, every now and then coming close to the neatly trimmed curls between Kim's legs, then sliding away, as if on a whim. Her fingernails were now drawing lines up and down the insides of Kim's thighs, as light as feathers, reaching up high enough to feel the wetness coating her legs, then returning to her knees, again and again.

Finally, Amy held her hips and bent to taste her. Kim sighed, long and shuddering, while Amy explored with her tongue. Kim rested a hand on the back of her head, guiding her to where she wanted her most. Amy followed Kim's lead, finding her center and sucking, her tongue flicking quickly. Kim yelled out. She was wet and slippery, and Amy filled her with two fingers while she worked her clit. Kim came hard, her hips jerking under Amy's hands. Amy lapped at her, loving the taste and smell of her, then moved up Kim's body once more, dropping kisses on her ribs, under the curve of her breast, at her collarbone.

"You're amazing." Kim's eyes glowed with satisfaction. She held Amy's face and kissed her, their tongues twining. Soon, her fingers stroked lower, sliding around Amy's clit. "Baby—you're so wet . . ."

"Yes . . ." Amy's hips twitched forward, encouraging Kim to

enter her. She was aching for her touch. She grabbed Kim and hauled her closer, kissing her fiercely, kneading every inch of skin she could reach. She could hardly breathe, and the rhythm of her thrusts was building too fast, but it was good, so good, but Kim was moving too slowly, her fingers rubbing small circles everywhere except right where they needed to be.

"Here . . ." Kim slipped one finger inside, keeping her thumb working back and forth over Amy's clit. Sensation poured through Amy, centering on the movement of Kim's hand, then spreading through her thighs, her stomach. Amy felt like she was teetering on the edge of the steepest cliff on the entire mountain. It went on and on, and somewhere far away her voice was begging for more.

"Please . . . Kim . . ."

Kim increased her rhythm, responding to Amy's words, bringing her to the edge and holding her there as long as possible. Amy moaned, her hips thrusting, and then she was falling. Pleasure exploded everywhere and she was completely lost. She tensed, her muscles clenching. "Ahh . . ." Delight filled her in long waves as she bucked hard against Kim's pumping fingers. Finally, she collapsed on top of Kim, letting her head drop to the mattress.

She lay for a long moment, enjoying the quiet and the taste of Kim lingering on her tongue, and especially the warm body next to hers.

"Hey . . ." Kim sounded as tired as she felt, and as happy.

"Mmm?"

"Best ambush ever," Kim said, rolling to her side. She lifted a hand and swept Amy's hair off her forehead. Amy snuggled into her arms, dropping a kiss on her lips.

"Hmm." Amy watched Kim sleepily, through half-closed eyes, and said, "I love you."

Kim smiled, quick and teasing. "Even if it's November twenty-first?"

"Every day," Amy said, snuggling into the sheets and closing her eyes. "All the days."

♥

"You're a dupe of the Valentine's Day conspiracy," Amy shouted above the roar of blasting air.

"I'm nothing of the sort." Kim buried her face in Amy's shoulder, clutching her arm in a death grip.

"You are. All this time it's been a front." Amy hugged Kim back, patting her reassuringly. "I'm a victim of false advertising. You promised me no romance today."

"This isn't romance, trust me. It's torture." Kim moaned and grabbed Amy tighter. "Can it be over now?"

Amy laughed. They were floating a hundred feet up in a hot air balloon, with the sun just rising. She stepped forward, and the world tilted beneath her feet. Wind rushed past her, sharp and cold. Above them loomed a bulge of red silk. Below them, the city was laid out like patchwork, with toy cars zipping along the roads. "This," she said, "is the most perfect Valentine's Day ever."

Kim cracked one eye open and gulped, taking a quick glance over the side of the basket, then she huddled in the center. "You're a crazy person," she said, "but I love you."

"That's all February fourteenth is about," Amy said, smiling broadly. "Even if it's just another day."

Lonely Hearts Club
Rachel Kramer Bussel

Valentine's Day might not seem like the ideal time for a one-night stand, but maybe that's only true if you've never met Teal. I'd never met her either before last night, never laid eyes on anyone as riveting as this one-word wonder who'd dyed her hair to match her name, or vice versa. I'd been planning to stay home and watch my favorite sappy romantic comedies (don't tell the other dykes, but I secretly thrive on *Ten Things I Hate About You* and *The Wedding Singer*, with the occasional *Chutney Popcorn* thrown in to maintain a little bit of queer street credibility), brewing up a batch of my favorite homemade spicy popcorn, and cracking open some ice-cold beers. But at six, just when I was about to sink into a long, luxurious bubble bath, my best friend, Amber, called, begging me to come out to the local dyke bar, Kitten, to hang out and keep her company. I love Amber like a sister, but sometimes we need some time apart. I told her so, and she whined, "But it's Valentine's Day," except it took her about a minute to get all the "a"s out in "day."

"C'mon, it'll be fun, and maybe you'll even meet a hottie of your own."

"I doubt it," I grumbled, my mind fixed on my huge green ceramic bowl, from which I could practically taste the popcorn, even though I hadn't popped a single kernel yet. I looked longingly at my plush purple couch, the biggest purchase of my adult life and most prized possession. I often crash out on it rather than my sturdy, but simply average, bed, sinking into its soft cushiony folds, curled up with a fat pillow beneath me, the TV blaring. But Amber was right; tonight was the one night of the year that most sane people didn't choose to be alone, and while it would likely just be me, her, and the handful of other single dykes we saw every time we went out, the only thing I had to lose was my record of reciting every line in those films by heart.

I went over to my closet, trying to figure out what to wear. I have everything from jeans, boots, and tank tops to the girliest, frilliest of dresses. Usually, I opt for something in between, not wanting to tip my hand immediately as to just how butch or femme I truly am because, when I'm honest with myself, I fall somewhere in between and can play it up either way. I love my arms, the way the biceps curl upward out of them, like a newly awakened kitten peeking out into the world for that first glimpse of morning. My muscles are just there, latent, waiting to be shown off. But, then again, so are my breasts. They're fairly large, 38D, but whenever I tell any of my friends that, they do a double take. "Really?" they ask, looking from my tits to my face, and back. They hold back on the second part, but I can read it in their expression: *They look smaller to me.* Ah, but looks can be deceiving; nude, my breats sit atop my chest in all their ripe, womanly glory, but for the past year, I'm the only one who's gotten to see them bared.

I settled for my favorite bra, a sturdy beige push-up adorned with delicate lacing, under a plunging black scoop neck T-shirt, the kind that looks casual but cost more than most of my jeans. I pulled out my favorite pair, the ones I would live in if society found that socially acceptable, the only pair I have that make me like my legs and my ass *more* after I put them on. I swept on some lip gloss, and brushed out my hair, and that was it. No jewelry or unnecessary accessories; I didn't want to look like I was trying too hard. I looked down at my bare feet, which I've always considered my worst feature. There's nothing wrong with them per se; I'm just not much of a foot fan. But they looked fairly decent, and almost against my better judgment, the nails had been painted bright red by a particularly aggressive woman at the salon. I slipped into medium heels, the ones halfway between leave-me-alone and come-fuck-me. They hugged the curves of my feet, but also seemed to say "buyer beware" to any woman who approached me.

I grabbed my jacket and purse and walked the three blocks to meet Amber. She was leaning over the bar, her ass sticking out, yelling something to the bartender over the music—*Cannonball* by The Breeders, totally random but somehow fitting for Kitten, where you could hear everything from R.E.M. to Lauryn Hill to Bratmobile in the course of a night. I walked up to Amber and slid my hand over her left ass cheek, giving her a playful squeeze. She squealed, then batted my arm in a playful swat.

"Stop it! People will think we're together, and baby, I'm on the prowl tonight," she said, before sliding a glass over to me. She must have had the beer waiting just for me.

"Thanks," I said, picking up the frosty mug and turning around to survey the scene.

It's a small room, completely unremarkable, the walls filled with marginalia from the last decade of lesbian pop culture, everything from Ellen to Melissa to, now, Portia and the like, the newly minted dykes who sometimes play hide-and-seek with their identities but captivate us nonetheless, with the occasional rock babe like Joan Jett thrown in. It was like a teenager's room with its overabundance of tacked-to-the-wall eye candy, and that was pretty much the vibe that came with Kitten—you just knew it would never graduate and change its name to Cat. I'd been coming here so long I felt like the great aunt to all these little girls flailing their heads to the music without a care in the world, but I still stopped by on occasion.

And then, as my gaze did a slow pan, I paused. There was a girl who looked nothing like any of those around her, who couldn't have stood out more if she'd been in one of those *Sesame Street* "Which of these is not like the other?" puzzles. Her hair cascaded down her back, but also stuck up and out. It seemed to be everywhere, and it was a blazing turquoise, a color only found in nature in the stone of the same name. She had on heavy-duty eye makeup, husky rings of black with silver, glittery lids. Her outfit was an amalgamation of silver, black, purple, and that wild teal again, all streaks and rips and layers; what could have been several tops; a micro mini; ripped fishnets; and thick boots. She was drinking something bright red, probably the night's holiday Kool-Aid-inspired special. She was doing the same thing I was—looking around, as if bored—when her eyes caught mine and stayed there. She looked me right in the eye and raised her brows, then panned all the way down my body, and back up. She kept her eyes locked on mine while she finished her drink, not chugging it, but slowly sipping, taking each cold sip as if she needed it to remember the taste. She wasn't my normal type—too punk, too young, too wild—but I liked that she could be so direct. I was always hearing about how, "Remember last year? That girl Holly liked you, and she said hi to you and you said hi back, but then she was waiting for you to ask her out and you never did . . ." or some variation on the theme, and I was sick of it.

I had an urge to ask her a thousand questions—What's your name? Where are you from? What do you do?—all the usual biggies, but I refrained, letting her set the pace. She was a creature, more wild animal than normal girl, and I suddenly needed to see what lurked behind her blazing eyes. When she finished her drink, she brought her lips to mine by way of introduction. They were cold and beery, but somehow sweet, and I let her tongue slip into my mouth and slide along mine.

"I'm Teal," she says. "You don't recognize me because I'm not from here. I go to school a couple hours away, but I'm older than most of the students there, and just can't stand to be around all of them going all mushy and gooey on Valentine's Day. But that doesn't mean I want to be alone, so I hop in my car and drive until I get to wherever it is I think I'm supposed to be. And tonight it was here. With you," she says, her voice going deep as she presses her body up against mine.

I could feel all the textures of her clothes and jewelry, a nipple ring poking through the soft cloth of her various shirts, the roughness of her fishnets against my leg, her boots sliding along my ankle, and I liked it all, liked the way Teal went after what she wanted without thinking twice.

I looked down at this wild child, so far from my typical girl, but something about her attitude appealed to me. It wasn't love at first sight, certainly, but I knew I had to have her, and vice versa. I reached around and squeezed Teal's ass through her skirt, eager to see just what I could do with it. We stopped kissing and I stared into her blue eyes, took in her bright lips, now wearing the remnants of my gloss. I was planning to take her home, but she tugged me toward the bathroom, and I figured that was as good a place as any for a Valentine's hookup.

Once inside, the small confines served us well. There was no room to spread out, so our bodies seemed to naturally morph together. I kept trying to grab her ass again, but she had both hands tangled in my hair, pulling it so my head leaned back. We were fighting over each other, over who would be the first to give way, let go, submit. Finally, I gave up. Much as I coveted her ass, I was starting to buckle, my knees shaking as she tugged on my hair while her other hand made laps around my skin.

She pulled me so I faced the sink, my hands grasping the edges for balance. She pressed her fingers up against my cunt, through my jeans, and I moaned, feeling myself release a trickle of juice and watching in the mirror as my face got more and more flushed. She lifted my shirt just enough to reach the lacy edges of my bra, peeling them down so my breasts hung out over the wire rims of the bra, large and bursting with need. She tugged on my nipples, hard, pinching them tightly until another trickle emerged. Teal leaned up against me and bit the back of my neck, little nibbles one on top of the other interspersed with licks from her fast-moving tongue that drove me mad.

"Are you ready?" she asked, and I nodded, tears forming in my eyes at the maddening pace she was taking—the long, meandering cruise around my body this smart-mouthed little vixen was clearly enjoying. "Good," she said, her voice hinting at something promising.

She gently undid my jeans, tugging them down so I stood with my top pushed up, tits hanging out, jeans slung down around my ankles. I shut my eyes, not wanting to see how open I was to her. She stepped back, kissed my ass around the edges of my panties, her tongue darting along my crack and then lower, where my panties were already wet. She came back up and trailed her warm tongue along my cheeks. She was so soft and sensual that I wasn't prepared when her hand reared up and smacked my ass. She spanked me, first one cheek and then the other, clearly experienced in the art. My ass burned with the delicious pain, the sting that quickly built upon itself and had me dripping into my poor panties.

After she deemed my ass sufficiently reddened, she stopped and pulled down my panties. I kept my eyes firmly shut, sure that they'd be a sopping heap by now. I spread my legs as best I could in that position, and she dove right in, her fingers pressing into my wet, aching hole. That's how I felt; not so much like a woman connecting with a new lover on some deep, emotional level, but like a woman with a hole that needed to be filled, and Teal was just the girl to do it. Her silent, probing fingers pushed deep inside, quickly discovering exactly how wet I was. I didn't realize how tightly I was gripping the sink's edge, or how my body had tensed up until her whispered command, "Relax."

And I did. I let go completely, let the tears fall down my cheeks, let any shred of composure I still had fall the way of my panties, let go of everything except the feel of her fingers inside me, twisting, searching, seeking. I let my breath go, let it come out in ragged, uneven shudders that seemed to bubble up from deep inside. I looked at myself in the mirror, my bare face now blotchy and sweaty, and the tears streaming as she worked her fingers just so. Then I clenched my teeth, spread my legs just a tiny bit more, pushed back against her, fucking those magical fingers right back as we danced to our own special rhythm. It had nothing to do with love, but don't be fooled into thinking it did anything less than rock my world completely. When I came, I thought I might break that sink—and I didn't care. It would have been worth it for the way my body trembled, the way everything halted, then sped up, then halted again, my pussy a tornado of need as she touched my core and coaxed every last drop of desire out of me. It would have been worth it to look behind me and see her arm moving up and down, to realize I'd let this stranger, this beguiling creature, take me on a delicious trip without wanting anything more than these few stolen moments.

We cleaned up, pulling on our clothes, washing our hands, trying not to look at each other too closely. Then we stepped outside and I followed her to where she'd left her coat, by the door.

"It's been fun, but I've gotta run. See you around. Maybe next year," she said, taking my hand and depositing a handful of candy hearts, soft and slightly melted, the tiny words blurred.

I put them in my mouth one by one, savoring their tart sugariness, feeling my body come down off the rush that Teal had made in me. Amber had been right—meeting Teal beat watching videos any night. I looked down at the last heart, peered at it until I could make out the letters reading Lonely No More. I savored the candy, and the words, which for now, rang true.

Happy Valentine's Day, indeed.

Encounter
krysia lycette villón

Years ago I was deemed a pillow queen, a label I held onto willingly. It's apparent by the heart-shaped note you left me that you agree—your directions are concise, precise, and direct. I like it. A lot. We should not have made plans to meet on this February night because of all of its implications, but I'm choosing to come to you anyway, abandoning my hold on proper boundaries.

And so I am here with you. I got the room. I got undressed. I waited, though I had only to wait a few minutes for you to arrive. All as you requested.

A single bedside lamp gracefully illuminates my sun-kissed skin and somehow manages to darken the otherwise mediocre ambience of this hotel room perfectly. I am only visiting this port town and gay mecca from Arizona for a few days. You live here now, having left Chicago years ago after completing your doctorate.

I am seated on the edge of the king-sized bed. You walk slowly toward me. Button-down shirt still crisp even after 9 to 5, sleeves rolled up and arms free of all jewelry. My eyes slowly graze over every inch of what is exposed of your clothed flesh. Skin dark, smooth, hairless. You haven't aged but for those few white hairs mingling with the others by your temples. You stand before me, your denim-covered legs between my own. Eyes fiery. Body cocked. As you begin to lean forward, I find my hands reaching up to stop you. They grab your hips, get caught momentarily on your black leather belt, then slowly move upward. Your body is so unlike mine. Tight, taut, cut, yet soft. You do not have these same curves to your figure. You plan your living arrangements based on the proximity of the local gym. Your hips are narrow, your waist small. I unbutton one layer and remove it. As expected, I expose a bright white undershirt that still carries the faint smell of bleach despite your attempts at masking it with fabric softeners and detergent. As I pull your shirt up, you flex your already flat stomach at the sight of my lips coming close. I kiss it, drag my tongue around it. My fingers reach the edge of your sports bra and take your lycra-bound breasts into my hands. You hide them so well. You suddenly pull your T-shirt off, breath now ragged. I look up at you, pull myself to almost standing, my mouth reaching for the place where I think your nipple might be, and you pull back. You smile.

We've been here before. I know what you like, but I like to push your limits. Though our lives have changed, this is one thing that has not. I want to see if you'll let me get a little further this time. I sit back down. You take your bra off for me, throwing it quickly behind you. You release them and your large, and now less supple, breasts sit playfully in front of my lips. Nipples hard. I feel your hand at the back of my neck, pulling me forward, as you offer me one nipple. One of my hands reaches for the other breast, while the second caresses your muscular back. This is new.

You were the one who made me this way. Deemed me. Taught me about boundaries and how to play with them. Safely. We were both young college students, still teenagers, but you always seemed more aware of your own body and your desires. Your body was almost entirely off limits. This only made you seem more sensual to me, never detached or self-hating like my friends believed. I could never explain it enough to them. How I felt physically bound by you, but mentally freed. I could allow myself to be your instrument. I had never felt so alive. It was with you I shared my first orgasm. It was with you I began to understand the complexity of my womanhood and how it differed from yours. Bodies became bodies. Genders became performances and expressions and realities. Sex became groundbreaking and revolutionary. And I became yours until it was time for us to go our separate ways. We promised one another friendship some day and only until now, a chance meeting in a chance local dive at a chance moment in time, have we had the opportunity to fulfill our promise. I want nothing more than to be your friend again. Your sweetheart. Here. Now. As you've asked.

I shift my weight so our legs alternate, putting me at an angle to your stance. The hand that was on your back now makes its way toward the front. I am pleasantly surprised to feel the length of your shaft against your own thigh, held tight by your boxer briefs. As I push up on it, stroking you, I hear a small noise release from your throat. Your hips rock forward to meet me. I sit back fully. I straddle your legs again as you still stand in front of me, and begin to unbutton your jeans. You pull back. Unbutton. Unzip. Release your dick for me. Saliva collects in my mouth. I'm ready for you.

I take just the tip first, pump my mouth over it to get your hips in motion. I hold you at the base, then begin running my tongue up and down your shaft. I use my hand to spread all the wetness around, with the tip of you in my mouth, and when you get wet enough for me I take you in a little deeper. A little deeper. Then a little deeper until I have almost all nine inches in my mouth and throat. I can already feel my pussy begin to throb. I always wanted you like this, but when we were last together the pressure of the lesbian feminist agenda kept us from asking for what we really wanted—butch cock—and so you made love to me with what your body had to offer. Now I get to do the same and offer you all that my body has to give.

I stop, stand, and turn you around by the waistband of your jeans, pushing you down on the bed, on your back. You have this sly smile on your face as you watch me. My hair is loose, long, and black, sweeping along your legs as I undress you. I take your boots and socks off, and strip you of your jeans. You remove your briefs. And then I am standing in front of you. You lying down on the bed, legs slightly open because I'm standing between them, and your dick standing straight up for me. The black leather straps spanning out from the base of that beautiful creature between your legs makes you a work of art. I want nothing more than to embellish you with my mouth. As I begin crawling over to you, to wrap my lips around you again, you whisper to me to come all the way up.

I do, memorizing your form against this quilted bedspread. You kiss me, your lips slightly cold from breathing heavy, but still sticky with your lip balm that smells of cocoa butter. You grab my hair by the base of my head, pulling it hard. I do the same, squeezing my hand between the pillow and your short afro. My fingers grab enough of it to expose just enough of your neck for me to get a quick taste. You start to push me upward, kissing my small, caramel-colored breasts, my stomach soft from two children and fifteen years as a single mom, directing me to sit on your face. I begin to do as you wish, my hands steadying myself on the edge of the faux headboard bolted into the wall. I flip around to still give you what you ask for, but also to take what I want. I move so fast I almost knock the southwestern-themed, sand-painted print off the wall. As I get closer to your dick, I notice that where there ought to be hair, you have shaved clean. This is new. Your pussy lips already glisten with moisture, and I can smell your sweet scent. At that moment I feel your tongue divide my lips.

"Damn, baby. You're so wet."

I can barely hear you as you begin to suckle me. My cue. I wrap my hand and lips around you again and begin to match my rhythm with yours. Even with your mouth buried in my pussy I can hear you moaning. I can feel it too.

I start to go faster when I feel your hips rocking with me and your attention begins to waver from my pussy. You hold your hips suddenly still, and I can hear you repeating something over and over. Is it "oh" or "now"? I don't know. And then you push me off of you, leaving me on all fours, confused by your sudden absence. You abruptly and forcefully pull me back to you, my knees toward the edge of bed, my feet just hanging off. I stay motionless while you walk to the window, tugging on the black-out curtains. A sliver of afternoon sun falls across the bed, across my backside. You come back to me quickly, leaning up against me so I can feel your dick in the crack of my ass. You pump slightly into me, then lean back to view me. The heat in the room now seems oppressive. I feel moisture forming at the small of my back. You reach between my legs, circling my clit with your fingers, sliding them back through my slick lips, and then insert three fingers inside me. We can both hear how wet I am for you.

"You have such a pretty pussy, mama. Like a flower. Blossoming for me. She likes me, I can tell."

You don't fuck me hard, you massage me, hitting my G spot when you feel like it. I am open. Head foggy. I can hear a song building in my throat, but I don't understand my own lyrics. I keep my ass up in the air, but my arms collapse, my head falling to the mattress.

You stand back. Tell me not to move. I can feel you looking at me. I hear you spit on your dick and can see you stroking yourself from between my legs. You walk slowly up to me, take the tip of your cock and place it at my opening. You tell me to touch myself. You don't move, but I do. I'm rocking, trying to feel the pressure of your dick on me, in me, but all I can get is your tip. Immediately, I bring my right hand to my clit and begin to rub it slowly. We stay like this until you feel me pushing back into you. I am mumbling to myself, whispering, whimpering. I start begging. I can almost feel your smile as you quickly thrust up into me. I can't help but suck my breath in loudly. I am so tight. You fuck me with short thrusts, pulling back slowly so I can feel the head of your cock running up and down all my ridges. The heavier I breathe, the deeper and faster your thrusts become, until your hips are slapping up against my ass.

You know I'm about to come when I suddenly stop moving as much. I feel this tightness in my stomach, this heat spreading from between my legs. I'm screaming out to you now, telling you I'm coming, and that's when I hear you too. Grunting. Holding my hips tight. Slamming into me hard, so hard it hurts and feels good at the same time. It's like a fire spreading wildly across a dry plain, the flames bright enough to momentarily blind me, paralyze me with all emotion.

Somewhere, in the background of my body, I can hear you. Your breathing quick, with short grunts, then a stillness of sound. You thrust hard one last time, holding still inside me until it passes. Then your hips continue to slowly pump into me, riding through my aftershocks, and yours too. We finally come to a stop, and you pull out of me gently, putting your hand over my pussy, slowly smearing my lips with the juices of my desire for you. This is your way of giving me back to myself, allowing me to love myself, be my own Valentine, like the saint for whom this day is named. And when I pull your face to mine, kiss you slowly, you know I am doing the same.

We collapse into each other, slide ourselves up onto the bed and spread out. The sliver of light, now reddish with the setting sun, cuts across you as we lay face to face and I am reminded of how deep and dark your eyes are. When I think of you, I don't remember much of our youth, only the fire. As if reading my mind, you speak softly to me about those college days and graduate school nights, poetry readings, and unspoken connections that had remained so until today. You touch my stomach and ask me about my children, and I know this is the beginning of a beautiful night. The beginning of a beautiful friendship.

Falling In
Jennifer Lawicki

Just as the night before, and the night before that, the pink neon sign on the front of the Harem Lounge and Nightclub flickered dimly through the front window of the now sparsely populated bar.

Valentine's Day Drink Special: 2 for 1.
Shot-Girl Wanted.

Any other night would have found the place packed from wall to wall with hot, writhing bodies on a quest for the perfect one-night stand. Such behavior was perfectly acceptable in a bar like this—could even be considered the norm.

But not tonight. Not on February 14th.

As clichéd as it sounded, it was a day for love. The kind of day that brought old lovers back together for one last tryst and new lovers together with the thought that maybe, just *maybe*, something pure and true could be found in such an imperfect world.

Perhaps there was some kind of secret magic behind *Valentine's Day* that caused people to think there was love to be had . . . they just had to reach out and grab it.

Nevertheless, for every believer there is a naysayer, and that was exactly how Maya had decided to classify herself. Valentine's Day was just an excuse for retailers to sell overpriced chocolate and flowers to unsuspecting consumers who fell for the whole charade. She wouldn't let flowers and lace and teddy bears fool her. She had seen the bad side of too many relationships to ever believe that a single commercial holiday could convince Cupid to draw back his bow.

Maybe she felt that way because she'd been working at the bar for too long. There was something about listening to random patrons complaining to her about their love problems that seemed to close her off from the idea of *love* even more than her own past experiences had.

It wasn't to say that she didn't believe in love. In fact, she thought that she had found it on more than one occasion. But she certainly hadn't planned on getting her heart broken time and time again by people who thought monogamy was just some kind of wood.

She often wondered if she hadn't put herself in that situation just by the conditions in which she lived—bartending at one of the hottest gay bars in all of New York while finishing off her college degree. Sure, she was able to resist the hundred or so come-ons she received during the course of a single night. But then . . .

Then there were those nights when she'd fallen into the eyes of a stranger . . . had been influenced by the warmth of the alcohol she served and the heat of the sea of bodies in the place . . . had let herself get caught up in the idea that something true could grow out of a meaningless encounter with a stranger who had caught her attention.

Hell, maybe she could have even learned to find such a situation acceptable as a means of maintaining some kind of human companionship.

But then she had met Jade.

Tall, tanned, with long dark hair . . . gorgeous, funny, smart, full of wit . . . completely perfect. And by far the biggest player she'd ever met.

Maya had watched the alluring girl make her way through the bar patrons night after night, a new conquest made with every visit. She was intrigued by her, fascinated by the way the brunette temptress wooed and won over every woman she had set her sights on.

Never had Maya thought the exotic girl would pay her the least bit of attention. She would watch her from her station at the bar, secretly hoping the gorgeous girl would just look her way, give her a simple nod of acknowledgement.

It almost seemed one night as if it was fate when four waitresses called in sick at the same time, leaving the club packed full of thirsty patrons and only two bartenders. Maya trotted from one end of the bar to the other, feverishly serving up drinks to the voracious hordes shouting and waving money. She barely had time to look up into the crowd, let alone to have any type of conversation with a person besides, "What can I get ya?" Her paltry three months of bartending experience hardly seemed to be a benefit on a night like that.

Only when Maya heard the most sexy, sultry voice call an order across the bar did she manage to look up. She froze for a moment. There before her, in all her beauty, was Jade, closer than she had ever gotten to the girl before.

An emerald gaze. A smile. A nod.

Maya was taken aback that the object of her fantasies for so long now had finally noticed her. Acknowledged her. It only took her a moment to realize she was still frozen in place until she saw Jade wave her hand back and forth, trying to get her attention yet again.

Shy by nature, Maya shook her head to break the spell, sending her hair cascading across her shoulders. She chuckled to herself, embarrassed at how silly she must have appeared.

"Sorry," she said with a smile, moving a stray hair away from her eyes. "It's kinda crazy in here. What can I get ya?" she asked as she put her hands on the bar and leaned closer, straining to hear the sultry voice over the crowd.

Jade smiled, giving Maya an obvious once over before leaning in across the bar so their faces were only inches apart. Maya could feel Jade's breath warm upon her cheek.

"I can't help but notice that you're kinda swamped here . . . I've been waiting in line for almost thirty minutes."

Maya smiled shyly, shrugging her shoulders as she pulled back slightly. "Sorry. To say we're understaffed is an understatement. The day before Thanksgiving is always crazy, and four girls called in sick. This is hell!" she joked, popping the top off of a few bottles of beer as she talked. "But . . . you've got me here now. What would you like? It's on the house."

She focused her mind back to what she was doing, trying not to get too lost in the emerald-green eyes of the girl in front of her.

After a moment or so passed, Maya finally looked back up, eyes frantically searching the front of the crowd for the girl who seemed to disappear into thin air. Just as she felt the disappointment start to wash over her, she glimpsed someone hop up onto the bar and leap down into the work area.

She spun quickly to see Jade standing there in her tight black jeans and green tank top, running a hand through her ruffled hair, then straightening her top. Bewildered, Maya could only stare at her.

"I used to tend bar in Soho. This crowd is a piece of cake," Jade said with a wink as she searched behind the bar for a bottle of tequila and started pouring shots as they were ordered from across the bar.

Maya was about to protest but figured there would probably be nothing she could do to dissuade this woman, who always seemed to get what she wanted. She'd gladly share her tips if Jade could help make the night easier.

They didn't get the chance to talk much during the night as the busy pace had kept constant, but they did manage to keep stealing glances out of the corners of their eyes, share winks and smiles any time they came face to face, rub up against one another just right as they passed through the tight confines of the bar. It wasn't until four in the morning, as the bouncers ushered out the last of the intoxicated patrons, that the two girls could finally lean back against the bar and relax.

"Fuck . . . that was intense," Maya sighed as she ran her fingers through her hair, her top riding up to reveal a toned stomach she was proud of. She opened her eyes to catch Jade gazing over at her with a smirk on her face, obviously checking her out. Never had Maya felt so naked under anyone's gaze before. Feeling her cheeks redden, she could only mutter, "Umm, thanks for your help. You didn't have to—"

Jade cut her off. "I know I didn't have to. I wanted to," she said, her voice raspy from yelling all night long. She took a few steps closer, keeping her eyes locked on Maya's, grinning as Maya became more and more nervous as every inch of distance closed between them.

Maya leaned back as Jade came right into her personal space, the smile on Jade's lips confident as she placed her hands on either side of Maya. Jade had the height advantage as her brilliant green eyes stared down at her.

Only a few moments passed before they broke eye contact and began to passionately kiss, tongues dueling and teeth nipping as their hands blazed trails up and down each other's arms and back. They were lucky everyone had vacated the bar because nothing and no one could have stopped the passion that flared up between them. They both felt something in that instant, and neither one of them could fight it.

Their first encounter behind the bar of the Harem Lounge was quick and intense and hard, leaving both craving more of one another. Sure, to anyone else it was probably just a case of old-fashioned fucking, but Maya was sure they couldn't feel the passion and intensity behind every kiss, every touch, and every taste that she and Jade shared.

The relationship they shared, if you could call it that, continued on for a few weeks. Maya held onto the belief that something good or true could develop from some really mind-blowing sex. She *knew* there was something more between them. On more than one occasion, she had woken up in the middle of the night to find Jade watching her as she slept, which made Maya pretty sure that Jade felt the same thing.

They got along extremely well. As they made the nightly walk from the bar to Jade's apartment, they'd laugh and hop around, acting like two young kids without a care in the world. They'd almost always stop at the convenience store to get a can of whipped cream and a jar of cherries, both smiling secretly as they paid for the items, knowing full well they were the perfect toppings for the best sundae in the world that involved no ice cream whatsoever.

They would then go back to Jade's apartment, fuck against the door as soon as they walked in, play a bit with the whipped cream and cherries, fuck again on the bedroom floor, and then end up on the bed for the night.

There was no cuddling or any other kind of shows of pure affection. As much as Maya wanted to press herself close to Jade and wrap her arms around her, she didn't want to take a chance on pushing Jade away with something she didn't seem ready for. The closest they got to affection was the toe-curling kiss Jade would give Maya before she left in the early morning for classes.

"I'll see ya later, gorgeous," she'd say, then watch Maya walk down the hallway before closing the door and going back to her daily life.

As the days passed and the holidays quickly approached, Maya started to feel like the words "I love you" were definitely being felt by the both of them, but they were both too intimidated to say them.

One night as she lay dozing in Jade's bed after another round of animalistic fucking, she was surprised to feel soft fingertips caressing the small of her back as she lay on her stomach. She slowly opened her eyes to find Jade awake and watching her again, one arm extended so she could gently touch Maya's lower back. Jade made no effort to stop, so Maya kept quiet for as long as she could.

Out of the blue, Maya finally uttered a few quiet words. "Yunno, you're allowed to love me . . . if you want."

Jade's fingers stilled on Maya's back, as if she was contemplating what Maya had said and what exactly Maya was offering to her. She pulled her hand back to her side and sat up, wrapping the sheet around her naked form. A few moments of awkward silence passed before she spoke.

"I don't want to," she said, her tone devoid of emotion as her eyes stayed focused on some random spot across the wall.

Stunned, Maya could say nothing. She felt the flush of embarrassment creep across her body as her eyes welled up with tears that she dare not let fall.

And that was pretty much how it all ended. The two girls remained in bed, awake but unmoving, until the early hours of the morning. Maya silently got up from bed and got dressed, letting herself out of the apartment without saying goodbye.

Maya went to work that night with trepidation, fearful of running into the stunning temptress for whom she'd let herself fall so deeply. To her surprise, Jade never showed up to the bar that night. Or that week. Or for the next month and a half, roughly. Maya couldn't be absolutely sure Jade had never showed up over Christmas or New Year's Eve because Maya had left the city to be with her family for the holidays. But over a month had passed since she had returned, and there was still no sign of Jade.

Part of her was relieved that she hadn't run into Jade. She knew that seeing her and watching her go home with other girls would be rough. She needed the distance to help get over her case of puppy love. But another part of her was just . . . sad, and lonely, and hurt. As obscure as their so-called relationship had been, she thought they had a true connection—that more was said by their comfortable silence than any words could have ever voiced.

Most days, Maya did pretty well, ignoring any niggling

thoughts of the other girl. Work was busy enough that she was too preoccupied to sit and wallow about the past. But then there were nights like tonight—Valentine's Day. The bar was pretty dead. Most couples went to romantic dinners in fancy restaurants and horse-drawn carriage rides at sunset. The few patrons scattered around the mostly empty bar were either lonely singles like her or the regulars who came almost every night as part of their daily routine.

Maya rolled her eyes as she watched one couple at a table in the corner, holding hands across the table while smiling and giggling at one another. She had pretty much convinced herself that relationships like that didn't really exist, and if they did, they didn't last.

Not wanting to watch the overt display of affection anymore, she yelled to the other bartender that she was going into the back to get another case of beer. She walked slowly to the back room, taking her time and generally moping around before grabbing a case of random beer and heading back to the bar. She almost dropped the case when she walked out to find Jade sitting at the bar, looking directly at her. Her breath caught in her throat as she instinctively used one knee to keep the case of beer from crashing to the ground.

She took a moment to collect herself before placing the case onto the bar, then turned to face Jade, a fake smile on her face. "Hey, Jade," she said, trying to hide how nervous she felt.

"Hey," Jade replied, keeping her gaze locked on Maya. "I was just . . . kinda . . . in the neighborhood."

"Oh," Maya answered back. "Great. Nice to see you. So, um . . . what can I get for you?" she asked as she opened the case of beer and started to empty it into the cooler, trying to keep herself from looking up into the beautiful green eyes she remembered so well.

"Actually, I'm not really here for a drink," Jade said.

"No?" Maya asked, still avoiding Jade's eyes. "Just here to chase tail, then? Kinda slim pickings tonight, Jade. Maybe you should try someplace else."

Jade shook her head, looking more nervous herself at Maya's nonchalant words. "No, that's not it." She fell silent. "Maya . . . Maya, please look at me."

Maya stopped what she was doing, steeling her shoulders before turning to face Jade, her smile long gone. She raised an eyebrow, waiting for Jade to say what she had to say. It gave her a thrill of pleasure to see the normally cocky lady killer so unsure of herself. Jade nervously shredded a cocktail napkin before looking at Maya.

"I'm not good with this emotional stuff. I never let my feelings get involved, 'cause that way I can make sure I never get hurt. I'm sorry if I hurt you in the process."

Maya scoffed a little, then started to turn back to what she'd been doing. She was stopped mid-step by Jade's next words.

"I didn't want to love you, but I can't help it. I've been trying to avoid it and run away from it these last few weeks, but I can't anymore." She hesitated only a moment before standing up on the bottom of her barstool to reach across the bar and grab Maya's hand. "I know what I want—you. Will you be mine, Maya?"

At that, she pulled a single red rose from behind her back and held it out to Maya, smiling tremulously as she waited for Maya's response.

Maya stood completely still, staring at the red rose offering. So many thoughts ran through her mind. She was both scared and excited at the prospect of finally having something *real* with Jade. Sure, it was a big risk. Then again, what's life without taking some risks?

Letting a smile cross her face, she took the rose, letting her eyes meet Jade's as she breathed in the flower's sweet scent. "That depends," she responded playfully as she stepped closer toward the bar that separated them. "If I say yes, can we maybe have a sundae together?"

Jade smiled wide, but before she could answer, Maya spoke again. "And maybe breakfast in bed, too?" She watched Jade closely to see if she would catch any signs of anxiety or hesitance.

Still smiling, Jade let go of Maya's hand only for a moment so she could walk around the bar and grab the bartender's jacket. "I'd love that," she said as she held up the jacket for Maya, who maneuvered into the jacket, holding up her long hair and then letting it drop against her back as she turned to face Jade.

"Let's go."

The two girls took a slow walk to Jade's apartment, both comfortably quiet as they strolled hand-in-hand down the familiar path. But it was different this time; they could both feel it. It wasn't going home to be wild and crazy and nasty and naughty, though they were both aware that was where the evening would likely lead. It was going home . . . to start something new. Something meaningful. Something true.

As the two girls approached the small store where they normally bought their sundae toppings, Maya was surprised to find Jade tugging her past the front entrance. She stopped in her tracks, giving the girl a questioning smile. Jade smiled nervously, looking suddenly shy. She shrugged her shoulders a bit, trying to look nonchalant as she kept tugging Maya past the building.

"I dunno. I thought maybe . . . we could go down to that ice cream parlor on Grant Street and get a real sundae. My treat."

Maya smiled softly as she nodded, finding Jade's sudden sweetness quite endearing. Her smile widened as Jade brought their interlaced fingers up to her lips to place a soft kiss on the top of her hand even while they continued their walk down the street.

The trip to the ice cream parlor and back to Jade's didn't take too long. They giggled at the strange looks they received. After all, it was quite unusual to see two people walking down the snow-slushy streets of New York City in the middle of February with ice cream cones in their gloved hands.

The silence between them became a little less comfortable as they took the elevator up to Jade's apartment. It wasn't the thought that they were going up to the apartment to have sex that was making both of them edgy. It was the fact that it could possibly be more than that. That it *was* more than that. There was no more running from or searching for love. They had already found it. Now they just had to learn how to accept it.

At the twelfth floor, they exited the elevator, still holding hands. At her door, Jade reluctantly let go of Maya's hand to unlock and push it open. She walked in and stood aside, allowing Maya to walk in. They had been in this position many times before—Maya against the wall next to the door, Jade pressing her close as they kissed hard and fast. There had never really been any true emotion behind it before. Passion, yes. Emotion, no.

Maya automatically backed up against the door, looking up at Jade through her eyelashes as she unbuttoned her jacket and let it fall to the floor. The other girl quickly followed suit, unzipping her jacket and pulling it off, tossing it over onto the couch. She took a step closer toward Maya, letting her tongue flick over her bottom lip while she held eye contact. As Maya reached out her arms and slipped her fingers under the hem of the Jade's shirt, Jade stopped her.

"Wait," she said quietly, her voice almost pleading.

She took another step closer, cupping Maya's face with one hand and allowing the other to interlace with the fingers that played with her shirt. She tentatively brushed her thumb along Maya's cheek, smiling as Maya rested her cheek into the palm of her hand. Slowly, she leaned in and brushed her cheek against Maya's, breathing in deeply as her lips grazed her skin. She pulled back for just a moment to look into Maya's deep brown eyes before leaning in to finally taste her lips.

Their kiss was delicate and chaste at first, both getting used to the feel of one another's lips again. The thought of how badly she had acted made Jade wince a bit, realizing her own stupidity had almost ruined something this good. She had been trying to save herself from taking a fall, but she realized now that she didn't need saving—she needed to jump in with her eyes closed, and, with any luck, she'd land on her feet, with Maya at her side.

Their kiss deepened as Jade let her tongue play gently with Maya's. She groaned when Maya sucked on her tongue. Slipping her hand around Maya's lower back, she pulled the girl close and gently nibbled on her lower lip.

Then, much to Maya's surprise and delight, Jade was leading her away from the door and down the hallway to her bedroom. She ran her fingertips lightly down Jade's arms before working her fingers just under the hem of Jade's shirt. Jade's chuckle let her know it was okay now to push a little further. In one swift movement, she slid Jade's shirt off and tossed it aside onto the floor. Kissing passionately once again, they moved quickly to the bedroom, where Jade began to tug on Maya's shirt.

"Off," Jade mumbled into the kiss.

Maya happily obliged, smiling against Jade's insistent lips.

"Better?" she asked.

"Getting there," Jade replied as she easily flicked open the buttons of Maya's pants, then stripped them off her before turning her attention to Maya's soft neck.

Maya tilted her head back, giving Jade more access to suck and kiss along her sensitive skin. She moaned, fumbling with the zipper of Jade's pants. Jade broke away from her long enough to remove her pants and reveal she wore no underwear.

"Anxious?" Maya said chuckling, then gasped as Jade pushed her back onto the bed.

"Have you seen yourself in a mirror lately? Of course I'm anxious. You're fucking gorgeous," Jade said as she scooted them up higher on the bed and looked into Maya's eyes like she was going to devour her. The look was enough to make Maya shiver.

"You feel so good against me," Maya said breathlessly as she wrapped her arms around Jade's back, pulling her close as they kissed, hard and deep.

"Is that what you want?" Jade asked, as she kissed her way down Maya's jaw to her neck, flicking her tongue over the soft skin there before sucking on it lightly. "To feel me against you? My pussy dripping against yours as I fuck you with it?"

Maya groaned and closed her eyes, nodding furiously because she couldn't seem to speak at the moment.

"Okay then, that's what you'll get," Jade said, as she began to kiss her way down Maya's body, leaving a wet trail down her chest and stomach.

The scent of Maya's hot, wet arousal goaded Jade to kiss her through her red, and now thoroughly drenched, panties. She kissed lightly at first, teasing just above her clit before sucking the material into her mouth, making Maya moan and push against her.

Trying to remain cool and collected and in control, she placed one last kiss over Maya's panties before sliding them off, letting her fingertips graze Maya's thighs and sides as she slowly slid back up her body.

They kissed deeply again as Jade lay on top of Maya, positioning herself so their wet pussies pressed against one another. She kept her body perfectly still as she moved her lips to the corners of Maya's mouth and peppered light kisses there, lost in the sensation of their warm bodies pressed so intimately together. After several more soft kisses on Maya's lips and cheeks, Jade couldn't hold out anymore. She could feel Maya's pussy pressed against hers, hot and wet and ready. Maya's heavy breathing and squirming body urged her to take charge. Carefully, she used one hand on the bed to lift herself while sliding the other between them to first part Maya's swollen lips, then her own. They sighed and gasped as their hard clits touched, loving the way the teeniest bit of pressure was just a perfect tease for them both. Before Jade could even start to move her body, Maya wrapped one leg around her, pulling them even tighter together.

Jade grinned at the small gesture and looked into Maya's brown eyes as she slowly started to work up a rhythm, grinding their wet pussies together.

"Oh god," Maya groaned, clenching her eyes shut as she bit on her lower lip. She wrapped her arms around Jade's back and held her close, none too gently scratching her fingernails up her back.

Jade groaned aloud, moving faster and harder, loving the slick sounds of their pussies sliding together. Their breathing quickened as their hearts beat faster. Any other night, Jade would have had the music blasting loudly from her surround-sound speaker system, the pulsing beat rippling through her as she lost herself in a sea of sensations. But tonight, she needed to hear Maya—needed to hear her every gasp and breath and moan. She wanted to be completely and wholly aware of only the girl she had so stupidly pushed away and almost lost. She wanted to look into her eyes, hear her moans, taste her lips, feel her skin, and smell nothing but the heady aroma of their passion.

Feeling herself moving toward orgasm, Jade ran her right hand along Maya's side before gently coaxing the girl's leg from around her and pushing it forward a bit, making Maya's pussy open even more as she slid against it. She could feel their clits bumping perfectly now, each hard and wet against the other.

"Come for me," Jade whispered into Maya's ear, nibbling and flicking at her lobe with the tip of her tongue. Maya's warm breath against her face and neck was driving her crazy. "Come with me, baby," she urged.

"I'm so close . . . harder, Jade . . . I want to come with you . . . I want you to come all over me," Maya moaned, her breathing getting more and more ragged with every thrust.

She slid her hands down Jade's back to her hips, pulling Jade roughly against her.

"Fuck!" Jade groaned as she started to thrust her pussy harder against Maya's, feeling her starting to shake. She kissed her way from Maya's ear to her neck, kissing and sucking as Maya writhed beneath her.

Maya's sighs and gasps as she climaxed sent Jade over the edge, her body becoming rigid as she pumped her hips roughly a few last times. She came hard against Maya, their juices flowing together as they remained intimately pressed against one another.

She kissed Maya's neck and lips, trailing soft kisses on her lips and across her cheeks as their breathing slowed.

After a few minutes of silence, Jade finally rolled onto her back next to Maya, staring up at the ceiling as she pulled the sheets up to her waist. Tension filled the air as their old familiar pattern seemed ready to rear its ugly head again.

Maya fiddled with the top of the sheet as she stared ahead, not knowing exactly what was supposed to happen next. She knew what she wanted to happen—she wanted Jade to roll over and hold her in her arms all night, to fall asleep in the girl's arms. But she didn't want to come across as being clingy or needy, especially with their past history and how skittish Jade could be. Instead, going against what her body was willing her to do, she decided to give Jade a bit of room to breathe before they settled in for the night.

"Um, I just remembered that I forgot to put my rose in water. I should, um, go do that," she said more calmly than she felt, pulling the sheet aside so she could get up. Before she could even swing her legs over the edge of the bed, she felt Jade's hand holding her back.

"Wait!" Jade said, anxiety making her voice tremble. "How about you stay here with me, and I'll get you another flower tomorrow afternoon?"

Maya turned to her. Jade looked worried, as if she was afraid Maya would reject her. Maya smiled softly, laying back down and drawing the sheet up over her chest. She was just about to close her eyes, exhausted and ready to sleep, when she felt a pair of arms curl around her and a leg wedge between hers. She opened her eyes to find two of the most brilliant green eyes staring lovingly into hers.

"Happy Valentine's Day," Jade whispered, before resting her cheek on Maya's breast as they both fell asleep, content smiles upon their faces.

Something in the Cards
Vicky "Dylan" Wagstaff

I've never classed myself as a lucky person. Never won a raffle, found stray money in my path, or had any of my numbers come up on the lotto. Basically, any luck I ever had was more often than not . . . bad.

I'm not complaining. Not really. I have fun with my life. When I'm not working at the factory at least. The greeting card factory that is. Where I met Amy.

I'd been working there for about a year before she started alongside me in the production line. I'd been told to keep an eye on her, to show her the ropes. The place isn't big, and we don't have a technical job, but we have to make sure there are no faults in the cards before they get sent for packing.

That's our job. Me and Amy . . . pulling out from the line cards that are printed wrong or crumpled. When we spot them, we throw them behind us into a large plastic box that only gets emptied when it's full.

It's pretty full now because the old printer is on its way out, and that means lots of messed up cards. Christmas has just come and gone too, and now we're printing Valentine's Day cards. We're kept pretty busy in the run up to the holidays because we supply most of the local shops in the area here around Leeds.

I used to get really cheesed off when the printer was in full speed, all out and throwing cards down the line like they're going out of fashion. I would get dizzy trying to keep up, so I was more than glad when Amy came along to work beside me.

I was glad in more ways than one to be honest. Mainly because the minute Amy walked in the door, I was floored by her.

She stood out because she looked like she belonged somewhere on a beach in a bikini, playing volleyball, rather than throwing a tatty old apron on to watch cards fly past on a squeaky conveyer belt.

There were no lookers in the factory before Amy. I was probably about the nicest girl in the place, and that's saying something because the construction blokes down the street don't exactly whistle at me.

My hair is kind of short and messy, a dusky blonde that isn't going to dazzle anybody. I'm little and pretty skinny. Despite my lack of confidence about myself though, my mum always points out that I have a fine pair of striking blue eyes. But I think she only says that because I inherited them from her.

Amy on the other hand . . . She looked like some kind of angel when she strode up to tell me she was going to be working beside me.

The first thing I noticed was her long dark hair, almost black as it shone in the harsh lights above. Then her eyes . . . such a rich brown, shimmering as she smiled at me, a full open smile.

She said hello and told me her name, and I blinked, looking like an idiot as I tried to stammer out a welcome while I gazed up at her, noticing how her long slender body fit snugly into her clothes. I couldn't speak—my mind warning me that she's going to know right away I'm gay if I don't look away from her breasts. Then she starts chuckling.

That's right. She was giggling away at me as I mumbled my name at her. I didn't feel offended though, because it sounded so sweet. So unguarded and sincere. Her eyes were all lit up and looking at me like I was the only other person in the room.

Maybe I imagined it, I don't know. At the time I was sure I was just suffering from the fact I thought she was gorgeous, but I guess as time went on, I discovered that she didn't really smile that way at just everybody.

Anyway, she arrived about three weeks ago, and we've been working side by side ever since. I managed to not stutter every time we spoke, and she started telling me things about herself—about how bored she is of living in Leeds and how she dreams of traveling abroad. I heard all about how much of a pig her boyfriend is, and how much she wants to leave him, but is too used to being in a relationship. I tried to tell her that being single isn't all bad. We're both the same age—in our early twenties. There's no reason for us to be tied down.

I think she's finally willing to see that she doesn't have to sit at home every night with a boyfriend who has no clue what Valentine's Day is, let alone go out and buy her something nice to show how much she means to him.

"Hey, Rachel, are you gonna stare off into space all day or give me some help here?" Amy asks with that adorable chuckle to her voice.

I look up at her, blinking like a moron, as I try to pull my thoughts away from how much I've grown to really like her over the short time we've worked together. And I mean, *really* like her.

Maybe my luck is turning. She seems to like me too, possibly in a way that I could never have hoped for given the fact she's straight and has a burly boyfriend tucked away at home. There's just something in the way she seems to lean toward me when she speaks, and the way she giggles when I tell a lame joke that makes others roll their eyes at me.

Yes, I definitely feel something between us. Something more than friendship.

I feel something for her that I've tried not to think about too deeply when I lay in bed at night fantasizing about her because I couldn't possibly even begin to deal with the prospect of falling in love with her, knowing I most likely don't have a chance.

I can only hope fortune shines on me though, because looking at her now, with her beautiful brown eyes focused solely on me, I know I'm falling for her, and hard.

"Are you okay?" she asks, moving closer.

I force a smile onto my face that hopefully won't give away how I feel and wink at her, trying to find the tough girl inside me that doesn't do the whole swooning thing.

"Yeah, I'm fine. I'm just wondering why you're slacking though." I point to all the faulty cards that are too far down the line to go grab and toss into the overflowing waste box.

"Me?" she gasps in feigned disbelief, lifting a hand to her chest with the cutest shocked look I've ever seen. "It was you. I was . . . Rachel, don't force me to have to tickle you."

I turn my eyes back to the creaky old conveyer belt with the blur of cards going by, but I just know I look a little surprised at what she just said. We've gotten fairly close, but I didn't know we were at the tickle stage. The closest I had gotten to her was whilst placing a plaster on her finger because she had a nasty paper cut. Couldn't have her bleeding on those nice, crisp, white cards. But I recall those few minutes almost as if they had happened in slow motion.

I'm pretty sure I was practically shaking as I wrapped the small plaster around her ring finger, my own fingertips just brushing over her skin lightly as I did so. Her skin was so warm, and my heart was racing. I could smell the scent of her perfume like it was wrapped around me. Just under that bottled aroma though was purely her—exotic and captivating. And she was looking at me the whole time I was tending to her cut. I mean, really at me. Never looking away from my eyes.

My heart was going crazy for her that day, I can tell you. Like a thousand wild horses had been set free within my chest and were never planning to stop running.

"Okay, so you have to tell me what's going on with you, Rachel. You keep missing the cards with the blatantly obvious mangled Cupids and hearts."

It's true, I do. And they *are* pretty obviously mangled. One of them practically had two Cupid heads and would look much better as some kind of Halloween card than one you'd want to have arrive on your doorstep on Valentine's Day.

"I'm okay, Amy. I guess I'm just . . ." I don't finish the sentence because I can't come out and tell her that I'm distracted because of her.

Three weeks and I'm completely smitten with her. Three weeks of her smile and her beautiful eyes twinkling at me. Her sweet voice filling my head at night as I try to remember she's out of my league, taken, and being no more than friendly.

She stops flinging cards behind her and turns toward me, her hand coming up to rest on my arm, forcing me to look up at her.

I turn my body to face her more, and away from the cards shooting past on their way to the end of the line. I forget all about the cards and my job, though, as I stand gazing up into her gentle eyes.

She cocks her head slightly to the side and allows a soft, slow smile to curve her lips. If I didn't know better, I would say the smile was almost flirty. Like she's just become completely aware of something and likes the idea . . . a lot.

I almost stop breathing, wondering if I should joke off the fact that there seems to be something going on between us right now. I don't do that though, mainly because I really don't know *what's* going on.

If I was any good at reading signals I'd probably know, but I was always so bad at that. My ex girlfriend even said I could win prizes for being oblivious and inconsiderate. Maybe that's the reason why I always sucked at love. I just never found a way to decipher the small things like looks and touches, or feelings that were just there without explanation.

The way Amy is looking at me right now though, it's like she can see right into me. I can feel that. It isn't a subtle signal—it's practically a neon light. But I try to work through all the reasons in my mind why she couldn't possibly be looking like she was stepping that little bit closer to kiss me, because these kinds of things don't happen to me.

I can't seem to focus on anything other than her, though. The deep brown of her eyes softens the edges of my world, as she becomes all I can see. Her full cherry lips part slightly, allowing just a peek of her tongue as she wets them.

I do the same, almost without thought. Without conscious awareness of the fact that my lips were dry, and that my body was preparing for her to move just that one step closer as we keep our eyes locked, our world consisting of nothing but the two of us in an echoey landscape of clanking machinery.

She's almost close enough to fall into now completely, close enough to disappear into the depth of her eyes. And I'm enveloped in her scent again, my body coiling from the inside out with how much I want her against me.

I move ever so slowly toward her, so she's not the only one inching closer to bring us together. We're almost toe-to-toe. My face is near enough to hers to feel the warmth of her breath upon it.

I tilt my head up to compensate for our height difference, to seek out her lips with mine. My mind freezes temporarily to block out any intrusions that might tell me not to be foolish enough to believe she would let me kiss her.

Then just before that perfect moment, she pulls away abruptly, her eyes darting to the left. Her body recoils sharply as if I'd just pushed her away.

I step back. I sense the little devil on my shoulder mocking me for daring to think I had read the signals right. Then I notice the factory foreman striding over to us, looking far less than pleased as he waves his clipboard around dementedly, like a flag.

I understand right away why Amy had leapt back as soon as I catch what the foreman is yelling in our direction. The printing machine has stopped its incessant whirring, and people are slowly making their way out of the big doors that lead to daylight and freedom from the dusty atmosphere.

"What the hell have you two been doing all this time?" the foreman screams, as he stops at the box at the foot of the conveyer belt. The box that is meant to be full of unspoiled cards for retail, and not topped off by a nice array of misprinted and crumpled cards that should be in our waste pile.

I look at Amy, who's blushing bright red, and then back at the foreman as he stomps over to our station. I try to stutter out an excuse, but I'm pretty sure it'll get lost in his haze of anger. So instead I hold up my hands as he stops in front of us, and conjure up the best reassuring smile I can muster. His mouth opens and closes like an ill-mannered fish, finally settling on closed as I speak.

"Calm down," I say. "There's no need to panic. Only a few slipped by, and we can stay late and get them out of the box."

He blinks and narrows his eyes at me, shifting his glare and looking to my left at Amy, as she stands there like a naughty schoolgirl about to be told to expect a letter being sent to her parents. I glance her way too and can't help but find the sorry look on her face adorable, and I get caught up in it for a second.

I forget the foreman altogether as he's murmuring something about lights and keys. I'm too busy feeling my heart being trampled on by a herd of stampeding butterflies as I fall completely in love with Amy.

I can't help it. It hits me too quickly to duck and run like I've been doing for the past week or so. I can't possibly escape the fact that we've done nothing but laugh together, sharing stories and secrets as we spend all our time in each other's company here at work, growing close and secure with each other.

As I stand and gaze at Amy's flawless face, the foreman starts to shuffle away, still muttering to himself. Amy then turns to face me, a twinkle in her eyes as she smiles the warm open smile that I've never seen her bestow on anybody else.

She's breathtaking, and I'm captivated.

"Rachel, did you hear what he said?" she asks me with a chuckle as I just stand and grin at her. "He's going to turn off most of the lights, but we have to turn the last set off and lock up when we're done."

Trying to blink my way out of the daze I'm in, I notice she's holding out her hand. I look down at the keys shining in her palm. I take them from her slowly, my fingers brushing softly over her palm, and almost jump back from the way just touching her feels.

"Right," I mumble, worried that I'm getting all my wires crossed and plugged into all the wrong slots by thinking there could be something between us.

But then she shocks me by reaching out to touch my face. Softly. Barely touching me at all as she cups my cheek, then tenderly strokes her fingers down to my jaw line before moving her hand away, her eyes never leaving mine until she turns to head for the end of the line.

I stand in silence as I let out my breath slowly, suddenly aware that I've been holding it. My skin tingling where her fingers had been. I've never felt so much warmth from another person in such a simple gesture. It was like she was telling me not to worry so much, or maybe that she feels a little of what I do.

I really don't know right now. What I *do* know is that I've never felt such a connection to anybody before in my life. It feels like we fit together perfectly, and I hope to God it's not all just in my mind.

"Come on, it's your fault we're stuck here when we could be on our way home," Amy calls from where she's standing, sifting through the good cards for the bad.

I can't help but grin because there's no malice to her words at all. She never really gets angry with me, even when I steal the last sandwich from her lunch box. Amy is probably the sweetest girl I've ever known.

Softly laughing to myself at just how smitten I've become, I make my way down to join her, noticing how quiet and still the factory is all around us. How the darkness seems to blot out the rest of the old place, leaving it seeming like our little space bathed in the light from directly above is all there is.

As I reach her side, I notice Amy has already started to make a little pile of cards at her feet. I say nothing about the way we just almost kissed, or the way she just touched me.

As we rummage through the box, our eyes keep meeting in that cute embarrassed way I would mock other people for doing. There's suddenly so much tension between us, like a static charge as we almost brush against each other whilst bending to remove the misplaced cards.

My heart is jumping in my chest, and maybe I'm going crazy . . . but I'm almost sure I can hear Amy's heart pounding the same. Like it's falling into the same rhythm as mine as our glances become looks, and the looks become held and almost tender moments where our eyes are diving into each other, looking for clues.

I daren't speak right now because I'm pretty sure I'd just blurt out something about how much I think about her, feel for her already, and want her. How much she makes my skin feel like ice, ready to melt at her touch.

I don't want to scare her away. I can sense that she's reacting to me in ways that *have* to mean she's thinking similar thoughts, but I don't want to push it. I don't want to push *her* away.

So we search through the box, littering the floor with the unwanted cards that will never fulfill their purpose. The tension between us palpable. Like we're both looking for release, even if that release is just to speak.

Pulling the last slightly crumpled card from the pile and tossing it on top of the others, I bend down to scoop them up in my arms. Amy bends with me, catching the few I fail to gather up, smiling almost shyly at me as we stand and walk over to the waste box.

We both stop at the box full of the forlorn-looking mass of rejects, dropping our lot onto the overflowing pile. As we both reach out to stop them from sliding right off the top and down to the floor again, our hands touch. Just a slight brush that lingers— lingers enough for me to hold my breath just as Amy takes a sharp one. I don't move as my eyes glance down to where we're touching.

My heart almost beats right out of my chest as she tentatively slides her hand over the top of mine, her fingertips grazing my knuckles as her warm palm rests on the back of my hand. She pauses there, not quite holding, just touching, the subtle movements of her fingers sending tingles all along my arm.

I don't react at first until she looks over at me, the deep gold flecks in the brown of her eyes catching the light and my attention as I turn my head slightly. Then her fingers slowly wrap around mine, and I know I'm not the only one feeling this thing between us. We're both drowning in each other's gaze. There's no hope now of stepping away from the obvious.

Taking a chance that it's the right thing to do, I move to face Amy completely. Swapping my right hand for my left to take hold of hers again, with more intent. More purpose as we find ourselves impossibly close. Our chests rise and fall to the tune of the hungry look I can now see for certain in her eyes.

I can feel the heat of her skin drawing me closer. And I can see now that she's holding herself back, just as I am . . . but I don't have the willpower to hold back any longer. So I call up my courage and close the small distance between us, crushing my lips to hers without warning.

Instantly she's pressing up against me. Her lips, her body, flush against mine, as fear loses out to desire.

Our hands atop the discarded Valentine cards clasp together, fingers entwining. My other hand reaches up to hold her face gently as our kiss grows bolder and deeper.

Her lips are so sweet. So soft and yielding as we taste, tantalize, and seek more from one another. And as she opens her mouth slowly, allowing my tongue to enter, I realize I've never felt so completely overwhelmed by the soft slide of tongues and lips as I am now.

She tastes incredible, like I knew she would. Her tongue is shy in seeking out mine, but all the more alluring and perfect for it. Kissing her a little harder, unable to hold back any longer, I hear a soft moan escape her and I'm instantly wet with desire.

I pull back slightly, sucking lightly on her tongue as I do so, causing another moan that has me pushing my hips up against her. Craving more contact.

Without speaking, without asking why, what if, yes, or no, I push Amy up against the box of cards, her backside just resting on the edge as I trail my fingers up from where our hands were entwined. Up the inside of her arm, over the top of her shoulder to her neck. Then I allow my fingers to slide into the hair at the base of her neck, my other hand doing the same, I put everything I am . . . everything I have, into kissing her.

I want her to know what she does to me. How each look she gives me . . . every smile . . . has me melting. Swooning. Falling.

Her arms hold me tight against her, and lips and tongue giving me back everything I'm giving certainly has me believing that this is not just me. This is us. Wanting each other just as much, with no doubts or hesitation.

Everything around me is blurring into nothingness as she becomes all there is, dominating all my senses.

I feel her hands slowly move to my lower back. Her fingernails catch on the fabric of my shirt, causing me to arch forward slightly, my body settling between her legs as they part for me. Her breasts are moving over mine with every breath she takes, as if purposefully caressing my nipples with hers. And my nipples are hard for her. Straining toward her. Aching in the same way they have every night since I met her.

Fitting snugly between Amy's thighs as she shuffles her backside up onto the box so her feet leave the floor, I trail my lips from hers, down to her neck, just wanting to taste her skin. To discover as much about her as possible.

Her fingers slip under the hem of my top, and I know for sure that she's not going to leap away any time soon, screaming that I was taking advantage. I can feel in her questing hands and hear in her soft sighs as I place wet kisses in the hollow of her throat . . . that she's not going to freak out suddenly.

I'm certainly glad about that because with all my dreaming and thinking about her, I'm so worked up I could push her down onto the cards right now and show her just how gorgeous and sexy I think she is.

As soon as the thought crosses my mind of course, I can't stop thinking about doing just that. And she's pulling me against her body like she needs me as close to her as possible, so it's not really helping me think about backing off and waiting.

I don't want to wait. I want her. I need to make her feel what I'm feeling.

Delicately I suck on her neck. Tiny whimpers escape her lips and drive me nuts as my hands move to her sides. My palms glide over her ribs, upward and inward slowly, just waiting for the signals or the words to make me stop touching what I've desired so much.

I don't just want to throw her down and fuck her though. That wouldn't come close to what I feel. What I crave. With Amy, I want to love her slowly and surely. Show her with every touch and kiss I can offer how I've fallen madly in love with her.

Just to make sure I'm not going to make any mistakes, however, I pull back slightly, licking my lips. Looking into her eyes, so dark and intense with desire I almost feel naked before her. I halt my hands just under the curve of her breasts and go for broke.

"You're beautiful, Amy. Inside and out. And I want you," I tell her. The words are loud and clear, though I spoke in a hushed whisper.

She smiles. That smile that almost has me bursting with feeling. "I'm all yours," she whispers back, making my insides tumble over and over as she grips the last of my resolve and tugs it firmly away. "I was yours right from the start."

I feel a rush of heat that must be my heart pumping more than just blood around my body, and I feel like I could grin the biggest grin I've ever been known to. In fact, I probably am doing just that, if the way Amy is looking at me is any indication.

I don't care though, because I can see in her eyes, as well as know in her words, that she feels the way I do. That she really is mine—that whatever connection I had felt from the start is real and true.

Without worry now I lean back in to kiss her. A little softer this time, trying to convey to her that I'm not just in it for a one-time deal. For the way she looks. For nothing more than a notch on my bedpost.

She must understand that because she's kissing me back in just the same way, and I'm sensing more than just need and desire from her as her hands gently cup my face, thumbs tenderly rubbing over my cheeks.

With nothing stopping me now in my desire, I move my hands up over Amy's breasts, allowing the weight of their fullness to settle in my palms as she takes a deep breath at the touch. Our tongues halt their quest to know each other fully as our lips barely move, just brushing lightly together in a pause for us both to adjust to this more intimate contact.

I rub a little over her with my palms, feeling her nipples stiffen against them, pushing into my hands in a plea to tease them. I comply and run my fingers over their hardness, pressing into the sensitive flesh.

I feel Amy bite her lip, and I kiss over her jaw line to her ear, placing small caresses over the delicate shell as I breath harder in reaction to the way her body moves against me. I know I should take things slow. I know we should do this elsewhere—not in an old factory on a stack of cards—but I need her now.

Continuously trailing my lips over the silky skin of Amy's jaw and neck, I cautiously move my right hand down from her breast, my fingers tripping over the material of her top as I feel her stomach tense at my touch.

I'm pretty sure she must know where I'm heading, but she's not making a move to stop me. Instead, she pulls me in tighter as she moves her hands further up under my top, holding me close. Her fingernails scratch with just the right amount of pressure to have me groaning every time she does it.

My underwear is soaked with how much I want her. And I have to discover if she's in the same state. I have to feel if her quiet moans and sighs are the only affect I'm having on her, so I move my hand over the outside of her jeans, touching the material lightly, gauging her reactions to make sure I'm not jumping ahead too quickly.

I find out I'm not going too fast at all as Amy lifts her hips to feel my hand slide over her pussy, over the top of her jeans.

"Fuck. Rachel, I want you. I've wanted you from the moment I saw you. Please, just take me."

The words came out husky and bold.

My eyes rake over Amy's body and I can see she's probably more wound up than me. She leans back a little, one hand resting behind her on the cards, her brown eyes locked on mine as my palm presses into her ever so slightly.

She closes her eyes for a second, then a wanton moan comes from deep inside her. A call to me to give her what she needs.

Moving so I have room to maneuver, I let my hands travel to the zipper of her jeans, tugging on it, pulling at the dark material as she lifts her hips. Her backside rises off the cards, spilling some to the floor in our rush to free her. I don't hesitate in pulling down her underwear too, gripping the waistband in my fingers along with her jeans, and helping her wriggle until they slide down her legs and to the floor, kicked off along with her shoes.

I allow my gaze to wander then, roaming up over her legs to the place I want to worship with my tongue as I instantly see how wet she is for me. The insides of her thighs glisten with arousal. Her pussy is shaved smooth and looking like the most delicious treat I could ever hope to enjoy.

I know right then that I have to taste her. I have to feel the silky pink flesh on my tongue and lips. Fill my mouth with the delicious taste of her.

I glance at her face, catching the need in her eyes, and move in closer to her again, in between her legs. My hands softly stroke her thighs as I lean in to kiss her once, before lowering myself to my knees.

I don't think she was quite expecting that because her eyes went a little wide. But as I slide my hands up the insides of her tanned thighs, close enough to her wet sex to be completely intoxicated by her scent, she relaxes.

She spreads herself wide for me, her legs falling open as she leans back on the pile of cards. She's beautiful. And offering herself to me. So I place kiss upon kiss up the insides of her thighs, taking my time as I reach the glistening juices seeping from her pussy.

Not wanting to miss a single sensation, or a single taste, I kiss right on top of her swollen lips. Right over her dripping hole as she gasps loudly in the quiet atmosphere. My lips linger, just pressing over her, my whole being wanting me to push my tongue inside her right now, but my mind telling me to go slower. To savor her because she tastes like heaven.

I allow the tip of my tongue to slip between her folds and over her soft pink flesh, but her grasp on my head makes me realize Amy isn't going to allow me to keep it slow. She's trembling already, one hand firmly stroking through my hair and pushing me into her.

I smile a little and run the flat of my tongue from the place she's wettest, open and wanting me. Then up over her clit, making her groan out my name.

That spurs me on. I want to hear her say my name over and over.

Pressing against her, I flick my tongue over her firm little clit, circling it gently with the tip, then licking harder over it. Her hips are moving in time with me, her breathing shallow and loud. Sexy sighs and moans drive my tongue deeper between her parted folds.

I hear her moan my name again as I grip her thighs and push

my tongue inside her. Her pussy is so soft and warm, so wet for me. I feel her wetness spilling out of her and into my mouth, over my tongue and down my chin as I try to fill her pussy completely. Her hands pressing on my head encourage me, and I slide in and out of her faster and harder, fucking her with my tongue.

She tastes more amazing than I could ever have imagined. I thrust my tongue inside her, wanting to touch as deep as I can. Then I feel her pussy grasping at me as she shudders, moaning ever louder as she starts to come. I groan into her, aware enough to find her clit with my thumb so she comes harder for me. Rubbing over it as she calls out my name, her juices gushing into my mouth, as she writhes beneath me.

I drink her down, sucking on her pussy. Wanting more of her. Loving that she's given this gift. Loving her more and more with every whisper of my name, and every shudder that I feel as she catches her breath. Kissing her pussy softly now, her fingers curl through my hair, urging me to stop licking her and to stand up.

"Rachel," she says, "come here."

I reluctantly pull away and rise to my feet, wondering only briefly how she'll react to the taste of herself on my lips. She leans her body into mine as I kiss her deeply.

"Rachel," she says softly, and I smile against her lips after a few moments, wrapping my arms around her protectively as she does the same. Then I feel something warm and wet on my cheek.

Leaning back a little I notice the shimmer of tears in Amy's brown eyes, but before I can ask what's wrong, or worry about why she might be crying, she silences me. Whispering words that I really wasn't expecting.

"I love you, Rachel."

I feel my heart flip in my chest like it just took a dive from a great height and was caught by hands that I feel, from deep within me . . . are going to keep it safe.

"I love you too," I whisper back, feeling it with every fiber of my being. Feeling like my luck has turned at last.

Finally, I can rest now, knowing I have somebody in my arms that I would give my life to keep safe and happy, no matter how complicated things might get when she breaks from her mundane past.

Despite the short time we've known each other, I truly feel that we're connected. And I'm the luckiest girl alive.

Rose-Colored Glasses
M. C. Ammerman

Ah, there you are, my friend. Are you ready for our little Valentine's love story? Good. Let's put on our red-lensed, heart-shaped glasses and step through the mists of time to find our setting.

Here we are. As you can see, we are standing in the middle of the supermarket, late in the evening on Valentine's Day, looking across to the deli/seafood counter. The manager and the other workers have left; only two young women remain. Behind the counter, to our right, is Brenda. She's been on her feet all day, filling the seafood bins with half-frozen shrimp, weighing portions of salmon to which color has been added, and taking orders for party platters on the telephone. Her feet inside her Keds are sore, the blue polo shirt all store employees are required to wear smells fishy; her hands are red and raw from washing and re-washing and handling icy seafood. Still, if one looks very, very closely, one might almost think there is a gleam of excitement in her surprisingly blue eyes, and one might notice how frequently she glances down the counter to her co-worker in the deli section.

Behind the deli portion of the counter is Gretchen. Like Brenda, she's a big, round, solid girl with sore feet and red hands. Her arms are strong from working the slicer over and over again nearly every day for the four years since high school, and her blue polo shirt is covered with a fine sprinkling of American cheese bits. From where she stands, she can see the bakery counter, and she has been looking all day at the Valentine's cookies and cakes out on display. She might pick something up before she leaves, but she's not sure. Her mother would enjoy it, but neither of them should really eat so much sweet stuff, especially her mother. Besides, it would be too pathetic. She has no Valentine of her own, and probably never will. She doesn't want to be reminded.

Brenda, watching, sees Gretchen sigh, then amble into the back for plastic wrap. It is time to start the clean-up, but Brenda has something to do first. She reaches behind a box of plastic gloves and pulls out a red rose; moving very quietly in spite of her aching feet, she quickly drops the rose on the slicer and scuttles back to her seafood display. When Gretchen returns, Brenda is buried deep in the glass cabinet, scooping shrimp into a plastic bag, apparently absorbed in her work, though a certain redness about her neck might be a clue if Gretchen wants one.

As Gretchen moves back toward the slicer, Brenda watches through the glass walls of the seafood case. She sees her stop, stare, and reach out a hesitant hand. Brenda quickly looks away as Gretchen gazes wonderingly around her, then picks up the rose.

"Brenda?" Gretchen says.

Brenda swallows hard and slowly pulls herself out of the case, her face flushed. "Yeah?" She faces Gretchen with what she hopes is an innocent look, but Gretchen is still peering around the store in a puzzled fashion.

"Somebody left this on the slicer. Did you see who it was?" She finally looks at Brenda, whose color is returning to normal. As

Brenda hesitates, looking at the linoleum, her tongue apparently not working, Gretchen suddenly wakes up.

"Oh."

Brenda glances up and sees that Gretchen has caught on. An agony of doubt assails her as she wonders just what will really come of her foolhardy gesture. What if she'd made the wrong assumption? What if—

Gretchen smiles shyly. "Thanks. It's . . . really sweet of you."

Whew. The doubts retreat, and Brenda's face turns red again, but she's smiling, too. "I'm glad you like it."

They stand staring at each other for a moment, until Gretchen suddenly realizes the time.

"We'd better get going, I guess. We don't have much time to clean up." She puts the rose carefully on the shelf with the box of plastic gloves.

"Uh, yeah."

They return to work, both moving with practiced efficiency until everything is neat and clean and the lights are off. As they stand at the time clock, Gretchen holds the rose up and sniffs it, admiring Brenda's blue eyes more openly than she'd ever done before.

"It's a nice one," she tells Brenda.

"Yeah, they had them over in produce when I came in. I bought it at lunch. I just . . . well, um . . . would you like to go out? We could go to Denny's or something and get a sandwich." Brenda tries to appear casual.

"Um, yeah, that would be nice," Gretchen says. "But I should call my mother. I don't want her to worry."

"Sure. You can use my cell phone."

They clock out and exit by the back door. Gretchen calls her mother to tell her she's going out with a friend, something she's almost never done, but her mother accepts it with good grace. Indeed, if Gretchen could see her mother's face, she'd see how happy this makes her.

Soon the two women are sitting in the fluorescent ambience of the local Denny's, being served by a pimply faced, skinny boy who has known Brenda since grade school. Harry sees the rose, but, with unusual sensitivity, makes no mention of it. Instead, he pours on the charm he usually reserves for parties of elderly ladies who come in for lunch. Gretchen smiles warmly at his amusing banter, and he suddenly has an insight into why his old friend has apparently been smitten. Gretchen's not a supermodel, he thinks, but she's pretty, and her smile is real, not fake. He glances at Brenda and sees her smiling at Gretchen almost adoringly. He has seen Brenda smile many times, but not like this. He takes their orders and tells the cook to be quick with them, that they're special customers of his. It's a slow night, and the cook obliges with surprisingly good humor.

In their booth, the two women talk of the many things they've talked about before behind their counters—movies, CDs they did or didn't like, their pets. Gretchen's mother has a Chihuahua that Gretchen can't really stand, and Brenda has a cat. Gretchen says a cat is better than a little yappy dog any day. They laugh, and Brenda, feeling both bold and nervous, reaches out and squeezes Gretchen's hand under the table. Gretchen is momentarily surprised, but doesn't pull away. She swallows hard as her eyes meet Brenda's, and the warmth of the touch grows.

Finally, they are finished with their meal, during which Harry has been considerately attentive, hovering delicately in the background, attempting desperately to make the evening special in any way he can. Brenda has been a good friend to him, and he likes Gretchen very much. He gives Brenda a thumbs-up sign as they are leaving; both women see him and giggle. He blushes, but sees Gretchen's face light up delightedly, and doesn't regret the gesture.

"So, well, I guess I'll see you tomorrow," Gretchen says as they stand by their cars. Neither wants to leave; they are holding hands openly now. It is dark in that part of the lot, and it's empty. Brenda looks into Gretchen's eyes and hopes she's right about what she thinks she sees there. She pulls gently on Gretchen's hand, and feels no resistance, so she reaches a hand up to touch her cheek.

They lean toward each other, awkwardly, but manage to brush their lips together in a quick kiss that leaves them both nervous and giddy.

Brenda takes a deep breath. "Uh, well, uh, maybe you'd like to come to my place?" She sees Gretchen's eyebrows go up. "Well, it's only ten, and you did say you'd like to meet my cat." Gretchen is silent. "If you don't want to, it's okay. I mean, I don't want to rush you or anything," Brenda mumbles.

Gretchen smiles and squeezes her hand. "Well, I do want to, really. I just . . . well, I never . . ."

Brenda takes a shuddering breath. "Yeah. Me, neither." They eye one another a moment, then laugh nervously.

"Well, let's go, then," Gretchen says, feeling reckless. "Maybe we should find out together," she says softly. Brenda's eyes widen, and both laugh again.

Brenda drives ahead, leading Gretchen to the duplex she shares with her brother. They bought the little house years ago with the money from their father's life insurance policy. Brenda does most of the work around the place, which suits her brother, who travels a lot as a salesman. Brenda tells Gretchen all this as she unlocks the door.

"He's in Asheville right now, seeing a client," she tells her.

They step inside to be greeted by a sleepy gray cat. The house is sparsely furnished, but the sofa is big and squashy, and Gretchen sinks down into it, looking around and admiring Brenda's attempts at decorating. Brenda doesn't have much money, but she does have the sense to surround herself with healthy plants, solid furniture, and simple color combinations. Gretchen feels comfortable here, and begins to relax. Brenda comes out of the kitchen with two glasses of iced tea and places them on the coffee table. She sits on the sofa, not too close, and an awkward silence falls. The gray cat jumps up and begins a sniffing exploration of the guest. Soon, both women are petting the cat, secretly delighted when their hands brush together. The cat and the iced tea are quickly forgotten.

Brenda shifts closer to Gretchen and takes her face gently in both hands; she hears Gretchen's breathing quicken, and feels her own heart thumping madly. She has dreamed of this moment for months, planning each movement, but has doubts that she can get it right because she has only her imagination to rely on; but she remembers that Gretchen is even more unprepared than she is, and decides to just go for it, gently.

Gretchen sees the warmth in Brenda's eyes and thinks about how kind those eyes could be, and how they sparkle with glee at any funny thing that happens in the store. She remembers the gentle sympathy with which Brenda has always listened to her when recounting her mother's various health problems, and how helpful she is each day as they work to keep pace with customers' demands. Her heart seems to expand within her chest as she realizes she is in very caring hands.

Their lips meet, and this time, neither pulls away. The softness surprises them both, but the surprise is quickly replaced by a driving hunger as the heat registers, and both feel an ache between their legs. They part, both gasping from the intensity of their feelings. They embrace tenderly; Gretchen feels shaky, and Brenda soothes her with gentle murmurs, stroking her hair and thinking about how good it feels to take care of this woman, who she knows has spent so much time and energy caring for a sick mother and for two tiny nephews whose divorced parents have little time to take them out to parks and playgrounds. She has longed to show Gretchen how special she thinks her, and now has a chance. She feels the other woman's trembling subside, and plants quick, gentle kisses on her neck, below her ear. She feels Gretchen's touch on her side. Their mouths meet again, open this time, and their tongues search, shyly at first, then with increasing boldness, exploring one another's mouth with pulsing energy.

Brenda feels a wetness between her legs, and boldly brushes her hand against the side of Gretchen's breast. As the other woman gasps, she strokes more firmly, moving her hand around to cover as much of its roundness as possible. Even through the layers of clothing, she feels the hidden nipple harden, and her groin aches even more in response.

Gretchen is momentarily stunned by the touch. She moans softly, burying her face in Brenda's neck, amazed at the feeling and heartbreakingly grateful for it. She reaches down to place her hand over Brenda's, holding it to her breast, silently agreeing with the gesture.

Brenda slowly stands, pulling Gretchen up with her, and together they make their way upstairs, slowly, stroking one another's bodies gently until they reach Brenda's bedroom. Brenda has a big brass bed, bought with hard-won savings, and covered with soft pillows. They part long enough for Brenda to light a candle on the dresser. They sit on the edge of the bed and kiss again. Brenda slips a questioning hand beneath Gretchen's polo shirt, but pulls it away quickly as Gretchen jumps.

"Sorry—"

"No, it's okay." Gretchen takes Brenda's hand and places it on her waist. After a moment's hesitation, Brenda slips her hand back in and feels the warm skin beneath, runs her hand over the soft mound of flesh that hangs over Gretchen's black work pants.

Gretchen's head drops self-consciously. "I guess I should lose weight, huh?" she whispers.

Brenda puts a gentle finger under Gretchen's chin. "So should I, but we aren't going to do that right away, are we?" She grins. "Besides, I'm used to it. I wouldn't know what to do with some of them damn skinny women we see at the store."

Gretchen laughs in spite of herself, and slips her own hand under Brenda's shirt, realizes the shape she feels really is familiar, and forgets her worries.

Brenda tugs gently at Gretchen's shirt, and begins to pull it up. Gretchen raises her arms and soon the shirt is off, and Brenda is embracing her, kissing her. She feels the hooks on her bra disconnect, and her large breasts are released. Brenda pulls away, taking the bra with her, and Gretchen inhales, seeing her own naked chest rise. A second later, warm hands cover her breasts, and she gasps a little as a tingle shoots through her loins. The hands squeeze, gently, as she closes her eyes and swallows hard. Brenda's hands slide around to her sides, her fingers gently rubbing the red marks where her bra has cut into her skin, something Gretchen herself does nearly every day. She leans forward into Brenda's strong arms and kisses her gently on the lips, placing her hands on Brenda's neck. As she strokes first her neck and then her short brown hair, she feels Brenda's hands come around to her breasts again, this time teasingly brushing her nipples until she throws her head back, lifting her breasts into the touch. She almost falls backward but Brenda catches her and pulls her down on the bed.

Gretchen plucks at Brenda's shirt with an inquiring grin, which is met with a sly smile. Brenda sits up and removes her shirt, but before she can begin to remove her bra, Gretchen surprises her by lifting up the elastic and pushing the bra up over her breasts. She lies back, letting Gretchen stroke her nipples, softly at first, then more firmly; finally, she sits up and unhooks her bra. She rolls toward Gretchen and gently moves her hands aside, placing her mouth insistently on Gretchen's left nipple, sucking and licking more and more strongly as she hears Gretchen begin to moan. She plants kisses over every inch of flesh she can find, before reaching down to undo Gretchen's pants. Gretchen makes no move to stop her; she is floating in sensations she's never felt before, only dimly aware of Brenda's actions. Brenda keeps up her sucking, her mouth on Gretchen's left nipple and her left hand pinching the right one; her right hand works at the zipper and then gently begins pulling the pants down. Somehow she manages to sit up long enough to pull Gretchen's pants and underwear down, then goes back to her breasts, stroking Gretchen's round belly and thighs gently, wonderingly, giddy with excitement and happiness.

Gretchen, vaguely, thinks she should be returning the favor, but can't seem to decide what to do. Brenda seems to be perfectly content with what she's doing, so Gretchen decides simply stroking her partner's breasts is enough for now. She'll do whatever Brenda wants when the time comes. She feels a sudden, tickling sensation between her legs, and realizes Brenda is stroking her pubic hairs so lightly they nearly stand on end. She can hardly bear the feeling but wants more. Brenda strokes more firmly, rubbing now, and Gretchen opens her legs, hardly knowing what she's doing. A shy touch causes her to nearly twitch off the bed; as Brenda's fingers continue moving, she calms a bit, but her breathing is rapid, and she is very still, hardly believing this is happening to her as the gentle but unyielding fingers slip a little inside her, finding the wetness she knew was there.

Brenda realizes, as she feels the wetness under her fingers, that she hasn't really believed until that moment that Gretchen is as into this as she is; now she knows the woman is just as excited as she, and the knowledge makes her bold. As she pushes very, very gently with one finger, she feels Gretchen rock her pelvis upward, a tacit permission that she takes advantage of, slipping her finger deep inside her partner, following it with a second finger, and then a third, at which Gretchen whimpers just a little, but rocks even more. Brenda has never felt so powerful before as she thrusts her fingers rhythmically in and out of her lover. At the same time, her heart nearly explodes in her chest as she watches Gretchen's face, her eyes closed, her mouth parted, her breath coming in gasps, and her chest heaving. She kisses Gretchen's belly and pinches a nipple between her fingers, smiling at the groan of pleasure she elicits, more pleased than she could imagine at giving this woman so much pleasure. She slowly pulls her hand out, and slides her fingers up the wet crevice, searching delicately until she finds the tiny mound of flesh she knows is there. As she touches it, Gretchen cries out sharply, so Brenda pulls back a moment to let her settle, then touches it again, causing Gretchen to shudder. She thinks a moment, then places her fingers gently back inside, but reaches her thumb up to brush the wet nub as she thrusts again. Gretchen begins writhing beneath her, crying out softly. Finally, she stiffens, her breathing quick and shallow; with a cry she goes limp, and

Brenda feels a pulsing against the fingers she has pushed deep inside, accompanied by a rush of liquid. She lays her head on Gretchen's belly and gently pulls her hand out. Curious, she licks her fingers and decides she likes the taste. She's glad; she hadn't been sure she would.

Gretchen lies on her back, her chest heaving, her mind racing. She is facing the sudden realization that for the first time in her life, she's been touched intimately by another person, her body entered and brought to orgasm by someone other than herself. This, after her earlier gloomy thoughts of never having a lover of her own, is too much, and the tears start. Brenda is instantly holding her close, cuddling her and telling her it's all right.

"It's just so . . . I mean . . ."

"It's all right. You don't have to tell me," Brenda says. "It's like, real intense for me, too. I just hope you're not mad, or . . ."

"No! No, I . . . it . . . was wonderful," Gretchen sniffs. "I feel, well . . . like you really care," she whispers.

"I do," Brenda whispers back. "A lot. I just wish I could've told you sooner, but I wasn't sure you'd be interested, you know? And then we were looking at that magazine . . ."

Gretchen giggled. "Yeah. I guess I just figured it would be okay to kind of let you know. I trusted you not to judge me." Their eyes meet. "I was right, huh? You're probably, like, the most nonjudgmental person I know. That's what I like about you. One of the things, anyway." She watches Brenda blush, and realizes how cute that is. And remembers that turnabout is fair play.

"In fact, I think maybe I should show you how much I care about you," she whispers softly. "If I can, that is. I'm not sure I'll be as good as you . . ."

Brenda blushes more deeply and looks away, embarrassed. "Well, it's not like I have anything to compare with, you know. I'm just so happy you're here," she says, almost inaudibly. Gretchen feels her heart melting and rolls closer, brushing her lips against Brenda's.

"I'm glad I'm here, too," she says. She kisses her lover again and again, feeling the heat rise between them once more, and lets her hands play over Brenda's breasts. She knows Brenda is more reserved than she, quieter, and is delighted when she finally elicits a moan of pleasure from her. She takes Brenda's nipple in her mouth and sucks experimentally, feeling it turn harder under her tongue as she swirls it around, moving the little hairs that grow in a circle there. She reaches down to Brenda's pants, and almost laughs when Brenda gets up quickly and takes them off, tossing pants and underwear into the corner of the room.

They lie together on the bed, Gretchen gently touching her lover everywhere, stroking her thighs and finally entering her with her fingers, thrilled with Brenda's shivering reaction to the touch. It makes her want an even greater reaction, so she kisses the other woman's strong thighs and finally spreads her legs.

"You don't have to," Brenda pants, realizing what Gretchen means to do, and not wanting her to be turned off, but Gretchen reaches up and pinches her nipple, hard, and she stops talking. Gretchen's own cunt is wet again; she wants to try this, to see if she'll like it, if Brenda will like it. She buries her face in a mound of pubic hair, a little confused as to where to go next, but brings her hands down and gently moves the hair away; as she does so she sighs, which causes her partner to gasp, so she breathes directly on the flesh before her, hotly, and is rewarded by another gasp, and a shudder. Her fingers gently part the folds that hide Brenda's clit, and she stretches her tongue, hesitantly, to just brush the pink nub with the tip. She feels Brenda jump slightly, and grins involuntarily. The next stroke is more deliberate, and she forgets her self-doubt as Brenda begins to cry out and struggle gently beneath her. More confident, she grasps Brenda's hips and holds her down as best she can. She is trying to be creative; she starts out licking, then begins a gentle sucking that causes Brenda to thrash about, and Gretchen almost loses her grip. She relents for a while, licking again. She tries to place her tongue inside Brenda's cunt. The other woman is moaning and mentioning God several times a minute. Gretchen begins sucking again, and Brenda can no longer speak.

All too soon, Gretchen feels Brenda stiffen and shudder, hears her cry out softly and then begin panting. She licks gently, causing a little shudder each time, until the trembling stops, and Brenda's hands are pulling her up into a tight embrace. Both are crying, a little, this time, and Brenda is whispering in her ear how wonderful it felt, how wonderful Gretchen is, and how much she loves her. Gretchen finds herself saying the same things, and they lay like that for a long time, until sleep claims them.

The next morning, Gretchen has to try to explain her nightlong absence to her mother, who is upset and worried, but is mollified when she sees the radiance in her daughter's face. She has been concerned for a long time about the girl, who had come out to her only a few months before, after they'd argued about Gretchen's not having a husband and Gretchen telling her plainly that it wasn't her figure, it was her preference that kept her unmarried. Her mother knows Brenda from having visited her daughter at the deli counter, and knows she's a good girl. She hopes it will work out.

Customers visiting the deli/seafood counter begin remarking about how nice it is to shop there. The workers are so friendly and personable that it's a pleasure even if they have to wait in line. The other workers, and even some of the management, figure out what's going on, but no one says anything because deli workers are hard to keep, the customers are happy, and no one's causing any trouble.

After several months, and following negotiations with Gretchen's mother and Brenda's brother, Gretchen moves into Brenda's half of the duplex. They have the usual wrangles over where to put the sofa, and what to name the new cat they found in the alley, and who's not eating right, but they are as happy as most couples in the world, and find that every day life is a lot easier to deal with now. The people around them see two nice women who work hard and save their money and do the same sort of things everyone else does. Some realize the full meaning of the situation, and some don't, but it doesn't matter to Brenda and Gretchen, who think the world of one another, and who love to celebrate Valentine's Day best of all the days in the year.

That's our story. Hope you liked it. Oh, by the way, you can keep the glasses.

Cupid's Needles
Melinda Johnston

"Hey. A question for you," she said, looking up past the brim of her cowboy hat and taking a drag off her smoke. The tiny bar didn't allow smoking inside, so smokers dotted the sidewalk outside. I didn't smoke, but I'd stepped outside, knowing I'd run into Liv.

"Yeah?" I said. *Yes*, whatever it was, *the answer was yes*. I'd had a frantic crush on this woman for ages.

"Have you ever tried play piercing?"

I blinked. "Once."

"And?" She cocked a carefully groomed, pierced eyebrow at me.

"It was fun. Why?"

She took another drag from her cigarette, then flicked the butt onto the street. "Well, there's a fetish ball coming up for Valentine's Day, and I'm doing the artwork. It'll be auctioned off for an AIDS charity. I'm doing a series of photos of people pierced by Cupid's arrows." She looked at me. "I still need some models.

I'd love to put a few needles in your back, and take some pictures. Would you be into it?"

It took me a second to unstick my tongue from the roof of my mouth. "Yeah, I'd love to. Um . . . yeah," I said, oh so suave. If it involved her touching me, I'd let her wrap me in snakes. Which wasn't impossible, in fact. She owned an albino boa constrictor named Percy that was the mascot for her piercing shop. I'd met him, and her cat, when I'd hired her to add another few holes to my ears.

"Are you free next Saturday afternoon?" she asked.

"Ah, yeah," I said, trying very hard not to leave my mouth hanging open.

She nodded and extracted her card from her chained wallet. "Around two?"

"Yeah," I said. So much for my degree in English literature. "That works for me."

"Great," she smiled, and, making a drinking motion with her hand, disappeared back into the bar.

I could barely concentrate all week. Liv was, to my taste, the most beautiful woman I'd ever met, as much because of her enormous charisma as because of her hazel eyes and gymnast's body. I'd never known anyone whose spirit was reflected in her face quite as vividly. I wanted her desperately, but I'd never managed to say anything about it. Every time I worked up the courage to finally talk to her, she'd be with another girl, or I wouldn't run into her, or I'd just plain chicken out. Now she'd talked to me. I knew her invitation was about her art, but still, there was no knowing what might happen.

I spent most of Saturday morning trying on and rejecting outfits. By the time I'd put on every garment I owned, and settled on my usual uniform of jeans and a black turtleneck, I was late.

She met me at the door with a purring tabby curled under one arm. She hugged me with the other, then dumped the cat into my arms. "Here, take the boy. I'll finish getting everything ready."

The cat, Mr. Lew C. Fur, didn't care who cuddled him, as long as someone did. He purred like a Softtail engine as I scratched his neck and ears, while I followed her through her art-strewn living room into the spare room set up as a piercing shop. The walls were covered with several paintings, solid black, on which women's shapes, variously entwined, had been carved into thick, glossy, black paint with a palette knife. In a few places, a faint red glow showed through.

"Careful, they're not all dry. So much paint, they take months," Liv warned me, as I moved to take a closer look. She was swabbing an elaborate black and chrome dentist's chair with bleach.

"So, what does the art for this project look like?" I asked, still clinging to Mr. Fur, an animated security blanket.

"Here," she said, handing me a pile of 8-by-10 black-and-white photographs. "For the party, they'll be projected on slides, then we'll auction poster-sized prints."

They were stunning. In one, a tattooed, 1950's pin-up of a woman posed with her legs sprawled. An arrow laced together the large silver rings that pierced her labia, three on each side. In another, a skinny boy with sinewy muscles was Saint Sebastian, bound to a tree, with arrows piercing him all over. In a third, a girl in a mermaid costume had a tiny feather-tipped fish hook through her bottom lip, while a burly, fisher butch stood poised with a net. I'd known she was good, but these were art.

"Liv, these are incredible. Wow! Thank you for asking me to be part of this."

She shrugged, a pleased grin flirting with the corner of her lip. "Thank you." She moved to take the cat, brushing my nipple as she did so. I nearly hit the floor. "You don't want cat hair in a piercing. Out, Lucy Furball." She winked at me. "His drag name."

"Of course."

She went to her small sink to scrub her hands with a stiff brush. Turning the tap off with her elbow, she dried her hands and slipped on latex gloves.

"How do you want me?" I asked, trying not imagine all the possible answers, lest it show on my face.

"I'm going to put these in your back," she said, gesturing to a pile of needles. The protective paper had been barely stripped back, and black feathers had been hot-glued into the plastic tip where a syringe usually attaches. She looked at me. "They're no longer strictly sterile, but I autoclaved the feathers and did it with gloves. Is that okay?"

"It's fine. I'm not at all worried," I laughed, gesturing at my scratched-up arms. I'm a klutz, and I work in a bakery, which is far more physical than most people realize, so I'm usually covered in scratches and bruises.

She set the chair back to an incline, and dropped the arms out of the way. What a cool toy. "If you take your shirt off and lean forward against the back, will you be comfortable?"

"I should be." I stripped off my shirt and bra and straddled the chair. I braced myself for the shock of cold vinyl, but she'd thoughtfully directed a space heater at the chair, so it was warm. I could comfortably lean forward against the padded back and rest my head on my crossed arms. "This is fine," I said. It was more than fine. The pressure of the chair against my breasts and abdomen increased the crampy, zinging, sexual buzz I'd felt all day at the thought of her touching me. I was hard put not to rub against the chair.

"Oh," she said, holding up her gloved hands, "I should have asked you if you'd like anything before we get started. Water? Soda?"

"No, I'm fine."

"All right then." She smiled, her gap-toothed grin transforming the severe beauty of her strong, androgynous bones. Liv was a chameleon, her face changing completely in different lights, different moods. She soaked cotton in alcohol and swabbed my back with it. I shivered at the cool tingle. "Relax," she said, her hands kneading the permanent knots in my shoulders. "This won't hurt . . . much . . . unless you want it to." She wiggled her eyebrows at me.

"Well . . ." I bit my lip, looking into her hazel eyes. "A little pain never hurt anybody."

She laughed and lightly slapped my back. She picked up a needle, and I sensed the change in her as she began to concentrate on her work. She gently stroked a spot on my back, then rested her palm on the spot. "I'm going to get you to take three deep breaths on my count, and on the third, I'm going to slip this in. Okay?" I nodded. "All right . . . in . . . out." I breathed deeply, feeling the heat of her hand radiate into my back. "In . . . out." Her voice was soft, far more gentle and feminine than her punk-ass appearance. "In . . . and . . . out."

I felt the sting of the first needle pierce the skin of my shoulder blade. It was just a small sting, quickly soothed into a point of heat by her fingers lightly resting on the spot where the needle slid under my skin.

"You okay?" Liv asked, her hand stroking my back.

"Oh yes. I barely felt that."

"I can make you feel it more, if you want it that way." A top's intonation slipped into the professionalism of her voice. If she kept that up, I was in trouble. I'm a top myself, even though I do like pain, but I'm willing to switch if another top is strong enough to make me. I wanted to act up and see what would happen.

"That's all right," I gasped. I had to clear my throat before I could continue. "This'll do just fine."

She smirked, then led me through the breathing again. She slid the next needle in close to the first. Then another, and another. As more and more needles were placed in my back, Liv dispensed with the elaborate breathing. By this time, the endorphins coursing through my system overrode the sting of each new needle. My back hurt, but it was in no way unbearable. It felt a bit like a skinned knee after the initial pain has worn off—hot, slightly stinging, but something I could easily ignore. What I couldn't ignore was the euphoria mounting in me. With each tiny break in my skin, endorphins flooded my bloodstream.

Endorphins are always released whenever the body is hurt, but they are usually busy coping with the real pain. When you trick the body into being hurt, under circumstances your mind is prepared to accept, if not welcome, endorphins are still released, but this time, you get very, very high. Screw heroin. This is the good stuff.

"You're not feeling the pain much, are you? You haven't made a sound."

I shrugged, regretting it instantly as the needles across my back pricked. "This feels more good than bad," I said.

I can take a lot of pain. Besides, although I'd never tell her, I had to be pretty far gone before I'd let myself moan. Some kind of butch bravado, I suppose. My thoughts must have shown in my face because she ran her fingers, hard, over the ridge of submerged needles along my back. I grunted a little, as much from the hit of endorphins as the renewed pain. Damn her.

I'd been concentrating too much on sensation to pay much attention to what pattern she was placing on my back, but as she touched it, I was aware of the curve taking shape on my shoulder blade. I craned my neck, trying to see, but Liv flicked her fingernail against a needle. "Hey, no peeking," she said. She gentled her hand and caressed my back. "It looks beautiful. We've still got a lot to go, though. You're still all right?"

Liv's voice, always soft, had deepened, become slightly breathy, husky. Had she become as turned on as I was?

"I'm much more than all right," I assured her.

She patted my back and grabbed another needle. I lost track of how many she was inserting. Her movements were gentle, rhythmic, as she rubbed my back, slid in a needle, then soothed the spot with her palm. I was lulled into a trance. I was so high I felt as though I was moving rapidly, anchored only by the heavy, flooded feeling of my pelvis, pressed against the dentist's chair, aching with need. If I closed my eyes, I could see sparks against my eyelids when she inserted a needle, feel a warm glow when her hands massaged unmarked skin. I drifted, lost in sensation, when a flare burst on my back. I moaned, a far more sexual sound than I had planned on allowing myself.

"No sleeping," she laughed, releasing the needle she'd twisted to get my attention. She leaned in close so that all I saw was her warm hazel eyes, and paused, an inch from kissing me, her warm breath stirring the tiny hairs on my cheek. My eyes closed.

"Ow!" She'd flicked the needle again. I caught her by the shirt. She pulled away, and the faded black fabric stretched, almost enough for me to glimpse her breasts. "There'll be none of that, missy," I said, twisting her shirt to bring her closer.

She cocked an incredulous eyebrow at me. "Did you just call me 'missy'?" She pulled her shirt free and stood with hands on hips, in full pissed-off top mode.

"I sure did, missy," I said, straightening up to grab her. Bad idea. It was the first time I'd tried to move since she'd started with the needles. As I wavered, she grabbed me, guiding me back down onto the chair. I grasped it, grateful for its stability in a room that had suddenly tilted.

"Here, take a sip." She held a bottle of Gatorade, with a straw, up for me to drink. I sipped, making a face at the taste. "It's gross, but it'll help." She stroked my hair. "Just breathe."

Her strong fingers found the tight spot at the back of my skull. She breathed in and out with an exaggerated sound, and I followed the rhythm she set, in time with her stroking of my neck. The energy in my back, disturbed into jagged waves of nausea, settled back into an electrical effervescence. She leaned in, and kissed my temple. I turned, catching at her lips before she turned away. We brushed lips, ever so lightly touching, until she ventured a soft tongue tip. I opened to her, and we kissed, deeply. Her hands gripped my hair. I clutched at her back. I was twisted up, half falling off of the chair, when she disentangled herself and pressed me down with a squeeze to my shoulders.

"We should finish this before we start anything else," she said, trailing a fingertip down my spine. "That is, if you're okay. I only have a couple more needles to go. But if you need to stop, it's fine."

"No." I had to clear my throat before I could go on. "I'm fine. Keep going." I paused, willing myself to come up with something more than a monosyllable. "I always finish what I start."

She met my eyes and smiled. "So do I."

I was so high, I barely felt the last few needles. I only realized she was finished when I heard the snap of her gloves as she peeled them off. Liv walked away from the chair and picked up her camera. I heard the click of the shutter as she snapped a few shots.

"Do you think you could walk if I guided you? I set something up in the next room."

I nodded. "Yes, if we go slowly."

She put her hands under my arms to help me sit up. The room tilted slightly, then righted itself with a swaying motion like wine settling into a glass. I waited a moment, then slid off the end of the chair and stood. The warmth of her body next to mine almost made my knees buckle, and I felt her arms tighten around me. After a moment, secure in her grip, I was fine, and walked with only a mildly drunken list into the next room. In a corner filled by a wedge of sunlight from the west-facing window, she'd pinned a swath of red velvet to the wall, letting it pool in soft waves on the floor. "Can you lie down on the velvet?" she asked.

I did, moving as one would expect with forty needles sticking into my back. I lay down, resting my head on my arms. I felt something cool and very soft touch my back. I looked up. "Rose petals," she said, hitting me square in the face with one. I growled. She winked, and scattered the rest of the petals around me.

She moved behind me, and I heard the click and whirr of her camera as she took a rapid series of shots. I heard her rustle around. "Could you look over your shoulder at me?"

"Oh," I squeaked. She'd removed her shirt. Her breasts were small and high over a well-muscled stomach. Half of an exquisite, black orchid tattoo peeked out over her low-slung waistband, just to the side of that most delicious muscle, the tight diagonal ridge of oblique that male swimmers often get, and woman rarely do. I was suspended for a long moment, trapped by a visual orgasm.

I became aware of the rapid click of her camera, as she laughed at me. "Well, you're topless, so I thought it was only fair," she giggled, photographing my lust-struck countenance for posterity. "Maybe you'll want to show these to our grandchildren."

Did she just say "our" grandchildren? Was she serious? I couldn't speak. I just lay there, watching her as she moved around, taking pictures from different angles. I only hoped I wasn't actively drooling.

"Close your eyes," she ordered, and I did, listening to her move about. I felt her close to me, then felt her soft breath on my ear. "Open your eyes." Her head was close to mine, her hazel eyes swallowed by enormous pupils. We kissed. Her hand cupped my jaw, fingertips brushing the hollow behind my ear. My hand found her breast. The firm mound fit perfectly into my cupped palm. I could feel her powerful pectoral muscles flexing under the soft flesh. As I shifted slightly onto my side, her hand came up to squeeze my breast, more than twice the size of hers. I moaned and wrapped my arms around her.

I sank back, pulling her with me. "Ow!" I yelped as the needles poked into my back.

"Oh, are you all right?" she asked, turning me over to check for damage.

"I'll live, I think."

I looked up at her, woebegone, all dignity lost. She smirked, and giggled. I giggled too. In a moment, we were both convulsed in laughter, me sprawled on my stomach, feathers poking out of my back; Liv kneeling over me, small breasts quivering with her laughter.

"Come on," she gasped, "let's get these out of you."

She helped me up and guided me back to the chair. She scrubbed her hands again, snapped on a fresh pair of gloves, and picked up her sharps container. "Do you like it fast, or slow?" she asked, fingertips dancing on my sore back.

"Umm, start slow, and we'll see." My voice was low, husky. She gently grasped a needle, and slid it out. I grunted. I felt an odd sort of release as it moved. It stung, but the small pain was soon swallowed by the endorphins that roared through me with renewed force. The needles were quickly removed, then she grabbed the alcohol.

"This will sting," she warned.

"Ssss." My breath hissed through my teeth. Sting, indeed. As the bite of the alcohol faded, though, my back felt light, as though years of tension had been lifted from it. I sat up, stretching and twisting, enjoying the way my back felt free, easy. But I knew I'd be sore tomorrow. Liv, still shirtless, stowed away the last of her equipment, then turned to me.

"So," she said.

"So," I said.

We looked at each other, bashfulness striking us both at the same time. She was so exquisite my heart hurt to look at her. Her muscles were so developed that she seemed stocky despite her slight build, and yet she looked so vulnerable standing in front of me, pale skin gleaming, black hair tousled like a little boy's. If I didn't say something, I'd break apart.

"Liv," I whispered, trying to force air past the lump in my throat, "you are so beautiful, and I—"

"No." She touched my face. "Shh, you don't have talk."

"But I do." I grabbed her hand, looking at it rather than her face. "I have had the most painful crush on you for ages, Liv, and I can't play with you unless . . ." I risked a quick look at her face. It was blank. I swallowed. "Unless . . ." I faltered, scared to go on. She was too quiet.

"Unless what?" she asked. I could feel her eyes on me, but I didn't dare look up.

"Unless it means something. I want you so badly I think my brain will explode if I don't get to touch you, but I don't think I could handle it if we make . . . if we . . . and then nothing." She squeezed my hand a little, and I managed to look into her eyes. "Don't worry, I'm not going to show up tomorrow with a U-Haul, but I feel too much to be with you unless you feel something for me too." It came out in a rush. I looked at the floor, sick at what I'd said. I'd scare her. No one said such things. We barely knew each other.

"I've been watching you," she said, voice low.

"I . . . you have?" I managed a glance at her eyes. They seemed bright, almost blue.

"I've been looking at you for months. You always seemed so cool, so self-contained. I wasn't sure how to get to you." She half smiled, then bent nearer to my ear. "I volunteered to shoot these pictures because I thought I might be able to entice you over here. I knew you'd be into this."

I clutched at her neck, pulling her against me, burying my head against her soft breast. "I'm not cool. You are. You are the most amazing person I know. It never occurred to me that you'd be interested in me," I said, holding her as though a strong wind was trying to tear us apart.

"Silly." She grabbed my chin and forced my head up. Her eyes, glowing blue, bored into mine. "I think you are amazing." She laughed. "So I guess we're both amazing," she whispered, touching the trail of tears that suddenly appeared on my cheek. "Agreed?"

"Agreed." I said, my voice shaking. I couldn't take it anymore. I picked her up and sat back on the dentist's chair, cradling her against me. I pulled her up, then bent my head to her breast. As I flicked her nipple with my tongue, she moaned, and I almost came, just from the sound. Her hands rubbed my head, caressed my earlobes, and squeezed my arms as I bit and sucked her nipple. Her fingertips found my breast, and I moaned into her as she drew teasing lines on my skin.

"This won't do," she cried, jumping off of me. My heart stopped, but when she took my hand, it started again, the beat loud in my ears as she pulled me toward her bed. We both shed our pants and fell on the bed, too eager to worry about our socks. She pressed me down, draping herself over me, fishing for something on the floor beside her bed. She came back with a double-sided dildo, a sleek black silicone V. Her hand slid down to my thighs, and felt the moisture that had overflowed.

"No need for lube," she purred into my ear. Her fingertips gently brushed my hair, then parted my lips.

"Oh, Liv," I moaned, "please, please touch me." Her finger slid inside me. I dug my fingers into her back as she curled her finger into my G-spot, making me close my teeth on her shoulder. With one smooth move, she slid the dildo inside me. I was so open, there was no resistance.

"Ah," I gasped at the sight of the dildo curving between my legs as if it had always been there. I grabbed her by the waist, pulling her under me as turned over. "Now it's my turn."

I slid my hand down her side, over her hip. She was so soft, yet so muscular, it was like caressing sun-warmed ivory. Her hair was trimmed, neatly, something I never had the patience to do. It was also soaked. The sudden rich smell of woman that filled the room as I moved my fingers into her cunt made me feel faint. All I was aware of was the smell of her, and the feeling of warmth and wet that met my hand as I caressed her labia for the first time. My body had vanished. All that was left of me was my hand, my nose, and my brain, no longer capable of thought, only of processing sensation.

Her nails ripping into my sore back recalled me. I growled into her ear, "You better behave."

"Or?"

"Or this," I whispered, my tongue flickering at her ear. I slid over her, and guided the cock into her. As it slid in, I felt as though I was falling, sinking, until I came to rest against her, as close as two people can get. I paused, wrapping my arms around her, just feeling our connection. The dildo might have been a jumper cable, transmitting electricity between us. She wrapped her legs around me, and I began to rock against her, following the rhythm of her hips as she moved under me. I kissed her, sucking on her bottom lip in time with my thrusts. I raised myself slightly off of her so our nipples brushed together as our hips rocked. She pulled me back down against her.

"No, stay here, touching, as much of you touching as much of me as possible," she whispered.

"It's always the bad asses who are the sweetest romantics," I told her, nibbling her earlobe.

"Oh yeah?"

"Yeah."

She tightened her legs around me, flipped me over, and had my arms pinned before I could react. Fun with Judo. "Oh my, I'm trapped. Whatever shall I do?" I said, looking up at her, biting my lip. If she thought being on top put her in control, she had another thing coming. I thrust upward, lifting her with my hips. Despite her strength, she was so small I could lift her easily. I circled my hips, playing with her, and her grip loosened enough for me to twist my hand free. I rubbed her clit and she rode me, grinding herself down on the dildo and my fingers. She let go of my other hand, and I played with her nipple. As I twisted it, her back arched. She started making soft little cries. Every sound she made set off a firecracker in my uterus.

"God, Liv, you sound so good. Let me hear you," I begged, my fingers flicking at her clit. "Please, Liv, please."

As I begged her, she seemed to let something go. Her cries grew wilder. She rode me harder. Her every moan brought me closer to the edge. At last, she dug her fingers into my hair and screamed, her whole body convulsing. As she screamed, I exploded, arching up into her.

We collapsed together in a tangle of limbs. Liv reached down to gently extract the dildo. She tossed it off the bed.

"Meruph," her cat mewed, as he went to investigate.

Liv looked at me, "The cat—"

"Is . . . is chasing . . ." I gasped.

We both convulsed again, in laughter, each clasped to the other's breast.

It wasn't until I got home late the next afternoon that I realized

I hadn't seen what she'd done to my back. I stripped and looked into the bathroom mirror. A few small bruises dotted my shoulder blades from the needles she'd twisted, but most of the marks had disappeared, or at least faded to the point that I couldn't see them in the mirror even by craning my head over my shoulder. I'd have to wait and see.

She wouldn't show me the pictures, no matter how much I tormented her.

"You'll just have to wait and see," she said. "And if you don't stop whining, I'm going to Photoshop in a moustache and devil horns."

On February 14th, we walked into the fetish ball together, both draped in leather. The black-and-white slides flickered onto the walls. The mermaid. Saint Sebastian. And then me. In black and while, sprawled out, my eyes huge with lust, and love. On my back, Photoshopped to the scarlet hue of fresh blood, were the feathered arrows. In the shape of a heart.

I looked into her eyes. "I love you, too, Liv," I whispered, clasping her to me. I held her, and we swayed together on the dance floor for a long, long time.

Rock Star Valentine
Lynne Jamneck

She lived on a ranch in Arizona. I liked to scream into a microphone in front of thousands of people.

Depending on how you choose to look at it, the situation could have gone really bad—or really excellent. Ha—you'll have to stick around to see the end result. You might just be entertained.

So anyway, there I was with my axe, my couldn't-give-a-shit attitude, and my band, along with buckets of Kool-Aid and beer on our private circus of a tour bus on our way to stomp through a special Valentine's gig in LA at the Whisky a Go-Go. We were the opening act for *the* new, hot shit Indie rock band, Dött Kalm, who hailed from Seattle. They were being touted as the best thing since Nirvana, so naturally we were stoked about being on the bill.

We'd been driving through from Phoenix where'd we'd just finished a short string of fucking amazing shows, successful bordering on the insane, so we were all pretty frenzied and hyped. There had been fans backstage telling us we should have been the main event instead of the opening act! I'd been strutting like a cock of the walk for a whole week.

So there we were: me, Kristen, Shari, and Alice, hammering our happy way down the open road, joined by Lenny, our tour manager, and Lou, the bus driver.

By just looking at her, you'd have taken Lou for a severely insane woman. She had these fucking ripped muscles and a semi-permanent scowl on her face. We saved some money on hiring her all those months back 'cause she doubled as a bodyguard. She was only supposed to come along for the first tour, but she's been with us for almost a year now. Truth be told, Lou was the proverbial hooker with a heart of gold. Her insides were actually made of marshmallow. But crikey, could she drive that bus!

Lenny wasn't all that fond of her because of mainly two reasons: She'd punched him once because he dared criticize her driving skills—he had a shiner for a week—and she tended to score better with the girls than he did. That was his own fault though because he could be an abrasive bastard when he wanted. But he was an excellent tour manager, so we kept him around. His saving grace.

So again, there we were. Driving.

We were all about three beers down—except Lou, of course—and taking the piss out of Kristen because she seemed to be the band member who attracted the biggest number of groupies. I swear, she could give the eighties Madonna an earful, and then some. Chicks threw their underwear at her on a regular basis; she didn't even have to be on stage for that to happen. On the street, at bars having a drink, leaving her hotel room . . . What is it about drummers? Although, to be fair, I had a huge crush on Debbie Peterson from The Bangles when I was a teenager, so there you go.

At one point our dialogue jackknifed and everyone started to ask me for *my* sexual scorecard. Of course, I refused. Kiss-and-tell has never been my thing.

I know, I know. You're gonna give me a sly grin and say, "Oh come on! Be a sport!" The truth is, I just don't connect to groupies. Kristen connects to them in a very real, very special way. Seriously—having four orgasms a night is very fucking real, and very fucking special.

But me? After spending two hours hollering out the moral fiber of my soul, all I want to do is get in bed with a good book and a cup of Milo. Okay, fine, sometimes I spike the Milo. Happy? No really—I'm a bit of an armchair detective. I would have loved to have been a writer. And if any of this gets out to the paparazzi, I'll know where to come look. I have a reputation after all. Thanks to the media. I don't know where they get what they publish. They're so full of shit.

So there we were—driving and taking the piss. I'd just managed to steer the conversation back to Kristen's multiple orgasms when the bus suddenly hiccupped, careened, and then swung violently, followed immediately after by a loud *BANG!*

Everyone grabbed their beer bottles first—force of habit—and watched as the rest of everything on the table went flying. Cigarettes, Zippos, jerky sticks, whatever. It all crashed. I heard Lenny swear violently but mutedly. Lucky man—he was in the lav.

Lou yelled, "Hang on kids!" from the front—really, an unnecessary instruction. I heard the flap-flap-flop of the burst tyre and the bus complaining. Then—miracle of miracles—everything was quiet and stationary.

No one moved. I looked at Alice, Shari, and Kristen, all three still clutching their beer bottles for dear life. Then Shari carefully asked, "What the hell just happened?"

"I think the tyre blew," Alice breathed. I almost laughed at the grave look on her face. Narrowly escaping death will make everything seem funny.

"Aw, crap!" Lenny stumbled to the front of the bus, a perfect half of a CD in each hand. "My Pearl Jam CD's shot to shit!"

Alice made a face and muttered, "Thank God."

Kristen chipped in with, "Eddie Vedder always was inferior to Kurt Cobain." She managed to say it just loud enough for Lenny to hear. She meant to do so, of course. He gave her a disdainful look, and the two of them were about to launch into yet another argument when Lou yelled from the driver's seat, "Shut it, the two of you!"

Everyone froze.

Lou continued. "Okay, better. The tyre's blown, no shit. I'm not even going to make the effort of asking whether you're all alright because you're already—what am I saying—*still* bickering like children. I am going to go outside to have a cigarette and survey the damage, and you'd all better hope the cell phone gets reception out here. Don't any one of you dare come out there unless you have something constructive to say." With that, Lou grabbed her cigarettes from the dashboard and disappeared outside.

"Jesus," Kristen complained, "wrong side of the lezbo-bed."

Lenny momentarily forgot about his CD. "Yeah, totally."

"Shut up, Lenny. No one asked you."

Kristen waited defiantly for a retort. Thank God, he had the sense to give it up. Shari lit a cigarette and looked at me. "Dylan, you're going to have to go out there."

"Excuse me?"

"Go talk to Lou."

"Why am I always the one who has to go make nice when you all are responsible."

"Because you're the cute boy-butch, and Lou relates to you."

"Oh, fuck off. You're all just too scared is all."

"Too right," Alice said, smiling sweetly.

I knew I wouldn't get out of this one. Bloody hypocrites. Every single one of them have admired Lou's pecs from afar, but when it comes to the crunch they all flake out. Well, I had no such qualms. Lou and I had a thing—a communicative bond. Plus, we both secretly pined for Famke Janssen.

I left the lot of them to their devices and went to find some semblance of sanity with Lou by the side of the highway. She offered me a cigarette, which I happily accepted.

"Thought you quit," Lou said, striking the match.

"I did," I replied, inhaling.

"You want the bad news first or last?"

"What the hell—I'm going to have to hear it eventually. Shoot."

Lou squinted down the desert highway. "Tyre's busted beyond repair. We don't have a spare."

"Fuckity-fuck. You said there was good news?"

"The cell phone's got reception. We're about thirty miles west from the ranch of a friend of mine. She's on her way to pick us up. Once we get there, I can phone LA to make the necessary arrangements."

I slapped Lou on the back and grinned. From inside the bus rose the sound of discontent. Lou sighed.

I asked, "We're not going to make it to LA on time though, are we?"

Lou pitched her shoulders.

"Kristen's going to be pissed."

Lou snorted. "She's always pissed about something."

"True. But I mean—*Valentine's Day*—at the *Whisky*, packed to the rafters with dykes."

Lou laughed. "You're right, she's gonna be *bruised*!"

I started laughing. "Now she's going to have to spend Valentine's Day on a ranch! Kristen—Miss Fancypants!" We really let it rip then, until suddenly there was a clatter behind us and there was Kristen, a half-full bottle of Chivas in one hand, waving it about as she spoke.

"What the fuck's so funny? Stop fart-arsing about and let's get the hell out of here! Have you guys changed the flat?"

At that moment I heard the crunch of heavy tyres on the dirt road behind the bus. Lou jumped to her feet. Kristen's jaw muscles worked irately. I had the distinct feeling someone was about to have a hissy fit of budding rock star proportions.

And right there was when my whole trip changed.

The ranch girl—Lou's friend—was called Jack.

I know, it sort of gives Jack and Jill a whole new meaning.

Jack drove a weighty, beat-up, dust-covered 4x4 of some sort. Thank God all our equipment was being transported by a separate truck. I would have been loathe leaving all of *that* stuff in the middle of nowhere.

Everyone was terribly upset about the whole affair, but Lou just hustled them onto the open back of the four-wheeler. Kristen bitched about being treated like cattle. By then, no one was really listening anymore. Lou shooed me into the passenger seat, next to Jack, saying something like, "Come on, don't be shy," and Alice, overhearing, added "Yes, Dylan, don't be shy" and then the whole fucking lot of them tittered like rejects from a carnie fair.

I glanced sideways to smile and make nice with Jack, and I swallowed hard.

Oh Jesus, was I in trouble.

Jack's house sat squat in the middle of nowhere and was so big I thought at least ten other people must be living in it. One of them certainly being Jack's girlfriend. That's right—my gaydar was jumping off the screen. I felt Jack's dykey aura graze my kneecaps all the way back to her house.

Forget about it, Dylan. Women like that—they're never single.

Lou had somehow persuaded everyone in the back to a naff, out-of-tune version of *Nights in White Satin.*

"So," Jack said as she manhandled the gear stick forcefully and winced at the noise from behind, "you're a rock star?"

I gave her my famous camera smile and said "Well, *rock star* might be jumping the gun a wee bit."

"You're British?"

"Luckily." I cocked my head toward the troop in the back. "The rest of 'em's all Yankees."

She kept her eyes on the road. "Lou said you're in a band."

"Well, we're a little more than a band. Kitty Litter Days—that's our name. We're supposed to be opening for Dött Kalm at the Whisky tomorrow. In LA. It's a Valentine's Day thing."

"Don't know them either."

"Not into music that much, are you?"

"Actually, I'm a big music fan."

"Just not ours, I guess." Aw, shit. *What the hell, Dylan?*

Jack took her eyes from the road just long enough to give me what I assumed was a superior smirk. "I guess not."

Well fuck you, lassie. Poor taste comes in all shapes and sizes.

Just before Jack looked away I saw her eyes skip right down to my thighs, down—then back to the road.

So that's how she wanted to play it? Fair enough. I'll just see about her little game.

"I want my, I want my, I want my Valentine's gig!"

"Kristen, dear—how many times have I told you not to bring up Dire Straits in my presence."

"Shari, just what the hell is wrong with Dire Straits anyway?"

"The name sorta says it all, really."

The drive to Jack's house had come to a merciful end. We were all sitting outside on the verandah, smoking cigarettes, drinking beer, roasting like piggies in the sun. I was starting to get a headache.

"Dylan, where has Lou disappeared to?"

"Do I look like I baby sit the bus driver?"

"Bus driver slash bodyguard."

"Wise ass. Pass me one of those cigarettes."

"I thought you quit."

"I did."

"I know a secret," Shari piped up again. I knew that lilt in her voice; she was about to say something lascivious.

"Dylan's got a super hot crush on Jack."

"Oh for god sakes . . ."

"Oh yes, you do."

"Please—I got the distinct feeling she doesn't care much for us musician riffraff."

"Bullshit. She's playing hard to get."

"Give it up, Alice."

"Jack be nimble, Jack be quick, Jack come over here and suck my—"

"Oi!"

"Al's right," Kristen piped. "You think we couldn't pick up on the *sexshual* attraction between the two front seats of that car despite the bad seventies MOR music Lou had us singing? And by the way—she checked out your ass when you got out of that rattling jeep, Jack did."

Alice handed me another cigarette. "Suck on that, honey. Yeah, I know exactly what Jack wants for Valentine's Day."

Yeah, I had a reputation. It was part of the gig. And all right, there was *some* truth to it. The girls and I'd been together as Kitty Litter Days for the better part of four years. We were all crossing over the horizon into Thirties Territory. Except of course Kristen, bless her. Denial was an integral part of her daily routine.

When I was in my early twenties I had a raging libido. Late bloomer, see. I figured I had to catch up on all those confused schoolgirl days. These days I've come to appreciate the payoff of being selective. In fact, since becoming all fussy about whom I have sex with, the libido's become even stronger. Problem was, I tended to select people who were either totally wrong for me or totally unavailable.

Like Jack.

She actually seemed to be single, but really, she was *so* wrong. The combination of Jack and Dylan was wrong. I determined this through various illuminative conversations:

She thought Keith Richards was a superior guitarist to Eric Clapton.

Her bookcases were stacked with books by Freud.

Jack thought I was full of shit. She told me so.

I told Jack I was full of shit and proud of it.

It wouldn't be good.

How fucking irritating was it then that every time she opened her mouth I felt all fuzzy and my insides tingled. She'd be standing there, ignoring me baiting her, trying to be insouciant and all I could think of was how fucking amazing Jack's T-shirts seemed to fit her . . .

Valentine's Day. Here it was, and we were a long way from LA.

I woke up the next morning in the most comfortable bed I'd slept in for ages. I checked my watch. It was just after 9:30. Christ, why had I slept so late?

Save for the languid chirp of a bird outside the window, everything was lazy quiet. It was positively surreal. I wasn't used to the luxury of calm. I was even naked except for my DKNY boxers. After a long night, I would generally just tumble into bed still dressed. I must have slept something crazy because I couldn't remember a thing about the night before.

There was a soft knock on the door. I pulled the covers up. "Come in!"

It was Jack. She had on a worn-out pair of jeans and another mouth-watering T-shirt. Wow. I wondered if she had them custom made. Yeah—they were that good. Could any woman's breasts look that fucking perfect? Apparently, at some point in her life, Jack had been to a Rolling Stones concert, or so the shirt proclaimed. Ergo her fondness for The Keith.

I couldn't remember when last my hormones experienced such turmoil. I might not be the love-em-and-leave-em kind of girl I used to be, but women normally responded to me quite differently than Jack was. Usually, they threw themselves at me. And I'm not saying that to inflate my own ego. Some things were just the way they were.

"You're such a dyke," Jack smiled. She looked more at ease this morning. Relaxed.

"Excuse me?" *She saw you staring at her breasts for god's sake.*

"I mean the tattoo on your back."

"When did you see my tattoo?" I'm pretty sure I would have remembered if Jack had been anywhere near my lower back.

"You don't remember last night? All that bourbon?"

I was truly perplexed and just a little bit bewildered. Jack was enjoying it, I could see.

All these years have hardened me to the effects of too much alcohol. I felt fine. Not like I'd been drinking excessively. But it was true, I could remember absolutely zilch about the night before . . . Oh *fuck*.

"Don't worry your pretty little head about it," Jack smiled from the bedroom door. "I've seen plenty of naked women before."

And then she was gone, and I smelled the distinctive flavor of freshly baked bread and had the sudden, striking feeling that I'd somehow been trapped in a Martha Stewart Valentine's Special. Except a way sexier version, because outside my door, Jack was in the kitchen.

Had it been the way she had said, *The tattoo on your back?* Alternatively, perhaps it was simply her statement of naked women that now had me imagining all sorts of things.

The cell phone on the bedside table vibrated loudly, and I caught it just in time before the little modern miracle tumbled off the edge of the table.

"Lou, is that you? What the fuck—are you driving? Where the hell—and is that Alice?" I heard a scuffle and then the phone on the other end of the line changed hands.

"Kristen? Where the hell are you? I hear a car. Are you driving?"

"Well, technically speaking, I'm not driving. Lou's driving. She organized a car from a rental agency."

I couldn't believe this. "And just where the fuck are you all going?"

"Well, we thought that, since we're not going to make it to LA in time, we might as well drive back to Phoenix and check out the nightlife some more. I have a few phone numbers from our shows and it is, after all, Valentine's."

"What about me? You left me here!" I heard Alice laugh uproariously in the background. I was going to kill them all—slowly.

"I'll have you know, Dylan, that it was mostly Lou's idea to leave you there."

"Lou? I don't believe that."

"Yes, Lou. I get the sneaking suspicion she was trying to match-make again. She'll never admit it, of course. She hates being thought of as romantic. Besides, why take you with us when all you'll do is end up in a motel room with one of those thick, brainy fucking books you're so fond of reading. Your legions of fans would have a continental fit."

"There's nothing brainy about whodunits, Kristen."

There was another scuffle and then Alice was on the phone. "Dylan, come on. We know and *you* know that woman wants you to jump her bones and you want to do the same. It's a win-win situation. And don't argue with me. I saw the way the two of you were looking at one another in the kitchen last night. Lightning could have conjured in there."

"Alice, she called me a delinquent."

"Yes, and you called her a cultural idiot. Ra-ra, yadda, yadda—you may as well have ripped one another's clothes off right there."

"Oh, pffff." I couldn't think of a clever comeback.

"Have some fun, babe. It's Valentine's Day. I'm gonna get off the phone now 'cause Shari wants to play strip poker."

"Alice—Alice!" The phone line went dead. *Shit.*

This was the type of thing that happened when the people you spent the better part of your time with knew you too well. I got dressed, not bothering to put on shoes, then followed my nose to the kitchen.

Secretly, I've always wanted to live on a ranch. There's just something about it—horses, hay, cowboy-girls, chaps, and the smell of leather. What's not to like?

"Hungry? Breakfast's almost done."

I realized that I'd been standing in the kitchen doorway, staring. She was sexy as hell. Strong, lithe body and hands that always seemed to be busy with something. The night before it had been the ingredients of the paella she'd magically dished up for us and delivered with the bonus of four bottles of fine red wine that would put the best, cockiest California grape to shame.

"I'm starving, actually."

This time the smile on her lips seemed amused rather than arrogant. She'd done up her sun-flecked, honey hair in a simple but dead-sexy ponytail that trailed along between her shoulders. There were telltale flour tracks on her jeans.

She made me want to lay her down and undress her slowly, savoring her even slower. I could easily get lost in those arms forever. Fuck fame. Who needs it?

"Would you sit down? You're making me nervous." Jack pulled out a chair. "They left you here, didn't they?" She was working with the oven, and when she opened it, the warm smell of fresh bread billowed out.

"How'd you know?"

"You sounded very indignant on the phone."

"Oh . . . fuck."

She laughed, and for some reason the sound went directly for my groin. It was like honey. "I don't bite, you know."

"You seemed to want to last night." I wished I had a cigarette handy. I felt nervous and excited and out of control. "You were chomping on me last night about not knowing my Bartok from my Beethoven."

She closed the oven, then placed the fresh bread on a cooling rack, giving me a sexy smile. "Well you don't, do you?"

"Guess not."

"I guess I don't like crowds. I would have liked to pick your brain a little further, but . . ."

"I know. Kitty Litter Days . . . us girls together can be a handful."

Jack took off her oven mitts and tossed them on the table. Before I could say anything else she was right next to me, and then she swung her leg over mine and sat down on my lap. *God*, she smelled good. Like summer heat and home. Her hands on my hips felt weighty and light at the same time.

"You're really confusing me here, Jack." It came out mostly as the nonchalant joke I'd intended for it to be, but it was also the truth. The night before I'd been pretty sure she thought I wasn't worth a second glance.

Jack's hands moved up slowly, her hands leaving hot, tactile trails on my skin. Her lips were slightly parted and her eyes were black, dilated pools.

"Confusing me and turning me on."

"That's normally what happens when I sit down on a girl's lap."

My hands were on her legs, above her knees. The washed-out smoothness of her jeans felt pretty fucking sexy on the palms of my hands. What do I do to her? What does she like?

"The bread's gonna get cold."

"I'll make some more."

"Okay."

"Do you like it when I touch you there?" Her hand was splayed high up on my thigh.

"Oh, yes. Uh-huh."

I didn't dare move.

"I don't know what it is about you, Dylan, but I've been thinking the most foolish things ever since you got into my car out there on the highway."

"How does that feel?" My fingers touched her stomach, and I could sense the coiled muscles beneath her skin.

"Here." She took my hand and moved it to her breast. The nipple hardened against my palm. I touched her there only briefly before both my hands snapped down to the small of her back and scooted her nearer.

"Jack—where did you get that name anyway?"

"It's short for something, of course. I'll never tell."

"How'd you get it?"

"A girlfriend at school. She said . . . I should have been a boy."

"Silly girl. She didn't know, of course."

"Dylan?"

"Come on . . . what's it short for?"

"Happy Valentine's Day."

She kissed me. Her lips were warm and soft. I felt like I was in someone else's fantasy.

Both her hands were flat against my thighs now, and as her fingers squeezed, my muscles contracted, my thoughts spun. Her arms curled around me. Our bodies fit together perfectly. Jack was warm and soft, like her kisses, which had turned deep and penetrating while her hands moved down to my knees.

Jack said, "I think I might like you."

"Shit, I think I might like you too."

I don't know how we made it to the bedroom. Jack's bed was still unmade, and it pleased me to realize she wasn't the perfectionist I had taken her for. I flung her down on the bed and crawled on top of her while she pulled off her shirt, the bed sinking beneath our combined weight.

We couldn't seem to stop kissing. I could have tasted her for hours. Her tongue was hot, and she made me crazy the way she kept pulling me down on her.

I wanted to get her clothes off. All of them.

This day had started in such a peculiar fashion. First, I get ditched by my mates. Left on a ranch with a woman I was sure hated my guts, and now here I was, having heated, steamy sex with said woman.

Jack. Oh, Jack. The sound of your name in my head makes me want to do things.

"Careful . . ."

My T-shirt fell to the floor, making Jack smile at the sight of my other tattoo—a black snakelike curve that ran down my flank and disappeared down the front of my pants. She made no mention that she'd seen that one too.

When I stuck my hand down the front of her jeans, her lips touched mine and she expelled hot air into my mouth. "I knew you'd feel this good," she breathed.

"Do I? Jesus, you feel awesome."

"I'd love to see you on stage."

"Jack, I think I could fucking fall in love with you."

"What?"

"Let's take these off." I popped the buttons on her fly, making her laugh as I pulled her pants off in one smooth *swish*.

Jack pulled me back on top of her. She ran her hands along my skin and said something about my back being sexy, and me being confident and butch and being the reason she dropped her knickers so quick. I said her knickers were sexy but won't she please take them off so I could do my job better.

Both Jack and I were unhurried, but all set to explore one another's bodies at a pace that satisfied us both. Her hands were firmly on my arse, and somehow the effect of her being totally naked and me still having my jeans on made me believe I somehow had the upper hand. Or maybe, just maybe, it was the other way around.

She moved her hips, slowly. Playing me and enjoying the look in my eyes that wanted to tell her *leave it to me entirely to please you* but at the same time found it such a turn on that she wanted me to get my rocks off at the same time. And she kept urging me to go deeper, which drove me fucking insane. It quickly became hot and sweaty and hungry and we fucked despite—or because—of our reckless sentiments.

I have strong arms. I can lean over a woman forever.

I was starting to sweat, the short hair of my fringe clinging to my forehead. Jack reached up to wipe the errant hair from my eyes. Her hand was warm against my head as she pulled me down. I tasted the saltiness of her skin and her mouth—and mine—her lips opening to let in my tongue and her breasts, warm, rigid nipples pressing against mine. Her legs were still up, high around my waist, holding me tight.

She said something that sounded like "come on" and kicked her feet against the mattress.

My hand reached out on impulse to hold her down as I pulled

myself up. She tried to free herself but I wrenched her hand away, pinning it above her head against the wall. Jack's back arched, hips reaching up to meet mine where they stayed, locked in a hot, perspiring clinch with my hand in between.

Her eyes were closed and she was smiling. I fucked her slow and tight and deep until my eyes started to swim and my heart crunched inside my chest and I felt I was going to pass out from the sheer thrill of her nails raking across my back and her having to keep quiet by sucking—biting—on the moist skin of my shoulder. There were going to be sexy welts all over my back.

"Ow, fuck—" I eloquently exclaimed at the pain as she scratched my arse and bucked into me, shuddering as she grabbed fistfuls of sheet between her fingers.

I collapsed on top of her, spent, breath racing. "Fucking, crikey . . . woman."

"Whoever said the British were shy about sex?"

"Not me—"

"No, you certainly are not."

I kissed her. "What now?"

Jack said, "First things first. I'm starving."

I kissed her again. "I should hope so. I don't work this hard for nothing."

It's such a horrid fucking cliché. Yet I suppose clichés are clichés for a reason; otherwise, they wouldn't be clichés, right?

Jack was indeed single. Well, up to the point where I rode onto the scene on my Rock 'n' Roll horse.

I fell for her lock, stock, and barrel, plus all the other juvenile things that people say when their emotions take them for a ride. It must have had something to do with the fact that it had been Valentine's Day. Dangerous, all this romantic BS.

Jack didn't sell her ranch. I mean, okay cool, fine, clichés are al right and all in its place, but let's not go overboard here. Instead, I moved in with Jack.

Come on, gimme a break! Besides, I'd been renting in the city, a bachelor's pad that they overcharged me on rent and where people banged on my door at all hours of the day and night. The Arizona light was an inspiration to my songwriting anyway.

Lou insists she hadn't planned on setting me up with Jack, but that blown tyre . . . She said it was fate. I always knew there was more going on in that head of hers than people gave her credit for.

The only problem Jack and I now have is arguing over whether the 14th is Valentine's Day or our anniversary. She always wins, though. I'm a sucker for giving a woman what she wants.

When the Lights Go Down
Therese Szymanski

"I want to make love with you," I said, looking right into her beautiful blue eyes. Her eyes were as deep as the ocean, filled with eternal kindness and understanding. There was a pause as she returned my gaze, and it felt as if our souls were touching. I felt her look as a caress.

She brought her hand up to my face, gently guiding my lips to hers. I felt the soft brush of her lips against mine, the warmth of her breath on my cheek and the sure pull of her arms around me, bringing me in closer to her. I sighed and gave over all control to her.

I closed my eyes and leaned in toward her, letting her guide me down to the couch. Her weight on my body was reassuring, comforting. Even though Val was in incredible shape, her breasts still felt plush against me, her thighs soft against mine. Our bodies intertwined as the kiss continued, my hands exploring her back, pulling her in even closer. Our bodies fit together like Legos. I arched up against the hard thigh wedged between my own legs, pressing against my pussy. I wanted to be naked under her, having her take me.

I wanted her to fuck me—hard. I didn't care who was watching.

I ran my hand through Val's thick hair and enjoyed this moment, for that was all it would ever be. For no matter what physical sensations she created within me, even now, with her lips against mine, with her body on top of mine, feeling more right than anything had ever before in my life, some part deep within me was longing for something more, for something else—and we both knew it.

The lights dimmed as the melodic notes of k.d. lang's "Miss Chatelaine" began to dance through the air. Our kiss deepened, our bodies moved against each other. When the lights were totally out, and applause drowned out the song, we jumped to our feet and ran through the upstage door into the green room.

"I can't believe this is the last night," Val said as she pulled off her shirt and bra. I glanced appreciatively at her pert breasts and flat stomach while I changed my own costume. She had an amazingly feminine body for someone who could come off as so butch. It was amazing what clothing could do—even the biggest butch could look quite femme when she took her clothes off.

"You two did great!" said Jesse, the director, as she came backstage. "And we're really gonna rock 'em in act two, right kids?" she continued, glancing around at Jennifer, Mark, and Kelli, who comprised the rest of the cast.

I felt a sudden fear that after tonight I'd never see any of these incredible people again. Jesse must've read my thoughts because just then, as the rest of the cast began their excited chatter while changing their own costumes, she turned toward me.

"You *are* coming to the bar with us tonight, right Lara?" she said, running her hand back through her short, black hair as she gazed unabashedly at my half-naked body. "It is V-Day, after all. We still need to hook you up with someone."

"Which bar?" I asked nervously as I tried to nonchalantly cover some of my body. I was wearing only panties.

"The Rainbow Room," she replied, glancing up at my eyes.

Val must've misinterpreted my blank look. "C'mon, Lara, it's closing night *and* Valentine's Day—you can't dis us on the cast party!"

Wearing only her flimsy silk underwear, she jumped at me and quickly began tickling my ribcage, causing me to drop my hands and expose my breasts. I folded over, trying to escape Val's fingers and hands as I laughed my ass off. No one seemed to notice as she trapped me on my back while still tickling me.

No one except Jesse, that is. Her dark eyes were turned toward us, a slight grin touching her face. A grin or a smirk, I couldn't quite tell which.

So there I was, wearing only my panties, in a roomful of people of both genders, stretched out on my back with a half-naked woman sprawled over me tickling me.

The first time I ever saw Jesse was the day I auditioned for this show—six months ago. I had just come out and had seen the call for auditions in the gay paper I'd found at the local women's bookstore. It had seemed like a very good way to meet some women. Lesbians. Real lesbians.

I showed up for the second night of auditions. I tried to stay near the back of the theater, but even from there I saw her, and she saw me. Those dark, intense brown eyes slowly traversed my body from my eyes to my feet, with brief pauses in between, making me feel more like a woman than I ever had before in my life. Her grin was rather cocky, with a bit of a snarl, an element of playful kidding about it as she slowly assessed me.

She was clad simply in washed-out blue jeans, heavy black boots, and a worn black leather jacket with a simple white T-shirt. One hand loosely held a clipboard; the other was hooked by its thumb in her hip pocket, adding to her cocky attitude.

"I haven't seen you at auditions before," she said, striding toward me. She put a hand on my arm to lead me up to the front, right next to the table she'd set up for herself. Handing me an audition sheet she continued, "Have a seat, make yourself at home." My arm burned where it had ever so briefly touched the black leather covering Jesse's arm.

Years ago, when I had started thinking about women, I never would've admitted any sort of attraction to someone like Jesse, but, now, knowing what I was, and having her standing mere inches in front of me, I felt a sweat break out on my brow and a weakness in my knees. I suddenly imagined those very strong arms wrapped around me, that powerful body taking control of me, overwhelming me . . .

I sank gratefully into the proffered seat, my entire body shaking, and noticed a dampness between my legs. I had never experienced such an immediate reaction to anyone before in my entire life. Her every word and look seemed like a caress to me—an intense and warm caress.

Auditions led to Val and I being cast opposite each other in the leading roles, which led to rehearsals and . . . everything else. It felt so right the first time Val touched me with her soft hands, pulled me in close and flirted with me throughout the entire act. I finally realized exactly what I had been missing all those years when I acted with men, when I dated men, except . . . except . . .

Except through it all was Jesse watching with those dark eyes and smiling that little grin.

Val was everything I ever thought I wanted in a woman—she didn't lose her femininity in her butchness, her hair was layered and feathered and reached her shoulders, her hands were gentle, she had a shoulder I could imagine crying on, arms I could imagine holding me throughout the night.

She was intelligent, kind, and available. I learned the latter right away for throughout the entire play I was supposed to be in love with her, even though my character didn't tell her till the end of the first act, but we flirted throughout it all, and sometimes, or oftentimes actually, when we stopped, she'd let her hands touch me, touch my thighs, my neck, my hands . . .

When she touched me I was on fire and I could feel her caress in every heartbeat, vein, and pulse in my body.

Then came the fateful night when Val and I first had to do the kissing scene. We tried the scene with ten different blockings that night alone. At times we just stood there, and her lips brushed first my neck, then my ear and my cheek, until finally I guided her lips to mine. I couldn't wait any longer, she was so close, so near, and I needed to feel her against me, needed to feel her lips on mine, to taste that luscious mouth.

The heat rushed through my body, down to my crotch. I could feel her pressed against practically every inch of my body. I held on to her neck, unwilling, unable to release that mouth, unable to give up that feeling I had so long desired.

I don't think anyone thought anything of it. They thought it was me playing with the blocking; well, perhaps maybe Val did think more of it. But suddenly I couldn't stand on my own legs any longer, suddenly my knees buckled and I was in Val's arms, and she was lowering me to the couch, laying on top of me, her thigh between my legs, my lips pressed desperately to hers, wanting her tongue inside me, wanting her to make love to me . . .

"And . . . lights down!" called Jesse from where she was sitting several rows back in the theater.

Val helped me to my feet, supporting me with an arm around my waist. "Jesse," she said, "I think I've figured out how you cast your shows."

"And just how is that, Val m'love?"

"You look at the women who've tried out and say 'Hmmm, would it turn me on to see her make out with her, or—hold on! Now her making out with her—that'd really turn me on! Yeah— you two are cast!'"

"Are you calling me a pervert?"

"Are you denying it?"

"No," Jesse said with that grin, before slowy eyeing me up and down. "Not at all."

After rehearsal that night, Val took me out for a drink, and then she took me home. She came into my apartment with me. We were barely in the door . . .

"I think we need to rehearse that scene a few more times."

Val pulled me into her arms, pressed her mouth against mine. My heart was racing. She picked me up easily and carried me into my bedroom, laying me down on the bed. I had never before felt so vulnerable. She sat on the edge of the bed, leaning over me, kissing me. Her lips brushed my lips, my cheek, eyelids, ears, and throat until they came back to my greedy mouth. I met her tongue with my own, urging her into me, needing her inside of me any way I could get her.

Her hand brushed my breast and I arched upward, wanting to feel her touch on my naked flesh, wanting her to touch me so badly I was almost in tears. She unbuttoned my blouse and pushed my bra aside. My nipples were already hard, rising to her hand, her palm, her warm mouth.

I ripped pitifully against her shirt, wanting to feel her skin against mine, wanting to feel her all over me. She pulled her shirt up over her head, taking her sports bra with it, then roughly pushed my legs apart, placing her breasts between my legs as she wrapped her mouth and tongue over my nipple, teasing it back and forth before she worked her tongue down toward the zipper of my pants . . .

I closed my eyes, feeling her all over me, feeling her heart beating against my throbbing pussy, feeling my soaked underwear pressing tight against it. She peeled off the rest of my clothes so I lay utterly and totally naked and exposed for her. She pushed my legs open even more, staring down at me before she ran her hands roughly up my legs, bypassing my soaked pussy and up to my breasts.

"Oh God," I murmured, "oh God, Val . . ."

I saw her. I wanted her to touch me, to be inside of me, to take me. She lay on top of me, the denim of her jeans rough against my skin, the tender flesh of her breasts like silk against my own. I felt her reach down between my legs and cup the dampness. I closed my eyes, breathing heavily, and arched up against her.

And then Val was gone. It was Jesse who slowly slid her fingers into me, Jesse whose fingers were making me feel so good, making me arch up against her. Those dark, velveteen eyes looked down at me as a wicked grin touched her lips. She winked at me.

"Jesse, Jesse," I moaned, riding her fingers, giving myself to her.

Her fingers left me. Jesse left me. Left me feeling empty. "Please," I begged, reaching down for her hand, opening my eyes . . . and seeing Val looking down at me with a raised eyebrow.

"Jesse?" she asked, her hair falling down over her forehead.

I tried to lift myself up, but found myself too weak to do so. Falling back on the pillows I sighed in frustration. I wanted Val so bad it hurt. I wanted her to continue, didn't want her to stop touching me, feeling me, tasting me, but it also felt so wrong. I wanted her, but I was in love with Jesse.

In love with Jesse. Val was almost everything I'd ever wanted in a woman, but Jesse was . . . Jesse was overpowering.

The way her muscular legs carried her easily onto the stage to demonstrate a movement, the way her tanned forehead creased when she was deep in thought, the depth of emotion she showed while explaining a character motivation to me . . . There was ever so much more to her than could ever meet the eye.

Val and I talked all night long, and after she left I cursed myself for letting such a woman get away from me. Now, weeks later on Valentine's Day, she was tickling me till tears came to my eyes, and Jesse stood watching us.

"Please, no, Val!" I yelled, trying to roll out of her reach.

"Only if you promise to come with us!"

"But I don't even know where the bar is at!"

Jesse looked down at us, obviously enjoying the spectacle we were creating. "I'll take you," she said simply, her voice deep. I felt more than skin-deep naked. I allowed my arms to fall slightly away from my breasts, offering myself to her. "After the show, just follow me to my place and I'll take it from there," Jesse said, her eyes never leaving mine.

Jennifer walked up beside Jesse. "Now I know why you're so devoted to the theater. Where else can you get such a show for free?"

"Who'd want such a spectacle?" Mark said with a quick finger snap as he brushed by to get his tie and jacket for Act Two.

Jesse watched me for a moment longer, but this time she wasn't looking into my eyes. If my nipples weren't already rock hard, they were now. I was aware not only of my nakedness, but also of my panties and of how much I wanted them off.

Val winked at me.

All I could focus on during Act Two was going home with Jesse. Seeing her place. Seeing how she lived. Seeing her bedroom. I hoped she'd leave on her black tank top for the bar—I loved seeing her strong arms, thinking about them around me, holding me, fucking me.

Energy was high throughout Act Two, with everyone excited about closing the show, and about going out and dancing our asses off that evening. Even the couples had decided to forgo the usual romantic Valentine's dinner for two and come to the bar. I was worried about what would come after this evening—whether or not I'd ever see any of these people again. I couldn't imagine not seeing them all practically every day. I couldn't imagine not knowing when I'd next be seeing Jesse.

As planned, after the show, after we changed back into our street clothes from our costumes, talked with the audience and did the obligatory mingling, I followed Jesse back to her place. Her black Bronco seemed to fit her energetic lifestyle, and her neat Royal Oak bungalow seemed just the sort of place I could imagine her living.

I was right behind her as she unlocked the front door. A large, 100-pound or so yellow Labrador retriever greeted us.

"Don't worry about him, he's just a big puppy."

"What's his name?" I asked, kneeling down to pet him.

"Elroy." She opened the back door, and he bounded outside. "Just let me change my clothes and I'll be right with you. Make yourself at home."

I glanced around the unadorned living room, admiring the polished wooden floors, the leather sofa and maple furniture. Jesse apparently liked a simple arrangement of quality goods.

"Do you mind if I check my e-mail quickly?" she called from an office off the side of the living room.

"Go ahead," I replied, following the sound of her voice into the neatly appointed room. Jesse had changed into a red silk shirt and tight, well-worn blue jeans with yet another pair of heavy black boots. The glow from the computer monitor lit her face in a slightly eerie light, casting an even more ethereal image upon her than my already overwhelmed imagination ever could.

Her fingers danced across the keyboard as she glanced at a few messages and typed off replies. The swift, sure movements of her digits were mesmerizing. I could imagine her stroking me with those long fingers, touching me with those gentle, yet strong and competent hands . . .

She turned and caught me staring. She stood and stepped toward me. "And to think that the cast has been wondering which way the wind blows . . ."

I tried to back away from her, but stumbled instead. Jesse caught me in her arms.

I pulled away.

"I'm sorry," she said. "I forgot about you and Val."

"Val and I are just friends." I knew I sounded like an idiot.

"You sure about that?" Jesse asked, raising an eyebrow. She ran her fingertips lightly up my arm, causing goose bumps to break out all over my body.

How could I tell this incredible woman that Val made me sweat, while she, Jesse, made me into a bowl of jelly? How could I explain the difference in lust versus love? Between friendship and . . .

She cornered me against a wall. "So, you're not sure about that? Does that mean maybe you'll be *my* Valentine?"

I wanted to scream at her to take me. I wanted to throw myself into those incredible arms and let her powerful body take me however she wanted. Instead, like an idiot I said, "Yes. I mean, no. I mean yes, I'm sure about that . . ."

Suddenly her lips were against mine, her body pushing me

against the wall, her thigh lodged between my legs, pressing into my wetness. I had been wet all night, waiting for her, wanting her. If being naked in front of her got me so ready, God only knew what her actually touching me would do. I knew I could come in almost no time.

I groaned as her tongue forced its way into my mouth, as my body arched into hers, as our bodies melded together.

She pulled away. "Have you ever been with a woman before?"

I looked down, not saying a word, still holding on to her, not willing or able to release her. I didn't know what to say.

"Is that a yes . . . or a no?" There was a twinkle in her eye.

"I . . . I'm not sure."

"Did you go all the way with her?" She ran her finger along my collarbone, inside my blouse. "Did you get naked with her?" Her finger dropped down, hooking the front of my blouse, inching ever so slightly into my bra. "Did she feel you up? Make your nipples hard? Make you wet?" She took my breast in her hand, playing her thumb over my already hardened nipple.

My legs were rubber. I couldn't stand much longer.

"Did she touch you here?" She reached down further. I groaned and pushed my crotch into her hand. "Did you let her inside of you?" Her face was in my neck, her voice a whisper against my ear. I was pressed against the wall, her body tight against me the only thing keeping me standing. She knew precisely what she was doing. "Did she taste you? Make you come?"

"No," I said.

"What?" Her breath was warm on my ear.

"No. She didn't taste me. She didn't make me come."

She knew the effect making me say such things would have on me. She was a master violinist and I was her instrument. Without ever really touching me she knew everything about me.

"I want to make love to you. Will you let me do that?"

She was now looking deep into my eyes, touching me more intimately and deeply than she ever could with her hands, her body.

I nodded.

She picked me up as if I were a feather, her strong arms cradling me, my head resting against her shoulder, and took me upstairs to her bedroom. The entire upper floor of the bungalow was her bedroom. She laid me down on the bed and reached across me to turn on a lamp.

"I want to see you."

She played her hands across my hair, brushing a few stray strands out of my face, then down my cheek, running her thumb over my lips.

I lay there, watching her, watching the expressions cross her face, seeing the concern and feelings—maybe even love—in her eyes. I felt comfortable, more comfortable than ever before in my life. It felt right to be lying in Jesse's bed about to make love with her.

Her fingers toyed with the buttons on my shirt; she was in no hurry. "We won't do anything you don't want to . . ."

I silenced her by sitting up and placing my lips against hers, wrapping my arms around her and bringing her down to lie upon me. Her lips traced a path down from my lips, down my neck, down between my breasts, as her nimble fingers quickly unbuttoned my blouse. She smiled briefly when she saw my bra—white and adorned with red hearts, my secret acknowledgment of the day—then expertly undid my bra to expose my breasts. Her lips teased the extended nipples that were so eager to greet her tongue, which whipped back and forth across them. Her tongue toyed with one nipple while her fingers squeezed the other.

"Oh, God, Jesse," I said, eager to get out of the rest of my clothes, eager to feel her skin against mine. I wanted to feel her inside me. I wanted to be hers. "Please, I need to feel you," I said, struggling against her shirt.

She sat up and pulled off her shirt and bra, then pulled me into a sitting position long enough to strip off my shirt and bra.

"You are so beautiful—your breasts, your mouth, your belly," she whispered into my ear as she pushed me back to the bed. Her breasts were soft against mine, her skin softer than anything I had ever previously before imagined.

Using her teeth, she undid the zipper of my jeans, then played with my navel ring, tugging gently, teasing me with her tongue. Her hands and mouth were everywhere at once.

I lifted my hips to allow her to pull off my jeans, socks, and soaked underwear. I lay there, naked under her gaze, as she sat up and stared at me. I had never felt so exposed before in my life, nor had I ever felt so comfortable.

She leaned down to kiss me as her hands trailed down my body. Our tongues met in my mouth, and then, as I had never before done in my life, I opened my eyes and looked deep in hers . . .

Our eyes were still locked as she slowly trailed her fingers up and down my wet slit, then inserted first one finger, then another, inside of me. The intimacy was incredible—Jesse penetrating me in the most private way, being inside me while looking deep in my eyes. It felt as if our souls were connected, as if our innermost parts were coming together.

I don't know if I was more heated by her touching me like I had never been touched before, or by watching her watching me while she caressed me.

She kissed my neck, her fingers still toying with me, squeezing my clit gently, while her lips traveled down my body. Her tongue danced across my skin as I squirmed under her. I arched my chest up, begging her to take the erect nipples in her mouth again, needing her everywhere at once. I wanted more intimacy with her than I had ever before experienced in my life, than I had ever imagined before in my life.

I pulled her naked body against mine, enjoying the warmth of her skin, the pounding of her heartbeat against my breast. Her hands were warm as they played with me, as my hips began to arch up against her, wanting still more.

Her mouth trailed down over my belly, and I felt her warm breath against me before I felt, for the first time in my life, the warm, sweet wetness of a woman's tongue against my clit.

"Oh, God, Jesse!" I screamed as I went further than I ever had before, her tongue tracing my clit, flicking it back and forth. She groaned with the taste of me as she lapped me up, as I groaned with her, moaning and writhing under her ministrations. This was what I had wanted ever since the day I first saw her, ever since she first cast me in the play . . .

I looked down in the dim light and saw her mouth against me, saw her looking up at me . . . Our gazes met and held. The heat that had been coursing throughout my body suddenly focused between my legs. Her tongue on my clit, sucking and licking, caused all my blood, all my life to focus right there.

I spread my legs wider, opening myself up to her even more. I reached up to grab the headboard, spreading myself totally for her. Her tongue was inside of me, then flicking back and forth over my swollen flesh. The nucleus of heat that had gathered between my legs grew, coursing down my legs, bursting up into my stomach . . . and it grew with every stroke of her tongue. She worked me up and down, tasting me, eating me, taking me . . .

"Jesse!" I yelled as my world was split apart, as I tossed her body across the bed . . .

A few moments later I lay in her arms, feeling her hands trace circles over my bare skin, caress my hair, stroke me.

"Lara, there's something I want you to know . . ." she began, turning my head so our eyes again met.

"Shhh," I replied, laying my fingers against her lips, afraid of what she might say next.

She gently removed my hand and reached across me to turn the lights down. "I love you. Happy Valentine's Day."

Cuban Heat
MJ Williamz

The dream was fading. Yet it seemed to continue. I felt myself waking up, but could still feel the Tahitian beauty from my dream working her magic between my legs. From somewhere between consciousness and sleep came the feeling of a mouth working on my cunt, licking and sucking, devouring me. Still not fully awake, my hands moved down to investigate, and felt the silky softness of Tanya's blonde mane. Tanya was my latest bedmate. She must have interpreted my hands on her head as encouragement, because her tongue stepped up its pace between my legs.

"Nice try, baby," I said sleepily, grinning to myself. The only time Tanya got between my legs was when she could sneak down there while I slept. After all, I am stone. "Get up here and lay next to me."

Pouting, she did as I'd instructed. I leaned over her to kiss her hard on her mouth, the taste of myself fanning the flame she'd started.

My hand made its way down to one voluptuous breast. She

moaned as I caressed it, alternating kneading its fullness and teasing her nipple. She let me know she liked it by frantically entwining her tongue with mine as she grabbed my hair.

I pulled away from her, letting my lips follow my hand as I kissed downward, appreciating once again the softness of her, the way she felt under my mouth, how her skin quivered as I left little kisses all over. I kissed below her belly button, stopping briefly to gaze longingly at her pink swollen wonderland.

I slowly lowered my mouth to her, reluctant to tear my gaze away, but needing desperately to taste her. I breathed deeply of her scent as my tongue slid easily inside her warm wetness, lapping at the juices that were flowing there. I stayed inside briefly before moving my mouth to her slick and swollen clit. I closed my mouth around it and sucked. Harder and harder I sucked, while my fingers moved in and out of her. She arched her back, pressing herself into me as her whole body tensed before she toppled over the edge and floated into orgasmic bliss.

Moving up to take her in my arms, I kissed the top of her head and ran my fingers through her soft hair.

"So, CJ, I've been thinking," Tanya threw at me.

Looking down, I saw her focusing on my breast. She was playing with a nipple, and couldn't seem to tear her eyes away from it.

"What were you thinking?" I asked warily. Tanya thinking and not meeting my eyes didn't strike me as a winning combination.

"I just want you to know that I really don't expect anything from you for Valentine's Day."

My heart stopped. Wide awake, I realized that I had a definite problem. The fact that she even mentioned Valentine's Day meant she was reading way more into this than was there. Just because we slept together a few nights a week, didn't make it a "relationship" and it certainly wasn't something to be celebrated on Valentine's Day. Saint Valentine was the patron saint of love. If there was a patron saint of lust, I could see celebrating it with Tanya, but definitely not love.

We had been sleeping together for about six months, since

meeting late one night at the gym where the attraction was instant and mutual. We were in the shower at the same time and I couldn't keep my eyes off her. She made a special point of washing her hair an extended time, keeping her arms above her head so I could have a clear view of her luscious, full, double-D breasts. After she'd rinsed her hair, she kept her eyes locked on mine as she soaped up her body—spending extra time where her legs met. Once appropriately lathered, she grabbed a razor from her shower kit. She held it up and looked at me, asking if I cared to help.

Not about to turn down an opportunity like that, I knelt before her and shaved her mons before taking one leg and placing it over my shoulder as I drew the razor along the tender skin between her legs. I had to be extra careful to avoid her lips, already protruding with desire. Once I had her completely smooth, I ran my tongue along her swollen lips before slipping it inside her.

I sucked on her lips, pulling both into my mouth while my tongue lapped over them, determined to taste everything she had to offer. I pulled myself away and led her to the bench, where I pushed her down and nestled back between her legs, not caring if anyone walked into the locker room to catch us. I immediately took her clit between my teeth and sucked on it, while my fingers slid into her tight wetness. She groaned as she put her hands on the back of my head, pressing my face into her as her hips rocked against me. I had three fingers inside her when she finally yelled out as I brought her to the first of several orgasms that night.

Sure, I reflected as I laid there contemplating her comment. Tanya was an incredibly sensuous woman and I loved having sex with her. But Valentine's Day? That was something else completely. I debated how to respond. I knew that if we did anything, I'd be misleading her in a very cruel way. On the other hand, if I *didn't* do anything, I was sure she'd cut me off. What a choice. When it hit me that Valentine's Day was the next day, I knew I had to think fast.

"Oh, Tanya, didn't I tell you? I'm goin' out of town for a few days."

"You are?" She propped herself up on an elbow and finally looked me in the eye, her green eyes glittering dangerously.

"Yeah," I said, sliding out of bed and reaching for my clothes. I needed to get out of there. "I thought I told you."

"Where are you goin'?" she asked.

"Going?" I knew what she meant, but chose to feign misunderstanding. "I'm gonna head home. You need to get ready for work."

Fully dressed and not wanting to continue the conversation, I kissed her before she could say anything. "I'll give you a call when I get back, okay? We'll talk then."

Before she could respond, I let myself out and caught the elevator to freedom. I almost hailed a cab, but opted instead for a walk in the cold, early-morning air, hoping to clear my head.

Pushing my hands deep into my coat pockets, I was once again amazed at how someone like myself from warmer climes could feel so comfortable there in the cold, snowy Northeast. Although, as new flakes began to sting my face, I found my mind drifting back to years gone by, reflecting on how I came to live up there in the first place.

I was eighteen years old and as hot blooded as any young Cuban. Growing up a Mendez had its advantages and disadvantages. The advantages of having a Mafia *Padrino* for a father were numerous—freedom to go where I wanted without worrying about anyone giving me any trouble; money to spend without thinking; and living in a mansion with so many rooms that I could do just about anything I wanted there without ever getting caught, or so I thought.

The disadvantages mirrored the advantages, really—someone always keeping an eye on me when I hung out on the streets, so my freedom was mostly perceived; the never-ending lectures about how my parents should make me get a job and earn my money the way everybody else did.

Of course, being female, that last threat didn't mean much to me. My father would never sink to having his daughter actually work for a living, at least that's what I'd been brought up to believe. So, life was pretty good for me as a high school senior with my whole life ahead of me. I was baptized, or cursed, depending on your point of view, with the name Carmelina Juanita Mendez. My friends called me CJ.

That particular spring afternoon, I strutted down Calle Ocho after school like I owned the place. Very aware of the admiring stares being cast my way, I hid my eyes behind my dark sunglasses so no one could see my response. I stood tall as I walked confidently into the pool hall that my uncle owned. As *Tio* Carlos came out to greet me, he took one look at me dressed in black jeans and a black tank top and stopped in his tracks.

"*Dios Mio*, Carmelina," he pleaded. "Must you dress like a man?"

"I'm not dressed like a man," I shot back, taking my glasses off to look him in the eye. "I'm dressed like *me*."

He hugged me then and mumbled that he'd never understand. As we broke from the embrace, I again met his eyes, casually flipping my black bangs out of my eyes. I was the tallest woman in my family. At five feet eight inches, I stood almost as tall as most of the men. I knew they thought it disrespectful for me to meet their stares, but I enjoyed the feeling of power it gave me and did it every chance I got.

"*Tio* Carlos, have you seen Maria around?"

Maria was a part-time bartender there—and part-time playmate in my bedroom. She was older than I by a couple of years, only stood about five-foot-two, and was as beautiful as she was adventurous. Her skin was the color of dark caramel, her eyes black as ebony. She wore her thick black hair long; so long it hung to her waist. In bed, she'd often sit on top of me and her hair would fall forward covering her breasts, so it tickled my face while I suckled on her. Thinking about her was getting me wet. I needed to find her.

"Sorry, Carmelina, Maria doesn't work today. I haven't seen her."

"Shit," I mumbled.

"*Excuse* me, *Senorita?*"

"*Lo siento*. I'm sorry. I gotta go. I'll catch you later."

My shades back in place, I left in search of someone, *anyone* who might be fun for the afternoon. I headed straight for the *taqueria*, hoping Maria might be there. Instead, I saw Kellianne Harrison—the girl I'd been in love with since second grade. Kellianne was everything I wasn't: blonde, blue-eyed, short, feminine . . . and straight. She looked out of place there, as one of the only *gringas*, but didn't seem to mind. She called even more attention to herself as she stood and waved at me.

"CJ! Over here!"

Like I wouldn't have seen her anyway. I walked over and sat next to her.

"Whatcha doin?" I asked her.

"I'm working on my calculus homework. I was hoping you'd be here to help me."

"Kellianne? Are you serious? Have you looked outside? Spring has sprung, lady. There is so much more to life than calculus."

"Easy for you to say," she said, turning her baby blues pleadingly to me. "You're going to USF in the fall. Some of us are still trying to make the grades to get into a good school."

"I'm flattered," I said, wondering if she had any clue how I felt about her. "Okay, what are you working on?"

The next couple of hours flew by. I helped her with her homework, but it was pure torture having that body so close to me and not being able to touch her the way I wanted. And she smelled so good. By the time the study session was over, I was a hormonal mess. She thanked me for my help and walked away, swaying her hips and teasing me excruciatingly.

Accepting that I was going to spend the afternoon alone, I headed home, let myself into my wing at the mansion, turned on my stereo and lay on my bed with my brother's *Playboy*. Not more than a half hour had passed when someone knocked on my door.

Assuming it was my annoying little brother, Juan Jr., or Johnny, I took my time opening it.

On the other side of the door stood not Johnny, but Maria.

"I heard you were looking for me," she purred, walking past me and making sure to rub her breasts against me as she did.

I closed the door and turned around to find her shirt off and her hands removing her skirt. I walked to her and pulled her close, pressing her naked breasts into me as I kissed her hard on the mouth. I met no resistance—her mouth opened immediately and our tongues wrapped around each other.

My mouth moved lower. I had one full breast in my mouth when my door burst open and in walked Johnny.

"What the fuck?" he bellowed.

Frozen with surprise, it took me a second to stand up and say, "Johnny! What the hell are you doin' here?"

"I can't fuckin' believe this!" he yelled, leaving my room at a run.

Shaking, Maria left immediately and I paced my room for the next hour or so, until it was time for dinner—we always ate dinner as a family—to wonder what my punishment would be. Johnny, a year younger than me, had always been jealous that I was the first-born. Not that it mattered. I was, after all, female, and therefore undeserving of any rights a firstborn male would have. But Johnny was threatened by and jealous of me, and I was sure he'd run straight to my father to tell him what he'd walked in on.

When dinnertime finally arrived, I walked into the formal dining room and was not surprised to find my father already seated there, alone.

"Hey Dad." I tried to sound calm. "What's that?" I asked, pointing to a packet at my place.

"It's everything you'll need." His response, though spoken quietly, set off a warning signal deep inside me.

"Everything I'll need?" I repeated, hoping my nervousness didn't show. "Such as?"

"Open it!" he commanded.

I did. As I reviewed the contents, he ran a narrative for me.

"You'll find your high school transcripts and diploma. Congratulations. A smart girl like you. Not too surprising, really, is it that you graduated early?"

I glared at him, unsure of his exact meaning, but knowing from his tone that I wasn't going to like anything I'd find. I went back to the contents of the packet.

"An airplane ticket," he said matter-of-factly. "You'll be flying to New Jersey tonight."

Looking up at him again, it took all my self-control not to walk over and slap him.

"That's right, Carmelina. You will be starting school at Logan University Monday. It's a nice, private university and there will be plenty of family there to keep an eye on you."

Standing straight, I looked him in the eye and challenged him. "I am eighteen years old, Dad. I can do what I want. You can't send me away like this."

My father stood then, leaned on the table and met my eyes, his dark eyes as cold and hard as flint. "I can and I will! I don't care how old you are, Carmelina. You are a Mendez! You will not disgrace this family!"

My insides turned. I was afraid. But I wouldn't let him see it.

"Whatever." I tried to sound casual as I flipped my bangs out of my eyes. "You can think what you want, but I'm not going anywhere."

I sat down and shoved the packet aside.

"What's for dinner?" I asked.

My father sat back down and said calmly, "You'll be taking dinner in your room. A car will be here in two hours to take you to the airport. Pack what you can."

I couldn't believe he was serious. I didn't know what to say. I just sat there.

"You are excused," he said, not looking up from his plate.

"But, Dad . . ." I tried.

"No buts! Get out of my sight."

"Dad," I pleaded.

He looked at me then and said, "If it's the money you're worried about, don't. I will send you money every month from now on. You will be taken care of."

He was adding insult to injury. I was too angry to speak. I didn't trust my voice, terrified I would cry in front of him.

"Now GO!" he yelled. Realizing I had no choice, I got up to leave the room. I was at the doorway when he said, "And Carmelina?"

I turned, "Yeah?"

"Don't ever come back."

"Huh?"

"Ever. I never want to see you in this city again."

That had been twenty years ago. And I'd never been back, following his orders. I lived comfortably in New York, having moved there after graduating from Logan with a degree in marketing. My father continued to deposit money into my account monthly, as promised. I made good money running my own ad agency, but I let him keep giving me money. I figured it was the least he could do for me. And it let me take lavish vacations and spend extravagant amounts of money on the women I bedded.

The route to my apartment led me right past all the high-end department stores. Their windows were all decorated in hearts, all red clothes on display. A florist's window held oversized bouquets of roses. Valentine's Day. My thoughts returning to the present, I was confronted yet again with my Valentine's Day dilemma. I had told Tanya I'd be out of town. But where would I go? Money wasn't the issue, obviously; it was more a question of where did I feel like going in February? Not exactly my idea of the ideal month to travel. But if I stayed in the city and anybody saw me and it got back to her . . . well, there went my current playmate.

"Shit," I muttered under my breath, kicking snow out of my

way and forging onward. I still had about twenty blocks to go and spent every last step thinking of where I could go just to get out of town for a few days. As the snow began falling anew, my mind kept drifting back to Miami. I felt drawn to go back. But, did I seriously want to go there? What would I do there? What would my father do if he heard I was back in town? How would he know I was back in town, I argued. I was sure he'd stopped watching for me by now. And I didn't have to go anywhere near the old neighborhood. The thought of South Beach in February was suddenly very appealing. Clothing optional on the beach, warm sunshine. No responsibilities, no commitments, no Valentine's Day issues. As I entered my building, my mind was made up. I was finally going back to Miami. I stopped by the desk and asked the concierge to book me a flight that night. Miami, I thought to myself as I rode the elevator to my suite. Home. No, I corrected myself. Not home. This city was my home. Miami was to me, like every other tourist, a vacation destination. Nothing more.

I awoke the next morning in my private bungalow at Le Cotier, an exclusive resort on South Beach. I had arrived late the previous night, so only took the time to check in before falling dead asleep to the unfamiliar sound of the surf outside my window. It took me a moment to realize where I was that morning, but the warm sea air drifting over me quickly reminded me. I stretched, feeling relaxed and safe, miles away from New York and Tanya. I didn't even let the worries of my father finding out I was there intrude on the beautiful morning.

I made myself some coffee and sat on my private patio, looking over brochures I had picked up in the lobby. I had no plans, but some of the touristy ideas in the brochures made my stomach turn. I flashed back to the term *turistonto*, synonymous with easy mark, a clueless fool meant to be taken advantage of. That's the way we felt about them when I was a kid.

One brochure that caught my eye was about the Lincoln Street

Mall. Lincoln Street was said to be family friendly, with lots of restaurants, art galleries, and nouveau shoppes. It seemed as good a place as any to start my vacation.

Once showered and dressed, I checked my reflection in the mirror, pleased with what I saw. My white linen suit fit on my slight frame perfectly. I felt somewhat "Miami Vice," but I looked so good with the black T-shirt hugging my body, that I had to smile. I was fairer than many Cubans, but still had the brown eyes and black hair and light olive skin that contrasted with my teeth for a smile that lots of women found irresistible. I wore my thick hair short, slicked, and parted on the side, with my bangs long enough that I still had to brush them out of my eyes on occasion. It was a habit I'd discovered that women found endearing and I was in the mood to endear myself to as many women as I could.

I was looking good and feeling good as I left my bungalow, walked up past the main hotel, crossed Ocean Drive and made my way to Lincoln Street. People were out in droves that February morning. The tables outside the cafés were filled with people enjoying their coffees or early lunches under the warm Miami sun.

Having determined to walk to the far end of Lincoln Street and work my way back, I passed many trendy spots, smiling at all the scantily clad ladies I saw. They were everywhere. Tight shorts, tighter tops, short skirts with bare midriffs, long, flowing skirts with bikini tops. I was in heaven, I thought, grinning to myself and thinking of the fun I was sure to have that evening. South Beach would be a smorgasbord for me and I planned to taste a little of everything.

I was about halfway to the end of Lincoln when I saw a shop named, "The Other Side of the Rainbow." The name, combined with the rainbow banners out front, made it impossible to resist walking in. It turned out to be more of an art gallery than a shoppe. There was a register just inside and to the right, where a twenty-something brunette with long hair and dark eyes smiled at me as I walked in.

"Is there anything I can show you?" she asked innocently

enough. I caught myself before replying that her tight halter top, combined with the air conditioning, was showing me two very nice perky nipples that I'd like to see more of.

"Actually, this is my first time here. I saw your sign and had to come in. The work in here is impressive," I said, looking around at statues placed strategically throughout the store and paintings that hung tastefully on the wall. There was much on display, but there was no sense of clutter.

"So, tell me what I'm looking at, please," I said to the bronzed beauty.

She came around to stand next to me. "You're looking at art."

"So I see," I replied, appreciating her sense of humor.

She laughed. "These are works from both well-known and unknown gay and lesbian artists only."

I nodded. "Impressive."

"Mm-hm," she agreed. "And even more impressive is that only a small portion of the proceeds go to the artists. Of course, having their work exhibited here is worth far more than money," she added. "The majority of the proceeds is split between AIDS research and breast cancer research."

I arched my eyebrows. "*Very* impressive," I said. Needing to play devil's advocate, I turned to the young woman beside me and asked, "And what about you? Surely some of the proceeds go to pay you and the rest of the staff here?"

"We volunteer," she countered.

"You volunteer?" I repeated, cynical enough to have a hard time believing what I was being told. "And the owner? Surely he skims quite a bit off the top?"

A voice from behind me said softly, "*She* doesn't skim. She pays the bills here. The rest of the proceeds are allocated as Alicia said."

I turned to find a beautiful blonde woman, about my age, dressed in a sharp-looking beige skirt suit. The pale blue blouse under her open jacket swelled temptingly, but I knew better than to ogle. This woman was obviously all class. She had been standing with her hand outstretched, as if about to introduce herself. Her eyes grew wide as they met mine, and her hand dropped to her side.

"CJ?"

I was certain I didn't know this woman. I would remember a stunning woman like this.

"Have we met?" I asked, barely able to get the words out.

"It's me, CJ. Kellianne."

"Kellianne Harrison?" I asked. Damn! She'd grown into one fine-looking woman. I quickly checked for, and didn't see, a wedding band. Still, to be safe, I said, "Oh. It's probably not Harrison anymore, though, huh?"

"Oh yes, it's Harrison," she replied.

I stepped forward and my arms were around her before either of us could react. Her arms circled me, pulling me close, pressing her body into mine. It was a moment I had fantasized about for years.

Pulling back, I took her hands in mine and looked into those blue eyes that had haunted me throughout my youth.

"Damn, you look good, Kellianne."

"Thank you, CJ. So do you. The years have been kind to you."

I took my hands away from hers, put one hand in my pocket and brushed my bangs out of my eyes with the other.

Kellianne laughed. "Still doing that, huh?"

"Yeah," I grinned. "I can't seem to lose that habit." Determined not to lose my cool, I decided to try another approach.

"So, you volunteer here, too?" I asked.

"In a manner of speaking, I suppose I do. I own it."

"You own it? Wow! I'm impressed." I was a bit confused, though. I had assumed the owner would be family. "Where did you get the idea for a place like this?"

"Well," she began, "I wanted a way to raise money for good causes, plus I think we need a way to showcase gay and lesbian artists. We need to support each other. And if some heterosexual dollars come our way too, so much the better."

"*We?*" I asked. "You mean . . ."

"Yes, CJ. I mean I'm a lesbian." She laughed. "You don't have to look so shocked."

"Yeah, well, I guess people change," I managed. I was beginning to feel like a total idiot. Where was the suave butch who no woman could fluster?

"Yes, we do." She smiled. "Now, are you going to take me to lunch and tell me whatever happened to you? As I recall, one day you were helping me with homework and the next you were off to some private university or something, never to be heard from again."

I offered her my elbow and she slid her hand through it. "Yeah, well, it's kind of a long story, but I'd love to buy you lunch."

Kellianne immediately suggested we cruise up to Calle Ocho and check out some old haunts. I convinced her otherwise, telling her the tale of my last miserable night in the city twenty years ago, as we walked along.

"Your dad kicked you out for being *gay*?!" She was appropriately appalled.

I laughed, covered her hand with my free hand and told her it was no big deal. After all, it had been a long time ago.

She rested her head on my shoulder then, a gesture that seemed so natural. As we made our way back up Lincoln to the beachfront, we talked about everything—our families, our lives, our likes and dislikes, our jobs, walking like we'd been lovers for years. I was both aroused and content having her so close. It felt so right for her to be on my arm, and I realized I still desired her with the same longing I'd had as a teenager.

That longing was accentuated by the sights on the beach. Granted, topless bathing was permitted, but there were several women who had opted to bathe au natural. All shapes and sizes were out there, each one a tribute to the wonder and beauty that is a woman's body.

Although the bathing beauties were whetting my appetite, none held my attention like the woman on my arm. I leaned over and kissed the top of her head. Her hair was soft, clean, and smelled of roses and lavender.

She stopped walking and stood facing forward. For a moment I was terrified I'd blown it.

"That felt so natural," Kellianne whispered.

"It did," I agreed, wanting her with every ounce of my being, but afraid I'd scare her off if I let it show.

"Where are you staying?" she asked.

"At Le Cotier."

"Mmm, fancy," she said, leaning her head back on my shoulder and turning us in the direction of my hotel.

As I closed the door to the bungalow behind us, I felt like a teenager on my first date. I was a nervous wreck. She seemed so calm as she walked through my temporary digs, checking out my view of the beach, inspecting my personal effects in the bathroom.

"Everything meet with your satisfaction?" I joked.

She came back into the bedroom and stood in front of me, removing her jacket.

"So far, so good," she answered.

"So far?" I teased, trying to stay calm at the sight of her breasts straining against her flimsy blouse.

Her hands went around my neck, her fingers playing with my hair. I moaned as I tipped my head back, enjoying the sensation of her fingers.

I rested my hands on her hips and looked into those blue eyes, trying desperately to read her mind. Was she just playing with me? Did she want me as badly as I needed her?

"So far," she replied, and I felt pressure on the back of my neck as she pulled my mouth to hers. "I have a feeling it's going to get much better," she whispered, just as our lips touched.

Our first kiss was tender, soft, almost tentative. A struggle waged inside me—I wanted to kiss her harder, claim her as mine, leave no doubt in her mind how I felt about her. But I didn't want to make her uncomfortable, or make any assumptions that could possibly impede our progress.

I pulled away from her and looked into her eyes briefly, before kissing her softly, almost playfully again.

"Just how I imagined it," she said.

"Really?" My ego soared. "You've imagined kissing me before?"

"Many, many times, my strong, smart, sexy CJ."

My mouth covered hers again, this time with no pretense of tenderness.

I helped her onto the bed, kissing her hard as I sat down beside her; I felt her shaking in response.

Her arms around my neck pulled me close, urging me to kiss her harder, her tongue dancing in my mouth. Her mouth was so warm and moist and responsive, just as I knew the rest of her would be.

I gently laid her back so she was underneath me. We continued kissing, alternating between tenderness and passion, wanting each other so desperately, but determined to make this last. She began to arch her back, pushing herself up against me. I lay on top of her, relishing the feeling of our bodies fitting together.

I slowly kissed my way down her cheek, just under her jawbone, into the hollow of her neck. Her hands held my head, running her fingers through my hair and making sure I knew what she wanted. As I kissed that tender spot on her neck, I began to unbutton her blouse, then pulled away to look at her. Her eyes, less focused, left no doubt in my mind that this was what she wanted. I peeled her blouse away and unhooked her front-clasp bra.

Her full breasts sprang free. I moaned involuntarily as I looked at the perfectly shaped mounds. Her areolas were pink and her nipples were hard. I looked into her eyes as I slowly caressed her taut nipples.

Her eyes pleaded with me to continue, so my mouth retraced its path down her neck as my hand slid under her skirt. I felt her shiver as I traced my fingers along her soft inner thighs. I could feel the heat radiating from under her panties and I marveled at her response to me. Arching her back, she pressed herself into my hand, her crotch wet against me.

I kissed her again as my other hand slid behind her back and unzipped her skirt. She lifted her hips, allowing me to remove her skirt and panties in one fluid motion. My resolve to make her wait, wanting to increase the sexual tension weakened. I couldn't wait. And as I gazed at her nakedness, her legs seemed to open on their own, leaving her exposed to my hungry eyes.

I stood up and quickly removed my clothes, anxious to feel her skin against mine. Her eyes glittered with desire as they traced a path from my face to my nipples, down my flat, firm stomach and stopped at the dark triangle of hair between my legs. She reached out and squeezed my nipples.

The need to have her was complete. I lay back down on top of her, breast to breast, catching my breath as they met. I slowly rubbed my chest back and forth against hers, holding myself up so only our nipples touched as we kissed long and deep

I began to trail kisses down her cheeks, along her neck, down her chest to take one erect nipple in my mouth and twirl it with my tongue. Her gasp let me know I was on the right track.

Moving to the other nipple, I brought my knee up between her legs. She squeezed her legs around me and I pressed into her, encouraged by her wet heat, while I kissed all around her breasts— over, under, sucking and licking her nipples. I moved back so I could trail kisses down her stomach to the tip of her closely trimmed hair. Over and over, I licked and kissed until she was writhing in anticipation.

"Please," she urged.

Smiling, I made my way lower, letting my tongue circle and stroke her clit. The urge to be inside her was strong and she was so soft and wet and warm when my tongue entered her. Deeper and deeper I thrust my tongue in her, pulling her to me and loving the feel of her moving against me. Her quivering body and ever deepening moans told me that she was nearing the edge, so I moved my tongue back to her clit. Harder and faster I stroked her, becoming more and more aroused at her response. She moved frantically against me, pressing into me until she suddenly cried out as she grabbed my head to hold my mouth on her. My tongue continued its pace as her body was racked with one orgasm after another as she called out my name again and again.

I teased her clit softly as she came down from her final climax, then licked my way back up the length of her body, before I kissed her again. Our sweat-slicked bodies squished together, and she laughed, pushing me gently away. She looked into my eyes and I looked into hers, marveling at the love I saw there. How wondrous was that after all these twenty years? I pushed a damp blonde curl off her face and kissed her softly before taking her into my arms to just hold her.

She curled into my body as if she'd been there forever. This was what I had wanted my whole life. I couldn't believe Kellianne was finally in my bed. In my life.

"Mmm . . . Happy Valentine's Day to me," she murmured.

I did not greet this reference to Valentine's Day with panic. Rather, I felt like I finally was where I needed to be on Valentine's Day. And I was definitely with the right person.

"Happy Valentine's Day is right," I said, rolling back over on top of her, our mouths meeting again, our tongues dancing with newly fueled passion.

Make Love To Me
Ellen Tevault

"I don't know if I can do it." She paused and glanced toward my side of the bed with her back still to me. "Be with a butch that won't let me show her how much I love her." I thought I heard her voice crack and wanted to reach out to her.

Over the years, some femmes have pushed until one of us tired of the pushing and left. For some reason this time was different. I didn't know why or how, but it was.

"I can't," I said, feeling her pull away. "I'm sorry."

The thick silence between us smothered me. It was one of the very few times since that horrible night years ago that the threat of tears made my throat tighten. I clenched my eyes shut to prevent the tears from escaping. I don't know why I held onto them as if they were secret treasures.

Another night, she kissed her way down my body and stopped at my belly button. I knew she had stopped because she sensed my body stiffen the closer she came to my "down there." She sighed, and I stroked her hair, feeling her breath on my stomach.

The next morning, she cooked eggs for breakfast. I smiled

when I saw her standing there with her long brown hair wet from her shower, dancing to the beat of whatever tune played on the radio. No matter how late I'd be for work, I couldn't resist grabbing her sashaying hips and nuzzling her neck.

"Good morning," she said, turning to return my hug. "I love you."

I felt her warm breath on my neck when she spoke the words. "I love you, too," I said, kissing her forehead.

We performed this little ritual for over a year until I decided to tell her.

I stood at the dresser, shaking from our ritual of me denying her. I saw in the mirror that she had her back to me, lying on the bed.

"I was . . ." I paused and let out a shaky breath. "Raped."

I didn't turn around to look at her. I didn't want her to get mushy and mother me; I wanted to keep my protective barrier up. I needed it.

I heard her shift on the bed. "I'm sorry," she said. "I . . ." She never finished the next sentence, but after that night, she didn't push again.

A few months later, with Valentine's Day approaching, I peeked into her drawers to check her size and then jumped into my truck to go find the perfect gift. I searched through several stores to find lingerie in her size. Disappointed in the collection of plus sizes, I panicked and called a friend.

"Try She Bops. That's where my girl buys all her stuff," my friend said. "I'm glad to hear you two are doing good."

"Me, too," I said, turning my truck toward the store mentioned. "Thanks for the tip."

"No prob. Big day, isn't it?"

"Yeah, Valentine's Day and our anniversary," I said, stopping at the light to turn into the shop's parking lot.

"We knew it. We said you'd be a great couple when we fixed you up."

"Yeah, one blind date I'll never regret. Gotta go." I pulled the truck into a spot. "I'm here."

Inside the store, I looked around and felt overwhelmed by the selection. I hated to shop, but I trudged forward, determine to find her something special. I picked up a red lace bra and panty set, imagining it against her creamy flesh.

"May I help you, sir?" the store clerk asked, sneaking up behind me.

I jumped and turned around. "I'm not sure if this is the right size," I said, holding the set out to her. I felt her eyes travel up and down my body several times. I knew the look on her face; it was the gender-questioning disgusted look.

"Is it for you?" she asked with the I-hate-being-tricked tone, which I usually hear when people realize they have mistaken my gender.

"No."

She walked away.

I stood there for a minute, watching her, trying to decide if I wanted to patronize this store after all. But they had the right sizes, so I returned to my examination of the bra and panty set. I made a fist and put it inside the bra's cup to see if it would fit her, wondering all the while why girlie clothes couldn't be sized easily like men's.

"May I help you?" another sales clerk said. I stared at her and then glanced over her shoulder at her co-worker. She glanced back and said, "Oh, don't mind her. That time of the month, I think." She giggled as if we were old friends sharing an inside joke. "So, is this for your girlfriend?"

"Yeah, but I'm not sure I have the correct size." I handed her the set and dug into my pocket for my cheat sheet of the numbers I'd found on the bras and panties in her drawers.

She looked at the paper. "I see. This will get you in trouble. Definitely too big." She smiled as she hung the bra back up and retrieved a smaller size.

"I was thinking maybe pink instead," I said, looking around for something similar in a softer color. "She likes pink."

"Oh, I know what she'd like. Let's go over here," she said, walking in another direction. "Do you want something specific?"

"I really don't know," I said, shrugging.

She smiled the poor-butch smile that femmes have. I smiled back and raised my eyebrows as if to say she had me pegged right. Holding up a bra and panty set in bright pink with embroidered hearts, she asked, "How about this? It's her size." She held it up to her body to give me an idea of how it'd look.

"I like it. Are you sure about the size?" I flashed her a sheepish grin.

"I'm positive. I wouldn't want to get a stud in trouble with her femme," she said, leaning toward me. "Understand?"

"Now I get it. I'll take it."

"We also have matching nail polish. Would she like that?" She held onto the set and walked toward the cash register.

"She likes me to paint her nails for her," I said. I shook my head, feeling the blood rush to my head, and knew my face was bright red. "I can't believe I told you that."

"Lucky girl. Anything else?" She rang up the lingerie and the nail polish. "We have complimentary gift bags for the special occasion." She held up the gift bag for me to see the heart surrounding the store's logo. I nodded, and she packed it for me with tissue paper. It looked better than if I'd wrapped it myself.

"Flowers next," I said to myself, as I placed the package on the seat next to me. I backed the truck out and headed off to the florist. I had a fabulous dinner planned for our special night, and wanted everything to be perfect.

Returning home with groceries and a dozen pink roses, I busied myself with preparations for the big night. After I put the groceries away, I cut the stems of the roses with my pocketknife like the woman at the florist had instructed. I searched all the cabinets but couldn't find a vase. I gave up and dug a large coffee creamer jar out of the trash. I washed it out and ripped the label off.

"It'll have to do," I said out loud, arranging the roses in it and praying they wouldn't tip over. "I hope she doesn't notice."

I threw a white tablecloth over our card table, which we used as a dinner table, and folded red cloth napkins. I tried a fancy fold, but they kept flopping over so I just folded them in half. I placed the roses in the center of the table, surrounding them with votive candles in little glass jars. I put matches on the table to light them later.

I stepped back and studied my table. I sighed and decided it'd have to do. "Time to make dinner."

Eventually, I slid the homemade macaroni and cheese into the oven to bake next to the chicken breasts. Usually I used boxed mac and cheese, but tonight deserved better. After I had everything on or in the stove, I lined up my vegetables for the salad. I tore the lettuce and chopped carrots, tomatoes, and green peppers. As I chopped onions and fought back the tears, she came home.

"I didn't expect you yet," I said, wiping the onion tears from my eyes with my sleeve.

"Oops," she said, hiding something behind her back. "I thought you said to be here at seven."

I looked up at the clock and said, "Shit."

"It ain't that bad." She looked around. "Is it?"

As I rushed to assemble my salad, the smoke alarm buzzed. We both turned toward the stove and saw smoke pouring from the oven. I ran over and yanked the door open. "Damn it," I said, grabbing a potholder and pulling the macaroni and cheese out. The cheese had dripped over the casserole dish and burned on the bottom of the oven. "I wanted everything to be perfect," I said, sliding the dish onto the stovetop.

"It is," she said, hugging me from behind. "We have each other."

"I think it's still edible," I said, stirring a spoon around the pasta and cheese sauce. "Now I know why I prefer the boxed kind." I took out the chicken breasts.

She giggled and said, "Me, too."

"I guess we'll eat what we can." I put a chicken breast on each plate, along with the pasta and the salad in bowls. "Go sit at the table. I'll bring it out."

"Ooh, what service. We should do this more often."

"Hush," I said, swatting her behind.

"Mmm, the flowers smell great," she said, leaning into the buds. "Did you get them at the grocery store?"

"No, I bought the good kind. I actually went to a flower shop."

"Boy, I'm being treated like a queen tonight."

"Hey, I beg your pardon. I always treat you like my queen," I said, putting her plate before her.

"You're right. My mistake." She lifted a forkful of the pasta and sniffed it. "It smells delicious, honey."

"I hope so." I turned to the screeching smoke alarm and said, "Shut up." I fanned away the smoke until it stopped and took the battery out once it did.

I'm not sure the food was great, but she said so anyway. I didn't eat much. I fidgeted with my napkin and wondered how the night would go. I had a special gift for her, in addition to the panties and bra.

"Are you going to light the candles?"

"Oh, crap. I forgot," I said, jumping up to get the matches from the kitchen.

"Honey, they're right here," she said, holding them up. She struck one and lit the candles on her side of the vase. Out of the corner of my eye, I saw her pause when she noticed my makeshift vase, but she didn't say anything.

"What are you smiling about?" I asked as I lit the candles.

"Nothing," she said, looking up from the vase to me. "I love you. This has been a great Valentine's Day."

"It's not over yet. Plus, it's our anniversary. We had our first date tonight three years ago."

"Yeah, the whole purpose of that party was to fix us up," she said, smiling. "Can you believe a Valentine's fix-up party?"

"We were the only single people invited. Remember?"

"I wonder what they'd have done if we'd brought dates with us."

"I don't know. Shit themselves."

"Probably."

"I have something for you," I said, jumping up to get the gift. I raced around looking for it. Where was it? I looked in every room.

When she returned to the table with her gift bag, she asked, "Did you leave it in the truck?"

"I bet I did. I must have had too much in my hands. I'll go look."

"I'll be here," she said, taking another bite of her salad. "We have all night."

I found it on the seat, waiting for me. I snatched it up and raced back into the house. When I sat down, I was breathing heavily from exertion, nerves, or both. She had moved the roses off the table and to the kitchen counter.

"Slow down. No need to kill yourself, honey," she said, reaching across the table to pat my hand. "Everything is great."

"I tried, but I forgot dessert." I sighed, thinking about the cupcakes I'd planned to buy.

"That's okay." She slid her bag across the table to me, and I pushed mine toward her. When she saw the logo on the bag, she said, "Oh, wow, I've heard great things about that place."

I held my gift in my lap and waited for her to open hers. She pulled out the tissue paper and glanced into the bag. "Oh, honey," she said as she pulled out the bra and panty set. When she held it up to herself, I noticed that it looked prettier next to her than it had on the salesclerk. She smiled at me, her luminous eyes sparkling with pleasure.

"Do you like it?" When she nodded, I said, "There's matching nail polish in the bag."

She looked in the bag and pulled out the polish. "Ooh, you'll have to paint my nails for me, so I can be pretty for you."

"You're always pretty."

She blushed and looked down for a minute. When she regained her composure, she asked, "Aren't you going to open it?"

I dove into my bag with both hands and took out a package of tank tops and some boxers with hearts on them. I laughed. "I almost bought myself some of these to wear for you."

"You're kidding?"

I held them against my hips to show her. "Don't you dare ever tell anyone about these."

"Honey, every butch in town is probably getting some for tonight."

"That's beside the point. They don't need to know I have any silky ones."

"Ugh, Macho Butchism."

"Hey, what about it?" I walked around the table to pull her out of her chair. She snuggled against me as I wrapped my arms around her.

"Let's go to bed," she said, looking up at me.

"I thought you'd never ask."

We blew out the candles and walked to our bedroom, holding hands. Once in the bedroom, I felt like every breath I took came from an increasingly smaller windpipe. I pretended it was just another night, but I knew differently. After we discarded our clothes, we crawled into bed as usual and cuddled. I kissed her neck and caressed her breasts. She kissed my neck. I took a deep breath.

"Make love to me," I said, feeling a flush spread across my face and throat as my heart beat faster.

In response, she reached her arm around my waist, trailing her hand down my back and over the curve of my ass. I shivered at her touch. She paused with her hand on my bare bottom and looked into my eyes, which pleaded with her to understand what I was offering her. I was offering myself with no boxers, no strap on, and no barriers—just me. I hadn't given that to anyone in years. She smiled and moved her hand up to the center of my back, a safe place to be touched. At that moment, I hoped that meant she understood.

"Are you sure?" she asked, staring into my eyes. I opened my mouth to respond, but nothing came out. She studied my face for the answer.

When she kissed me, I appreciated her assertiveness. She pulled me to her so our whole bodies touched. I trembled as she trailed kisses down my body. She sucked my left nipple, fondling the right one with her fingers as both nipples hardened at her touch. She switched to suck my right breast, and her hand traveled down my stomach to my inner thigh. My legs automatically parted at her touch.

She kissed and licked my stomach, kneading the roll of flesh in her hands as she kissed. She didn't know it, but her soft lips gently touched every spot where my rapist had punched me, yelling, "You fat bitch. Stupid pig. Damn dyke." With every agonizing blow, he'd screamed another insult. She kissed away the fifteen-year-old wounds. I wanted to scream, "NO!" but instead I clenched my eyes and mouth shut. A tear escaped down the crease of my crow's feet and rolled down the side of my face.

I gasped as she kissed and licked my inner thigh where he'd bitten me. It was as if she knew where all the invisible wounds were. When she paused, I saw her glance up from between my legs. I wanted to stop her, but I fought back my panic and didn't.

After a short pause, she parted my lips for kissing and stroking. At first, I refused to feel the pleasure, but then I wanted to get lost in the feelings. I didn't want my mind to travel back to that horrible night, the last time I was this open and vulnerable for another person. I closed my eyes, willing myself to think only of what her fingers and mouth and tongue were doing to me—pushing aside the memory of the sight and smell and feel of the man who'd attacked me.

"You're so beautiful," she said.

I opened my eyes to find her looking at me, and felt a blush heat up my face.

She laughed softly. "Don't tell me the big, bad butch has never been told that before."

I tried to close my legs. The words "beautiful" and "ugly"

bounced back and forth in my mind. With the word match screeching through my mind, I shivered and stiffened.

"I'm sorry," she said, brushing her lips across my thigh where I had her trapped. Because of the fog, I didn't know if she was apologizing for teasing me or for what he'd done to me.

I reached down to stroke her hair to reassure her that I didn't blame her. When I brushed away a brown wave of hair, I saw a tear rolling down her cheek onto my thigh. I opened my legs again to loosen my grip on her. Stepping into my comfortable protector role, I reached down to pull her up on top of me and wrap her in my arms to soothe her sobs.

"I'm really sorry," she said again. Her breath felt warm on my skin.

"I know, sweetie." I brushed her hair away with my fingertips and kissed her forehead. She looked up at me, her face wet with tears. Her mouth found mine and nibbled my lips. My hands danced down her back to her round ass. As our kiss deepened, I cupped my hands around her cheeks and pulled her closer to me. We separated, gasping for air.

For a short time, she laid her head upon my breasts. She teased my nipples with her mouth and fingertips until they throbbed on the brink between pain and pleasure. A demanding whisper rolled around in my mind, saying, "Release me. Release me." Its echo became more intense the more she teased. Soon she resumed kissing her way down my body over my roll of stomach. Her kisses had more determination as she found her way back to her spot between my legs.

I shivered when I felt her tongue brush across my clit. I gasped as she slipped her fingers into me. I tensed, expecting to feel violated, but as she easily pumped her fingers in and out of me, her gentle caresses finally healed the mental and emotional wounds of my brutal rape.

Fighting back tears, I gave myself into the pleasure, moaning as I thrust my hips forward to meet her entry. This time there was no rigid body with my mind somewhere else looking down onto the scene. All of me invited this woman inside. My walls gripped her fingers, not wanting to let them escape. My body begged for her touch as I arched higher to take her deeper into me.

As my body arched up to her, she sucked my clit into her mouth and rolled her tongue around it as if she were savoring a delicacy. I shuddered, and my body spasmed with my orgasm, rushing from my body like a prisoner released. I collapsed and laid there, panting, feeling her kisses on my sensitive skin and the hug of her arms around my thighs.

Suddenly feeling naked, I said, "Come here."

She crawled up my body and kissed me. Realizing I felt exposed, she snuggled against me and covered us with a sheet. Her soft lips nuzzled my neck as her gentle fingers stroked my arm.

I could feel my body relax totally as all my pent-up fears and insecurities seemed to flow from me. I squeezed her to me and sobbed, unable to say the words I wanted her to hear. As if she read my mind, she kissed my forehead and said, "I love you, too."

At that moment, I knew she understood.

Sweet Thing
Joy Parks

Watching Petey Ginoa knead bread dough is like watching a thing of beauty.

Watching her do it when she doesn't know anyone is watching her is even better.

First there are her hands, which are large but not too large; peachy pink hands that get washed soft over and over again everyday, strong with short square nails and slightly knobby knuckles, the kind you get when you crack them too much. And flour. I don't think I've ever seen those hands when they weren't covered in flour. Strong hands, but not rough at all. Hands that can shape delicate flutes on a tartlet crust or fix a tiny broken motor on a mixer or, I believe, unfasten a button so slow and perfect, sliding a finger down the space between breasts, sliding past a slight mound of belly, sliding down. I take a gulp of Fair Trade fresh-ground something or other to keep me still and watch how she grabs a hunk of sunflower rye or cornbread with organic red pepper slices, or whatever delightful concoction is in her bowl today, and drops it onto the breadboard, her hands dancing it into a perfect round, her fingers disappearing inside, then out, inside again. Kneading. Needing. I watch those fingers turn and poke and stretch the dough. I feel heat welling up between my thighs, try not to squirm. I watch her with my lips parted like I'm waiting for a kiss.

And then she stops. I hold my breath. She pushes up the sleeves of the white shirt she's wearing beneath her apron and begins to knead some more, flexing her perfectly shaped muscles, girl muscles, but firm and healthy and strong looking. The kind of arms that make you wonder what it would be like to be inside the circle of her body, feel those muscles tighten and press against you. What that would be like? That close.

It's warm in here and the windows are sweating from the steam of the kitchen, still morning cold outside. I should go. I should get up and walk out of here as best I can and get to work on time for a change; the walk would do me good right now. If I could just stand up.

I could watch those hands for hours.

Yeah, I know I've got it bad. And I don't quite know what to do with it.

Everyone back home told me I was going to hate moving to a small town even if it's the only place I could get a job. That's because in a small town everybody knows everybody's business and I'd have to watch my Ps and Qs they said. Because growing up in the city and having the natural luck to get away with a whole lot of stuff, I didn't have to work very hard at being discreet. Who was going to know and who was going to care?

So I've been laying low, working at the library as the junior librarian in training, trying to make it look like I'm far more interested in learning how to organize the periodicals and start a community reading circle than I am running back and forth to Petey's all day to buy coffee. I can't sleep most nights now. I don't know if it's all that caffeine or the fact that I keep dreaming about those hands on my skin and have to get up and drink a lot of cold water just to keep from melting in my own heat.

But bless the gossips in town for helping me learn all about Petey. I guess some of them saw me spending so much time in the bakery that they wanted to warn me so I could be on guard and not fall prey to her seductions. Being that you'd never know from looking at me that I've dealt with plenty of seductions from women like Petey and enjoyed every single one of them. From the very first day I walked into her shop, if she'd ever even looked at me with half a hint that she might be interested, I'd have fallen on my back so fast I might have ended up with whiplash. It's funny being femme. Sometimes you hate the fact that no one knows and you have to go out of your way to make sure some butch knows you're available 'cause you look too straight. But the good ones know. The smart ones. They can look past the heels you wear to work and the lipstick and the clothes and silky underwear you love because it feels so sweet against your skin, and love all that about you, know what you are beneath your clothes, not just any woman, but special. One who would fall on your back for them, let them touch you all over, let them reach inside your body, fuck you hard and tender and whatever it takes to make both of you feel so good about what it is that you are.

But since I'm not so obvious to normal people, I got the whole deal on Petey.

Petey Ginoa is a legend in town. Everybody knows she's a lesbian even though nobody's ever seen her with any woman at any time. She's too smart for that—to get caught. It's a small town and she's got a damn good business and she'd be crazy to take a chance on losing it all. Petey's not her real name; it's Pia, which is the name on the sign above the door. Her father named the shop after her back when she was a baby. But everybody calls the place Petey's. They eat Petey's bread and take Petey's cake home for birthdays and baby christenings and stop by Petey's for coffee. Sometimes I think if not for her, the whole damn town would go hungry. Petey suits her more. That's just how it is with some lesbian children, the way they outgrow the names their mommas gave them, grow into something different, someone different, someone no one ever expected them to be. Taking a new name is like being born all over again into who they should have been all along.

Not that Petey's the kind of woman who'd think about it that way. She probably just realized she was becoming someone such a delicate name like Pia didn't fit. It made her feel uneasy. So she gave herself a more comfortable handle. I get the feeling she's the kind of woman who would do whatever she needs to do to feel okay by herself and not give a damn about what anyone would think.

I wonder if any of her lovers—who no one's ever seen—call her Pia.

Wouldn't seem right somehow.

I want to be one of those women no one's ever caught her with.

I want those hands needing me.

On a belt under her apron Petey wears a measuring cup that looks like it was made by Black and Decker. She wears clean, crisp, white pants that cup her fine ass just right, and a white button-down shirt with the sleeves rolled up to her elbows. She wears a full-length, white apron slung over her neck and tied real loose, and clean white sneakers that don't make a sound. Her dark hair is cut short and loose around her face, which seems a little tanned. Even in winter that hair curls up at the back of her collar when she's moving around the kitchen in the heat. That collar, those curls. I have to keep my hands in my coat pocket or flat, fanned on the counter, when I order my coffee. I look the other way when she slides the little waxed paper bag of cannolis my way, stop myself from reaching across the counter, stop myself from reaching out to touch her neck, smooth those curls. Touch her face real slow. I think her forehead would smell like butter, that her skin would be lightly glazed all over with a fine dusting of sugar, that if you put your mouth to her skin, you would come away tasting sweet.

I'm thinking Valentine's Day's my time to make my move,

'cause that's when everybody's all crazed over romance and hearts and flowers and wanting to be loved. And I don't believe Petey could be all that different from anyone else.

Today is Friday the 13th, and not a soul on the street fails to comment on it. I don't feel unlucky, just a little racy knowing I've got just today to figure out how I'm going to pull off the seduction of the town dyke. I wonder if she has a girlfriend now, but only for a minute, because something tells me no, that I'd sense it if she did and at this point it wouldn't matter if she was dating my own best friend. If I'd been in town long enough to have one.

When I hit the door of the bakery, I almost swoon. It's the clouds of moist heat that gather inside, rain on the window, plus the scent of something sweet and deep, along with something fresh, like fruit juice, underneath it. And there's Petey. She's behind the counter, smiling at me. It must have been my reaction to the aroma that wrapped around me as I came inside. I wrinkle my nose like I'm sniffing for more and look at her grinning, as if to ask what's making such a delicious smell. Her eyes are actually lit, wide and open, more so than I remember ever seeing them. She motions me over. I've never been that close to her aside from her pouring my coffee or taking my money when I paid for bread or muffins or those slices of all-natural Queen Anne's cake with caramel-covered nut crust swirled with spidery feathers of toasted coconut. Or crème brûlée custard on a toasted almond crust. Or shiny pecan buns, moist and slippery as the flesh of my thigh right now. I'm weak. I don't think she's ever really talked to me. Specifically to me. And she still isn't. I step up to the counter and she's still smiling and motions me even closer. I move in like I'm in a trance, move in for a kiss, to touch my lips to her cheek, her lips. Desire bubbles up within my belly, tiny flutters inside my cunt. Like wings. I wonder if she can see down my blouse, see my breasts nestled in the pink, lacy, silk demi-cup I bought mail order from Victoria's Secret just in case something like this ever happened. Catch myself when my eyes start to close. She raises a fork to my lips like a present, speared with a tiny piece of something pink and fluffy, like cotton candy covered in chocolate. Oh baby. She directs the fork toward my lips as I open them like a command, take the gift inside. Something sweet and deep breaks on my tongue; my mouth wells up with wetness. I think about the pink of it, pink like the tender underside of a breast set free, pink skin of a vulva, all shower-fresh and warm, my tongue roaming my mouth to seek out and find every touch of sweetness, the citrusy aftertaste a surprise. I worry about drooling. I swirl it around my mouth, take it in, inhale it. Most of your taste buds come from scent. I taste an orange cream chocolate like from the Fanny Farmer box at Christmas, but warm. I want to tell her it's like sex on a fork, but that's too bold, too early in the dance. She's close still, watching me, silent. I open my eyes wide now, finally able to open my mouth.

Then she speaks real low, her voice deep but clear against the clang of coffee cups and beaters in the kitchen.

"So, you like? It's blood-orange cheesecake iced with a bitter-sweet chocolate glaze. Did them special for Valentine's Day this year. It's the blood orange that makes it pink. They're in season right now."

She beams.

Oh the pride in her voice. Hands in her pockets, shoulders dropped back, slight smile drawing tiny lines around her lips like a frame. She makes me want to leap over the counter, pull her head down into the pink silk of my too far open shirt, whisper "you are magical," wrap my legs around the clean white apron over her clean white pants, beg her to take me right there, right on the kneading board covered with flour and dabs of bittersweet chocolate glaze.

It takes three more trips to the bakery for me to get up the nerve to do what I have to do. All that coffee and anxiety is making me feel dry-mouthed, and it's now or never. So while she's ringing up the roasted red pepper and cilantro quiche with butter crust that's going to end up being my supper, I finally manage to find my femme courage and make my intentions known. At least to one of us.

"So, what are you doing for Valentine's Day?" I ask her.

She looks down at the floor like I've caught her in a lie.

"Nothing," she says. She kicks imaginary sand with the toe of her clean white shoe.

I'm tempted to look down too, but I keep my eyes right on her, make sure she can feel them.

"How come?"

It hurts almost to keep my voice this even.

More kicking at nothing. I've turned her into a 12-year-old boy.

"I don't know. I don't go in for that sort of stuff. Romance and stuff. Phony."

Yeah, I think so too. If you do it their way. But I can't say that. Instead, I say, "Me neither. Maybe we ought to hang out and do nothing together."

She stops kicking. Goes still. I wait. There's a buzz rising in my ears. Bubbles flip upside my stomach, more tickle inside. I feel a coffee burp rising, wish it away.

She lifts her head, swings it up slow as if she's trying to get unstuck from something.

I don't think she knows. She doesn't see it. Too long stuck here in town. If she never saw my kind before, how would she know what I looked like?

Sweet thing, I think. You ain't seen nothing like me yet.

She finally speaks. "Sure. Why don't you come tomorrow night? I'll be here after we close."

She moves her eyes around the room as if to remind me, or maybe her, where she means.

I say I will. Like it's nothing at all. Like I'm not already thinking about what to wear, what looks best when it's taken off. Like I'm not planning what I'll scent myself with to draw her close, the way I want her to remember me when she first sees me naked and vulnerable and writhing beneath her. I smile and turn and take my steps just so, knees bent just so to roll my hips slow, knowing she's watching me walk out the door . . .

"I'll try to save us one of the cheesecakes—" I hear her call to me.

But I'm already out the door.

I manage to stay away from the bakery all day Saturday until the streets and the lights outside the bakery are dark and the moon is large, ringed with silver bracelets of cold. I can feel the air dry inside my lungs; it almost hurts to breathe. Inside it will be moist as always.

Petey's alone in the bakery. She's got an apartment in the back, but it's tiny and it's obvious she prefers being in the shop. The radio is playing low and I keep wondering if she knows why I'm really here. She's a little different now that no one's around. A little more animated. A little more herself, I think. The self she can't be when she's on display. We sit and I talk about nothing at all until there's a Johnny Rivers song on the radio and I start swaying to it without thinking about it. Petey grins at me.

"I bet you like to dance."

"I do." I smile. "Want to dance with me?"

There. I've said it. Turning point. No turning back. Either I'm in her arms or I'm out the doorway in the next couple of minutes.

"With me?" She acts surprised, but I've been around the block enough to know it's an act. "I'm not much of a dancer."

Wonder how many times it's started out this way.

"Come learn," I say. Stand up. Motion for her to come my way.

While Johnny is crooning on about the poor side of town, I take her hand, which feels as smooth and warm and clean as I knew it would and put it at my waist. I put my arm around her shoulder, resisting the urge to slide my fingers through the curls that have gathered there. She's sweating. Just a little. Grin and slide my other hand into the one that's dangling by her side.

"You want to dance slow, like this?" she asks. Goes limp. I feel a little like I'm being baited. I nod and try to get us synced up with the music.

All the time she's staring at me like I've grown a second head. And then she starts to laugh.

"You really want to dance that bad?"

I stop moving. That about does it. I'm sick to death of drowning myself in caffeine and eating twice my own weight in pastry to get this sad ass closet case to realize she's got a willing victim here. And now this. I feel my dignity slipping away like pearls on a broken thread and figure, what the hell. So I reach up and kiss Petey Ginoa square on the lips. I slide my fingers into those dark curls that have been as tempting as chocolate shavings for weeks; they feel like wet silk between my fingers. And I press my breasts into hers and slip my leg around hers, press close so she can't miss the kind of heat I'm giving off. I may not get what I want, but I'm definitely going to give her a taste of what she's missing. And after what felt like about three years, I let go of her and push her back onto her feet and stare at her as if to ask what she plans on doing next.

Petey looks at me sideways, almost like a glare, and if I hadn't seen that look in the eyes of plenty of women who remind me of Petey, I'd think she was mad at me. But that look's not about mad. It's about fear.

"You aren't exactly the shy type, are you?" she snarls low.

"You like shy?"

I'm looking at her straight in the eyes.

"No. Not necessarily. Just most people, most women that I've been with, they aren't full time like you. Mostly just sad women who want to forget for a little while that they're married to someone they can't stand being touched by. Others that just want a little vacation from their lives, a little adventure and when it starts to get over their head or there's a chance of getting caught, they run back to where they started. You're not like that. You're a different kind altogether, aren't you?"

Something about that makes me feel really proud, like I've just won a contest. So I'm her first real lesbian, her first real pure femme.

"And you like it?" I smile all coy. I know she does.

"I could get used to it," she says, non-committal. But then, before I have time to think about what that means, she is beside me, her arms around me, kissing me, her lips beating a tattoo down my neck, her pelvis pressed into mine, making me strain backward.

"I don't think you should look a gift horse in the mouth."

And she smiles. It's a new one, a little too knowing, but it's a beautiful smile. I'm all heady and fluttering from being so close to the one I adore that I hardly even notice when she pushes me upward onto the breadboard and hoists herself up beside me. I don't know if I am gift or being gifted, treat or being treated, but it doesn't matter. The flour on my back feels dry and silky and the air in the bakery is still warm enough from so many Valentine's cakes that I don't feel a chill at all as she slides off my sweater and pants, runs her fingers over the pearl heart trims of my red lace bra, kneads the knuckle of her thumb in the crotch of my red lace panties before she slides them over my hips and down to the floor, grinning all proud at the heat and wet inside my cunt, grinning at the way I press against her hand. She whispers "how long have you wanted this . . ." and my head falls back as if it's very heavy all of a sudden and I whisper back, "Forever, since I first saw you, maybe even before that."

And she shudders, that butch shudder of realization of being wanted by a woman. She unbuttons her jeans and slides them off, kicks off her shoes, wraps her arms around me as if I'm something that might slip away, and pushes me gently down on my back.

Petey Ginoa makes love even better than she makes bread and cookies and pies and cakes. She touches me all over slow, achingly slow, and kisses my face and breasts and belly with creamy wet kisses that make me ache and open my legs wide, press hard against any touch of hers I can just to get some relief. And when she finally slides her fingers between my legs, when my cunt overflows with want of her and opens easy and hot to draw her inside, she cries out my name high and surprised. And Petey Ginoa fucks as sweet as her eight-minute frosting. Her want is hot enough to make me feel the steam rising from her body, her fingers kneading me inside, her mouth hungry on me, her tongue tracing sweet glazed circles, rising at times so I see her mouth wet and shiny with me, while I cry out "Petey" and tug at those mythical curls at her collar and wrap my legs around as much of her clean, sweet, white cotton self that I can, try to take all of her inside. I can tell by her eyes and her moans and the way she keeps her lips on me, the way her fingers gather inside me, thrust higher and deeper without asking, simply taking, knowing it's freely mine to give, that Petey Ginoa has never had a woman want her wholly like this, has never had a real love to call her own. I arch my back, strain up against those strong knuckles slipping, twisting, filling me, those dear arm muscles straining to take me as I come screaming, shivering, crying out, grinding my ass hard against the smooth wood.

It's warm here lying beside the oven. Petey lies there silently beside me while I come back inside myself, her fingers resting on my hipbone, her cheek against my hair. I snuggle closer, the board is wider than you'd think to see it in the daylight, but I'm not afraid of falling. I'm facing her now, her shirt is open, her T-shirt and plain white underpants still on. I cuddle against her, kiss her neck, then place my hands at the bottom edge of her shirt, slide up slowly, graze her breasts. She catches her breath. Stops my hand. Holds it tight against her heart.

"Aren't you tired?"

It sounds like she's afraid I'm not satisfied.

"Not tired, relaxed," I whisper, "and I want to touch you."

She stiffens slightly beneath my hand. Her heart is beating. Hard enough to hear it, I expect to see it thumping up like a cartoon character when they fall in love. Or get chased by something wild.

"I . . . usually . . . don't . . ."

It hits me. Petey's used to nice straight girls who like to get finger-fucked all night but don't offer to give anything back. No touch back, no tongue back. That might make them gay. And I sigh.

"Do you want this?" I whisper. "Do you want me to love you?"

She turns her face away from me. Mumbles into her arm, into the makeshift pillow the dishtowel has become. I lean in to listen and there's only one word I hear.

Never?

Petey the butch goddess is a virgin?

Chaste despite sexually servicing what seems like a third of the married women in town, if you can trust the stories. Forty-something and never been touched. Jackpot, I think, but then I panic. For a split-second, I want to get up and "presto change-o" my clothes would be on and I would be gone.

But that doesn't happen.

What happens is . . .

First I roll my eyes upward and curse and thank the Goddess for making me brave enough to bring Petey out. All the way out.

And I remember everything I know about butches and sex and surrender and what that means and prepare for anything.

Then I slowly slip my hand inside the rib knit tee she's wearing beneath her open shirt and caress her belly with my open palm. She gurgles something low and deep inside her throat. Her stomach contracts under my touch, new nerve endings coming to life for the first time. I feel terribly powerful and daring. She settles her shoulder closer into me, stretches out her legs; I try not to think of her feet in her white sports socks hanging over the breadboard, but I do and I giggle. She smiles at me as she strokes my hair with her hand. Slowly, oh so slowly, as if her stomach stretched for miles, I take my time and slide my hand further up her shirt, grazing her breasts with my knuckles. She sucks in air, twitches. I can hear my own breathing and hers, imagine it rising up into the moist steamy air that sits inside the bakery. Joined at the breath, I think. I kiss her neck, kiss her shoulders, raise her

T-shirt further and bend to trace with my tongue the places my hands have been. Her skin is clean and sweet-tasting, and moist with heat. Glazed. All that sugar, all that goodness. She's moving down, rising up to meet my hand, still palm flat, my mouth, tiny sighs breaking from her mouth. My fingers find her breast; it's small and easy to cup within my hand and her nipple is firm as the dried currants I've watched her stir into dough and almost as dark. She gasps. I find my courage and rise up further on my side so I can move more easily. Gently, I gather her breasts under my hand. She likes a little more pressure than I would have expected, croons out soft little cries of want as I grasp her breasts, release them slowly, knead her gently as I have watched her do so many times. And eventually, when I'm not sure how much more she can take, I smile and kiss her lips and bend my face to her chest, sucking each hard curranty nipple, one, then the other, until her hips start to rise off the board. She's starting to get loud. With my mouth still on her, licking a trail over her breast, I retrace my path down her belly, further, further still, slipping my fingers beneath the waist-band of her cotton underwear, slowly over a mound of damp curl-ing hair, slowly, so slowly . . . She widens her legs to greet me and she is wet and slippery and smooth as pearls under water, she is open and gasping. In the dark, I imagine shiny deep pink—like the filling of the cheesecake she fed me before. And I need the sweet-ness. She's rising and crashing into my fingers, so hard and so new that I rise up and turn, stretching out, never moving my hand, use the other to push off what bit of her underwear still clings to her. Spread her open, slip a finger inside gentle, so gentle, and she yells something I can't hear, as if part of her is far away now. And I move inside her slowly as she wriggles all over the cutting board, and all of a sudden, I need to taste her. I throw my head down between her moving legs, trade my finger for my tongue. She is sweet there too, sweet and fresh and slippery wet as cream. I lap her up, suck her sweetness into my mouth, my tongue fluttering hard and fast, then soft slow inside her lips. I grasp her thighs on either side so I can hang on, stay with her, buckle in as if she's a wild ride in a small town midway and she cries out, loud, almost a scream and comes shaking and gushing wetness into my mouth, inside of thighs stretching, ass grinding, bucking under my tongue.

And she is done.

And for a few moments, she lies in my arms and we ride out her aftershocks with the heel of my hand nestled inside her lips and she sighs over and over, stretches arms out long and languid and pulls me close, and for a split second, I feel all Prince Charming come to curl up and sleep with the princess. Until she kisses me, tongue searching out all taste of her, until she rolls me onto my back, and I feel the wetness spreading out beneath me. I must have come too, when she did. She gathers up the wetness on my thighs and hair and slips her fingers inside me. Oh. One. Two. Yes. Three. More. Petey pushes my knees apart, spreads me wide open, lowers her still trembling body onto mine, grinds her wetness into mine with a fury I never expected and I wrap my legs around her hips, shelter her as she rides me hard, her hands grasping my shoulders, my body rising up to meet every stroke. She is gasping now, breathing loud and calling out, sweet bits and pieces of words whispered, fuck sweet wet baby, come, mine, mine, oh fuck, beautiful you, oh. And I feel the climb and rise of us both as she comes hard and loud into me while I lock my legs around her, grasping, grinding, shivering, up, up and over, screaming and trembling against her as she falls into me, done, head full of dark sweet curls, fine strands of burnt sugar candy, warm swirled over my breasts.

Valentine Dance
Cherokee Echols

"Hey Rett, you're going with us to the strip club tonight, right? I mean, we can't have one of the team missing out on Big Mike's birthday."

"Sure thing, Paulie, I'll see you and the guys at Baby Does around twenty-three hundred." Rett shook her head and turned back to the computer controls of the petroleum refinery she worked at. She wondered how the fellas would feel if they knew most of the dancers were lesbians and actually more interested in her than in any of them.

Rett dashed home for a quick shower and change before she headed to the club. After all, who knew—after the guys got drunk, she might get the courage to take one of the dancers to a back room for her own private lap dance. She knew she could never do it out in the open with all those slobs watching.

She put on a pair of starched black jeans, a white tank top to show off her well-developed arms, and her favorite pair of black boots. Taking one last look in the mirror, she ran her fingers through her short, wavy black hair, then grabbed her billfold and keys and headed out the door.

The ride to the club on her Harley was a bit cool without a jacket, but she loved the feel of the big bike between her legs. Besides, it was the only thing she'd had between her legs in quite some time. Between working full time and taking classes, she didn't get much time for socializing.

At the club, Rett pulled out a twenty to pay the cover charge. She was stopped by a leggy blonde who wore very little.

"Hey, sugar," she said, "I'll forgo the cover for a kiss."

Rett leaned in for the kiss, but stopped when she saw a truck full of her co-workers pull up. She sighed and handed over the twenty. "Sorry darlin', looks like I'm paying with cash tonight."

The blonde smirked and said, "Go on in, sugar. You can owe me later. Of course, I might have to charge interest."

As soon as her eyes adjusted to the dim light, Rett spotted the guys next to the stage, catcalling and whooping. Amidst much high fiving, she was informed it was her turn to buy a round of beers. Rett pulled out her wallet to pay the waitress, who had to deflect the hands of some of the fellas. Rett immediately came to her rescue by drawing their attention to the nearly naked woman on stage.

After several glasses of beer, Rett headed down the long hallway toward the women's restroom. The beautiful, dark-skinned waitress she'd helped out stopped her.

"I didn't get a chance to thank you earlier. I'm Vickie."

"Hi, Vickie, I'm Rett, and you don't have to thank me. It was my pleasure."

"It seems like all the guys you're with are having a great time tonight and really enjoying the lap dances."

"Yeah, we're celebrating the big guy's fortieth birthday."

"So, why haven't *you* had a lap dance?"

"You're kidding. In front of those apes?"

"How about I arrange one for you in the privacy of a back room? Consider it a thank you for protecting me from those goons." Vickie took Rett by the hand and led her into a room just off the hallway. "Just sit down and enjoy your dance."

Rett sat down and wondered if she should go to the restroom or just wait here. She'd barely started to get up when Vickie reentered, this time wearing a leather micro-mini, leather bustier, and thigh-high, spike-heeled leather boots. Rett sucked in a breath and sat up straight as soon as she saw her.

Vickie slipped a CD into a player and, in front of Rett, started moving her hips back and forth to the beat of the music. She ran her hands across her breasts, pinching her nipples and wetting her lips with her tongue.

Rett watched hungrily. "I didn't realize you danced, too."

Vickie straddled Rett's lap and whispered in her ear, "I don't. I'm only doing this for you."

Rett felt the warmth of Vickie's breath on her neck, and a flush of arousal surged through her. Vickie continued her dance, thrusting against Rett, who sat with her hands in her lap. Vickie rubbed her breasts in Rett's face, surrounding Rett with the scent of her perfume. Rett moaned with desire. Vickie, now wearing only her boots and a thong, had her back to Rett, and was swaying her hips back and forth. When she then bent over to thrust her beautiful round butt into Rett's face, Rett, without thinking, leaned forward and nipped it with her teeth.

Vickie whipped around, shaking her finger at Rett. "Not supposed to touch the dancers." The song ended and Vickie grabbed her discarded clothes, kissed Rett's cheek, and fled the room.

Several times that night, Rett tried to find Vickie again, but always just kept missing her or was unable to find her at all.

After that night, Rett couldn't stop thinking about Vickie. When she was finally able to make it back to the club, she'd been told Vickie was gone, and no one knew where. Next thing she knew, she'd gotten her bachelor's degree in chemical engineering and moved to a new job in a new place with a new home, forever losing hope of seeing Vickie ever again.

Rett heard the doorbell early one Saturday and trudged to the door in a pair of boxers and a T-shirt, not bothering with her robe. The smaller of her two new gay male neighbors was standing there with some fresh-cut flowers from his tiny garden.

"Well, good morning gorgeous," Bill said, holding out the flowers. "I swear, if I wasn't a happily married man, I would ravish you with the way you're looking right now."

Rett took the flowers. "Want a cup of coffee?"

"Sure. Why don't I make it while you put something on over those boxers?" he said, going to her kitchen. When she returned a few moments later fully dressed, he handed her a mug. "Here you go, baby cakes, a nice hot cup of coffee for my favorite hot lesbian."

"So what's up? What do I owe this early morning visit to?"

"Well, since you ask, I need a favor."

"What kind of favor?"

"My niece, Elspeth, just graduated from college. She's a hydro environmentalist, whatever the hell that is. All I know is, she's going to work at the same place you do."

"Elspeth? What kind of name is that?" Rett asked, smiling at Bill.

"What do you mean? It was my mother's. Besides, I think she goes by her middle name outside the family. My whole point is, I'd planned on having you both over for dinner to introduce you, but she had car problems and won't get here in time. I was hoping I could give her your name so she could look you up at work."

Rett, furrowing her brow, asked, "What exactly is it you want me to do when she looks me up?"

"Well for one, you could have lunch with her so she doesn't have to eat alone her first day at a new job. To thank you, I'll bake you a cheesecake and make my famous fettuccine."

"Yeah, sure. Why not? Here, give her my office number. Tell her to either give me a ring or drop by tomorrow and I'll take her to lunch."

"Oh thanks, sweetheart. I knew I could count on you." Bill looked down at the slip of paper Rett had handed him and read, "Baretta? What kind of name is that?"

"Very funny, it was my mother's. Besides, you know I go by Rett outside the family."

It had been hell all morning, and by noon, Rett was already tired, had a headache and wanted to eat lunch, but she hadn't heard from Bill's niece and thought she should wait until at least 12:15.

"Excuse me, Ms. Powell, I'm Vic . . ." The woman coming through the door stopped in mid sentence and mid stride.

Rett looked up and, to her wonder and amazement, there stood Vickie. Rett leapt to her feet. "Vickie!"

Vickie turned and practically ran back down the hall. Rett took off after her, catching her at the elevator.

"Hey wait, Vickie," Rett said. "Where are you going so fast? How did you know where to find me? You were looking for me, weren't you?"

"Looking for you? No! Well, I mean . . . yes, but I didn't know it was *you*! I was just looking for a friend of my Uncle Bill's."

"Bill? You're Elspeth?"

"Elspeth? Oh yeah, I guess Uncle Bill would have called me that. My name is Elspeth Victoria Redding, but I prefer Vickie."

Rett smiled broadly. "Well great, Vickie, I believe you and I have a lunch date."

"What? Oh no, I can't go to lunch with you." Vickie turned toward the elevator.

"Why not?"

"Because of that night at Baby Does. I'm just so embarrassed. Please just let me leave."

She jumped onto the elevator, leaving Rett wondering what to do next.

❤

That night Rett went straight over to Bob and Bill's. She punched the doorbell four times.

Bill whipped the door open. "Gorgeous! Where's the fire? Are you in that big of a hurry for the fettuccine and cheesecake I promised you?"

"Sorry Bill, listen, you have *got* to help me."

"Sure, what seems to be the problem? Oh hey, did you meet my niece? Quite a looker, isn't she?"

"That's what I'm here about. You have *got* to get her to talk to me."

"What are you talking about? Why won't she talk to you?"

"It's a long story that starts back in Oklahoma. She really ought to be the one to tell you about what happened. All I know is, I have to get her to talk to me."

"Okay, just slow down. Come inside and let's see what this is all about."

Rett followed Bill inside and told him and Bob all about meeting Vickie. She left out that it was at a strip joint, but did explain that Vickie seemed to think she did something embarrassing and so she ran out on Rett.

"Sounds like you like her quite a bit," Bob said.

"Yeah, I do. I can't explain it—we haven't even really talked, but I feel a connection with her."

Bill patted her knee sympathetically and said, "Well, I tell you what, how about I have you both over for supper Friday and you can talk to her then?"

"Aw thanks Bill, that would be great." Rett sat back on the couch and let out a breath she hadn't realized she was holding. All she had to do now was make it until Friday.

"Uncle Bill, I just love your and Uncle Bob's place. You'll have to come over and help me decorate my little apartment."

"Sure, sugar, I'd love that. Why don't you help me by setting the table?"

Vickie looked at the plates and frowned. "There are four plates. Is someone else coming?"

"Just a friend of ours we'd really like you to meet."

"As long as it isn't Rett Powell . . ." Just the thought of Rett made Vickie ache with want and embarrassment.

"Just what is the story there? She seems to think you should be the one to tell me." Bill intently watched his niece as she set the table.

"Oh, I can't, Uncle Bill, please . . . I'm sorry. Let's just say it was very embarrassing to find out we're co-workers."

"Well, we think she's very nice. She's quiet, works hard, and I don't see a lot of women running in and out so I know she's not a playgirl."

"Uncle Bill, it's not her coming over, is it?"

"Well . . ." Bill started, but then the bell rang and everyone looked to the front door.

"Oh please no, Uncle Bill," Vickie said.

Bill shrugged. "Sorry, it's too late now, sugar."

"Gorgeous! Come on in. Let me take your jacket," Bob said in the other room.

"Thanks, Bob," Rett said. "Something sure smells good. Hi, Bill. Thanks for having me over. Is she here?"

"Yes, she's in . . . Well, where did she go?" Bob said right behind her.

"What is it between you two?" Bill asked. "I just knew you would have gotten along and been fast friends."

"If I have my way, Bill," Rett said, "we're going to be more than friends. Where did she go?"

"Check to see if she went out on the back patio while I finish getting things ready for supper. Do you want a beer or glass of wine before you go out there?" Bill asked.

"No thanks. I just want to talk to Vickie."

Rett went to the patio. Vickie stood to the side, her arms

wrapped tightly around herself. Rett slowly walked toward her. "Hi, Vickie." Rett paused. "Won't you please talk to me?"

Vickie turned to face Rett, avoiding eye contact. "Don't you understand how mortified I am?"

"No, honestly I don't. What's the problem?"

"I gave you a lap dance."

"Yeah, and it was great. I've wanted to see you ever since."

"Why? Do you think I'll do it again? Strip for you? Dance for you? Do you think that's the kind of person I am? I was waiting tables at Baby Does to help put myself through school. The tips were good, but I *never* stripped and that was the *only* time I ever did a lap dance. I even had to borrow that outfit."

"First off, I think you are a very nice person. Second, I see nothing wrong with waiting tables *or* stripping if that's what it takes to get an education, and no, I don't expect you to do that again unless that is what you want. What I want—what I really want—is simply to get to know you better."

"I just don't think I can. I mean, you have seen me almost naked *and* you bit my butt!"

Rett grabbed Vickie by the hands. "Vickie, please tell me what I need to do to get us beyond this. Would it help if I embarrassed myself?"

"No, well, maybe . . . okay sure."

"All right then. What should I do?"

"How about you give me a lap dance?"

Surprised, Rett looked at Vickie. "Baby, I'm butch. Butch women don't traipse around half-naked giving lap dances."

Vickie pulled her hands from Rett's. "That's what I want. You said there was nothing wrong with it."

"Well, yeah, but I just can't do something that personal and out of character unless it was like Valentine's Day and I was in love."

Vickie dropped her head. "I guess, then, we have nothing to talk about." She quickly left through the back gate, running away from Rett yet again.

♥

Two weeks passed, and Vickie had successfully avoided Rett at work and felt perhaps Rett had given up on her. This brought Vickie both relief and sadness. She had been attracted to Rett from the first sight of her in Baby Does and wished she'd never given in to a moment of weakness and performed that lap dance. If she hadn't been so foolish, then perhaps she would have a date now.

Maybe Rett was right—she shouldn't be embarrassed. But then, why did she feel her cheeks get hot every time she thought about it? Oh well, tonight she'd have a nice dinner with her Uncles Bill and Bob and forget all about Rett and all the temptations, and distractions, she provided.

"Well, if it isn't my favorite niece. How are you, sugar?" Bill bear hugged her.

"I'm doing well. I've really been looking forward to your home cooking. I feel so bad about running out on you the last time I was here." She frowned. "Say, why are you guys so dressed up? You're making me feel ratty in my jeans and sweatshirt."

"Oh, we just thought it might be kind of fun to dress for dinner. How about a glass of wine?" Bill handed Vickie a glass of wine as the doorbell rang. Bill and Bob looked at each other, then at their watches. "Well, sugar, I think that's our cue. Food's in the oven and dessert is in the fridge. I hope tonight works out. Come on, Bob, grab our overcoats."

Vickie looked at them with confusion. "Hey, wait a minute, what the hell is going on? Where are you going? What are you talking about?"

Bill and Bob opened their door to leave, and Vickie saw someone just outside. "Oh hell, Uncle Bill. Please, not again!"

Rett walked in wearing a beautiful Armani tuxedo. In her arms, she carried two dozen long-stemmed red roses and a box of candy. Vickie couldn't help but think that Rett looked very handsome.

"Vickie, I'm sorry I had to get Bob and Bill to trick you into coming over here tonight. But please, just give me fifteen minutes of your time. Then, if you want to leave, I promise I will never bother you again. I also hope you will accept these from me. It's Valentine's Day, you know," Rett said beseechingly.

Vickie was moved by Rett's thoughtful gesture. "Okay, what is it you want to say?"

"Well . . . it's not exactly what I want to *say*. Here, sit in this chair."

"Why? I'm comfortable over here."

"Please, Vickie, just humor me for fifteen minutes."

After a moment's hesitation, Vickie sat in the chair Rett had placed in the middle of the living room. After ensuring Vickie was properly ensconced, Rett quickly hit play on the CD player. Taking a deep breath, she started dancing seductively toward Vickie, slowly removing her tuxedo along the way. Underneath the beautiful tux, Rett wore a leather bustier, leather hot pants, and thigh-high leather boots.

"OHMYGOD!" Vickie clasped her face in shock.

Rett continued her dance around Vickie until she had stripped everything off except her thong and boots. She straddled Vickie's thigh and rubbed her breasts in Vickie's face. "I'm doing this only for you," Rett said breathily.

She then turned around and threw her well-muscled ass into Vickie's face, where Vickie promptly nipped it with her teeth.

They were both breathing hard when the song ended with Rett standing in front of Vickie. "I would only do something like this for the woman I love on Valentine's Day. Happy Valentine's Day, I love you, Vickie."

Smiling at Rett with desire, Vickie placed her arms around Rett's neck. She murmured, "You truly do," in a voice thick with emotion. It was a statement not a question. She met Rett's eager mouth in a hot kiss, and their tongues dueled for possession of the other.

"Please come with me to my house," Rett said, tearing herself from the kiss.

Vickie could only nod. Rett threw only her jacket back on, leaving the rest of her clothes, and led Vickie out.

They'd barely made it into Rett's condo when Vickie pressed her up against the door and sought out her mouth with her own. They struggled with hunger and desire, desperately clutching at each other. Vickie removed Rett's jacket to work her way down Rett's chest with her tongue, but Rett gently pushed her back. Vickie looked at her with confusion.

"Wait a minute," Rett said. "I don't want this to go wrong, where I'll have to win your confidence all over again. I want you very much, but I don't want it to be a one-night event. I want Valentine's Day to be the day we remember as the first day of our life together."

Vickie cupped Rett's face in her hands. "Rett, honey, do you always talk this much? I think I'm going to die if you don't touch me, love."

The endearments weren't lost on Rett. She swept Vickie off her feet and carried her into the bedroom.

Rett placed Vickie by the bed and, with one motion, pulled her sweatshirt off. She kissed the pulse point on Vickie's neck, working her way up to gently suck on her earlobe before she nipped at the smooth skin along her jaw, soothing the bites with a gentle stroke of her tongue. She brushed her lips across Vickie's with a feather's touch. Her tongue softly traced Vickie's upper lip. Her next kiss was more forceful, causing Vickie to open her mouth to accept her insistent tongue. As their kisses deepened, Vickie undid the button and zipper on her pants.

She took Rett's hand and said, "Touch me . . . touch me here." She slid Rett's hand into her pants and gasped at her touch. Vickie moaned with desire as she took one of Rett's breasts into her mouth and began moving her hips with the stroke of Rett's fingers.

"Baby, let's move to the bed." Rett was breathing hard. She slipped her hand from Vickie's pants, making Vickie groan at the loss. Rett sucked the wetness from her fingers, slowly licking each one with her tongue, all the while looking at Vickie with hooded eyes. Vickie's legs almost buckled as she felt the blood rush to her already blood-swollen clit at the sight of Rett licking her fingers.

Rett finished undressing them both before she stretched out

beside Vickie on the bed. They got reacquainted with a passionate kiss that brought a moan from her. When they came up for air, Vickie pleaded, "Please, baby, don't tease me. I want you to finish what you started. I want your fingers in me again. I want your mouth on me." She placed Rett's hand between her thighs again while arching her back to bring their hips closer. Her hand moved down Rett's belly until it found wetness.

Rett gasped as Vickie entered her and began rubbing along her clit with her thumb. Vickie enjoyed the feeling of the blood-engorged labia and the little twitch she teased out of Rett's clit. "Do you want this?" Vickie asked in a whisper.

"Yes," Rett replied, panting. "I want all of you. I want you to taste me. I want your hot mouth on me and I want to taste you."

Vickie started kissing a trail down Rett's stomach until she found the hot wetness waiting for her eager tongue. She enjoyed the bristle of Rett's pubic hair on her cheeks and sighed with contentment, causing Rett to shudder from the hot breath upon her swollen, wet sex.

Rett pulled Vickie up by her arms to face her and looked deeply into her eyes, and said, "I want us to do this together. I want to taste your sweetness too." She gently pushed Vickie onto her back and twisted around to straddle her face while burying her own face in Vickie's pussy. Vickie's tongue quickly reached to stroke Rett's distended clit before Rett started her own exploration of Vickie's waiting center.

Vickie bucked wildly, pressing her hips forward to force her sex into Rett's face, all the while feasting on Rett's hot pussy. Vickie's thigh muscles tensed before her whole body suddenly shuddered, and she gasped through an overwhelming climax that brought Rett over the top with her.

After lying for a few moments with her cheek resting near the intoxicating source of her lover's sexual scent, Rett stretched out beside Vickie to draw little circles on her hip with her fingers, content in the afterglow of sex.

"Rett?"

"Yes?"

"Since I didn't get you anything for Valentine's Day, would you like me to give you another lap dance?"

Rett rose on her elbow to look at the beautiful woman lying next to her. "Honey, you have given me plenty. You have given me the greatest gift of your body and your love."

"But I would like to do this one more time for you; it's sort of what got us together. Do you understand?"

Rett hugged Vickie close. "I would love for you to give me another lap dance. But before you do, I want to do something, okay?"

"All right. I'll get ready and wait for you here."

Rett went into the other room, and when she returned to the bedroom, she carried a kitchen chair and a portable CD player. Vickie gasped when she noticed what Rett had strapped on.

"I guess you have a different version of a lap dance in mind?"

"Only if you want . . ." Rett ducked her head.

Vickie smiled seductively and said, "Hit the music for me."

Vickie began her dance in front of Rett. Running her tongue over her lips, massaging her breasts with her hands and swaying her hips to the music, she slowly undressed as she rubbed up against Rett while gyrating to the beat. She occasionally slipped her hand between her own thighs to flick a finger quickly across her clit. Soon, Vickie had nothing on but a smile, and she was breathing hard along with Rett who had been stroking herself between her legs. The scent of their excitement filled the air.

Rett saw Vickie's wetness trickling down her thigh just before Vickie threw her breasts into Rett's face, obscuring her view.

Vickie took the head of the dildo, rubbing it back and forth across her throbbing clit, before sliding the whole cock inside until she settled into Rett's lap. She began rocking slowly up and down.

Rett groaned aloud at the sensual image of Vickie pleasuring herself on her dick. She hungrily took Vickie's breast in her mouth and teased the nipple with the tip of her tongue.

Vickie tangled her fingers in Rett's hair, holding her tightly to her breast. With each thrust of Vickie's hips, the pressure pushed the base of the cock against Rett's clit, causing both women to go wild with arousal.

"Yes, baby, this feels so good. Harder, please harder."

Rett pulled Vickie's hips into her. Their bodies drenched in sweat, they thrust quickly together until they both shook and cried out in release. They collapsed into each other's arms to catch their breath and enjoy the ripples of pleasure that still surged through their bodies.

Vickie whispered into Rett's ear, "I would only do this for you."

She finally moved from Rett's lap and pulled Rett up from the chair. They wrapped their arms around each other and kissed deeply.

"Happy Valentine's Day, lover."

"Happy Valentine's Day to you, too. I can't wait to see what you give me next year. I wouldn't mind this becoming a tradition."

"Next year? I'm not done with you yet for this year," Vickie said as she tugged Rett over to the bed.

She's with the Band
Kristina Wright

It never fails. Every gig, there's one chick in the front row making eye contact that I can practically *feel*, sending the vibe that she's ready, available, and mine for the taking. We'd played the Harbor Bar many times, but I'd never seen the blonde before. She had on more eye makeup than a drag queen and platinum blonde hair almost as white as the low-cut halter dress that hugged her body like a condom on a strap-on. In other words, she was smoking hot. My response? I ignored her, singing over her head and refusing to make eye contact.

My bandmates were another story. Both of them were watching the blonde like they wanted to devour her for dessert. Men. They're pigs. Unfortunately, I'd never been much of a girl-band girl, so I was stuck with two horny single guys and the unlikely band name Bubba Chryst. Don't ask, because I couldn't tell you. I just remember it involved a bizarre theological discussion and a whole lot of tequila.

Groupies are a perk of the job, the boys say. Musicians get laid, it's a fact of life. I wouldn't know. I was never one for casual, bar bathroom sex before I had a girlfriend, no matter what they say about dyke rockers, and for the past three years I've been with Wendy—my amazing, conservative, executive girlfriend whose idea of good music is Michael Bolton, circa 1990. Believe me, I suffer for my taste in women every time we have band practice. What's a rocker like me doing with a girl like that, Nick and Jae ask. The answer is simple—she drives a Volvo, is hopelessly uncool, and wouldn't know a box of hair dye from a weapon of mass destruction, but she rocks my world in a way the music never will.

Wendy came to one of our gigs after we started dating. One was all it took. The music was too loud, the club was too crowded, the smoke was too thick, and she didn't like the way everyone, men and women included, were staring at me with lust.

"They *all* wanted to fuck you," she said after I got home that night. "Every single person in there wanted to fuck you."

"Not the boys," I said, referring to Jae and Nick. "They know I'm gay."

"Okay," she agreed. "Not them. But everyone else."

It wasn't true, of course. A lot of people come to hear us play with nothing on their minds other than Jae's drum solos or Nick's kick-ass vocals, never mind my killer guitar riffs. I didn't bother to argue, though. I knew there were a few people in the audience who would take me home and tie me up with my own amp cord if I let them. Of course, I'd never let them.

I was distracted by the blonde and missed Nick's signal to segue into the next song. He shot me a look from the other side of the small stage. I smirked and quickly fell into step. We have a play list, but he'll mix it up once in awhile, depending on the crowd. The place was packed and throbbing with energy tonight. It was an odd mix of twenty-somethings, a handful of older biker dudes reluctant to give up their drinking days, and a bunch of law enforcement guys unwinding after a long week. It was a good crowd. They were loving us, so I ignored the blonde and blissed out on the music.

By the time we finished the set about fifteen minutes later, I was ready to be wrung out and hung up to dry. We had a thirty-minute break before the next set so I hightailed it back to the poorly lit closet that served as a dressing room. Nick and Jae were right behind me.

"Oh man, she was *hot*," Jae said, stripping off his ubiquitous black T-shirt and pulling on another that looked just like it. "Aren't you at least going to talk to her?"

I flopped down on the small, battered loveseat that served as the only seating area other than a folding chair. "Hell no," I said. "That package is trouble waiting to happen. Besides, I've got Wendy."

Jae shook his head. "Do you believe her?"

Nick took a swig of the beer that had materialized right before we finished our last song. Bartenders are good to us low-paid rockers. "Wendy the accountant? Wendy who is fuckin' pissed you're working a gig on Valentine's Day?"

I was in no mood. "Hey, boys, if you like her so much, why don't you take her out to my truck and give her a good time for the next thirty minutes?"

"Sorry, kid," Jae said. "We're definitely not her type. She only had eyes for you."

"Then how 'bout you go jerk each other off for the next half hour and leave me the hell alone?" I snarled.

"What the fuck is your problem?"

Nick jerked his thumb toward the door. "It's hormones, buddy. Let's hit the bar and leave the bitch kitty to lick her wounds."

The door slammed behind them. Nick was right, I was sulking. Wendy was pissed at me for working on Valentine's Day. We'd been together three years and hadn't yet spent a Valentine's Day together. I hadn't been keeping track because I didn't much care for the hearts and flowers shit, but she did. A lot. Part of me said she should just suck it up and understand she was with a musician and I had to play when I could get a gig. Another part of me—that sappy, lovey-dovey part that I pretended didn't exist—wanted nothing more than to blow off the last set and head home to Wendy. I was caught between rock-and-roll and a hard place and it sucked.

I sighed as I rested my head on the back of the ratty loveseat, wishing I'd grabbed Nick's beer before he left. I'd already finished mine, but I needed another. I wanted to be loose for the next set, and really needed to drown my sorrows besides. By the time I got home, Wendy would have been tucked in bed for hours and I'd still be in a lousy mood.

There was a knock at the door. "Go 'way, boys. I'll be ready for the next set."

The knocking persisted.

"What the hell do you want?" My mood was definitely getting worse by the moment.

The door opened and I saw her blonde hair before I even saw her face. "Sorry, sweetie, you're not allowed backstage," I practically snarled.

"Are you sure?" Her voice was whiskey sweet and a little breathy, as if she were nervous.

It was the voice that did it. I sat up and stared at her, then shook my head. "Well, *damn*, come on in."

She closed the door behind her. "There's no lock."

"Nope. Is that a problem?"

She hesitated for a second, then shook her head, blonde hair skimming her waist. "I guess not."

"Come sit next to me."

The room was no more than six feet across, so she was sitting beside me on the loveseat in two steps. "Hi," she said.

"Hi, yourself. You like the music?"

She smiled, her red lipstick accentuating her plump lips. "I like *you*."

I couldn't stop looking at her. "You're cute."

She ran her fingernails, painted red to match her lipstick, up my bare arm. "You're hot."

I leaned forward and kissed her. Her mouth tasted like waxy lipstick and some fruity, alcoholic drink, but the bar served only beer and shots. "Where you been tonight, babe?"

"I met some friends for drinks after work and they started bitching about their love lives, so I took off," she murmured against my mouth. "I thought this place might be fun."

"Mmm." I wrapped my hand around the back of her neck and

kissed her hard, kissing away the wax and the fruit to get to her real taste. That warm, wet taste. "So, you were out cruising and came here?"

She shifted against me, and I could feel the hard pebble of her nipple against my arm. She nibbled on my neck, taking her time, doing it right. "You can't blame a girl for not wanting to be alone on Valentine's Day."

"Right." I slid my hand up the inside of her thigh, past the short hem of her dress. I realized two things almost immediately—she wasn't wearing panties and she was soaking wet. "God, babe, you're going to leave a wet spot on your dress," I said, as I slid a finger inside her.

She gasped, grabbing my wrist tightly. "It's the alcohol. It has that effect on me."

I slid a second finger inside her. "The alcohol, huh? I thought it was me that got you hot."

"You do," she said, barely above a whisper. "I've wanted you to touch me all night."

I slid my fingers out and trailed her wetness down the inside of her thigh. "Touch you, huh? That's it?"

She tried to pull my hand back between her legs. "Touch me, fuck me, get me off," she said.

"Sounds like a song." I grinned. I was thoroughly enjoying this. Maybe the boys knew what they were talking about. Having a groupie was turning out to be one hell of a perk. "I only have a few minutes."

"I guess you'd better fuck me quick."

She didn't need to tell me twice. I wrapped my arms around her waist to pull her onto my lap so she was straddling me. Her dress rode up high on her hips and I palmed her crotch, squeezing gently. She moaned, digging her nails into my shoulders.

I slid my fingers back inside her and pumped her hard. I didn't just want her to moan, I wanted her to scream. "Is this what you want?"

She nodded, swinging her blonde hair. "Yeah. Oh God, yeah. Fuck me."

I finger-fucked her fast and deep because I didn't have time to take it slow. She rode my hand, doing the work. All I had to do was keep my fingers inside her and she'd get herself off. With my free hand, I undid the knot of her halter and groaned when her breasts swung free. I caught a rigid nipple in my mouth and sucked it hard, harder than I should have, really. She only moaned louder and rode my fingers faster.

I didn't realize the door had opened until I heard Jae say, "Oh, shit. Oh, *shit!*"

"Get out," I mumbled around the nipple in my mouth.

The door slammed as the hot blonde girl straddling me arched her back and came on my hand. I kept stroking her until her cunt stopped undulating and she released her death grip on my shoulders. My hand was covered in her juices, and I knew I'd have bruises to show for my first groupie experience. Not a bad night, after all.

She collapsed against my shoulder, breathing hard. "Oh, my *God*, that was awesome."

I chuckled. "What about me?"

She looked up, blinking like a deer in headlights. Then she gave me a slow, wicked smile. "Sorry. Didn't mean to be selfish."

She slipped to her knees on the grungy carpet, working my belt loose. A knock on the door and Nick's gruff, "We're on in two," stopped her.

"Damn," I sighed. "Guess I'll have to wait."

She ran her finger up the inseam of my jeans. "After you're finished playing?"

"Hell yeah, babe." I stood up, pulling her with me. "You can stay in here. You need to clean up a little bit," I said, wiping a smudge of lipstick from her cheek.

"Hurry back."

Her breath against my neck as she hugged me sent a chill up my spine. "I sure as hell will."

I left her there, flushed and smelling like sex, to face the sentries standing right outside the door. Nick looked impressed; Jae looked pissed.

"What the *hell* was that?" Jae jabbed his finger at the closed door. "What were you doing in there?"

I tried to get past him. "Do you really have to ask? I thought you got a pretty good look."

Nick leaned against the wall, blocking my path. "What's up with you and the hot blonde?"

I shook my head. "Don't worry about it."

"I thought you said you'd never do that," Jae said.

His concern about my relationship that he had dubbed "Titanic 2" was endearing. I laughed. "Don't worry about me, okay?"

"Leave her alone, man," Nick said. "That's the first time she's cracked a smile since we got here tonight. I'm starting to think we'll both get out of here with our balls still attached."

"What about Wendy?" Jae is nothing if not persistent.

The door to the dressing room opened. My "groupie" stood there, blonde wig dangling from her fingertips, her short brown hair standing up in tousled spikes, full lips bare of lipstick. Her white dress was wrinkled and her eye makeup resembled a raccoon more than a vixen. She didn't look like a groupie anymore—she looked like the love of my life.

"What *about* Wendy?"

The look on their faces was priceless and totally worth whatever hell they'd give me later. I didn't have time to enjoy it, though.

I grabbed them both by their T-shirts and pushed them toward the stage. "C'mon boys, we have another set to play."

I looked back at my girl, grinning like a fool. "I'll see you *soon*."

"I can't wait." She smiled that slow, familiar, just-fucked smile I love. "Happy Valentine's Day."

Now *that's* the kind of Valentine's romance I like.

Where I'm Allowed to Kiss You
Pam Graham

To guarantee an outbreak of havoc, inform a gathering of CEOs that their cellular telephones are about to be confiscated for forty-eight hours. Six of the eight CEOs beginning their weeklong Sensitivity Excursion were balking strenuously at the news that their phones would be taken away.

While the men around her leapt to their feet with the unity of a pew full of Southern Baptists, Leigh Sparks remained seated at the walnut conference table—one hand in the pocket of her suit jacket protectively cupping her own phone, the other still calmly holding her pen poised above an open notebook. Doing without communication was, of course, beyond consideration. Leigh's mind paced and raced like the others, but she permitted herself no visible disclosure.

The other woman among Leigh's group slid coolly into the chair next to hers. "Pretend to share with me how incensed you are over this," the woman said, and shoved something into Leigh's phone pocket.

That made two hands, a cell phone, and something else in there, yet Leigh maintained the stillness of a stamp collection. She could feel that the other woman's hand was chilled.

Leigh struck an amicable, yet whispered, tone. "I *am* incensed. And I presume your violation of my personal space has something to do with a plan to thwart this seizure?"

Natalie Anson assessed Leigh approvingly. "As self-controlled as advertised, aren't you? Very good." Natalie squeezed Leigh's hand there in the pocket darkness. "I'll explain later. We're having dinner together tonight in my hotel room, by the way, seven-thirty, room three sixty-three. For now, take this cell." She pressed the tiny device into Leigh's palm. "When they collect them, you turn this one in. Keep yours." Her hand came out and patted Leigh's thigh. "Might want to turn off your real one and slip it into your underwear or something, just to be sure. I'll explain all this at dinner."

Natalie pushed away from the table, satisfied, and jumped into the most bombastic group of protesting executives.

Leigh tapped on Natalie's door at the appointed time.

Natalie wore the glow of victory. "Some coup this morning, huh? Do you realize we are the only two who retain the technology to call our offices freely?" She held a wine glass and took a sip. "The room phones have been turned off, you know. Let me get you some of this." She raised her glass and followed its lead to the bar. Over her shoulder as she poured, Natalie amended, "I mean, sure, the others can prostrate themselves before some stranger's room and beg to use the phone, but no privacy. And no incomings. Beautiful."

"Yes, Ms. Anson, you pulled off quite a neat maneuver. How did you know they'd take our phones and why did you so generously include me in your circumvention?"

"Easy answer to both questions—Albert, and Albert."

Leigh accepted a glass of red wine and took it to the sitting area where floor-to-ceiling windows slung above an overly groomed lawn that jutted to the edge of a tidy tree line. "I'm having a seat." She gracefully doubled her slender legs into a deep upholstered chair and settled back, pushing once at the front of her sleek, blonde hair.

Natalie dropped into the opposite chair. "Well, Leigh, and I'm calling you Leigh, so I might as well be Natalie, don't you think? Leigh, I promised you dinner and an explanation. Which would you like first?"

"The explanation."

Natalie draped one knee across the chair arm. "Damn. And I'm starving. Okay, here's the deal. I want us to partner up over the next seven days to make a clean sweep of all the challenges ExecExcursions throws our way. I want us, the female contingent, to kick butt."

"You're some kind of feminist?" Leigh surmised. Natalie's down-to-earth attire and the overall wholesome effect of her dense brown hair, which was allowed to fall in its natural waviness, hinted at an individualistic personality. And Leigh would bet those penetrating brown eyes were powered by strong ideals.

"To a degree, but not radical. Mainly, I'm someone who despises boredom. Now, we do this thing straight, no playing dirty and no tricks, and we're guaranteed a week that would make a CPA yawn. But we team up to gut the rest of those guys of their smugness, and what could have been a colossal waste of time becomes seven days of fun. Get it?"

Leigh had committed to this process, at the request of her board of directors, and planned to mine its intended value. "If that's how you feel, why bother coming?"

"Lost a bet. Look, Leigh, I'm chugging this wine like it's going to fill me up. But all it's doing is getting me high. How about we order dinner, over which I swear to convince you to play my way?"

Leigh sipped from her own glass, content in the knowledge the wine was landing on a stomach well-lined with the bread and cheese she'd eaten half an hour earlier. She smiled over the rim. "Please, order anytime you like. I'll have whatever you're having."

Over dinner, Leigh found out that Albert was Natalie's amazing assistant, a competitive intelligence genius who had uncovered the top-secret surprises ExecExcursions had in store for the group. She laid it all out for Leigh. The CEOs' cell phones would be locked away for forty-eight hours. During that time, the eight of them would be restricted to hotel premises. These and additional limitations were designed as a condensed basic training, meant to soften the participants' edges. Following those two days of restriction and intense psychological group encounter, would be the final five days filled with physical challenges. The executives would be released at midnight the following Saturday, allowing everyone to fly home Sunday morning and be with their sweethearts for Valentine's Day.

"Look, Leigh, all I'm asking is that we work together on the physical challenge stuff. Albert says you're a runner. Well, I'm strong and coordinated. Albert printed an outline of the challenge descriptions, so nothing's going to come at us out of the blue. Most of those guys are bloated like toads left out in the sun too long. Together, we could take every last one of the physical contests, I guarantee it."

Leigh liked Natalie. There was no reason she couldn't reap the program's legitimate benefits and indulge Natalie along the way. "Maybe we can bargain. First of all, I want Albert." Playfulness laced Leigh's voice.

"Can't have Albert. Anything else, but not Albert."

"I knew you'd say that. Okay, then how about not stopping at the she-women routine? Let's dominate the group encounters too. Did Albert get anything on those?"

Albert had sworn Leigh was an adventurer beneath the staid exterior she displayed. Had to be, he had reasoned, to make the daring corporate moves that highlighted her career. Natalie grinned and mentally saluted him. "Sure. Got all the information right here in my briefcase."

"Then we use our advance knowledge of the encounters to make it appear we're the most confident, sane, well-adjusted, clear-thinking humans who ever graced a group hug—and there will probably be lots of group hugs, you know, so brace yourself."

Natalie reached across the table over their nearly empty plates for a high-five. Leigh half-raised her hand before hesitating. "There's one stipulation."

"Always is. Name it." Natalie had expected strings.

"We truly test ourselves this week. Fully take on the challenges, all of them. Maybe not the way they were meant to be engaged, but we work very hard. And too bad if this sounds corny, but we walk away at the end of the week stronger than we are today."

"Is that all? No problem."

Folding her napkin, Leigh declared the meal finished and headed for the sitting area. "Now, bring those encounter exercises over here and let's get started on tomorrow's scam."

To say that Leigh and Natalie stood out in the encounters would be overmodest. As the eight executives jostled from the conference room on the evening of day two, in bubbly reunion with their cell phones, Natalie chuckled and commented under her breath to Leigh, "Beautiful. Even our singular nonchalance over getting the phones back didn't escape anyone's notice, you know."

Leigh shot her a sideways smirk. "You are psychotic in your need for superiority."

"I know, but I'm so *fucking* secure, it doesn't bother me in the least."

"Supper in your room or mine?"

"Yours. Thirty minutes to shower and change and I'll be there. Whatever you're having."

Natalie shoveled pasta as Leigh chewed thoughtfully and perused the handout they'd been given on the way from encounter that evening.

Leigh plunked a forefinger at the page. "Here's something that wasn't in Albert's summary."

"You sure? Do you want the rest of that garlic bread?"

Leigh dismissed the bread with a glance at her plate and a headshake. "I'm certain. It's this Private Emotional Challenge. His report didn't mention this." She paraphrased the explanatory paragraph. "Says we should each envision a situation we'd never expect to find ourselves in, something innocuous, but beyond our normal emotional range, and then push ourselves to experience it. We don't announce what it is or give any feedback to the group. It's entirely personal."

"Hmm. You're right, Albert didn't tell me about that one."

Tossing the pages onto the table, Leigh said, "There's little here to prepare for tomorrow. Pitiful. Their abuse of the word 'challenge' is criminal."

Natalie patted her full belly. "Too bad. Defeating the encounters wasn't exactly riveting, but it had its moments. Are we now staring monotony and tedium in the face?"

"Maybe not. Let's get to work on the Personal Emotional thing." Leigh picked up the new handout again.

"Get serious, Leigh. They won't be checking up on that one, so we skip it." At times, Natalie could not believe Leigh's earnestness.

"No. Finding a good one might be our only way around your dreaded sentence of five more days of boredom." Leigh kicked the foot Natalie dangled over her chair arm. "Let's do you first. Think of a situation that would scare the emotional shit right out of you."

"No such animal." Natalie examined her fingernails. "I am scare-proof, emotionally speaking."

"Doubt that, but let's wait on you, then. Me first." Leigh took a pad and pen from the counter and returned to her seat. "Okay, think in terms of categories. Ah." She nodded once, smartly, and began to write. "Confrontation. Affection. Inferiority. Competitiveness. Sexuality. Honesty. Okay, that's enough to work with. Now, which category to examine first."

"Sexuality. What's your sex life like, Leigh?"

"What's yours like, oh Natalie of the panic-proof emotions?"

"Easy question and easy answer. Two boyfriends, casual, for convenience. No commitment in either direction." Natalie batted her eyes mockingly. "Quite a rational arrangement all around."

"Not as rational as mine. No boyfriends."

"What the hell do you do about sex? Well, I know what you

must do, but once in a while don't you feel like it'd be nice if there were a second party involved?"

"Not at all. Because pregnancy would be so disastrous, I used three kinds of protection. Diaphragm, condom, spermicide, and I was on the pill besides. Any poor guy I went to bed with was basically glory-holing."

Natalie snorted.

Leigh continued, "Two years ago, I flushed my pills and dumped the spermicide into the fish tank—made them swim really slowly, by the way." Leigh checked that Natalie was properly amused. "Took some scissors and acrylic paints to my diaphragm, added some feathers, and fashioned a lovely dream catcher to hang over my bed. Gave my case of spare condoms to the Goodwill, and that was the end of that. Been merrily dating myself ever since."

"You're lying."

"Only about the spermicide. I'd never endanger my fish. They're extremely expensive."

"Then your emotional thing is easy. Get yourself some protection and have sex with a real live guy for a change. After two years, that would probably feel kind of 'out there,' wouldn't it?"

Leigh gave Natalie a derisive look. "Talk about unoriginal."

A wicked grin overtook Natalie's face. "Did I say a real live man? Pardon. I meant to say a real live woman. We take you to a lesbian bar and find you someone to bring back for the night. Do not tell me you wouldn't get a surge of anxiety to find yourself alone with a woman for sexual purposes."

Natalie was astounded to see that Leigh was weighing this proposal. Then Leigh actually said, "Might work. It would certainly not qualify as a cop-out." Leigh shifted to the next order of business. "Now you. Yours has to be at least as good as that."

Natalie was invigorated. "I get to go to the bar with you, right? I won't get in the way, promise."

"Of course. How could I make you stay behind when it was your idea? Now, come on, yours."

"One thing for sure, it's not going to top yours."

Leigh's turn for wickedness. "Unless . . ."

Natalie registered Leigh's drift. "Unless, nothing." She put up a forestalling hand. "Wait, now, listen. It's not the woman part, really. I just feel icky about being intimate with people I don't know. Even drinking after them, or using their hairbrush or anything. It's not an emotional trigger, it's just unappetizing."

Leigh considered for half a second. "Forget the lesbians. We'll have sex with each other."

"Are you crazy?"

"What's the problem? You're constantly eating off my plate and finishing my orphaned glasses of wine. Or have we stumbled upon something that intimidates you too much? What happened to your panic-proofness?"

"Nothing. I mean, no." Natalie blew out a full breath. "I'm game if you are."

Leigh stood and unfastened her belt as she crossed the room, on a bed trajectory. "Let's go, then."

"Now?" In her entire life, Natalie had never emitted such a girl-squeal.

"What else would we do with the rest of the evening? Not like we need our sleep before tomorrow's harrowing challenges, is it?"

"Not at all." Natalie told herself to buck up. If she were going to do this anyway, might as well do it with as much bravado as Leigh.

Leigh carefully hung her blouse over a chair back, then folded her khakis and laid them on the seat. Natalie, standing on the other side of the bed, fumbled with her fly. "We don't even know what we're supposed to do here. Or do you?" Natalie was suddenly suspicious she'd walked into a trap.

Leigh was long and lean and incredible to look at naked in the faint light of a small lamp across the room. Natalie also noticed that her posture was as relaxed as if she'd been fully clothed.

Leigh laughed at the suspicion. "I don't know what I'm doing either. But how difficult can it be? I mean, we know where we want to go, and we know generally how to get there. Need help with that zipper?"

"I've got it." Natalie finally freed herself from her jeans, then her T-shirt. Unlike Leigh, she had no additional articles, like underpants or bra, to navigate.

Leigh chivalrously motioned for Natalie to get under the covers first. Once they were both in bed and assiduously not touching, Leigh said, "Sorry, I should have asked if you needed to use the bathroom or anything first."

"No. Now what?"

"Let's see." Leigh rolled to her side. "Room dark enough, or should I turn out that lamp?"

"Light's fine with me. Can you believe we're doing this?"

"We *haven't* done anything yet." Leigh took the initiative. "Turn over."

She played her fingertips around the base of Natalie's belly until they were both breathing so hard she got up the nerve to brush across the soft hair below, then kept going and let her fingers wander up and down the inner muscles of Natalie's thighs, making sure to go too far up now and then. She whispered, "I'm unbearably excited without even being touched. How are you doing?"

Natalie gulped and whispered, "Just about paralyzed. Do more. I'm going crazy."

Obligingly, Leigh spread Natalie's thighs, one handed, and wiggled upward until she felt wetness. The slick, hot proof that she had fully aroused Natalie crushed any lingering timidity. Leigh adjusted her access angle slightly. "I could shove my finger into you. How would that be?"

"Perfect. God, hurry."

Leigh danced her fingers around the opening as if she would enter, but each time she barely penetrated the threshold before pulling back. The sounds this evoked and the way Natalie's slit chased after Leigh's retreating hand elated Leigh. After several rounds of such play, Natalie toppled Leigh and flipped her onto her back, then straddled her.

Sweat plastered Natalie's normally obedient bangs to her forehead and her eyes had a feral look as, breathing fast, she said, "Sometimes it's good to tease. But not now. I am begging you."

Eyes wide at Natalie's raw need, Leigh complied by pushing in smoothly, powerfully. After the shudder of relief combined with escalating thrusts of Natalie's hips, Leigh focused on filling her and sustaining the arousal, until all imperatives sharpened to a single demand—the vein-deep desire to watch Natalie come.

"Can you hear me, Natalie?"

Natalie was still astride, pushing frantically into each plunge of Leigh's hand. She nodded her drooping head in answer to the question.

"Good." Leigh maneuvered her thumb around to Natalie's clitoris. "Come hard for me, Natalie. Let everything go. I have you, and it'll be fine. Come hard for me."

Wet muscles clenched around Leigh's fingers as Natalie did precisely as she had been told.

Natalie was out cold for a solid twenty minutes. Leigh browsed some quarterly statistics and was about to take care of herself, when covers stirred on the other side of the bed.

Natalie's head popped out. "First time you ever did that, truly?"

Leigh peered over small-lens reading glasses. "Cross my heart. Not bad for a beginner, eh?"

Staring at the ceiling as she swept her bangs away from her face, Natalie laughed. "You ever get tired of running that company, you could make a nice living at it. Heck, *I'd* pay you."

Leigh turned her attention back to her financial report, saying, "No need to wake yourself. You may sleep there tonight. Won't bother me a bit."

"Yes I will bother you. More than a bit, I hope." Natalie scooted over beside Leigh and propped up on an elbow. "Lose the glasses and the numbers. It's your turn. You still naked underneath there?" She lifted the edge of the sheet for a peek. "Good. Now, turn off that light."

After such an ardent orgasm, Natalie was surprised at how quickly her body responded to the mere anticipation of returning Leigh's favors. First thing, she gently probed between Leigh's legs, explaining with sham apology, "Reconnaissance. Just want to see where we stand." Finding extremely hospitable conditions there, she stroked lazily. "Poor Leigh. Did you sufferwhile I slept?"

"No. Couldn't you see how fascinating those statistics were?" Leigh valiantly maintained a steady tone of voice.

"Well, good." Natalie went all the way in on the first push, taking Leigh off guard and shredding her breath to tatters. Natalie cradled Leigh's breast and guided the nipple to her mouth. She sucked a few times before asking, "Do yours have a direct link to here?" She withdrew and patted Leigh's clitoris, then dunked her fingers back in. "Mine do."

Leigh didn't, or couldn't, respond, but Natalie persisted. "Leigh, answer me. When I suck your breast does it feel almost like I'm going down on you?" Natalie demonstrated with a long, firm pull on the nipple.

Leigh managed, "Can't say for sure. You haven't done that to me yet."

Natalie's low laughter vibrated through Leigh's breast. "Astute observation." She recovered her soaked fingers and abandoned a very attentive nipple. Then, kneeling in its center, she surveyed the bed for extra pillows. "It has always been my opinion that to do this right, more care should be given to the comfort of both parties." She found two pillows in addition to the two Leigh already rested head and shoulders on. One she placed under Leigh's rear. "Comfortable?"

"Quite." Leigh telegraphed amused indulgence.

"Not stressing your lower back is it?"

Leigh shook her head. "Very nice angle."

The other pillow Natalie shoved under her own chest as she settled, on her stomach, between Leigh's thighs. There were a few technical adjustments before she asked, "Get you anything?"

"This should do it."

"I'm cozy and content, too, so take your time." Natalie noticed that Leigh's shoulders had been bared when Natalie pulled the covers down with her. "Warm enough?"

"Perfect." That sounded a tiny bit emphatic.

"Right. Here we go, then. Take all the time you want." Natalie was up for delivering the very best oral stimulation in the history of sex. How many times had she silently critiqued unsatisfactory performances? Lay thinking, detached, that she could do such a better job of it? Here was a chance to test the validity of her impatience with the men she'd known.

Natalie opened Leigh gently and pressed her lips against the pale pinkness beyond the folds. Scuppered by the sweetness of this hidden preserve, all Natalie could do at first was kiss there—kisses that grew more impassioned as she picked up the nuances of Leigh's scent. Kisses that forgot they were meant only for pleasing Leigh as they burned a streak of desire through Natalie's center. Before she even had the chance to use her tongue in the devastating ways she'd envisioned a tongue being used, Natalie felt Leigh's fingers lace themselves into her hair. Leigh tightened a moment, then fell still. Natalie abandoned the kisses to enclose Leigh and suck her with an easy, steady rhythm.

Leigh's descent from self-command was steep and consummate. Natalie had the sense that Leigh was spilling all over everything. Saying Natalie's name. Spreading herself wider while pulling Natalie closer in. Devouring huge volumes of air. Finally collapsing into her nest of pillows, panting and drenched with sweat.

Natalie was the one who fell asleep—again. She'd been dozing there long enough that when Leigh stirred and lightly rustled her hair to wake her, the cheek that had been pressing against Leigh's thigh had dried and stuck to it some. Still smelled terrific, though. It had been long enough too, that Leigh's unassailable coolness was back in place. Continuing to play with the ends of Natalie's hair, she said, "So, let me understand this clearly. If anyone in the room has an orgasm, you fall dead asleep."

Struggling back over to the far side of the bed, dragging her pillow with her, Natalie nodded. "Looks that way. What time is it?"

"Five to one. We're setting ourselves up for more challenge tomorrow than those activities should warrant."

"Yikes. Four hours left for sleeping."

Leigh pulled the pillow from beneath her butt and flopped it onto Natalie's stomach. "Almost be better to stay up straight though, instead of trying to wake up after only four hours."

"You *are* joking."

"You seemed to enjoy doing that. There must be more to it than one would think." Leigh deliberated. "And it's really only sporting to give those guys a handicap tomorrow. Not sleeping might level the playing field enough that we don't run circles around them."

Natalie propped her hips with the pillow and made room for Leigh to slip between her legs. Afterward, before sleep took her, she thought she heard Leigh say there certainly *was* more to it than imaginable.

They met the next day's demands effortlessly and with extraordinary good spirit, especially given their sleep deficit. During the short walk from the gym back to the hotel, two decisions were made. Showers should be quick, and supper could wait until they had done some work on their Private Emotional Challenge.

Leigh made it to Natalie's room twenty minutes after they parted in the elevator. An awkward moment tried to happen when they were finally alone for the evening, but Leigh skirted it with, "I think we were wise last night, not injecting a fictitious sense of romance into this with kissing and hugging."

Natalie weighed that and concluded, "Not like foreplay was necessary." She led the way and settled into one of the deep-seated stuffed chairs near the window.

Sinking fluidly into the fellow chair, Leigh shut her eyes and said through a smile, "What's on the docket for tonight, cruise director?" When Natalie didn't answer, Leigh's eyes opened. "So

you do have something in mind? Tell me." She flicked her gaze out
to the sunlit greens of the treetops across the lawn, then back to
Natalie, whose expression was now stained with the strength of
what she wanted. "Good God, tell me. You know I'll take care of
you."

"I'd enjoy seeing you . . . provide your own delight." Natalie
had indulged that day in several bouts of fitful reverie over the soli-
tary dissipation of Leigh's sensuality, until she found herself actually picturing Leigh's chosen means of tending to those matters.
She could see Leigh setting aside time, or perhaps scheduling it in.
What she couldn't imagine was Leigh climaxing alone. Leigh's
passion had repeatedly soared sky-high last night, and each time
she had invoked Natalie's name. Natalie had found that unex-
pected, as well as curiously affecting.

Unruffled by Natalie's request, Leigh slanted her eyes toward
the bed. "There?" The tone she struck was absolutely cordial. She
lowered her chin and glanced at her lap. "Or right here?" In preparation for whichever, she slid her belt's tongue from its buckle.

"Here."

Leigh opened her pants, closed her eyes, took a slow breath and
eased her hand beyond the parted zipper. Natalie watched Leigh's
fingers roam rhythmically beneath the thin, beige brushed cotton.
When Leigh's eyes fluttered briefly, Natalie tried to remember
whether she had ever known anyone with *light* brown eyes.
Tonight those eyes, set against Leigh's palest of blue linen shirt,
distracted Natalie from matters at hand to the wistful thought that
it would be nice to look deeply into them and say intimate, non-
sexual things. But that would violate the natural law of the universe
they had created. A universe that would self-destruct on
Valentine's Day, just three nights away.

Leigh's other hand, which had hung loosely over the chair arm,
curled and tightened. "I'm almost there, Natalie. On the very
verge. Would you like to tell me when I may give in?"

Natalie thought, *This is our intimacy. It's all we'll ever have.* She
said, "You want me to make you wait, don't you?"

Her eyes were closed again, but Leigh's hand had stopped moving. "So close."

"Look at me, Leigh." Natalie waited for her to look. "You think you're as excited as you can get without coming, but you're not. We're going to find out how close you can get. Start stroking yourself again. No, keep your eyes on me while you do it." When Leigh's breath and hand quickened, Natalie spoke again. "Now stop and bring your hand out."

Through a weak smile, Leigh observed, "You were right, I only thought I was close."

"Mmm hmm. Drive yourself to the edge again." When Natalie was sure Leigh could barely hold off, she said, "Later tonight, I'm going to lick you where your finger feels so good right now." Leigh flinched and Natalie warned, "Ah-ah, the game says you can't come until I say so." She allowed Leigh to settle before bidding, "Tell me what you have in mind for me tonight, I know you've thought about it."

The beat of Leigh's words fell into involuntary cadence with her fingers' movements. "On your hands and knees, in the middle of the bed, me inside you from behind." She closed her eyes while inhaling deeply, "Oh, God," then returned to Natalie's eyes. "I need to come."

"Not yet. Then what?"

Leigh wet her lips. "You'll push back hard, my other hand will support your stomach, you'll . . . I can't take this any longer."

"Yes, you can. I'll what?"

"You'll, I don't know, please Natalie, say I can come."

"Take your hand from your pants." Natalie wondered if a person could pass out from arousal because Leigh did not look very with it. "Okay, shut your eyes, go back in, and come when you like. I'll be watching. Enjoy."

It was an exquisitely drawn-out climax. Afterward, Natalie still couldn't conjure a true image of Leigh coming alone, without her, because she had said Natalie's name again.

When her will allowed, Leigh looked over at Natalie. "What

are you doing awake? Someone in the room definitely had an orgasm."

"Guess that blows that theory. Guess, too, you're going to request a similar performance from me?"

Rolling from her chair, Leigh assured sincerely, "I honestly don't think I could take it." She urged Natalie forward and climbed behind her in the chair, legs and arms around her, as if they were riding double on a sleigh. She unbuttoned Natalie's muslin slacks and slid her hand inside, precisely as far as she had into her own. As she began tracing slow circles in there, she said, "Don't hold back, and don't cooperate too much. Just watch that sun finish going down and bask in this." She dipped into wet heat. "Let's be very quiet, now. What a beautiful sunset."

They *were* quiet. And peaceful. At some point, Leigh almost rested her other hand atop Natalie's where it rested on the chair arm, but hesitated, hovering just above it to ask, "May I?"

Natalie thought, *Such a strange little world we've made. Access to my cunt goes unquestioned, yet she has to ask to touch my hand.* "Of course," she said.

In the months after their parting that Valentine's morning, it would be this night, these moments, that would stalk Natalie's dreams—awake and asleep. The nearness of Leigh's breathing, right next to her ear. The endearing scent of toothpaste still gracing those breaths. The way their cheeks touched now and then as Leigh varied her fondling. The stillness, except for the brushing of Leigh's knuckles against the inside fabric of Natalie's pants. And in the moment when the sun disappeared and Natalie gave herself up, the heartbreaking tenderness of Leigh moving her other hand over, holding it against Natalie's stomach until the tensing subsided.

When Natalie woke up, still in the chair, but before darkened windows now, Leigh was in the other chair, blithely eating a room-service dinner.

"What are we having?"

"Lemon-pepper chicken with buttered green beans and glazed carrots. You may have my carrots. Yours is on the table."

Natalie would have sworn something had changed between them, but Leigh didn't appear to think so.

By Sunday morning, when they'd arranged to meet for breakfast in Leigh's room before she departed for the airport, Natalie was admitting to herself that she didn't want a clean and forever break. Saturday, she'd sneaked off to the gift shop during lunch and bought a Valentine card. It was passably neutral, blank on the inside, where Natalie had printed, 'Thank you. I will remember.'

When Leigh answered the door, they agreed they both looked pretty great all dressed up for travel.

Leigh hustled off toward the bathroom. "Food's already here, dig in. I'll be right out."

Perfect opportunity for Natalie to slip the card into Leigh's carry-on bag.

After breakfast, Leigh was doing her final gathering and they were about out the door. Natalie mentioned the lovers' holiday.

Leigh snickered. "What a racket. Paying homage to the florists, card companies, candy makers, and all the other sellers of cheap symbols of being in a relationship. You know the ones I hate the most? Those creepy shiny balloons."

Feeling like Cupid caught in the headlights, Natalie snatched the card from Leigh's bag and sprinted to her room. It wasn't much of a sprint, they both wore heels. Leigh's pursuit was too close to shut her out, so Natalie desperately shredded the card into unreadable pieces.

Leigh reached around Natalie's body, grabbing at the destruction. "Hold on. Was that for me?"

The wrestling and card ripping escalated, and before they knew it, Leigh had rent a tear in the front of Natalie's suit jacket. Natalie slammed card confetti onto the bed and gaped at her ruined jacket, then popped all the buttons off Leigh's blouse with one exhilarating yank.

When most of their clothes lay in shreds across the bed, Natalie pushed Leigh back onto the pillows and spread her legs. The fierceness had gone, but urgency still ruled. Natalie lowered her mouth to Leigh one last time, thinking, *At least I am allowed to kiss you here.*

Leigh stood in the doorway afterward, wearing one of Natalie's T-shirts and a pair of her shorts. She chuckled, "Great finale, don't you think?"

Natalie refused to crack. "What else did you expect? Better go now, though. You know I need to sleep after that. You'll still make your plane, right?"

"If I hurry. Sorry you'll miss yours."

"Albert loves to fix these kinds of things."

Leigh hesitated before closing the door. "If that card was something kind of sweet, or whatever, I wouldn't have ridiculed it."

"I know, but it wasn't. It was lewd, so I reconsidered."

"Right. Bye then." And Leigh left smiling.

Natalie lay across the card and clothes debris on the bed and dialed her cell phone. "Albert, I'm going to miss my flight, can you get another? Thanks. Oh, and let me know when Leigh Sparks' plane is safely on the ground in Boston, please."

Dragging home from her office late the night of that next Valentine's Day, Natalie found a dark jumble piled in her front porch swing. Bending over the figure asleep there under a shield of Valentine talismans, she whispered, "You don't do anything halfway, do you?"

Leigh blinked conscious like a PC lighting up. "I try to be thorough, yes."

Carefully relocating a huge white shaggy dog with a heart on its belly that read 'Be Mine' to the glider, Natalie nodded.

Gift by gift, Leigh handed her the rest of the Valentine loot, cataloging, "Your heart-shaped box of chocolates, your 'Sweetheart' mug full of hard candy, your roses." She batted the mylar balloon floating above them. "And your creepy 'Be My Valentine' shiny balloon." The thing bobbed down and bumped her forehead. "And these." She held out a bag of roasted potatoes leftover from lunch. "They're cold, but that never stopped you before."

Natalie eased beside her in the swing and they stared at the glider full of red and pink capitulation to romance.

In a voice that could have been disclosing corporate secrets, Leigh announced, "I cry about you."

"I cry about you, too." Natalie nibbled at the potatoes. "So, what do you propose we do to fix that? Come on, I know you made a list."

"I was thinking just go ahead and inject romance into the whole thing and see where that gets us."

"So we get to kiss, hug, cuddle after making love, and hold each other while we sleep?"

"All that, and here—" Leigh dug around in her coat pocket. "I have a Valentine card for you." She held it out of reach. "But first, tell me what was in the one you tore up."

Natalie leaned forward and kissed Leigh's closed lips. She pulled back and smiled, looking into her eyes. "I saved all the pieces." Another kiss. "Tell you what, *next* Valentine's Day, I'll give them to you and reveal what it said."

Leigh put her arms around Natalie's waist and curled closer, then kissed her again and let her tongue slip in for a while before replying, "Or the next Valentine's Day, or the one five years from now, or ten."

Babalu
Nicolette Rivers

"It wasn't love at first sight. It took a full five minutes."

—Lucille Ball

As a child I loved old sitcoms. We're talking the vintage stuff with two loving parents, squeaky-clean kids, and a well-trained dog. I'd stare at the pretty housewife and long to be her. I knew I wanted the dress, the heels, and the pearls, but most of all, I knew I wanted the loving partner.

I would lie on my bed, sucking on a cherry LifeSaver, trying to block out the sound of my parents fighting in the next room. I'd imagine myself as one of those appealing women who had problems that would be fixed in half an hour and a spouse who brought home the bacon and wrapped her in strong, safe arms. That was my ideal, even in the days when I played the dutiful feminist. I only let a few friends know my true longings—and even they didn't know that sometimes, in my fantasy, the safe arms belonged to another woman.

My favorite show featured a wacky redhead who was always getting into trouble. Her husband would get mad at her and lapse into his native language, but it was clear he loved her even when she was at her wackiest. Sometimes when he was really angry he would threaten to spank her. On one episode they even showed him pulling her over his knee and, while they left the rest to the imagination, I could picture everything—including him wiping away her tears afterward.

I grew up and married Dan right out of college. My husband towered over me by a full 12 inches and loved to work out. Though he was roughly the size of a small house, he never seemed to get angry; however, he did master being quietly disappointed and extremely baffled by the woman he'd married. Most people would have called it a good marriage; we never fought, he tolerated Ricky (my dog), and he was a sensitive—although uncreative—lover. And he always remembered special occasions. As did I. Usually.

So why was I, the original Christmas-Shopping-Done-by-Thanksgiving Girl, spending Valentine's Day looking for the book my husband wanted? And why was I down to the last bookstore on the list?

I pulled up to Eva's Secret Garden, put a quarter in the meter, and prayed they'd have the book in stock. Because I hadn't began searching until the last minute, I felt a little scatterbrained about it and like I'd let Dan down *again*.

I walked into the bookstore, glancing around. It was quiet except for a CD player in the corner that seemed to be piping television theme songs throughout the store. I felt right at home.

There were only a few customers—all women—and the atmosphere was relaxed. I couldn't see an easily identifiable employee, so I began the search on my own.

To the slightly frenzied melody of a song normally associated with the cartoon antics of animals, I looked at the labels on the shelves—*Lesbian Erotica*, *Erotica: General*, and *Homosexuality and The Law*. Then I saw a book that promised it was the definitive guide to strap-on sex.

I examined Eva's a little closer and it all clicked into place: the all-female clientele, a display of rainbow bumper stickers, the sign in the doorway that stated the city didn't tolerate hate crimes, and the reputation that the city had for being welcoming to gay business owners. I started to laugh but quickly choked it back. Wacky redheads didn't cease to exist when the show was cancelled! I heard a voice behind me.

"Can I help you find anything?" It was a great voice—clearly female, but also deep and slightly husky.

I turned to see the owner of the voice . . . and my heart skipped a beat, then sped up. The speaker had amazing blue eyes that instantly convinced me drowning would not be a bad way to go. The eyes were bracketed by the very beginnings of crow's feet, which were so subtle most people wouldn't notice unless they were staring. They might not notice the freckles either, but I did. Which meant I was staring—and hadn't answered her question.

"I . . . no, I'm looking for a book. I'm thinking you wouldn't have it here."

She smiled then. "Oh, what's the name of the book?"

"*A Man for All Seasons.*"

The smile became wry. "You're right. We don't carry that book."

"Yes, well, I see that—I didn't know that . . . well, it didn't say in the phone book . . . See, the book is for my husband—the man I'm married to . . . What I mean is . . ." My voice trailed off.

Just then the theme for my favorite show began playing.

"I think I know just what you're saying. It's fine. Look around, though—you just might find something you like." I thought I saw a mischievous twinkle in her eyes.

"It's funny," she added, flicking her head in the direction of the CD player, "but you remind me of her."

"Sorry," I said, blushing.

"Wasn't complaining," she tossed over her shoulder. I watched her walk to the counter.

Even though it was clear they didn't have the book—even though it was clear I needed to hurry—I didn't leave. Instead I lingered, tried to act like a casual browser, and covertly examined the woman. All I needed was a trench coat and a shoe phone . . . but that was another of my favorite shows.

My behavior was out of the ordinary, but I was unable to stop sneaking glances at every opportunity. She was beautiful in this really strong and solid way, like Helga in the Andrew Wyeth paintings. She wasn't a waif by any means—she had to weigh at least 25 pounds more than me—yet there was something eerily compelling about her. Although she appeared to be in her early 30s, I could picture her as a mischievous tomboy—complete with skinned knee and slight sunburn. A female Huck Finn.

I loved how I could see the fine laugh lines on her skin as the sun streamed through the window and highlighted her face. Her hair was pulled back in a messy braid, but it was wonderful how those loose tendrils framed her face. I imagined replacing those tendrils with my fingers, caressing the ridges of her high cheekbones, then following the same path with my lips.

The strength of my reaction surprised me. I'd had the occasional—okay, more than occasional—fantasies about women, but I'd never felt anything like the longing that filled me when I looked at her. I wanted to be wrapped in her arms. I wanted her to want me. I wanted to make her smile again.

I forced myself to head toward the door, knowing I had no reason to stay. At the doorway, I saw a rainbow-colored pet bandana. It was perfect for Ricky and, to be honest, it would be an excuse to talk to her.

She was on the phone, talking about how someone was late and how she hoped she'd be able to make her bank appointment. She wasn't facing me, but I realized she also looked terrific from that angle as well.

When she hung up, I cleared my throat and said, "I saw something I like a lot."

She turned and looked at me with a raised eyebrow. The wry smile was back.

I held up Ricky's bandana. "My dog will love it."

"Ah." She reached for the bandana and our fingers touched. I shivered, then blushed because it was one *obvious* shiver. I barely registered the sound of the door opening.

"Sorry, Dalrymple. I got stuck in traffic," a grey-haired woman said, stepping behind the counter.

I laughed in vague surprise. "Dalrymple?"

"It's my last name. I'm Deenie."

"Christina," I said, handing her the first card in my wallet and smiling. I hoped I didn't have lipstick on my teeth.

"Nice to meet you, Christina. Is the Meadowdale Library a good one?" She handed me back my library card.

"Yes, very nice. I recommend it highly. Let me try this again." I took back the card and dug through my purse. Driver's license, blood donor card, appointment card for Ricky's vet, phone number written on a withdrawal slip from work. American Express—*thank you!* I handed her the card in what I hoped was a calm and ladylike manner.

She ran my card through the machine, fighting back laughter.

The other woman peered at the bandana. "If you like that, we have—oh, where did I put them?—rainbow collars. I meant to put them out yesterday."

The register purred out the receipt and, after hearing my name on Deenie's lips, I felt like purring right along with it. She handed me the slip and a pen.

Deenie winked. "It's okay, Cory—let's give Christina a reason to return."

I slid the signed slip toward her. "Oh, I can think of a few reasons." I couldn't believe I had said that! *Hello? Husband?* I told myself that a little flirtation wouldn't hurt anything.

"Good luck finding your book."

"My book?" I couldn't decide if her eyes were a true blue or more like an aquamarine. In the words of Elton John, though, hers were *the sweetest eyes I'd ever seen.* I could stop back for the collar in a couple days.

"*A Man for All Seasons.*"

"Right, right." I felt my face flush. "Of course."

I walked out of the store feeling like the very axis of my life had changed somehow, all the while telling myself I was just being ridiculous. After all, I was happily married.

That night I gave my husband some cologne and a pair of silk boxers. I also gave my other Valentine, Ricky, his bandana. Dan gave me a new day planner and a pair of slippers identical to the ones his mother liked to wear. They had no heels, no marabou, no sex appeal—they were the type with the elastic band that left lines around your feet and ankles.

"Are you okay?" he asked, noticing the reaction I tried to hide as I looked at the slippers. He seemed detached. It felt like he knew he was my husband, knew I was going through something, and knew it was his job to make an effort to show concern.

I tried not to sound defensive. "Sure. Why?"

"You just seem a bit off. I don't think you care for the slippers, you didn't get me the book I told you I wanted, and you bought my dog a bandana that will get him anally probed by every male dog at the dog park."

"Dan, that's absurd!" His *dog? Since when? Every time Ricky did the least little thing wrong he talked of taking "your dog" to the pound.*

"Christina, it's a joke." He sounded weary.

I took a deep breath. "I know, I know. I'm sorry." I got out of my chair and went to sit in his lap, like I used to do in the beginning of our relationship. He allowed it, but didn't wrap his arms around me the way that he once did. "Thank you for the slippers . . . and the day planner will really come in handy. I was just hoping for something a little more sexy and fun though."

"I figured that. I want you. I love you. I don't need you to wear sexy underwear. We've been married—what—a couple years now? We should be comfortable enough to not have to dress up for each other."

I closed my eyes and tried to find the right words. "I don't wear sexy lingerie because I feel I have to, or need to—I want to! I like dressing sexy, and I like being flirty, and I like bubble baths, and being silly, and doing crazy, whacked-out, spontaneous things!"

I opened my eyes again. "Dan, the truth is that—I get afraid sometimes that I'll never be the woman you want me to be." I stroked his cheek with the back of my hand, feeling his whiskers scratch my skin. "Do I make you happy—the way that I am?"

There was a silence that seemed to go on forever, but I suppose it always seems that way when an answer is so important. Dan's mouth tugged down slightly at the corners. I knew he was also being as honest as possible. "I accept that you have a tendency to become distracted and do some fairly silly things. When I married you I was aware of this, and while I thought you would mature by now, I'm not unhappy."

The truth hit me hard. It wasn't that he wanted me to be someone I could never be—that would take legitimate passion—he merely *preferred* that I be someone I could never be. That was so much worse, somehow.

I had tried hard to be the most settled 26-year-old in existence, and it simply wasn't enough. He wouldn't ever leave me over it, but if he had his way I would be even *more* subdued. I might as well be a china doll kept in a curio cabinet. He would never be an insensitive jackass like my father; he would merely be an insensitive jackass in his own special way.

I stopped myself. I was being unfair. He was being honest—and if he was not the man for me, I was not the woman for him. If one of us had failed, then we both had failed.

What did *I* want? To be wild and crazy and passionate . . . and adored. I wanted to be loved even when I was imperfect, even when I was a wacky redhead. I wanted a sex life that was not a negotiation but a celebration. I wanted him to put on the god-damned silk boxers. What did he want? I'm pretty sure it was a wife who—while perhaps not being *perfect*—didn't lock herself out of her car every couple months, found him the book he wanted, and wore the goddamned old-lady slippers.

I put my head on his shoulder and began to cry. I felt him begin to gently stroke my hair, just like he used to do. It was nice, but not enough.

A week later, Ricky and I moved out.

Sharp claws clutched the back of my shirt, pulling me up against cold metal bars. I gave a surprised yip and turned around to confront my assailant. It was Fred, a brown tiger cat with one torn ear. He purred and rubbed up against the door of his cage. A hardened criminal, he was clearly unrepentant.

I petted his forehead with the tip of my finger. "You need a nail trim, my friend. The key is to get potential adopters to take you out, not to have you pull them in there with you!"

I took care of Fred's claws, spent a few minutes straightening up the cat room, then headed to the front counter. It was ten minutes before the shelter was supposed to open, but several people already milled around the lobby.

I could hear the impatient click-click of high heels behind me and knew it was Karen, the shelter manager, running late for the "Adoptable Pet" segment on the news.

"Chris, be a dear and enter these donations into the computer," she said, tossing a stack of envelopes at me, never stopping for a response. *Click-click*, she was gone.

Good to be appreciated, I thought with a grin. I quickly typed in the first two donations, but when I pulled the check out of the third envelope my heart skipped a beat.

Deeanna Dalrymple. I couldn't be sure if it was Deenie, and yet I didn't doubt it. I wanted it to be her too much. It took me an extra long time to process the donation because my hands were trembling.

It had been six months since I'd been to Eva's. I'd been too busy moving out of my house, quitting my bank job, applying at the shelter, filing for divorce, and mourning my marriage. I'd also still been more than a little awed at the strength of my response that day. I'd needed the time.

I knew, looking at the check, that I had to go back to the store. I needed to know if the attraction was real or a strange chemical imbalance. Six months' worth of fantasizing about strong yet feminine hands spanking my ass pretty much demanded it.

"Can we go back yet?" a woman asked in a high-pitched whine.

I looked at the clock. Close enough. "Sure, let me take you back. What're you looking for? Cat? Dog?" I ushered her through the doors.

"I want a full-blooded puppy that won't shed, bark, or grow over twelve pounds—oh, and already housebroken," she demanded.

"You don't want a pet, you want a stuffed animal," I mumbled.

"Excuse me?"

"I said, 'Follow me, we have many wonderful adoptable animals.' Let me ask you, what if the puppy has an accident on the floor, or barks?"

"I'll bring it back. I just want it to be cute. I don't have a lot of time to deal with a bad dog."

"Almost all dogs—particularly puppies—make mistakes while they're learning. We offer training—"

"I don't have time for that. I suppose I can chain it outside."

"Okay," I said, knowing I would be refusing her application for adoption. Real love didn't demand constant perfection.

I also vowed to go back to Eva's on my next day off.

I tried to stay calm as I entered the store. I pretended to casually browse the shelves, all the while looking for Deenie. I saw that Cory, the other woman I'd encountered on my previous visit, was behind the counter, but there was no sign of the real reason for my visit. Finally, I grabbed a cookbook and a new collar for Ricky and headed over to pay.

"Did you find everything okay? You've been here before, right?" Cory asked.

I smiled. "Yes, and yes." I gathered my courage. "The last time I

was here there was a woman named Deenie who waited on me—"
My voice trailed off. "Is she here now?"

"No, she left about three months ago. She's trying to make a go
of owning a coffee shop. It hasn't opened yet, but I can tell you
where it will be." She lowered her voice and leaned closer. "You
like her, huh?"

"No. I mean, she was just very helpful, and I wanted to thank
her."

"Sure. You sure dressed cute to deliver your thanks. Let me give
you directions to the coffee shop. That way, when it opens, you
can thank her there." Cory gave me a conspiratorial wink.

I knew I was busted and could feel the heat creep into my
cheeks. "Sure, that would be great. So does she have a partner . . .
in the coffee shop, I mean?"

"Nope, no partner. I guess she just never found the right one.
Maybe you have someone in mind?"

I walked out with the slip of paper in my hand and a debate
raging in my head. Was I a redhead or a mouse? Hadn't I tried to
blend in my whole life, always aiming to do the respectable thing?
Wasn't my new life about rebelling against that?

My marriage ended because I didn't want to hide the fact that I
was passionate and impetuous and needed someone who would
value that about me—not look at me and wish I was someone I
could never be. In times like these, often a woman's best bet is to
ask herself one question: WWLD—What Would Lucy Do?

So, would a wild, impetuous, passionate woman wait for
months to start what could be the best relationship of her life—
providing the other woman was willing—or would she use the
copy of the receipt for the shelter donation to go to said woman's
house? I knew that would be either "impetuous" or "stalker."

I would soon find out, I told myself, popping a cherry LifeSaver
for luck and praying on my worn copy of *Bridget Jones's Diary*. (I
revere two saints—Lucy and Bridget.)

The house was small and neat. I thought it could use a few
flower beds, but other than that I fully approved. Not that I had a

right to approve or disapprove, considering I might be leaving in the back of a police car, but a couple of rose bushes would be nice.

I knocked on the door, hoping she would be home and taking heart when I heard music coming from the house, hoping I wasn't making a major mistake, hoping I looked okay as I fluffed up the skirt of my dress—which was a modern-day version of the type that my sitcom heroine preferred. Just hoping.

Then she opened the door and my mind went blank. She looked amazing, and I was afraid I looked like a moron—and a stranger. I knew I would have to reintroduce myself.

She blinked a couple of times. "Hello, Christina. Why are you on my porch?"

Okay, no reintroduction. Also, no hope to just pretend that I was a Jehovah's Witness—I wouldn't need the *Watchtower* that I'd brought, just in case. I knew I should just explain to this woman why I was on her porch. I should have planned something, anything. Why did I suddenly feel like I was in front of a huge conveyer belt that was going by extra fast? And why did I think I would be telling someone at some point that it had "seemed like a good idea at the time"?

I had some 'splainin' to do.

Deenie stood there patiently. I noticed the collar on her blue chambray shirt needed straightening and my fingers itched to fix it—but I didn't want to be presumptuous.

"I work at the animal shelter—I used to work at a bank, but I quit there because I wanted to work with animals. Anyhow, you sent a check—but you know that—and it was really nice . . ." I faltered.

"You came here to thank me personally? It was only twenty-five bucks." She looked mock-perplexed, and very amused.

"Well, yeah, thank you, but that's not why I'm here. I'm here because you said I looked like that woman from the show. No, that's not it either. I'm here because—actually I have no idea why I'm here, other than it was great meeting you, and I left my husband. Not specifically because of you, that would be crazy. Then again, I'm standing on your porch, and that might seem crazy too.

Maybe we need to just let go of the whole discussion of my sanity."

"I wasn't the one who brought it up, and I haven't had a chance to say much. I'm not sure it's a discussion, in the strictest sense of the word."

"Right, sorry. Would you like to have a discussion? Maybe not about my sanity, but about anything? Books? Animals? Rose bushes? Reruns of old shows?"

"Would you like to come inside?"

"So you can call the cops? That's not necessary, I'll leave peaceably." I turned to go.

"No, so when I kiss you the neighbors won't stare."

I turned back.

"Still want to go?"

"Not so much, anymore."

She held her front door wide open. "Come in, Lucy."

"My name is—oh, right!" I walked inside. "You like me too, huh?" I asked as she closed the door.

She laughed and moved closer. "What makes you say that?"

"You're planning on kissing me, you knew my name after six months, *and* you remembered you told me I reminded you of you-know-who."

"Yeah, well, you still look like her, you're dressed like her, and you still have the same . . . um, personality. It would tend to jog one's memory." She ran her index finger along my bottom lip. "And kissing you just seems to be the best way to give your vocal chords a rest."

"So you don't like me a little?" I whispered.

"Nah, I like you a lot." She kissed me, and I knew then that every other kiss in my life had missed the mark completely.

"Wow, that was . . . wow!" All my nervousness melted away.

"Shhhh. I'm trying to concentrate." She lightly kissed the corner of my mouth. "Cherry LifeSavers," she murmured.

"You can taste it, huh?" I asked against her lips.

"Yes, and your tongue's bright red. I like it."

I pulled her closer, breathing in the clean, simple scent of her.

"Mmmm, get used to it, because I like LifeSavers and I love kissing you. I refuse to give up either one."

"You're getting pretty bossy all of a sudden," she said, running her hands down my back and onto my ass, making it clear who was in charge. My breath quickened.

She stepped back and took my hand, leading me to her bedroom. It was simple and uncomplicated, like the woman who slept there.

"Do you want this, Christina?" she asked, giving me a chance to turn back. I knew then I was right about her—she was someone who deserved and wanted all the things that I'd waited so long to give someone.

I sat down on the edge of the bed. "All my life." She smiled. God, I loved her smile, and the way it made her eyes light up.

She sat down next to me on the bed and caressed my cheek. "Since the moment I saw you, I knew we'd end up like this."

"Me too, and that's why I brought you a present."

"Honey, if it's *A Man for All Seasons*, I appreciate the thought, but disagree with the sentiment."

"Nope, no book, although I saw this one that claimed it was the ultimate guide to . . . well, another time." I stood up and slipped off my dress to reveal my heart-covered lacy bra and panties. "Happy Valentine's Day!"

"You're six months late, Lucy." She grinned and pulled me onto her lap.

"No, it's perfect! I spent February fourteenth with the wrong person, and it wasn't right at all—it's perfect that I should have my *real* Valentine's Day six months later. And I want to have Valentine's Day be our anniversary." I pouted.

"You seem pretty confident I won't strangle you in the next year. At least we won't have trouble getting a reservation. Very nice present, but I didn't get you anything."

"That's horrible! How will you ever, ever make it up to me?" I asked, teasing, even as I took her warm hand in mine and pushed it toward the wet between my legs.

She stroked me through the thin material of my panties for a moment, then slipped her fingers beneath the elastic. To touch my *very* wet heat. If I wasn't so damned horny I would have been embarrassed. Instead, I made a sound that could only be labeled as encouragement.

I loved being across her lap. The material of her jeans and shirt rubbed across my skin, and that, combined with her fingers, was driving me absolutely wild. There was something so erotic about the thought that I was really offering myself to this woman, allowing myself to be vulnerable in a way I'd never been before.

We'd spent so little time together, talked so little . . . yet, my trust in her was total, absolute, complete. My desire for her made me completely open to her—holding nothing back.

But I quickly learned she was ambidextrous. Much to my amazement and enjoyment. While one hand was doing truly magical things between my legs, the other deftly undid my bra.

She tossed it aside and it landed on a framed slingshot. I was about to ask her what she was doing with a framed slingshot when she started pumping two fingers in and out of me. I lost all sense of reason.

She pressed me down into the mattress, trailing kisses down my body. When she reached my belly, I tensed—wanting . . . willing her to go lower. And she did. *Thank God!*

It was amazing. My husband had gone down on me over the course of our marriage, but it'd never been as mind blowing and as exhilarating as this. Not even close. It was as if she cherished the femininity of me and had to show it by going to the source. I guess that might be sappy, but it's also true.

All my life I'd bought into the notion that I needed a man to complete me—that if the boy inserted tab A into slot B, I'd be a happy girl. Then why had sex before this moment made me feel empty and unconnected—wondering why I felt alone?

My friend, Asia, would say that Deenie had "mad skills." I actually went cross-eyed at one point. And uttered phrases that would be completely out of place in a black-and-white sitcom but flowed from my lips as fluidly as my desire. Fortunately, instead of getting my mouth washed out with soap, this only seemed to encourage my lover.

When I came to my senses, I realized I needed to somehow return the favor, but let's face it—I was functionally a virgin. And nervous all over again. As I was thinking about all of this, she slid her dampened face back up my torso and gave her lips back to me. She began to use her fingers again, and between that and her diligent attention to my nipples, she soon had me incoherent once more.

I was simultaneously thrilled and conscious that I still wasn't all together sure what to do. This is what I'd dreamed about for practically all my life—being with someone that really *got me*. Deenie not only *got* me, she *had* me for as long as she wanted.

I realized that all the nervousness was just more of the same old feeling not-quite-good-enough. I wouldn't carry that baggage into my future. Deenie had slipped out of her clothes. She was so beautiful, I began to tremble.

"Are you okay?"

I smiled and gazed into her beautiful eyes. "Never better!"

"It's fine if you want to stop for now. I know this is all new for you."

"I want to please you more than anyone else ever has before. Redheads are the jealous type, you know—and I won't be content until I've erased the memory of all other women. Show me how!"

"You're being bossy again," she said. Taking my hand, she began to show me. Soon I was immersed in the rich taste and scent of her. Later, she said I was a natural—and she wasn't just talking about the hair color!

Afterward, we cuddled together. "Would now be a good time to ask why you have a slingshot in a shadowbox on the wall?"

Deenie blushed for the first time since I'd met her. "My sister gave me that. When she was in seventh grade and I was in eighth, a couple of boys were picking on her. I knew I had no chance to whip them, but I also knew I was a good shot." Deenie shrugged. "Tracy kept it and gave it to me in the shadowbox as a housewarming gift. What are you grinning at?"

"That's just soooo sweet. And you gave money to the shelter."

I knew it was perhaps a little early to be proud of my girlfriend, but what can I say? She's amazing.

"Can we talk about something else?"

Amazing *and* modest.

"Okay, moving on . . . you said earlier I was being bossy, but I really only have one demand. You'll have to accept the men in my life."

"Excuse me?"

"Ricky and Fred."

"Tell me they're your gay best friends."

"I have my suspicions about Ricky, but I think Fred's straight. They're my dog and my cat. After I actually adopt Fred."

"Ah, okay. I accept your children."

"Good. Now, what's the number one thing you want me to support you on? I want to be a good girlfriend."

"I'm opening a coffee shop."

"Yep, I know!"

She stared at me.

"I'm not a stalker. I swear. Um . . . go on!"

"I play guitar, and I'd like to perform at the coffee shop. I would love your support."

"Of course! Hey, I sing a little. Can I be in your act?" I smothered a mischievous grin, and then gave an impromptu rendition of the *Brady Bunch* theme.

When she was quite through gaping, she asked, "You're kidding, right?"

"Why?"

"Lucy always wanted to be in her husband's show."

"Right, but she couldn't really sing, and I can."

"Uh-huh." She planted a kiss on the tip of my nose.

"No, really, I . . ."

"Don't make me have to spank you!"

Now, I can't really sing and I didn't really want to be in her act, but I'm no fool. So I asked again.

Takeoff
Cleo Dare

Jordi hated it when her boss stuck her with a travel assignment. Particularly because she'd gotten travel duty three times in the past two months and the anticipated travel period would include Valentine's Day. Not that she had anybody special to share it with since Deneene had left her at Christmas for a woman she'd met at a BDSM play party. Jordi was not as bold as Deneene. She certainly wasn't ever going to be bold enough to have *that* kind of sex.

"Aw, come on, George." She tried not to whine, but failed. "Give it to Susan. She's eager and she hasn't been out of the office in three months."

"No, Jordi. It's yours."

"Damn it, George. It's not fair. Where the hell is it anyway?"

"Albuquerque."

"Is that in the U.S.A.?"

"Don't be such a smartass, Jordi. I don't understand you sometimes." He stood up from the conference table, scowling and shuffling his papers into order. "Most people consider travel a perk."

Unable to help herself, she rhymed in her head, "and most people consider you a jerk." He glared at her almost as if he'd heard her thought. But she knew she'd lost the battle so she offered him a flat "whatever" smile before he turned on his heel, the flabby bulk of his butt shifting as he walked away. She stood up, slamming shut her own notebook.

Mary, the InServices corporate secretary, would have to make the travel arrangements for Jordi more or less immediately because the computer exhibitors conference was only a week away. She headed straight for Mary's office.

Fortunately, other than shipping the displays to Albuquerque, there wasn't much preparation involved, and Jordi had done it all a hundred times before. She knew when she made the request that Mary would remind her, as always, to save her receipts or the company wouldn't cover her travel costs. As if Jordi couldn't remember.

After finishing up with Mary, Jordi drifted back to her own office. What George would never understand—jetsetting playboy that he fancied himself—were the real reasons she hated travel: the days of enforced loneliness, the upheaval in her daily schedule, the small cruelties imposed by having to share close quarters with dozens of strangers ill-suited to each other, and the hurry-up-and-wait nature of airports.

Jordi was certain that somewhere in the corporate offices of the major airlines were sadists who manipulated schedules to ensure connecting flights landed at gates as far from each other as possible and that the time allowed to reach a connecting flight was calculated precisely to ensure that while the traveler could not actually complain, they would feel great anxiety about making their flight.

With all the new security since 9/11, there was the added pleasure of stripping down for complete strangers and being wanded while other complete strangers looked on. If that wasn't enough, there was always the potential thrill of being arrested or of experiencing the whole airport being shut down.

When the miserable day—a rainy, dreary Valentine's—arrived, Jordi packed her bags, and called a taxi. At the airport, she, of course, forgot to ask for a receipt, which meant $20 out of her pocket right up front. When Jordi returned, Mary would shake her thumb at her in her distinctive "I told you so" gesture.

The Houston airport was as she remembered it: dull grays and blues, as if the designer had somehow attempted to reconcile the opposite colors of the Civil War. All the little gourmet coffee stands and sales boutiques sported mixes of red and white carnations; some offered gigantic pink candy hearts on sticks for sale, but Jordi didn't think the color uplift was doing much for the airport and even less for her spirits.

Valentine's Day shouldn't be flaunted in the face of lonely hearts like herself, she decided. Disgruntled, she located her gate and plopped herself into an uncomfortable seat, mostly because there weren't any comfortable seats.

The sky outside the windows depressingly mirrored the gray and blue around her, and Jordi hoped there would be no difficulty getting the plane off the ground. The decor of the plane, too, she noticed when she boarded, was gray and blue. Was gray and blue supposed to be calming? Was that the idea?

Well, it wasn't. She wondered who designed the interiors of airplanes and noted, as she always did, how old the American fleet of aircraft was becoming, how cynical and bored the flight attendants were, and how unfriendly the faces of those already occupying seats were, as if to say, "I've staked out my territory; don't you try to take if from me."

Jordi located the number of her row, lifted her hefty carry-on into the overhead compartment, grabbed a blanket, banged her elbow on the way across the tall seats in front of hers to reach the window—wondering how travelers who weighed more than her lanky 115 pounds even got into the seats—and slid her attaché case beneath the seat in front of her, in compliance with the endless rant of the attendants over the intercom.

She glanced out the small scratched window and saw what she

always saw—miles of oil-stained concrete and men wandering around in orange safety vests who never looked busy but were apparently there for some purpose. She settled the blanket across her legs, pressed the recline button on her chair arm, and pushed back in her seat, closing her eyes.

Flying was a recurring nightmare she faced because of her job. She wasn't actually afraid of going up into the air; she was, instead, completely fatalistic about it. Very few planes crashed, but those that did tended to kill everyone. It was luck of the draw, and after the fifth flight she made for InServices, she just stopped worrying about it. There was nothing like familiarity to breed contempt.

There was a rustle to her left and Jordi's eyes flickered open. A woman was sliding across to settle into the seat beside her. She was broad-shouldered with olive skin and a mass of dark curly hair. She was a few inches shorter than Jordi.

"Hi," she said in a richly timbered, pleasant voice as she sat down. "They don't give us much room, do they?"

"No," Jordi replied, "they don't." It was impossible not to eye her seat partner. Her tight-fitting, maroon T-shirt showed off muscles that could only have been developed by power lifting, and high rounded breasts that were not large, not loose—even without the bra she didn't seem to be wearing—but just kind of no-nonsense and practical. Her black jeans fit snugly on what Jordi supposed were equally well-muscled thighs.

But it was the woman's smile that sealed the deal, and she choose that moment to turn its full wattage on Jordi. Certain of Jordi's body parts that had lain dormant for a long time sat up and took notice. Shit, she thought, and tried to return the smile but assumed it came off lopsided from lack of practice.

"So," the other woman said conversationally, "what's in Albuquerque for you?"

Jordi's ears relished the pleasing timbre of the other woman's voice. It was like soothing music. She laughed out loud with delight. It was a sound she hadn't heard from herself in a long time; it sounded foreign to her ears, certainly rusty, definitely forgotten.

She felt herself falling into the other woman's gray-blue eyes. Maybe she had been wrong. Maybe gray-blue was actually a rather attractive color.

"What's so funny?"

"Funny?" Jordi asked. "Was I laughing?"

"You most definitely laughed." The woman smiled again. She had a small dark mole just above her lip on the left side, which complemented her olive complexion. Jordi wondered if she was Greek or Italian or maybe Middle Eastern. Did people from those ethnic groups have gray-blue eyes?

The woman's brows drew together just slightly, but the smile remained and then took on a coy, questioning cast. "You're not saying anything."

Jordi was flooded with a sensation of sunshine and flowers, like a great wind had blown them into her body. It was impossible to fall in love in three seconds, she reminded herself. She knew that. Everyone over the age of 16 knew that.

"I, um . . ." Jordi felt as though she were floating. She knew the plane was still at the gate. It hadn't even started to taxi. People were still getting on board. She could see them coming down the aisle.

Whoa, she stopped herself and her runaway imagination. This was just a woman being pleasant. She probably wasn't even gay. That was when, glancing down, she noticed the Human Rights Campaign yellow-and-blue sticker on the carry-on the woman had stowed beneath the seat.

So what? Gay or gay-friendly didn't mean available.

"There," the stranger said in that deep sensual voice, pushing back her seat to match Jordi's, "that's better."

Jordi desperately wanted to hear more of that voice. "I could ask you the same thing," Jordi said, settling on a safe topic of conversation.

"What's that?" The woman's penetrating gray-blue eyes looked into hers again, and Jordi felt herself swimming.

Oh, God, she thought, feeling her breath come out in a pant, just take me here and be done with it. She forced herself to concentrate, afraid that the words she was thinking would spill unwittingly from her mouth.

"Um, what's in Albuquerque for you?" She prayed the answer wasn't "my lover." Although the woman was traveling on Valentine's Day, she wasn't exactly carrying flowers or candy. Of course the candy could be in the carry-on.

Hell, maybe she *was* available. Jordi knew her thoughts were tumbling around in a highly disordered fashion, but she had no idea how to stop them. What difference did it make if the woman had some other lover? They were hardly going to make love in the plane, were they?

"Training," the other woman replied.

Jordi calmed down and focused. "Really? What do you do?"

"I'm an aircraft mechanic."

"Wow! An aircraft mechanic? So you'd know how to fix this monster if it crashed?" Jordi gestured toward the rounded ceiling over their heads.

The other woman laughed, and Jordi felt a swirl of emotions start in her belly and move up into her chest. They were warm excited emotions. Desperate emotions of longing. And an even more desperate need for touching, for kissing, for being held. For love.

She had heard of people making out on airplanes, but she had never thought it happened to real, proper, cautious people like herself. Now it seemed like the most natural thing in the world. She imagined herself slipping her hand between the other woman's jeaned thighs and sliding it up to her crotch . . .

"Well," her seat companion said, still giggling, "not if it crashed! It would be a little late then, don't you think?"

"Huh? Uh, good point. You're right, of course." Jordi's face flushed.

"You still never told me why you're going to Albuquerque."

"Oh, trade show. My company designs specialized sales and inventory software for corporations. I have to man—woman, really—the exhibit."

"By yourself?"

"Yes. It's pretty easy to do. We ship the display by UPS and they deliver it to the site. I just set it up, demonstrate the possibilities, sign up customers, and Bob's your uncle."

"I actually have an uncle named Bob," the other woman said.

"Speaking of which," Jordi asked, "what's your name?"

"Sam." The woman turned those glowing eyes in her direction again. "Short for Samantha. You?"

Jordi loved the name immediately. Sam. It was tough, it was butch, but it was still playful. Playful and practical and unpretentious. Much like Sam's breasts, which Jordi wanted to cup her hands around. Maybe slide her thumbs over the nipples. They would become erect . . .

"Jordi," she said, extending her hand. To her shock, Sam raised it to her mouth and kissed it, instead of merely shaking it. Jordi melted in her seat, suddenly understanding why Victorian maidens fainted (besides the confining effect of their corsets, of course).

"Sorry." Sam smiled, placing Jordi's hand back in her lap on top of her blanket. "I couldn't help myself. If you want me to get another seat . . ."

"Oh, God, no." Jordi couldn't believe the pleading sound of her voice. Sam's ears perked up.

"So, you aren't minding the attention?"

Jordi's mouth was too dry for her to answer. The steward was in the aisle holding up a sample seat belt and explaining how to fasten it. Jordi knew he was talking but she couldn't hear him.

Sam raised the seat arm dividing them, extended Jordi's blanket to cover both of their laps and, reaching for Jordi's hand, brought it toward her and settled it on her thigh under the blanket. "Does that feel better?"

"Yes," Jordi whispered, feeling as though her hand had been

seared by its contact with Sam's jeans and she dare not move it, "but not nearly good enough."

"Indeed?" Sam's eyebrows raised.

A second flight attendant was coming down the aisle, checking to see that their seats were in the upright position for takeoff. If she suspected where Jordi's hand lay, she gave no indication.

The plane started to reverse from the gate. Sam's hand cupped Jordi's chin and turned her head toward her. Before Jordi could react, Sam's lips were descending to flutter lightly across hers. A moment later, their softness was pressed against her and she felt a swirl of dizziness as her body sank into the seat.

The flight attendant had stopped at their aisle. "You'll need to bring your seats forward for takeoff."

Sam disengaged herself from Jordi's lips and Jordi found herself looking up into the attendant's hard, unamused glare. She sat up and pulled her seat forward, wanting to straighten her hair, straighten her clothes, straighten her life perhaps even, but knowing it was impossible.

The flight attendant had moved on. The plane had turned and they were now bumping forward, lumbering toward the runway. Sam's finger was tracing a line down her arm.

"We should stop, really," Jordi said hoarsely. "I read an article about this."

"Really? About women making out on aircraft?"

"No. Just making out on aircraft. It's frowned upon. Some passengers have even been sued."

"Are you serious? All the way to fucking?"

"In some cases, yes." The word "fucking" made a flush of heat and a rush of wetness pool between Jordi's thighs. "Maybe in Albuquerque—"

"That's hours away," Sam whispered. "I want you here, right now."

The plane had come to a tremulous halt, as the pilot waited for permission to access the runway.

"There's no one else in Albuquerque, is there?" Jordi thought it was silly that she needed to know. This was hardly love, it was sexual desire. Well, of course, it *could* be love.

Oh, hell. Jordi's thoughts were in a whirl again. It was Valentine's Day, for Pete's sake. Did she have to put that much pressure on the day, on this other woman? Wasn't a little kissing and touching okay? Did she really need an Act of Congress to kiss a stranger on an airplane?

"Nobody there, nobody in Houston, nobody anywhere else." Sam's mouth was answering, but Sam's hand was already beneath the blanket, caressing the short sheath of black polyester that was Jordi's universal travel skirt.

Before Jordi could decide what she did or didn't want, Sam's hand had slipped beneath her skirt and was making its way toward the top of her thigh-high stocking.

Jordi turned to press her body against Sam's torso to hide her face. She was strung between lust and embarrassment, but the warm soft feel of Sam's body under her hands caused lust to win out. Sam's high, rounded breast was a quarter of an inch from Jordi's mouth and she grabbed the nipple, cloth and all, with her teeth and sucked it into her mouth.

"Uhh," Sam grunted in surprise. Her fingers were sliding along the several inches of naked flesh between Jordi's thigh-highs and the soaked cotton of her panties.

The captain's voice came indistinctly over the intercom, mumbling something about being cleared for takeoff. The plane lurched forward, then turned, entering the runway.

Sam's hand deftly shifted Jordi's panties aside, and her fingers sank into Jordi's heat and slickness.

"Oh, baby," Sam whispered, her fingers stroking up and down Jordi's soaked flesh, circling and pulling at Jordi's clit. Jordi moaned against Sam's breast, her hands clutching Sam's waist.

The plane accelerated down the runway, picking up speed for its impending leap from the earth. Sam's tongue was at Jordi's ear, flicking across the exposed sensitive ridges of cartilage. At the same instant that Sam's tongue entered Jordi's ear, her fingers slid deeply into Jordi's pussy.

The plane, roaring down the runway, performed the everyday miracle of liftoff, its wheels grudgingly releasing from the earth-bound concrete. Jordi, her body bucking into climax but constrained by her seatbelt, strangled a cry of exultation against Sam's shoulder, hoping the sound was lost in the vibratory noise of the plane's engines.

The plane continued to climb into the atmosphere until it leveled and Sam sensed Jordi's breathing had calmed. "Now that," she whispered, easing her dampened hand from beneath Jordi's skirt, "is what I call a takeoff."

Jordi's moist, happy eyes met hers. "Do you think they have candy hearts at the Albuquerque airport?"

"Probably. I think there's even a hotel."

"Indeed?"

"Yep. Maybe there's a Valentine's Day special."

"Umm," Jordi mused, "what we probably qualify for is the Mile-High Club special."

Sam laughed, her gray-blue eyes sparkling. "I'm not sure we qualify. We were hardly even aloft when you had your own version of a liftoff! But look," she pointed out the scratched oval window, "we're above the clouds now and—"

"—the sun is shining!" Jordi looked out, grinning from ear to ear.

"Happy Valentine's Day, Jordi."

"Happy Valentine's Day to you too, Sam." She gave this intriguing stranger, whom she most definitely wanted to know a whole lot better, a soft wet kiss on the cheek. She knew she would not find gray-blue, and certainly not flying—and hopefully not Valentine's Day—depressing ever again.

Valentine's Day Surprise
D. D. Cummings

My lover, Sophie, and I were celebrating our first Valentine's Day together, and I wanted to do something that would blow her mind. A coastal city girl, Sophie was wild and uninhibited, whereas I, coming from the farmlands of the Outback, was more on the conservative side. I decided it was time for me to change, to spice up my side of the relationship, and I knew just how to do it.

As I finalized the arrangements, I anticipated her reaction. She would be excited. Like a child, she would beg me to tell her where we were going, what I had planned, what I would do to her. I smiled to myself, my body tingling, knowing this would be a night we would both long remember.

I'd been with a few interesting women in the past, but no one could compare to Sophie. Her spontaneity, her zest for life, her passion with every project she undertook, and more importantly her love was overwhelming. She loved nothing more than surprising me, whether it was a home-cooked dinner or a trip to the mountains to ride horses and camp under the Australian sky.

She was attentive and considerate, a quality lacking in many of the women I'd dated. There wasn't a day that passed that I wasn't thankful for having met her. That was why today was so important to me. She had to know just how much I loved her.

I ordered a limo to take us to her favorite seafood restaurant. I'd requested a corner table in a secluded area that was thick with lush plants, and as we were shown to our seats every eye turned to stare at her. As she sat, she crossed her long legs, which made the front slit in her dress drop open to expose her luscious thigh. She winked at me knowingly. To me, Sophie is the most beautiful woman in the world. She loves attention and people admiring her sensational body, and I must admit, I love it too.

But tonight I wanted a bit of privacy for what I had planned.

She smiled across the table at me, her eyes sparkling mischievously. I hoped she had no idea what I was up to. There was no need to look at the menu or wine list. When the waiter came over, I ordered for us both—the garlic prawns appetizer and lobster entrée for her and a swordfish steak entrée for me. Her dinner preferences were one of the few ways she was predictable, and that's what I was counting on. Seafood made her horny, and I wanted her very horny. I watched her lips curve into a smile as the waiter poured glasses of Dom Perignon champagne.

"Mmm, I'm impressed," she said.

"So you should be," I whispered.

She wrinkled her nose, the bubbles from the champagne obviously tickling her nostrils. I opened my handbag and placed a gaily wrapped box before her. Eagerly, she ripped it open to find a red velvet box. Inside were the most exquisite diamond earrings I'd ever seen. Her face lit up, her eyes shining, brimming with unshed tears. She loved them as I knew she would, and I delighted in slipping them into her earlobes.

"They look beautiful on you," I said, kissing her neck.

"Oh, darling, I feel dreadful now. My gift can't compare to this, and you'll have to wait until we get home," she pouted.

Her berry-stained lips mesmerized me; for a second I forgot

where I was. I ran my fingers over the swell of her breasts and watched her tongue flick out at her top lip. She pursed her lips, smiling at my boldness as I carefully pulled down her décolletage, exposing most of her. A nipple peeked over the top of her lacy chemise. She held her breath as I flicked at it, watching it harden under my touch.

Her eyes darted about the room before she sighed with longing, her breasts rising and falling. I slipped my hand further inside, cupping her breast with my palm. I knew she was excited, excited by the risks I was taking in being so open, so demonstrative, in public.

The waiter was hovering with the garlic prawns. I watched a flush of color stain Sophie's neck as I asked him if he'd ever seen a more beautiful breast.

"No . . . er . . . no madam, indeed I haven't," he spluttered, as he laid the plates carefully in front of us.

Sophie ate greedily, giggling as the butter from her prawns dribbled down her chin. I devoured her looks lazily with my hungry eyes. A couple at a table nearby was whispering. I was sure they'd seen me slip out her breast, seen the waiter flush as I exposed and tweaked her nipple, but I didn't care. I was pleased to have them watching us, to have them see what they were missing out on.

She licked her lips, butter glistening in the corner of her mouth. I dabbed at the butter, letting my finger slip into her mouth. My pussy throbbed as she seductively sucked on my finger, her tongue rolling around while her eyes flashed over me. I whispered how much fun it was going to be to fuck her with the huge black dildo I'd bought her. As she threw her head back and laughed, I slid beneath the tablecloth.

"What . . . what do you think you're doing?" she gasped, shocked that I would be so bold.

I knocked her legs apart, and she eagerly inched herself forward so her arse was resting on the edge of the chair. Folding up her silky dress to expose a flimsy G-string, I heard her gasp as I pulled the fabric hard, ripping it away from her gorgeous pussy. I slipped the G-string into my pocket.

Her labia glistened with her juices as her fingers pulled the hood back over her clit, the nub already hard and inviting. Slowly, I licked her outer lips, leaving her clit alone. In and out of the folds my tongue danced, driving her wild. She pushed her pelvis forward, begging for me to nuzzle in, to drive her crazy like I always did, but tonight I wanted her to wait.

"Come on, baby," she begged, her juices flowing from her.

I lifted the cloth to show her what I'd been hiding in my other pocket—a diamond necklace to match the earrings. She gasped and nearly sat up, but I held her down.

"Oh, my God, let me see it," she begged.

"No."

"Please."

"Later," I whispered.

I began to inch the necklace into her hot pussy. As each diamond slipped inside, I pushed until it disappeared, with only the safety chain dangling from her. Now I licked at her clit, heard her moan and licked harder, my tongue zoning in on her before my teeth grazed and nipped at her flesh.

"Are you all right there, madam?" a man's voice said.

"Er, yes," she whimpered.

"Is there anything I can get for you? You look quite flushed." It was the waiter.

"She's just fine," I mumbled from beneath the table, my mouth never leaving her pussy.

He stuttered, and I heard him walk away quickly. Sophie half lifted the cloth, her chest heaving, a sure indication she was about to come. She squirmed on the chair as my finger rubbed her frantically. Just as her pussy began to contract, I stopped.

"Hey, not yet. Don't stop," she moaned. "I was just about to come."

"I know," I said, quickly slipping back into my chair and straightening my clothing.

Her hand flew down to finish herself off.

"No," I said, grabbing her arm. "You're not to come. You're to leave the diamonds there all night. If you don't hang onto them and they slip out, you can't have them."

"But baby, I need to come and I want to see them."

"Here, your lobster is coming. You'll have to wait and climax later." I chuckled as the embarrassed waiter placed our food in front of us. "Another bottle of champagne," I ordered, as he scurried away.

"What's gotten into you tonight?" she giggled.

"I thought it was about time I took charge. Made a few decisions."

"Hmm," she said. "I like the new you."

When the waiter returned, I made a point of sniffing my fingers as he opened the bottle. "Hmm, you smell delicious," I said, licking my fingers while he watched uncomfortably.

"I can't believe you did that," Sophie giggled.

I could barely take my eyes off her as we ate our meals and drank most of the champagne. Sophie's face was flushed. My hand slipped between her thighs. She was wet, very wet. I tugged at the safety chain, and she laughed. The couple at the next table was watching so I lifted the edge of the cloth up and placed it on the table. This way they could see Sophie's open thighs, her naked snatch, and, if they were lucky, perhaps even the twinkling of a diamond.

The man choked on his drink and his companion looked over, obviously furious when she saw what he'd been staring at.

"Would you like a taste?" I said, leaning toward her. "It's an acquired one. Just ask your husband. Once you've tasted pussy, you'll never want a cock again."

"How dare you!" she said.

She called for the waiter, but I dropped the cloth and looked stonily at her while Sophie asked for the check. "I've had enough," she said. "I just want to go home to bed, to give you your Valentine surprise."

As we strolled past their table, I lifted the back of Sophie's dress and ran my hand along the crack of her arse before giving her a light slap, then let the dress fall. I pulled the G-string from my pocket and dropped it onto the man's lap.

Looking over my shoulder, the outrage on the woman's face was comical, but it was the look of envy I noticed more on the face of the man. In the back of the limo, Sophie was all over me, tugging at my trousers, yanking them down far enough to grab at my G-string, trying to slip her fingers inside my pussy. I pushed her away, kissing her passionately, but this only inflamed her. She straddled my lap, freeing her breasts and thrusting them into my face, accidentally ripping her dress in her haste.

I sucked at a nipple, smacking her arse before running my fingers down her crack. She pulled me in closer, suffocating me in the process. The limo swerved, making me realize the driver was probably watching in the rear view mirror. Emboldened, I tugged at the chain dangling from her pussy.

"If I pull them out they're mine," I said.

She quickly sat back down, pouting as she did. I took her hand and smiled, wondering what she had in store for me. She loved to surprise me and even though I did a pretty good job of surprising her tonight, I was eager to experience my own.

She was out of the limo and up the steps to the front door before the driver could come around to assist her. I paid the driver and went inside. She slammed the door shut and was all over me, her hands touching and exploring, her mouth kissing, her teeth nipping at my mouth. She peeled off my silk shirt and crushed my massive breasts, smothering her face in my cleavage.

"Ready for your surprise?" she asked, pushing away from me.

"Yes," I said, disappointed she'd stopped.

"It's in the bedroom, on the bed. Quick, go look. I'll bring us in a drink."

Entering the bedroom, I saw two packages lying on the middle of the bed. I picked one up and tugged at the ribbons, then lifted the lid and found a set of handcuffs and a blindfold resting on a red satin pillow. The other package held a red lace teddy and a garter belt with stockings. A handwritten note instructed me to get changed, blindfold myself, and wait in the middle of the bed.

Smiling as I stripped out of my clothes, I glimpsed myself in the full-length mirror. I was tall, with voluptuous breasts and a great arse. When I was younger I'd wanted to be a model, but my breasts were so big that no one could ever get their eyes beyond them. I didn't care because I didn't want men ogling me anyway, so instead became a fashion designer. I spend all my time fitting women in sexy clothing. That's how I met Sophie.

As soon as I laid eyes on her a little over a year ago, I knew I had to have her. She was a runway model for one of my shows. There was an instant attraction, which isn't all that unusual when you work with models. The girls are all friendly and flirty, but with Sophie it was different. A spark ignited in me as soon as I touched her, and from that day on we've been together.

Finished with my reminiscing, I put on the garter belt and nylons, followed by the teddy. She'd made the perfect choice. The teddy was cut high on the side and low in the font. My breasts were practically spilling from the plunging décolletage, my nipples rigid through the fabric. My long black hair cascaded down over my shoulders and back, and I must admit I'd never felt sexier. The tease in the restaurant had me eager for more of her. Positioning myself in my must alluring pose, I blindfolded myself and lay back, hoping I didn't have long to wait.

"Hmm, very nice," Sophie purred, as she sat on the edge of the bed. "I don't want you to make a sound okay?"

"Uh-huh," I said.

"Shh! Not a sound. You're to do exactly as I say, and I will do exactly what I want. Understand?"

I nodded, pleased she was taking charge. I smelled the strong aroma of brandy as she brought a glass to my lips. I sipped the fiery liquid as it burned its way down my throat, inflaming my body and my desire. She spread-eagled my arms and cuffed me to the bed. I lay there waiting for what seemed an eternity. Music filtered through the intercom system. Then hands were roaming over my body, touching my curves, caressing my breasts, pulling the décolletage down further to totally expose my breasts.

I breathed deeply, loving the feel of her hands on me, enjoying the attention. The meal, the champagne, and now the brandy relaxed me further. I was in the mood for some sensual loving, and just as she tugged at my nipple, the other breast was attacked with ice. She had the cube in the palm of her hand and ran it over my flesh. I yelped from shock and cold, feeling my skin dimpling as the water dribbled under my arm.

"Shh," she whispered, "not a sound."

More ice was lavished across my torso, and then what felt like more than one pair of hands were roaming over me. Goose bumps covered me as I gasped for air. My skin was numb from cold so I wasn't sure what was going on. Her hot mouth attacked my cold nipple, bringing warmth and suckling me like an infant, drawing up my emotions, lulling me into a false sense of peacefulness before my legs were shoved apart. I heard the material of my crotch rip, and then ice was thrust inside my pussy. I wrestled against the hands, trying to pull my legs back together, but gave up quickly after a hard slap on the thigh.

I opened my mouth to scream, but a gentle finger on my lips reminded me of Sophie's command, so instead I pursed my lips together and uttered nothing. She slid ice against my lips, making me open my mouth so she could pop a small cube inside. It melted on the heat of my tongue. Then she dribbled more brandy down my throat, over my neck and breasts while she licked it all up.

I tugged at the restraints, wanting nothing more than to take her in my arms and ravish her with kisses. I desperately wanted to see if there was indeed another person in our bed and if so, who. How had she managed to organize this? Her tongue entered my mouth, then licked at my lips and chin before finding its way to my ear.

"I fucking love you, you horny bitch," she whispered, her tongue licking at my lobe, driving me insane.

It was wild. Fantastically erotic. The coldness of the ice and then the fire of the brandy was mind blowing. I was loving every second of it. Then her hands tugged at my teddy. I heard a loud rip as she tore it from my body. I lay there in only my garter belt and stockings.

Her fingers danced up and down that fleshy part of my thigh, the very top where the stocking ended, just grazing my pussy. I was crazy with desire, wanting desperately to tell her to hurry, to fuck me, to do whatever she wanted, and quickly. I pushed my pelvis upward, wanting her to finger me, but she held back, instead slapping my pussy hard, firing it up again before lashing it with more ice. The contrast of heat and cold was driving me crazy.

Now she was licking down my nylon-clad legs, sucking at my toes, which was something she never usually did. I dropped my legs open, my pussy gaping, begging for attention. I was desperate for everything at once, pleased as I'd always wanted her to suck my toes; pleased she was intent on pleasing me as I had pleased her earlier. Her tongue danced around my foot, over the instep, and then she was sucking my big toe into her hot mouth, rolling her tongue over it.

I wished desperately that my hands were free. I wanted nothing more than to finger myself, to pull the hood back over my clit and give myself a good rubbing. I was on the verge of coming, my pussy contracting as my juices began to flow.

I groaned, but stopped quickly. I didn't want to do anything to break the spell, to displease her. She kissed her way up the inside of my leg, stopping just before my pussy. I spread my legs further for her. I could feel her breath as her fingers pulled my lips apart. She slipped in more ice and then I think a finger or two. My lips were so numb, I wasn't quite sure of what she was doing, but the effect on my insides was fantastic.

Then she was climbing on top of me, her mouth licking and kissing, her hands touching me everywhere. She latched onto a nipple, sucked it into her mouth, while pinching the other cruelly between her fingers. I bit my lip, enjoying the pain as it turned into exquisite pleasure. My pussy throbbed with pleasure and longing.

Now she was back at my pussy, licking me, opening me up and devouring me, thrusting her tongue deep inside me. Her fingers found my clit and stroked that magical spot. I squirmed beneath her, enjoying everything she did, panting hard as my orgasm built.

Then suddenly she was over my face, pushing her pussy against my open mouth. I licked her, stretching my tongue, feeling the safety chain dangling from her. I'd nearly forgotten about the necklace, I'd been so caught up in what was happening to me. She ground her pussy against my face, almost smothering me. I tasted the sweetness of her and breathed in her scent. As she lifted herself from me, I grabbed the necklace with my teeth and felt the diamonds fall onto my cheek and slide off.

She moaned and thrust her saturated pussy against my face. I licked and sucked, lavishing into her. Suddenly another mouth was on my pussy. For a moment I just went with the flow, thrusting my pelvis up hard, wanting to be devoured and enjoying the fact that someone was giving me what had been my fantasy for years.

A threesome!

But then shock took over. Who was this person? I briefly thought of bucking her off, but Sophie was clearly into it too. And she was coming in my mouth. I sucked her greedily while my own orgasm built, and then my body arched and spasmed as I exploded into the mystery person's mouth.

Sophie, her juices dripping onto my chin and chest, maneuvered herself away. She attacked my breasts while this other woman continued to ravish my cunt. I'd never in my life been so turned on; orgasm after orgasm exploding from me, leaving me weak yet hungry for more.

Tugging at my restraints I wanted to beg to be freed, but I remembered Sophie's instructions so I gave up and tried to lay still, breathing hard but stifling moans, wanting desperately to at least see who had been eating me, giving me so much pleasure. I was drenched with perspiration, my body slippery and wet. Desperately thirsty, I nearly choked as Sophie poured more brandy into my mouth.

My mind was spinning, all my senses electrified. I felt the unmistakable head of a dildo against me. I allowed my legs to drop open. Who was wearing it, I wondered? I pushed into it, wanting my hands to be free, wanting to wrap my legs around the back of the woman fucking me. I did just that, digging my heels into the arse cheeks of my fucker. I spurred her on, loving every second of it. I could feel her hot breath against my neck, hear her grunting as she slammed into me again and again.

While I was being fucked so ferociously, my breasts and the rest of my body were ravished—pinched, slapped, and bitten. My out-stretched arms ached, the muscles sore, my wrists raw. I was almost out of my mind, my head thrashing about, trying to dislodge the blindfold. If only I hadn't tied it so securely! My mind spun with scenarios of who this person could be. Someone from work? One of the models? A call girl? Fuck, I couldn't believe Sophie had done this. The suspense was killing me.

It seemed like hours before my ravisher and I shuddered with mutual orgasms as she collapsed against me, my body sated, my pussy saturated. Slowly, she moved off of me as the handcuffs were removed and the blindfold untied. My arms ached, shaking with tension, while my legs felt weak, like jelly. My eyes smarted from the sudden light. I blinked, quickly trying to adjust as I scanned the room. There was no one in here, except me and Sophie. Her face shone with happiness, her eyes sparkling with pleasure.

"Surprised?" she laughed.

"Where . . ." I began.

"Shh," Sophie said, the dildo still strapped to her.

"Who . . ."

"No questions, okay?"

"But—"

"This is my surprise, and if you want one just as good next year, then don't ask questions."

"But—"

I watched her unstrap the dildo. I wanted to take it and fuck her brains out with it, but I was so exhausted. The bed was rumpled, the room in total disarray. I wondered for a second if I'd been imagining things. Had there been more than one other person? Surely not? I wished she'd videotaped it, wished I could see it all played back, relive it again.

"Baby—" I began.

She silenced me with a kiss. "I'm exhausted. Happy Valentine's Day, darling," she purred, snuggling into me.

I held her, my love for her overwhelming. How on earth had she managed to do this? My hand strayed over her breast and she sighed with pleasure. She cocked her leg over my hip, and my fingers sunk into her wet cunt. She smiled as she muttered how much she loved me, the words slowing as exhaustion took over.

Her breathing slowed. I felt the diamond necklace cold against my thigh. As I too drifted off to sleep, I heard the faint sound of a door closing. Smiling to myself I wondered how Sophie could ever top this Valentine's Day surprise.

Fantasy Valentine
Denny Evans

Steph barged through the office doors. She didn't need to look at her watch; she knew she was late again. Avoiding the glaring eyes of her supervisor, she hurried down the aisle between the long rows of partitioned desks to her section in the large, open office.

"Is she coming?" she puffed, plonking down behind her desk, opposite her best friend and colleague.

"No, you're safe," said Sue, stretching her neck to look round the partition. "She's been distracted. Looks like the new temp has spilt coffee over her keyboard; but honestly, Steph, you're gonna lose your job one of these days if you don't watch it."

"It wasn't my fault this time. There was a queue in the lingerie shop from here to Tokyo. You know, it never ceases to amaze me how many men storm the lingerie shops on their lunch break looking for a sexy Valentine gift, yet don't even know the size of their own wives' tits."

Sue burst out laughing. "What makes you think they're buying for their wives? Anyway I thought you were going to get Hazel something different this year?"

"I am," said Steph, grinning from ear to ear. "This," she said, holding a skimpy silk chemise against her chest, "is only part of her present."

"Hmm, very sexy, but isn't that more for your benefit than hers?"

Steph raised her eyebrows with a cheeky grin. "Nothing wrong with spicing things up a bit."

"And what's the other part of her present then, dare I ask?"

"That would be telling, wouldn't it?"

"Oooh, sounds naughty."

Steph grinned again, "It is! It's what you might say, naughty, but very, very nice."

"Oh shit, the old bat is coming our way. Quick, put that thing away before we both lose our jobs."

On her way home, Steph made one last final call to an old friend from what she would call her "wilder" days.

"Hi, it's me again. Everything still set for tonight? You know what you have to do? You won't let me down, right? Okay, I'll see you at seven."

Steph was pleased when she saw Hazel's car in the driveway. She laughed to herself, "Yep, that's my babe. It's Valentine's Day, and she's left work early, impatient as ever to see what I got for her. Probably been searching through the whole house."

Hazel must have heard the car door slam because she opened the front door before Steph even had chance to put her key in the lock.

"You took your time. I thought you were never going to get here."

"You're early, though I can't imagine why," Steph teased.

"You know why, you bitch. Come on, hand it over. Where is it?"

Steph stood tall and laughed as Hazel frisked her up and down. "If you carry on like this on the doorstep, we just might get arrested."

Hazel laughed as she pulled Steph into the house and slammed the door shut. "Now, you tease," she said, kissing Steph all over her face, "I know you've got something for me. Come on, where is it?"

Steph let her oversized, tatty shoulder bag slip down her arm and onto the floor.

Hazel's eyes gleamed. "Ahh!" She grabbed the bag, ran to the sofa, and started rummaging through it.

Steph figured Hazel knew it would probably be lingerie again. She herself would be the first to admit she wasn't exactly imaginative when it came down to surprises, but Hazel never seemed to mind. Her heart warmed as she watched how Hazel excitedly pulled the brightly wrapped box out of the bag. It was red, of course.

"Hmmm, what could this be?" Hazel said, with an impish smile. She opened the box and gently took out a delicate, cream-colored, lace-edged silk chemise. "Oh, Steph, it's lovely. Thank you." She stood and wrapped her arms around Steph, pressing her body close to kiss her warmly. "You spoil me."

Steph slid her hands down Hazel's back and caressed her buttocks, pulling her even closer. "You know how much I love you, don't you?"

"I think I'm getting the picture," Hazel teased.

"Well, I hope you have the picture babe," Steph said, sliding her hands farther down under Hazel's buttocks, "because tonight is going to be a very special night."

"Hmm, don't tell me you've finally gone and bought that new fan-dangle dildo that can do everything except the washing up."

Steph burst out laughing. "No babe, something much better."

"God! Now I'm really curious."

"Tonight, *ma chérie*, I have arranged to make your very own fantasy come true."

"*My* fantasy?" asked Hazel, wide-eyed.

"Yep," said Steph, enjoying the look of disbelief on her babe's face. "For the next few hours, just like in the fantasy you told me about, your body will no longer be your own. From this moment on," she continued with a quick kiss, "you are no longer Hazel, the receptionist, you are Hazel, the sex slave."

Hazel stared at her with bewilderment. Steph winked, thoroughly enjoying the moment. She had finally succeeded in giving Hazel a gift she had not expected.

"Your Mistress will be arriving in due time to come and take her pleasure from you, and I, just like in your fantasy, am going to prepare you for her."

Hazel appeared completely dumbstruck. Fantasy was one thing, but reality was something else. Steph smiled as she kissed Hazel's forehead, anticipating her thoughts. But this is what her babe had always fantasized about, and now Steph was gonna make it come true.

"It's time for us to start the preparations." She took Hazel by the hand and led her to the bathroom. "I want you to strip."

Hazel hesitated but obediently stripped and stood perfectly still as Steph eyed her up and down.

"You sure are one hell of a beauty, babe, that's for sure."

Steph cupped Hazel's soft, pear-shaped breast and sucked on its pink nipple until she felt it harden in her mouth.

Hazel moaned. "Ooh, you know how horny that makes me."

"That's just a taste of what's to come."

Steph turned on the shower and quickly discarded her own clothes. "After you," she said, signaling Hazel to step into the shower cabin.

Hazel stood with her face tilted to the refreshing spray of warm water, groaning softly as Steph kissed down her spine and bit gently into her rounded buttocks. "Mmm, you're making me more wet than I already am."

"Just remember, this is your fantasy and you are to do exactly as you are told. Do you understand me?"

Hazel nodded in submission.

Steph rubbed rose-scented soap between her palms and glided them down, around Hazel's shoulders, caressing the curves and hollows of Hazel's perfectly formed body down to her feet and back up to her thighs. Hazel opened her legs and curved her back, pushing her buttocks into Steph's lathery hands. She gasped as Steph rubbed gently between her legs. She arched her back even more, seeming to will Steph to rub harder and glide her slippery fingers inside her.

"Not yet, my lovely. You're gonna have to wait. Remember, you are no longer in control. Now, get dried off, then go sit on the bed and wait for me."

Within a couple of minutes, Hazel was sitting naked on the bed, waiting as she'd been instructed. Wearing nothing more than a semi-transparent, light-blue shirt, Steph entered the bedroom, then walked over to the dresser and took out a Lady Shave.

"You're gonna shave me?"

Steph stood over her with a mischievous grin. "It's your fantasy, remember? Now, lie back and spread your legs."

Without further objection, Hazel did as she was told. Steph looked down, smiling as the warmth of arousal stirred in her lower regions. "Now, that's what I call a pretty sight."

She knelt down between Hazel's open thighs and began, with careful precision and much delight, to remove the curly auburn hair that concealed the succulent and hidden fruits of her babe's female sex. Hazel squirmed beneath her touch, a low moan escaping from her lips.

When the last hair was gone, Steph leaned back on her haunches to admire her handiwork. Arousal throbbed between her legs. She pressed hard against her own sex to ease its ache, but temptation overcame her. *Just one kiss for good luck, then. I deserve that much at least*, she thought. She leaned forward and pressed her open mouth onto her babe's soft, naked labia, fighting back the temptation to pop her tongue just a little way in to taste the hidden nectar within. Hazel groaned and shifted forward, but Steph pulled back.

"Sorry babe, sometimes you have to be cruel to be kind."

"Was that it? You make me as horny as hell and then leave me like this?"

Steph winked at her. "Something like that." She nodded at the freshly shaved pussy. "Looks nice, doesn't it?"

Before Hazel had chance to say anything, Steph disappeared from the bedroom. Within a couple of minutes she returned to find Hazel lying on the bed with her knees bent and legs apart, softly stroking the smooth naked flesh of her hair-free pussy.

"How does it feel?"

"Incredibly sensual," she said, beckoning Steph to her.

The sight was almost too much for Steph. She wanted to go down on her there and then, but no, she had to be disciplined, she had to play the game. She had set things in motion and she had to see it through. She held up the chemise.

"Come on slave, it's time to dress for your Mistress. This is gonna look just great on you."

Hazel sat meekly on the bed as Steph dressed her in the low-cut, fine silk chemise, held in place with delicate ties on her shoulders. Steph then brushed Hazel's long, auburn hair and arranged it seductively around her face. She kissed her tenderly on her mouth. "We're almost ready, babe, but we'll wait a few more minutes before giving it the final touch."

Steph knew she had only ten minutes to spare before the Mistress arrived, so she quickly set about rearranging the position of the bedroom chair to the exact requirements of Hazel's fantasy. She dragged the chair out of the corner and shoved it to within two feet of the bed, directly opposite to where Hazel sat on the edge of the bed.

She couldn't help but smile at the expression on Hazel's face as she stared at the chair in front of her. It was as if she could hardly believe this was happening. For years she had told Steph about this fantasy, but now that it was really happening she didn't seem so sure.

"What if this all goes wrong, Steph? What if she doesn't even like me? What if I don't like her?"

Steph stroked her hair. "Don't be nervous, babe, just enjoy it. Do exactly as you do in your fantasy and everything will be all right."

"But Steph, will you really be able to cope with it? I mean, won't you get jealous? You know how you can get when someone else so much as looks at me."

Steph knelt in front of Hazel, cupped her face in her hand and kissed her softly. "This is my very special Valentine's Day gift to you, and I'm pretty sure you're gonna love it. If you don't, then we'll stop. Okay?"

Hazel nodded.

They heard the sound of a car pulling into the driveway. Steph took a deep breath and smiled. "Our guest has arrived. Now we can complete our preparations with the one last final touch."

She slipped her hand under Hazel's flimsy garment to pinch and pull hard on both nipples, making them stiff and erect. Hazel gasped, then let her breath out, long and slow.

"That's much better," Steph said, taking a step back to admire the overall effect. The soft silk fell around the curves of Hazel's sexy breasts and enhanced her hard, protruding nipples. Steph smiled, nodding her approval.

"You're a real temptress—the picture of seduction. I'm sure your Mistress will be more than pleased."

She leaned down to kiss her one more time before leaving the room to go collect their Valentine guest.

Steph beamed from ear to ear as the Mistress threw down her coat. "You look fantastic."

The Mistress did not reply to the compliment. Her face remained stern. "Take me to her."

Steph led the way down the hallway, smiling at the click of their guest's stiletto-heeled boots against the parquet floor. She knew Hazel would hear it too. Things were going according to plan and it felt good.

Steph entered the bedroom first, turned, and bowed to the figure behind her. "I bid you welcome, Mistress. Your slave is ready and waiting to please you."

Hazel sat bolt upright on the bed as the long-legged, latex-clad, goddess of desire strode purposefully into the room—a powerful figure of female seduction and unharnessed eroticism. Her full, rounded curves were exaggerated by a skin-tight, corseted outfit held together by crisscrossed laces, from her ample cleavage down to her crotch. The material was so tight, you could almost see the outline of her labia. Her face was partially covered with a cat-like mask that revealed only her piercing, predatory eyes and inviting, glossy, sensuous lips. She stood boldly with legs apart, her left hand on her hip, her right hand clutching a short leather whip.

"Is she ready?" Her tone was harsh.

"Yes, Mistress," said Steph. "Ready and waiting to serve you."

Hazel shrank against the bed as her Mistress walked over to scrutinize her for what seemed like an eternity. She looked down at Hazel's breasts, resting her eyes on the hard, tempting nipples poking against the silk. She placed the handle of the whip under Hazel's chin and pushed her head backward, then from left to right.

"She has good looks at least."

"Thank you, Mistress," said Steph. "I'm glad you approve."

Without taking her eyes off Hazel, the Mistress took one step back and sat down in the well-positioned chair. "Show me," she commanded.

Steph moved forward to release the shoulder ties of Hazel's chemise. The flimsy silk fluttered down to rest in folds around Hazel's waist. The Mistress stared silently at her, then reached out with her whip to slowly trace the outline of the firm, plump breasts in front of her. She stared into Hazel's hesitant eyes and flicked her whip sharply back and forth across Hazel's nipples.

The whip stung like a bee, but Hazel didn't flinch or make a sound, save for a quickly indrawn breath. Faint red marks appeared on the pale skin around her erect nipples. The Mistress sat motionless, watching for a moment before reaching out once again to flick Hazel's nipples even harder and faster with the tip of her whip. The whip felt sharp and cutting, but the feeling sent a wave of excitement through Hazel's body. Yet she managed to sit perfectly still before her Mistress, her nipples stinging and burning red as animal lust coursed through her body and made her pussy throb.

The Mistress settled back in the chair and continued to stare at her.

"Very nice! Show me more."

Hazel knew exactly what she had to do. Sitting straightbacked with her knees still pressed firmly together, she began to roughly caress her own breasts. She squeezed and lifted her breasts up in offering to the Mistress sitting so menacingly before her. Her Mistress' deep breaths made her full breasts heave, emphasizing her cleavage in the tight corset. Exhilaration surged through Hazel's body, whirling round inside her stomach before burning its way down to between her legs. The awakening sensation made her want to lift and knead her breasts even harder and pull her sore, red nipples tantalizingly toward the demanding eyes.

Her Mistress drew in a sharp breath as she forced her whip between Hazel's knees, pushing one leg away from the other. She purred as she caught a glimpse of Hazel's exposed sex. Almost impatiently, she flicked her whip from thigh to thigh, urging Hazel's legs wider apart. She gulped in air and let out a ragged breath, as she sat and savored the sight of Hazel's well-prepared, shaved mons. She reached out again with her whip to slowly caress the glistening lips, running its tip up and down the partly open slit, sending visible shivers of ecstatic delight through Hazel's body.

The Mistress brought the whip to her nose and breathed in its mingled aroma of leather and sweet female musk. She stared at Hazel, who stared back, all the while continuing to play seductively with her breasts. The Mistress placed the handle of the damp, sweet-smelling whip against Hazel's closed mouth.

Hazel automatically opened her mouth and closed her lips around it. She tasted leather and her own juices as she demonstratively sucked and licked the instrument of dominance. Any leftover feelings of apprehension disappeared as she felt the heat and wetness spread between her legs as erupting torrents of passion exploded within her.

The Mistress withdrew her whip, watching as Hazel continued to squeeze and pull on her breasts while she spread her legs even wider. Hazel licked her lips, liking the way it made the Mistress gasp. The Mistress smiled and reached out again with her whip, flicking it sharply against Hazel's thighs, leaving a trail of tiny red blots as she worked her way up to the sensitive folds of flesh. She breathed in sharply, flicking rapidly against Hazel's tender, reddening lips, then flipped her wrist so the handle of the whip once again slid up and down Hazel's throbbing split.

As the whip came to her mouth again, Hazel opened her lips to willingly accept the leather rod, sucking and licking without shame, staring defiantly into the sultry eyes of her Mistress. Thrills of excitement rushed through her, overwhelming her senses as she sucked and licked even harder, reaching as far as she could with her tongue along the hard, leathery shaft, seducing and tantalizing the latex-clad temptress before her.

The Mistress groaned deeply. "Show me more!"

As if on cue, Steph stepped up to Hazel and kissed her passionately, thrusting deep with her tongue and then biting Hazel's lips. Hazel groaned as she thrust her tongue deep into Steph's mouth. Abruptly, Steph pushed Hazel onto her back, then straddled over her with her back to her so she could push Hazel's legs wide apart, exposing her babe's bare sex.

Hazel fought the instinct to close her legs, letting herself stay wickedly wide open to this powerful stranger in front of her. She trembled and gasped as she felt Steph's fingers on her outer labia, pulling them farther apart to fully expose her throbbing, wet cunt.

Hazel could hear the Mistress breathe heavily and the unmistakable sound of friction against latex as she shifted in her chair. It pleased her to imagine the Mistress running the whip between her own legs.

"Give me more!" the Mistress hissed.

Hazel gasped as Steph gripped her slippery, swollen lips and pulled them even wider apart to expose her stiff clit and wet, glistening hole.

She heard the clatter of the whip on the floor, then felt the Mistress push Steph's hands aside as she gripped Hazel's legs and thrust her tongue deep into Hazel's cunt, licking and sucking hungrily. Shocks of ecstasy exploded deep within her. All thought and reason fled from her mind, leaving her only the sensation of the tongue that flicked and whirled around her clit, then glided down through her valleys to thrust its way deep inside her wanting hole. Hazel, crazed with lust, grabbed Steph's hips, pulling her back over her gasping open mouth. Steph quivered as Hazel's tongue searched hungrily through her folds for the hard, protruding clit.

Steph leaned back, digging her fists into the bed as Hazel sucked and licked frantically in rhythm to the Mistress's thrusting tongue. Hazel was soaring, her lust intensifying with every throb of the hard clit in her mouth, her mind swimming in the sweet scent of female musk, her skin tingling with the wetness that drenched her hungry mouth and trickled down her chin. She groaned deeply into the dripping cunt as she felt the sharpness of the Mistress's long manicured nails against her wide-open thighs and the sound of her groans with every forceful thrust of her tongue. There was no today, no tomorrow—there was only now, this moment of pure, unadulterated, lustrous pleasure.

She dug harder into Steph's buttocks and rammed her tongue as hard as she could into her hot, dripping hole.

Steph gasped. "Fuck . . . Jesus."

Hazel felt resistance as Steph's muscles clenched tight around her tongue, but she would not be resisted, she was ravenous. Driven by the relentless surging power of the Mistress, she drove her tongue harder and faster in and out of her lover's cunt.

Steph groaned from the pit of her stomach, rocking back and forth against Hazel's greedy tongue. "This is fucking hot stuff, babe, go for it honey, if this is what you want, take it, take what you want baby."

Hazel was losing control. Her legs started to tremble; she couldn't control it. A powerful, uncontrollable force was taking over her body, making her hips move up and down in unison to the Mistress's relentless tongue.

Steph cried out between panting breaths, "Hold on babe! Make it last. Hold on girl!"

Hazel tried desperately to distract herself, tried to contain the overwhelming ecstasy, but the woman between her legs ravenously sucking and licking, slurping and drinking, made it impossible. She screamed against Steph's sex, slurping and gulping down the sweet juice that flowed into her mouth, digging her heels into the bed to lift and force her pelvis harder against her Mistress's mouth, begging for release.

The Mistress pulled back, then flicked her whip against Hazel's inner thighs and red-hot cunt. It stung. It hurt. Flashes of pain bit through Hazel's consciousness and transformed into unrelenting ecstasy. She felt the wetness flow from her as the intensified sensations took hold and shook her whole being. Her body still trembling, she felt the Mistress's mouth and tongue once again eat her up.

The mistress, panting and gasping, pulled back again, then jammed two long fingers into Hazel's cunt.

Hazel's pulse raced. She felt dizzy, breathless. Beads of sweat broke out all over her body. Her muscles clamped tight around the fingers, her body crying out for more, crying for release. She felt the fingers against her G-spot. She couldn't breathe . . . she wanted it to stop . . . she wanted it to carry on . . . she hated it . . . she loved it. Brutally, the Mistress shoved a third finger, then a fourth, into Hazel's gaping hole. She pushed her hand in and out, unrelenting in her goal. Hazel moaned against Steph's pussy. She wanted to scream. The pain was excruciating, yet exhilarating. Her mind pleaded for it all to stop, yet her body craved more. She felt the gush of wet flow from her swollen, throbbing cunt. She gasped for air. Steph groaned as she ground her cunt against Hazel's face, her trembling release sending a flood of wet into Hazel's hungry mouth.

Hazel couldn't feel her own body any more. It had been taken over. It was no longer flesh and blood—just a cunt, hot, wet, demanding, hungry for release. She was dying. She was drifting, sounds and visions blurred into nothingness. She was floating higher and higher. There was no air, no breath. Her legs quivered, her vagina clenched. Sweat seeped out of every pore. She was going, she didn't know where, she was almost there, almost . . . Her cheeks flushed, her eyes closed.

"*Petit mort*," she whispered as her body tensed one last time before slumping into total relaxation.

The Mistress groaned, still drinking the juices that flowed from Hazel's hot, sore hole.

Hazel couldn't move . . . couldn't feel. Her body floated somewhere high and far away. When had Steph moved? She didn't know. It was all a blur, but Steph was beside her now, gently caressing and kissing her back down to earth. She slowly opened her blurry eyes to see the tall, dominant figure standing before her.

"Come on slave," the Mistress said, sitting back in the chair and opening her legs wide. "You're not finished yet!"

Hazel struggled to a sitting position and stared into her Mistress's eyes. Her eyes fell to the full, rounded, heaving breasts bulging out of their corset, stretching the crisscrossed laces to almost breaking point. She followed the laces down to the wide-open thighs and watched as her Mistress stroked seductively between her legs. She felt warmth spread once again between her legs as an overwhelming animal passion erupted inside her. She stared deep into the lustrous eyes of the demanding woman before her. Yes, Hazel wanted her and she was going to take and tame this powerful creature of wanton desire. She rested her eyes on the deep, sweat-moistened cleavage as she knelt down to seductively release the strings of the tight corset. She could feel the burning eyes of her Mistress staring down at her as the luscious breasts heaved under her hands.

A trickle of sweat ran tantalizingly down the deep cleavage. Hazel purred and leaned forward to lick up the salty moisture. The full breasts were soft and heavy against her cheek. She wanted them—she wanted to feel them in her hands, to take them in her mouth and devour them. Her clit tingled and throbbed and wetness flowed between her legs as an animal urge made her rip the corset open. The Mistress gasped as her naked tits with their hardened nipples fell into Hazel's hands. Hazel moaned and caressed the soft flesh, teasingly circling the large pink nipples. The Mistress quivered under her touch and arched her back, coaxing Hazel to take her in her mouth. Hazel could feel the Mistress's need, but she was in control now and she was going to make her wait. She stepped in closer between the woman's spread legs and rubbed her thigh against the wet glistening cunt. The Mistress groaned and shifted forward, pressing her clit harder against Hazel's thigh and digging her stiletto heels into the floor to lift and thrust her pelvis up and down. Hazel pulled her leg back, savoring and relishing the changing expression on the Mistress's face. It was almost one of agony. More and more wetness flowed down her thighs as she felt a rising sexual power over this dominant figure of female seduction.

The Mistress wrapped her leg around Hazel's thigh, trying to pull her back against her aching clit, but Hazel resisted and smiled mischievously. She was going to make her beg.

She placed the tip of her tongue at the lowest part of the sweat-soaked cleavage and slowly traced up and around the soft female form. She could taste the salty sweat and feel the heat against her face as she teasingly outlined and brushed her tongue softly over the hard nipples.

The Mistress whimpered and threw her head back. "Suck me, suck my tit."

Hazel took the nipple in her mouth and softly grazed her teeth along the delicate skin before flicking rapidly with her tongue. The Mistress squirmed in her chair and cried out again, "Suck me, suck me now."

Hazel closed her mouth around the nipple, sucking softly at first, enjoying the tease and every agitated squirming movement of the woman now in her grip. The goddess screamed for more.

Hazel moaned as she sucked harder. She could taste the sweat, smell its female scent, feel the nipple harden and grow in her mouth. This woman, who had so mercilessly taken her, was now in her power. She was the fuel for the flame, and Hazel was going to have her!

The Mistress panted and gasped. She shifted down in her chair, opening her legs as wide as she could.

"Now!" she screamed. "Give it to me now!

Hazel looked over to Steph, who was breathing heavily and rubbing her pussy in excitement.

"I'm going to fuck her."

Steph knew exactly what Hazel wanted. She fastened a harnessed dildo to Hazel's hips and filled her open palm with lube. The Mistress slid down further in the chair with wide-open, trembling legs.

"Now! Damn you, give it to me now!"

Hazel smiled. She heard the command, but she wouldn't be rushed. She was enjoying making her wait, having this powerful woman who was now at her mercy. She stared at her, taunting her as she rubbed lube up and down the phallic shaft. She held it firmly in her hand, letting it become an extension of herself.

The Mistress panted desperately, pushing her hips further toward the shimmering cock. "Give it to me!"

Hazel smiled as she rubbed the hard knob against her throbbing clit. The Mistress screamed and gripped Hazel's arms, her body heaving and jerking. "Fuck me!"

Hazel stared into her pleading eyes as she plunged into the Mistress's wet and hungry cunt. Her pulse raced to the sound of ecstatic cries as she thrust harder and faster with every stroke. Words screamed through her head that she dare not speak—*I have the power. I will fuck you. I will take you.*

The Mistress cried out, and grabbed Hazel's hair as her body began to tremble and shake uncontrollably. Hazel thrust harder and faster, with wild unleashed animal lust. Her body was drenched with sweat, her pelvis jerking with sharp, hard pounding thrusts into this now powerless woman. The woman gasped for breath, her open thighs closing around Hazel as her body shook violently to its ultimate release.

Hazel pulled out and put her mouth to the Mistress's swollen pussy to drink the orgasmic juices flowing from her. She licked and slurped and sucked until she felt the trembling legs grow still. Then she fell sweating and panting onto the bed.

The Mistress stayed slumped in her chair, her legs splayed out. "Now that's what I call a good fuck!"

Hazel giggled as she undid the harness and pulled Steph down onto the bed. "Now, that's what I call a real surprise present!"

"Did you enjoy your self, babe?"

"What do you think?" Hazel asked, as she placed Steph's hand between her soaking, wet thighs.

Steph laughed, kissing Hazel's sweaty forehead.

The Mistress rose unsteadily to her feet. "Well, looks like my job's finished, hey Steph? I'll think I'll get going and leave you two lovebirds to it." Steph made a move to get up but her friend stopped her. "Don't worry about me," she said, moving toward the door. "I'll just freshen up, then I'll let myself out."

"Thanks for everything. You were just great."

The Mistress winked at Hazel. "Believe me, the pleasure was all mine."

Hazel felt her cheeks redden and hid her face behind Steph's back. Steph laughed, pulling her in closer.

"Who was that woman?" Hazel asked.

"Oh, just an old friend from way back."

"Hmm, got anymore old friends?"

"No way. Over my dead body, babe."

Hazel laughed and kissed her warmly. "No worries. There's only one woman in my life."

Steph gently rolled on top of her and returned her kiss. "I love you," she whispered tenderly into Hazel's ear.

Hazel bit softly into Steph's neck. She could feel the racing pulse and the heat of her body. She traced the contours of her ear with her tongue, then sucked softly on its lobe. "You want me?"

Steph groaned softly. "You're not too tired?"

"For you, never!"

Steph lovingly kissed her neck, shoulders, and cleavage. She caressed and kissed her generous breasts before taking a swollen nipple in her mouth. Hazel groaned and arched her back. "I want you," she whispered.

Steph reached into the bedside cabinet to take out Hazel's favorite dildo, soft and pink. Hazel lay on her back and opened her legs wide to welcome her lover, groaning deeply as her partner, lover, and true friend entered her gently. She wrapped her legs around Steph's waist, and together they moved through time and space to the rhythm of their passions, climaxing together in an ultimate expression of their love.

"Happy Valentine's Day, Steph."

"Happy Valentine's Day, Hazel."

Valerie's Valentine
Sue Molyneaux

Valerie's wrists ached from all the typing she'd done that day, but Mrs. Galloway was a strict boss. If the report was not on her desk by the end of the day, as she had asked, Valerie wouldn't be back the next day. She sighed as she twitched her neck to get a little crack out of it, but never took her fingers from the keyboard. Valerie blinked a few times at Mrs. Galloway's handwritten scrawl, and quickly looked at the computer clock. Five minutes to five, almost quitting time, but it would be at least another hour before she got home. Snow had turned to sleet and hail, and judging from the way it pelted the windows, driving would be slow going.

Valerie didn't like working for Mrs. Galloway, but as a temp she had little choice about where to work. It was good money, and after her break-up with Sally on New Year's Eve, she needed the money. Good old Sally—caught messing with an unnamed blonde in the bathroom at the party. Valerie still couldn't believe how unapologetic Sally had been—five years wasted for a bleached blonde.

"What's with the sneer, Valerie?" Mrs. Galloway asked from the office doorway. Val stopped typing. Was she sneering? She looked at Mrs. Galloway, in her perfect suit with her perfectly coiffed grey hair, and smiled politely.

"I didn't realize," she said apologetically.

"Is the report typed?" Mrs. Galloway asked as she shifted her slight weight from one foot to the other.

"I'm almost done. I just want to spell check it one last time," Valerie answered. Mrs. Galloway nodded curtly and stepped back into her office. Almost quitting time on Valentine's Day, and Val was not looking forward to going home and burying herself in chocolate ice cream and a box of tissue.

She picked up the report and knocked on Mrs. Galloway's door. "It's complete," she said. "I've included the extra figures you asked for, and even added an appendix comparing your service ratings with five other competitors."

"You're a very hard worker, Valerie," Mrs. Galloway said from behind her large, oak desk. "I'll tell the temp agency that I need you for another week or so." Valerie smiled as she handed over the report. "I want you to call custodial services. My damned window is leaking again," Mrs. Galloway said as she pointed to one of the windows that looked out onto the city. The window had been fixed just a few weeks ago, but when Valerie inspected it, she saw a few drops of moisture.

"Right away, Mrs. Galloway," she said and went back to her own office. She made the call and decided to answer her e-mails while she waited. A flash of grey caught her eye, and she looked up from her monitor to see a handsome woman standing before her, grinning. Val blinked a few times, but said nothing.

The woman raised her hand to her own left breast. "Jeri. Custodial." She tapped lightly at the nametag on her uniform. "You called me?"

Valerie stood up and motioned for her to follow. Mrs. Galloway was on the telephone, but indicated they should come in. She then turned her back on the pair, and continued to talk. "Franklin, I don't think you appreciate the opportunity here. If we're first into the Japanese market with this, we can beat them at their own game."

Valerie tuned her out. "The window leaks," she said as she pointed out the few water droplets.

Jeri stepped so close that she had to brush up against Valerie to see the problem. She simply nodded and put her toolbox down. Jeri bent over and opened her toolbox, grabbed a rag, and lifted her head slightly. She was level with Valerie's crotch. She took a big sniff in.

Mortified, Valerie stepped back. She glanced at Mrs. Galloway, relieved to see she had not noticed. Jeri carefully wiped the water away from the corner of the window and inspected the caulking.

"It needs a new bead," she said quietly, so she would not disturb the woman on the phone.

Valerie nodded, watching as Jeri cut away the old caulk. She shook her head, wondering if she had imagined the custodian actually sniffing her like a dog. *Just my imagination*, Val thought. *You are so lonely you'll think up anything*.

"Time to caulk," Jeri whispered.

There was a wildness in her eyes that at once thrilled and repelled Valerie. Jeri reached into her toolbox, took out a small tube of caulk, and began to massage the tube to loosen the caulk. She made a point of either flexing her biceps or stroking the tube in her strong fingers before squeezing it hard enough to force the white goo out of the tip. Valerie could not help but lick her lips as she watched Jeri run a finger expertly along the caulk, smoothing it to seal the window properly.

"All done," Jeri said as she wiped her fingers on the rag. "Anything else dripping?"

Valerie set her jaw tight. Jeri was flirting with her! "No, that's all the custodial work that is required, thank you," she said as she motioned toward the doorway. Jeri nodded and grabbed her toolbox. Together, they walked out of Mrs. Galloway's office.

Jeri turned unexpectedly and was standing right in front of

Valerie. "If you find any excess moisture anywhere, just call, and I'll be up. Lickety-split," she said, with an emphasis on the last two words. Valerie glared and pointed to the doorway leading to the hall. Jeri left without another word.

"Got any plans for Valentine's Day?" Mrs. Galloway called from her office.

"Not really, I—"

"Good. I need you to rewrite your report. I want an ROI added to each feature documented, and include an analysis of the methodology used to determine the ROI. Before you go home."

Valerie's heart sank. "It's Valentine's Day," she said softly. She had been planning on a good cry and some chocolate Double-Chunk Creamy-Hunk ice cream.

"It should only take a few hours. And besides," Mrs. Galloway said as reached for her coffee, "the traffic is miserable and you'd just waste your time in rush hour. This way, you work, you get paid, and then you can miss the worst of the traffic."

Val nodded silently as she took her report off Mrs. Galloway's desk. Her boss was on the phone again, and she leaned back in her chair to get comfortable. It squeaked out a protest as Mrs. Galloway waved Val back into her own office.

Valerie sighed as she plopped down into her chair, adding the report to the pile of other papers that covered her desk. She rummaged through her desk drawer for one of the many candy bars she kept for just such an occasion, then sat back to enjoy a five-minute break before hitting the keyboard again. She savored every scrumptious bite as she let her mind wander.

Before she knew it, she was picturing what Jeri might look like in a tight, white tank top, muscles rippling and skin glistening. Valerie shifted in her chair, glancing quickly at the doorway. Mrs. Galloway had turned around, and was looking out the window while on the phone with yet another important person. Valerie turned her chair slightly, wondering what Jeri's lips tasted like, if her kisses would be soft, or hard. *Hard*, Valerie thought, *and hungry*. She lost herself in Jeri's make-believe arms and passionate kisses, and without realizing it, she had dropped her hand to her lap to stroke her own thigh.

Checking on Mrs. Galloway, she fiddled quickly with her skirt, hiking it up so she could masturbate. It wasn't the first time, although she usually did it when Mrs. Galloway was in a closed-door meeting. Through her pantyhose, Valerie rubbed her clitoris in slow circles, quickly falling into her own rhythm. She imagined it was Jeri's fingers instead of her own, swirling around, rubbing her, searching her out, leading the way for her tender lips. As Valerie felt her cunt swell and throb, she pinched her clit a bit to hurry herself to orgasm. Closing her eyes, she imagined Jeri's head bobbing up and down between her legs. She moaned softly as her body shook with her climax, her hands hidden from view below the desk. Mrs. Galloway was none the wiser.

Mrs. Galloway didn't leave the office until almost an hour later. Valerie watched out of the corner of her eye as her boss wrapped a scarf around her neck and buttoned her coat. Mrs. Galloway brushed quickly past Valerie and breezed out the office door with a quick "Happy Valentine's Day," over her shoulder. There was no indication that she felt guilty leaving Valerie to work on such a romantic day.

"Happy Valentine's. Jerking off in my office. Whoohoo!" Valerie mumbled after the door shut behind her boss.

Mrs. Galloway popped her head back into the doorway, startling her. "And my chair squeaks. Get it oiled. Call custodial and have it fixed before morning. If they send that woman, don't let her be in my office alone. I don't trust her."

"Yes, Mrs. Galloway," Valerie said. Her boss headed out the door once again. She waited until she heard the chime of the elevator, then called custodial services. Only a few minutes passed before she heard the elevator chime again. She hoped it was Jeri—"that woman," as Mrs. Galloway called her. Jeri seemed a little rough around the edges maybe—perhaps just a bit too masculine in the uniform—but she flirted, and, in Valerie's imagination at least, she was a perfect lover.

A few moments later, Jeri walked through the doorway and into the office. "Hey," she said with a nod. She tapped her breast again as she touched her nametag. "Jeri," she said.

"Yeah, hi, Jeri. Mrs. Galloway's chair squeaks," Valerie said as she led Jeri into Mrs. Galloway's office. Valerie loved to be in Mrs. Galloway's office in the evening, and she watched for a moment as the sleet hit the window and trickled down. The lights of the city 14 storeys below seemed to sparkle like stars.

"Nice view," Jeri said, startling her.

"Oh, yes," Valerie replied when she caught her breath. "You can see the bridge from here."

"I didn't mean the window," Jeri said as she walked slowly into the office. Valerie turned, hiding her smile as she tried to play it safe. "You've been working here for a while now, right? We spoke on your first day. I don't know if you remember, but you asked me directions to Mrs. Galloway's office," Jeri said. Valerie nodded, watching as Jeri crossed the office floor and rounded the desk. "I notice you work late a lot of nights."

"Yes. Mrs. Galloway loves giving me work at the last minute," she said, looking around. The room was still dark, lit only by the outside light, but she could see Jeri's intense eyes. "You seem to notice me a lot."

"I've always admired you," Jeri said, approaching Valerie so they stood toe-to-toe. "I mean, you must be pretty smart to work here in bitch face's office, and you're really beautiful."

Val blushed. Sally had stopped calling her beautiful years ago, and it was nice to hear again. Jeri stared intently and slowly raised her hand to caress Valerie's face. Her hands were rough, strong, and persistent. Without a word, Jeri leaned in to kiss Valerie, softly at first, then with more passion when Valerie kissed back.

"Oh my God, what was that?" Valerie shrieked. "Was that the elevator?"

"I didn't hear anything," Jeri said. They both waited, listening intently, but heard nothing. "I think it was your imagination," Jeri said as she reached over and grabbed Valerie's breast. She squeezed a few times, but Valerie pulled away, still convinced that Mrs. Galloway was about to reenter the office.

Valerie stumbled toward the big wooden desk and tripped, spilling a small container of pens onto the floor. She fell to her hands and knees to retrieve the rolling tubes of plastic. Jeri knelt down behind her, but didn't touch the pens.

Jeri put her arms around Valerie, leaning across her back, pressing herself up against Valerie's ass.

"You have got to be kidding," Valerie hissed, the pens forgotten. Jeri's upper body pressed heavily against Valerie's back as she began to play with Val's breasts. The urgency of Jeri's hands took her by surprise, and she waited, on hands and knees, a little unsure of what to do. Should she push the woman off, order her out of the office and get back to work? Or should she just shut up and enjoy herself for a little while. Her nipples hardened quickly under Jeri's tender caresses, and Val had her answer. She leaned back, pressing herself into Jeri's crotch, and closed her eyes.

Jeri kissed Val's back and shoulders, tugging slightly at her top with her teeth. Her hands wandered down the sides of Valerie's body, then pulled her blouse free from her waistband. Jeri slipped one hand in and easily cupped her breast, while her other hand fumbled with the side zipper on Valerie's skirt.

Val's body tingled, but she felt a bit of pain shoot up her right arm. She couldn't continue to support both her weight and Jeri's on her weak wrists, so she leaned forward and rested on her elbows.

Jeri pulled back slightly, whispering in Valerie's ear, "I think I know what you'll like." She suddenly pushed Val's skirt up over her hips. Valerie caught her breath, her heart pounding. The sleet pelted against the window in a growing frenzy.

Jeri swiftly pulled Val's pantyhose and panties down around her knees in one motion, then pushed at Valerie's shoulders. Valerie complied, bringing her shoulders to the plush carpet, while leaving her ass up high. She gasped as Jeri pushed her thighs apart with her strong hands. Jeri leaned in to run her tongue along Valerie's exposed cunt, lightly sucking her lips. Valerie moaned and pushed back, eager for Jeri's tongue.

Jeri grabbed Val's round ass, raising her a little higher so she could better bury her face into Valerie's cunt. Sticking her tongue out as far as she could, she tickled Val's clit. With her nose buried in Valerie's folds, she inhaled deeply. She licked and nibbled Val's labia, sucking them into her mouth.

"That feels good Jeri. Eat me. Suck me!" Valerie pleaded.

Val swayed from side to side as Jeri slipped her right hand down her thigh. Her fingers joined her tongue, spreading Valerie's swollen red lips and playing with her clit. Jeri withdrew her mouth and slipped two fingers quickly and deeply into Valerie. Valerie gasped and looked back for a moment, catching only a glimpse of Jeri's grey uniform before her vision clouded over with pleasure. Jeri's rough hands knew what they were doing. She slipped a third finger in.

Valerie moved in rhythm to Jeri's fingers as they thrust deeper and deeper. "You feel so good inside me. Go deeper, deeper," Val moaned, rocking back and forth on her knees.

"I want to go so deep inside I touch your soul," Jeri said. "You're so beautiful, you make me come just thinking about you."

With her free hand, Jeri began to massage Valerie's ass, squeezing her cheeks firmly, running her fingers lightly along the crack. Her right hand kept thrusting while her left carefully separated Valerie's ass cheeks to reveal her bright, pink hole. With her mouth just inches away, Jeri blew warm air over Valerie's butthole, then ran her tongue a short way along Val's spine. Her lips moved randomly across her back and ass. Valerie's cunt was getting wetter with each thrust, each kiss. Her juices started to trickle down Jeri's hand, making it even easier to slide in and out. She slammed her fingers hard into Valerie's cunt.

"Fuck me harder!" Valerie gasped as Jeri's arm pumped madly.

Jeri knew it was the right time. She spread Val's ass cheeks as wide as she could. She stuck her tongue deep into Val's asshole, rolling it around in her velvety smoothness.

"Oh God! Your tongue!" was all Valerie could moan as Jeri rimmed her.

Jeri thrust her eager tongue in and out of Valerie's ass. Each time her hand went in, her tongue came out, doubling Valerie's pleasure. As her fingers withdrew slightly, her tongue went deeper into Valerie's tight butthole, her face pressing up against Valerie's white flesh. She pulled her tongue out and sucked on Val's pinkness, her lips kissing and licking it as Valerie moaned with pleasure. She was readying that cute asshole for one last assault.

"I'm coming!" Valerie gasped as Jeri continued fucking her. With one hand pounding wildly inside her, Jeri slipped her thumb into Valerie's well-lubricated asshole.

"Oh fuck! Yes!" Valerie screamed. "Jeri! Yes! That's it—"

Valerie dug her nails into the carpet, letting the waves of orgasm spill over her as Jeri fucked her cunt and ass with passion. Her muscles tightened, making Jeri move her thumb in increasingly faster circles, pushing deeper inside with every turn, every thrust. Pressed up against Valerie's flailing ass, Jeri watched her come. Come flowed from Valerie's dripping cunt and down Jeri's arm. Valerie buried her face in her arms, moaning loudly as another orgasm, and then another, rocked her. She had never done anything like this—had never been ass fucked, and it felt good.

Panting heavily, Valerie signaled Jeri to slow down. Without lubrication, her ass was beginning to feel sore. She had the best fuck of her life, had let orgasm after orgasm wash over her, but was coming down now. She relaxed her muscles, letting Jeri's ever slowing motions bring her back to earth. Jeri withdrew her thumb first, then her fingers, one at a time. Valerie collapsed onto her side, still breathing heavily, and looked at Jeri.

Jeri laid down beside Valerie, tenderly brushing a stray hair out of Val's face, then leaned in to kiss her.

"Be my Valentine?" Jeri asked with a smile. Valerie swallowed, and grinned back.

"You bet," she said softly.

Jeri laughed and propped up on one elbow. "Good. Catch your

breath, my turn next." She kissed Val passionately, hungrily taking her in, and was surprised when Valerie pushed her away. "What is it?"

"I don't want to fuck you in the office," Valerie said. "Take me home, Valentine."

Roses and Strawberries
Barbara Johnson

"I just love this time of year," Meghan said as she eyed the five men who entered the store. "The problem though," she continued, "is that if they're coming in here, they're already taken."

Kate looked up briefly but continued removing pairs of sexy underwear from a shipping box and tagging them. "Why don't you go? I helped the last customer."

Meghan snatched the red satin from Kate's fingers. "There's five guys out there. I can't help them all." She giggled. "Though I wouldn't mind helping out the two blondes, if you know what I mean."

Kate rolled her eyes. She'd been regaled many times with Meghan's fantasy of a hot threesome with two athletic blondes. Didn't she know reality rarely measured up to the fantasy? "Okay, let's go," she said as she came from behind the counter.

She sighed. While this might be Meghan's favorite time of year, it certainly wasn't hers. Besides the fact that she was single on Valentine's Day, she didn't take a job at Intimate Secrets so she could deal with men. No, she worked in a lingerie specialty shop so she could check out the women. Of course, the kind of women she was attracted to usually didn't come into the shop, unless, as Meghan had so perfectly stated, they were already taken. Still, the sight of a woman's nearly naked body was always a pleasure, even if she was straight.

"Can I help you find something?" she asked as she approached a tall man. He wore a business suit and looked distinctly uncomfortable. She was pretty tall herself, but she had to look up at him.

"Um, yeah." He shuffled his feet. "I need to get something for a friend."

"A girlfriend?"

He looked away, then at Kate again. "Well, she's my secretary."

Hmm, he's having an affair, she thought. She glanced at his left hand. No wedding ring, but that didn't mean anything these days. Either he was married, she was married, or both were married. Just not to each other.

"Perhaps some nice lounging pajamas?" She led him to a display. "We have some lovely silk ones."

"I don't know . . ."

"They could be something she would buy for herself," Kate added helpfully.

He looked relieved. "Really? Okay then, yes."

In honor of the upcoming holiday, most of the pajamas reflected the appropriate colors—lots of red and pink, and white ones with little hearts. She showed him a pale pink set with delicate rose embroidery. "These are very nice. Appropriate for Valentine's Day and yet not so overt like the ones with the hearts."

He nodded.

"Do you know her size?"

He looked her up and down, then glanced over at the amplebodied Meghan. "She's about her size," he said, pointing.

Kate pulled out a pair of large, then led him to the register. While she wrapped the gift in pink tissue paper and placed it in a silver box with a pink bow, she couldn't help but wonder what his story might be. Did he truly love his secretary? What circumstances kept them apart? Would he go to another store to buy something for the other woman in his life? Jewelry perhaps? Would they both get roses?

"Thank you so much, Mr. Adams," she said as she handed back his credit card along with the package. If he was indeed married, it wasn't smart to use his credit card at a store where he'd not bought a gift for the wife. "I hope she enjoys the pajamas."

He smiled. "You've been very helpful. Thank you."

"Kate," Meghan called out, "can you come help me?"

She walked over to where Meghan played queen to the other four men in the shop. They were all flirting and laughing while she showed them various thongs. Meghan, with her pretty green eyes and lustrous red hair, was always a draw to the male customers. And her full bosom and curvaceous figure helped too. Unlike Kate, who had the long, lanky figure of a ballerina, though she'd grown too tall to pursue the dance career of her young dreams. Kate had also traded her traditional dancer's long hair for a pixie cut. People told her the shorter style brought out the highlights in her dark-brown hair, but she still missed the pleasure of seeing a lover's eyes light up when she used to let her hair down.

"Bob here," Meghan said, "needs a push-up bra and panty set for his wife. He said she's a bean pole like you."

Bob had the decency to blush. "No disrespect," he said.

"None taken," Kate said, while mentally she pushed him and Meghan in front of a train. She led him away from the group. "We have a new line of bras that came in just in time for Valentine's Day. Do you know your wife's size?" It was amazing how many men did not know their wife's or girlfriend's sizes, even the ones who had been together for years.

Sure enough, he looked sheepish. "Can't say that I do. You'd think I would since we've been married five years."

"You say she's about my size?" Kate felt her cheeks redden as his eyes strayed to her chest. "I'm a thirty-six B."

"I'm not sure . . ."

"She can always exchange it."

"She'll get mad if I buy the wrong size."

Imbecile, she thought, why didn't you just look in her drawer? "If that happens, tell her we didn't have her size in stock, but you didn't want to just buy a gift certificate because that's not romantic."

His eyes lit up. "Great idea. Okay, what have you got?"

She showed him several different bras, all satin with lace or embroidery. He picked out a black demi-bra decorated with red and black lace, along with the matching bikini underwear. Kate personally thought it was one of the more trashier styles the store sold, belonging more in a bordello than a suburban bedroom. But she'd discovered in her five years of working at Intimate Secrets that most men wanted their women to be whores in the bedroom, and the lingerie they bought mimicked what they saw in men's magazines and on film. And given that Valentine's Day was only two days away, the store's inventory for the past three weeks had reflected male tastes more than those of its normal female customer base.

"I don't suppose you'd be willing to model them for me?" Bob asked with a lascivious grin.

Kate smiled, wanting nothing more than to punch him in the nose. "Not allowed."

Laughter at the thong table drew their attention. Really, hadn't Meghan talked the other three into anything yet?

"I bet *she'd* model them," Bob said, pointing with his head in Meghan's direction.

"She's married with six kids," Kate said. "Her husband's on the WWF circuit, and very jealous."

Bob looked like he didn't believe her, as well he shouldn't because she'd lied. Grumbling under his breath, he paid cash for his purchases. It made Kate wonder if the bra and panty set was indeed for his wife. Meghan and her admirers headed for the register just as Kate finished up with Bob.

"Can you help ring these up?" Meghan asked.

Given that no one else was in the store shopping, Kate couldn't really refuse. She didn't say anything as she rang up pairs of flimsy thongs decorated with rhinestones. It would have been cheaper if the men had just bought rhinestones and glued them to their girl-friends' bellies, but she rang up the thirty-five-dollars apiece items and wrapped them carefully in pink tissue paper. One of the guys was buying a white and pink corset.

"You need stockings to go with that?" Kate asked.

"Oh, yeah. You have the kind with seams up the back?"

"I'll get them," Meghan said. She brought over several sizes. After some discussion, the man settled on a pair.

"So, still want to fuck the two blondes?" Kate asked, after the customers had left.

Meghan leaned her elbows down on the counter and shook her head. "Nah." She sighed. "Men are so predictable."

"That's why I don't like them."

"Sometimes I think you have the right idea." Meghan shook her head at Kate's look of surprise. "No, I'm not coming over to the other side, but lesbians seem to have a whole different take on relationships." She straightened up and looked directly at Kate. "Speaking of which . . . you got any special plans for Valentine's Day?"

"Nope."

"What about that last one? Trish something or other?"

Kate went back to unpacking underwear. "Didn't work out. Her idea of fun was a six-pack of beer in front of the TV set watching whatever sports event she could find. And once football season was over . . . Well, she was just miserable, especially because I don't have cable."

Meghan laughed. "Sounds like you gay girls have the same problem us straight girls do. Sports widows."

Kate laughed too. "Yeah, sometimes it does work out that way. What about you? Do you have plans with Jimmy?"

Meghan grabbed a pair of sapphire-blue panties and tagged them. "Well, we've only been going out about three weeks, so it's kinda premature to think he'd do something romantic, don't you think?"

Kate smiled at the wistful look on her friend's face. She touched her arm. "Maybe he'll surprise you."

The bell above the door tinkled just then. Kate looked up and felt the blood rush to her face. It was Tracy, her ex. Their breakup six months ago had been bitter and acrimonious. They'd managed to avoid running into each other in the intervening months. Kate couldn't help but wonder why Tracy would now so blatantly came into the store.

"What the hell are you doing here?" Meghan said, voicing Kate's sentiments exactly. She was well aware of everything that had gone on.

Tracy, ever smug, did her butch swagger over to the counter. "Why, I'm here to buy a Valentine's Day gift, of course." Her toothy grin reminded Kate of a crocodile. "You got a problem with that?"

Meghan hurried out from behind the counter. "I'll take this," she said, shooting Kate a sympathetic look.

Tracy twisted the knife. "I've got a sexy, new girlfriend," she said with a backward glance at Kate. "The best I've ever had."

As she watched them walk away, Kate could feel the tears in her eyes. She angrily wiped them away. It wasn't like she cared one whit for Tracy anymore. What she did or who she was with was of no consequence. But the memory of her humiliation when she'd discovered Tracy in their bed with another woman who turned out to be a street hooker . . . Plus, the fact that Tracy had been verbally, and at times physically, abusive . . . It made Kate wonder anew how she could have so thoroughly lost her reason during the eight months she and Tracy had lived together after two months of dating. She'd sworn afterward that she'd never again fall prey to the lesbian penchant for moving in with someone she'd barely had time to know.

"My girl's got the best body in the universe," Tracy was saying, loud enough for Kate to hear. "I want something to show off every perfect curve."

"Maybe you'd prefer Dreamscape over on Fourth," Meghan said. "I hear they have crotchless, edible underwear."

"You've got a smart mouth on you," Tracy said, the displeasure obvious in her tone. "But I've always liked you, Meghan, so I'll let that comment slide. So, what about this little see-through number here?"

"I have to get out of here," Kate muttered as she headed for the door, feeling guilty at leaving Meghan alone with Tracy. In her rush to leave, she didn't hear the bell or see the customer walk in until she ran headlong into a solid body. She went crashing to the floor, feeling like a total idiot, her arms and legs all akimbo.

"I'm so sorry," a vaguely familiar voice said. "Are you okay?"

Kate looked up as someone took her arm. "Chris?" Meghan had also rushed over, and she and Chris now each held one of Kate's arms to lift her up. "I'm fine," Kate said. "What about you?"

"No bones broken," Chris said with a laugh.

"Hey, can I get some help over here?" Tracy called out.

Meghan shot Tracy a venomous look before heading back over to her. Kate turned to Chris. It had been months since they'd seen each other, but boy, did she look good. As she looked Chris over, Kate couldn't help but smile as she noted the still-athletic body and the deep blue eyes that reminded her of Jamaica's coastal waters. Her blonde hair was a darker shade now, but still cut short to control its unruly curls. Most of Chris's sports activities took place on or in the water, so she had no time for bad-hair days.

Kate had always harbored a secret crush on Chris, one that continued even after their brief fling three summers ago. Neither one had been in a place where a long-term relationship was feasible, so they continued on their separate ways after an amicable parting. Kate had eventually moved on to Tracy, but Chris, as far as Kate knew, had yet to settle down with anyone, though she'd every once in a while hear she'd been seen with someone.

"What brings you by?" Kate asked.

"I'm looking for a special gift for a special girl," Chris said, her deep voice still able to send shivers of delight up Kate's spine.

Hiding an intense pang of disappointment, Kate led Chris into the store, taking care to avoid Tracy and Meghan. "Did you have something particular in mind?" Please, don't let it be the usual bra and panty ensemble, she thought.

"We're kind of new, so I was thinking maybe a nice robe." She laughed. "Not the terry cloth variety though."

"Hey, Chris," Tracy butted in, "haven't seen you around. Got yourself some hottie keeping you home these days?"

Chris looked at Tracy like she was a flea on a dog. "That's none of your business, Tracy. Why don't you just buy your stuff and get out."

Tracy made a sound in her throat. "No need to be so unfriendly." She turned on her booted heel and followed Meghan to the register.

Chris touched Kate's arm. Her touch sent an electric jolt through Kate's body. "You okay?" Chris asked.

"Sure," Kate replied, not feeling quite so sure. She led Chris to a rack of robes. "These came in yesterday. Silk on the outside and cashmere on the inside. Wonderfully sensuous to the touch."

"Is this something you would like?"

Kate ran her fingers along the lapel's soft edge. "Oh yes, I'd like it. Just about any woman would, I think."

"That's good enough for me. What color?"

Kate looked into Chris's blue eyes. She felt like she could drown in them. Chris was looking at her expectantly, her lips pursed almost like she was waiting for a kiss. Kate swayed slightly. It would be so easy to lean in and kiss her, she thought. She took a deep breath and closed her eyes to break the spell. She turned back to the robes.

"I think the red is a bit too obvious and predictable. White is too bridal, pink too girly." She pulled a robe off the rack. "Black is a classic, and the silk fabric softens the color, I think."

"I like it too," Chris said.

"So, should I wrap this up for you?"

"Please."

Kate was shaking as she walked back to the register. She was amazed at her reaction to this woman. The spark that had fueled their summertime affair was still there. She felt herself blush as she remembered the sex they'd had. She hadn't had anyone as good before or since. How could she have let Chris get away?

Somehow she got through the rest of the sale without making a total ass of herself. She watched Chris leave, admiring her tight backside in her form-fitting jeans, and wondered if she'd see her again. It probably would be better if she didn't. It would take a while now to get Chris out of her system as it was.

"You like that girl, don't you?" Meghan asked. Her green eyes sparkled mischievously. "I think you should go for it."

"She was in here buying a Valentine's present for her girl-friend."

Meghan tossed a pair of lace panties into the box. "Story of our lives, ain't it?"

Kate smiled. "Well, my life at any rate." She looked at the clock. "Time for me to go. Janice should be here any minute."

She collected her purse and jacket and jogged down the mall to the Godiva store. Trying to save money for a new car, she'd taken on a second job. When she saw the line of customers outside the store snaking down the aisle and around the corner, she groaned. Why did they always wait until the last minute to buy their heart-shaped boxes of chocolate? Though she knew on Valentine's Day itself the line would be three times as long, tonight was still going to be annoying.

More than an hour later, Kate looked up to see Chris again. She was speechless for a moment. Twice in one day? Chris looked surprised to see her as well. "You work here too?" she asked.

"Just trying to make some extra money," Kate managed to say. "I take it you want some chocolates to go with the robe?"

Chris blushed. She looked so adorable. "Am I being too predictable?"

"You can never go wrong with chocolate. Can I suggest something a little different from the usual heart-shaped box?"

"Of course."

"I know you've stood in line for a long time, but come back early the morning of Valentine's Day and buy the chocolate-covered strawberries. She'll love them."

"You don't think it's a good idea to buy them tonight?"

"Well, you could, but they won't be fresh."

Chris smiled then. It took Kate's breath away. "You gave me good advice on the robe, so I'll heed it again and come back on Friday."

"Happy Valentine's Day," Kate said.

"Happy Valentine's Day to you too."

Kate was breathless as she arrived at Intimate Secrets that Friday. She was terribly late, and hoped Meghan wasn't too mad. It was going to be a horrendous day, she knew. There would eventually be four of them working, but in the early-morning hours it would be just the two of them. She'd get off work at five and was lucky she didn't have to work at Godiva too. Not that it would matter if she did. It wasn't as if she had plans for the evening.

"You're late," Meghan stated, but she didn't seem too angry, though there were already several customers browsing the store. She flicked her wrist. "Those came for you."

On the counter stood the biggest bouquet of roses Kate had ever seen. There had to be at least two dozen of the pale, gold-orange blooms. They looked like a tropical sunset. She snatched up the card. For Kate, the sweetest woman I ever knew, it read. Meet me tonight at Bella Notte at 7:00. The card wasn't signed.

Meghan danced over. "Who are they from? You've been keeping secrets from me."

"I swear," Kate said, thoroughly confused, "I have no idea who these are from. I'm not seeing anyone. Not even casually."

"Ah, a secret admirer then." Meghan sighed. "I'd settle for a single rose from Jimmy right now."

"I'd settle for some attention," an irate customer blurted.

The rest of the day passed in a blur. By five, Kate felt frazzled beyond belief. She and Meghan skipped out before their boss could beg them to stay. The roses took up the whole passenger seat, but she managed to get them home without spilling any water. She was excited, yet anxious, as she hurried to get ready for her evening out. Who would she find at the restaurant? And was it coincidence that it happened to be her favorite?

She gave herself the once-over before she headed out the door. Her cap of brown hair glowed with a healthy shine. She ran her hands through it, thinking once again that she should grow it out. She turned sideways, admiring the burgundy velvet dress that flattered her lean body, though she was wishing right now for some of Meghan's voluptuous curves. She also wore three-inch black heels, which put her at almost six feet. Would her mystery date feel intimidated? She sat down as she had a sudden horrible thought. What if it turned out to be a man? One of her customers? She took a deep breath. If that was the case, she'd politely thank him for the sentiment and take her leave.

She shrugged into her nicest wool coat and headed out into the cold February night. It felt like snow. The restaurant parking lot was crowded, but she lucked out as someone pulled out right near the entrance. "I'm meeting someone," she told the hostess as she unbuttoned her coat and scanned the room. It was hard to see, for the restaurant had turned the lights down so low she wondered at anyone being able to walk around. Flickering candlelight played across the faces of the laughing and smiling couples.

At an intimate corner booth, she caught a glimpse of someone she knew. Chris! She groaned. She hadn't seen this woman in over a year, and now she sees her three times in the course of one week? She was sitting alone at the moment, her date most probably gone to the restroom. Kate couldn't help but stare. Damn that woman looked good in a suit and tie!

"Do you see your party?" the hostess asked.

Kate shook her head. Was this going to be some kind of Valentine's humiliation? Stood up by someone she couldn't even name? Just as she decided to leave, Chris looked up and saw her.

Oh no, Kate thought, as she tried to hide behind her purse. This is just too embarrassing. Oh God, Chris was coming over.

"Hello, Kate."

Kate lowered her purse. "Chris. What a surprise."

"I was hoping you'd show up."

Confused, Kate asked, "Me?" Then it dawned on her. "Oh my God, this is a double date. You're trying to play matchmaker."

Chris laughed. "Not at all. I'm only here with one person."

"Oh." Kate looked around the room. All the tables were filled. No one else sat alone looking like they were waiting for someone. She *had* been stood up then.

Chris took her hand. Her touch sent shivers up Kate's spine. She felt her cheeks flush as a red-hot desire seared through her. She gasped at its intensity and snatched her hand away. "I have to go!"

Chris grabbed her arm. "Please. Wait."

"I can't. Your date will be out of the restroom any minute now."

Chris laughed again. "Darling," she said, "my date is you."

Totally confused now, Kate could only stare at her, dumbfounded. This was a dream, right? She'd wake up any minute now and find out none of it was true. She shook her head. No, she remembered getting the roses and the mystery card. The long, frantic day of helping men buy last-minute gifts for their sweethearts. No, this was not a dream. It was very real.

"But—" Kate said.

"I'm sorry," Chris said as she led Kate to their table and took her coat, "I thought you had figured things out."

Kate slid into the booth. "I had no clue."

The waiter magically appeared with two Caesar salads. He poured two glasses of Dom Perignon before slipping discretely away.

Chris took Kate's hands into her own. With each touch, Kate's body flamed with desire. She squirmed in her seat, wanting nothing more than to abandon the restaurant and go home—to bed with Chris. How tawdry was that?

"Like my card said, you're the sweetest woman I ever met. I don't think there's been a day gone by since we split up that I didn't think of you."

"I don't understand. If you felt that strong, why didn't you say something before now? It's been three years."

"What can I say? I was an idiot. I don't even remember now why we decided it wouldn't work for us. Our chemistry was so hot, besides the fact that we love doing a lot of the same things and we can talk about anything." She gently stroked Kate's hand. "I dated so many women after you, and found them all lacking. I realize now it was because no one measured up to you."

Kate thought back to the women she'd dated, and to her ill-fated relationship with Tracy. She found that she felt the same way. No one had really measured up to Chris. No wonder her love life had been such a disaster. She pulled her hands from Chris's and took a sip of champagne to collect her thoughts. Their salads remained untouched.

"Maybe we need to make up for lost time," she said, licking her lips suggestively.

Chris's blue eyes smoldered. "I'm ready when you are."

Kate stood and pulled on her coat. Chris quickly called the waiter over and paid, then followed her out to the parking lot, where she pushed Kate against her car. Gasping, Kate opened her mouth to Chris's tongue, feeling the rush of heat between her legs as Chris thrust a leg between them. Beneath the unbuttoned coat, Chris's hands followed the lines of Kate's body, from her narrow hips to her small breasts. She kissed Kate deeply, then moved her mouth to Kate's sensitive neck. Kate moaned, feeling the jolt go from her throat directly to her clit.

"You're naked under this dress," Chris said as her hand went to the hem and then up Kate's leg. Her fingers found Kate already swollen and wet.

Kate groaned. "Please," she whispered, "let's go home. Now!"

Laughing, Chris opened the car door and helped her in. On the short drive to her house, she continued to finger Kate, who sat with her legs spread and her dress ruched up around her thighs. Her touch inflamed Kate even more, making her arch back into her seat as her body trembled with desire and longing, her breath ragged.

Abruptly, Chris stopped, making Kate moan in frustration. "I don't want you coming just yet, my love," Chris said as she pulled into the driveway.

They hurried into the house, kissing wildly as they left a trail of clothes and shoes across the living room and into the bedroom with Kate completely naked while Chris still wore boxers and a T-shirt. Soft music already played in the background, while dim lights cast a golden glow. Kate smiled. Chris knew well how to plan in advance. The bed was strewn with gold-orange rose petals, and sitting in the middle was a silver box wrapped with a large pink bow, which Chris swept off without ceremony before pushing Kate onto the bed. The fresh cotton sheets were luxuriously soft and cool against Kate's bare skin. The scent of roses enveloped her.

Chris urged Kate's legs apart and lay between them, while her hands explored the lean planes of Kate's body. Her mouth was hot against Kate's neck. Kate moaned loudly as Chris brushed finger-tips over her sensitive nipples, making them stand erect, then gasped when Chris's warm mouth sucked one in while her fingers twisted and pulled the other. The sensation was exquisite, sending a shock to her clit and making her stomach leap. She could feel the wetness flow between her legs, and her knees raised almost invol-untarily. Chris growled as her free hand traveled down Kate's body, across her chest, over her belly, to between her legs. Kate's knees stayed raised but fell open, giving Chris easy access to her wet center. Chris's fingers teased and played, making Kate squirm with anticipation.

"Don't tease me," she pleaded.

Chris laughed. "You are impatient, my love. Tell me what you'd like."

"You know me well," Kate breathed as she thrust her pussy up against Chris's fingers.

Chris kissed Kate, her fingers still playing with and teasing nipples and wet lips. Their bodies grew slick together as Chris stayed between Kate's bent knees, their breasts touching. Her mouth and hands working independently and together to drive Kate insane with want and desire.

"I still want you to tell me," Chris whispered into her ear.

"I like when you fuck me," Kate said, feeling her cheeks flush with embarrassment.

Chris kissed her neck, hard. "I like that too," she said, before she took a nipple into her mouth and sucked. Kate arched under her. Smiling, Chris fumbled briefly under the pillow, then brought out a bottle of lube. She quickly slicked up her hand. Kate, watching, took a deep breath, feeling her vaginal walls clench in expectation, feeling the waves of desire and lust flow through her again and again.

Chris ran her lubed-up hand over Kate's belly, trailing downward to slid her fingers between Kate's swollen labia, sliding up and down and teasingly in and out. Kate was breathing erratically now, pushing into Chris's hand, kissing and biting Chris's neck. "Please," she said. "Please."

With a groan, Chris complied, thrusting her fingers deep. Kate cried out as she grabbed Chris's hair, her senses reeling—mouth and fingers biting and tugging her nipples, fingers and hand filling her, leaving her craving more. She dropped her knees to the bed, her dancer's flexibility leaving her spread wide open to be taken and plundered. She screamed as she felt Chris's whole hand shove inside her . . . raked her nails over Chris's wide, strong shoulders . . . felt the rhythm of their bodies as Chris fucked her.

"Chris," she called, over and over. "Chris!"

"You like being fucked, don't you, my love?"

"Yes, oh yes. Don't stop!" Kate flung her arms wide, grabbing hold of the sheet. Her hips arched upward as she took in all of Chris's hand and some of her wrist. "Sweet Jesus!"

And then Chris's mouth was on Kate's clit, sucking and licking, driving Kate to the brink and beyond. Time swirled away in a rush of fingers and tongue and lips and hands. Kate felt her orgasm build, her whole body tensing. And then she was coming again and again—one, two, three, all in succession. Chris had been the only woman who could ever do that to her. She gasped for air, feeling her body as one big nerve of pleasure.

"Come here, you," she said finally, grabbing hold of Chris's short curls and urging her upward.

Chris slid up, grinning. Her mouth and chin glistened with Kate's juices. "Damn, you're still as hot as you were three years ago."

Kate felt herself blushing again. It was true that no woman had ever fucked her like Chris did. Not even Tracy, who thought herself the Don Juan of lesbians. Maybe it was that she didn't trust other women like she did Chris? To let yourself be that vulnerable was risky in more ways than one—physically and emotionally. She traced her fingers along Chris's strong jaw line, then pulled her in for a kiss.

"I think I love you," Kate said after their long kiss. "I think I've always loved you."

"I love you too. We were silly to split up," Chris said. She leaned over and grabbed something from the bedside table. "I heard from a good authority that you like these."

Kate laughed delightedly as she beheld the gold Godiva box. "Strawberries?"

Chris nodded. "Chocolate covered."

Chris opened the box and took out a large strawberry, placing it in Kate's open mouth. She bit down, laughing as she felt the juice squirt down her chin. Chris leaned over and licked it off, the feel of her tongue sending new sparks of desire shooting through Kate's body. She wrapped her arms around Chris's neck, holding her close, taking her tongue deep into her mouth. She moaned as Chris once again thrust fingers inside her. Chris kept kissing her mouth . . . her neck . . . the tops of her shoulders . . . fucking her with her fingers while her thumb played with Kate's clit. It didn't take long for another orgasm to ripple through her.

Taking a final shuddering breath, she gently pushed Chris from her. "Dear God," she said, "that's never happened before. Not so soon after."

Chris chuckled, grinning broadly from ear to ear.

"You're very proud of yourself, aren't you?"

"Yes," she said as she took Kate into her arms. "You want another strawberry?"

About the Authors

M.C. Ammerman was born and raised on the East Coast and now lives in Los Angeles. She's still not sure how she got there, but she's glad she did. She prefers the longer form of the novel, but admits she's finding short stories fun, and a lot easier to finish.

Rachel Kramer Bussel is Senior Editor at *Penthouse Variations* and a Contributing Editor at *Penthouse*, where she writes the "Girl Talk" column. She writes the "Lusty Lady" column in the *Village Voice* and conducts interviews for Gothamist.com and Mediabistro.com. Rachel's books include *Naughty Spanking Stories from A to Z*, 1 and 2; *Up All Night: Adventures in Lesbian Sex*; *The Lesbian Sex Book*, 2nd edition; and the forthcoming *Glamour Girls: Femme/Femme Erotica* and *First-Timers: True Stories of Lesbian Sex*. Her writing has been published in more than 60 anthologies, including *Best American Erotica 2004* and *2006*; *Best Lesbian Erotica 2001, 2004*, and *2005*; *Best of the Best Lesbian Erotica*; and *Call of the Dark*, as well as *AVN, Bust, Cleansheets, Curve, Diva, Girlfriends, New York Post, On Our Backs*, Oxygen.com, *Punk Planet, Rockrgrl,*

The San Francisco Chronicle, *Time Out New York*, *Velvetpark*, and others. Visit her Web site at www.rachelkramerbussel.com.

Australian erotic writer *D. D. Cummings* has been widely published, having had more than 150 short stories accepted for publication with companies such as *Playgirl*, The Score Group, *Swank*, *Hustler*, *The Best Lesbian Fiction 2006*, *The Hot Spot*, *Forum*, *Red Scream Magazine*, *Skin Deep 2* (Alyson Books), *New Woman*, *Diverse Publication*, *The Mammoth Book of Female Fantasies*, *Bettina's Can't Help It* (Collective in the UK), *Delicate Friction* (Haworth Press), and many more. Visit her Web site at www.extasybooks.com.

Cleo Dare is the author of *Melting Point*, a mystery novel, and *Cheek of Night*, a romance novella. Under the pseudonym R.C. Brojim, she wrote the first book in the Minority Fleet space adventure series, *Cognate*. Watch for *Brushstrokes*, her new Cleo Dare adventure; and *Faultless*, her next Minority Fleet installment in 2006.

Cherokee Echols was born in Kings County, California, and raised in Oklahoma. She received her B.S. in Criminology from OSU. She has worked in the petroleum industry since 1987 in several positions, including Emergency Responder specializing in High-Angle Confined-Space rescue. She likes anything she has to straddle (motorcycles, wet bikes, horses, and, of course, women).

Denny Evans: Who am I? Good question. Passers-by on the street in The Netherlands where I live would assume I was your stereotypical conservative woman, but in answer to their assumptions I can only smile and echo the old saying, "Still waters run deep." I enjoyed my story. I hope you do, too.

Pam Graham is a writer with a graduate degree in astrophysics. Put another way, she majored in heavenly bodies. Politics, animal rights, and the environment are chief interests. Hobbies include running and lifting weights. Pam lives in Kentucky with her partner of seventeen years. Visit her Web site at http://www.pamgraham.net.

Lynne Jamneck is a South African writer and photographer currently living in New Zealand. Secretly, she would have loved being a rock star, but since she cannot sing to save her life, the writing, which she seems to have some talent for, was the next best thing. Her fiction has been published in numerous tasty anthologies, including *Best Lesbian Erotica 2003*, *The Good Parts*, *Call of the Dark: Lesbian Tales of the Supernatural* (Bella Books), and *Hot Lesbian Erotica* (Cleis). The first book in her Samantha Skellar mysteries is available from Bella Books. She is the creator and editor of *Simulacrum: The Magazine of Speculative Transformation* (www.specficworld.com/simulacrum.html). She can be reached at lynnejamneck@xtra.co.nz.

Melinda Johnston is a Vancouver, BC, writer who has been published in *The Good Parts*, *Hot & Bothered 4*, *Xtra West*, and *Outlooks*. She has also made two digital videos and is working on a third.

Karin Kallmaker is descended from Lady Godiva, a fact that pleases her and seems to surprise no one. The author of more than 20 novels (including the award-winning *Sugar* and *Maybe Next Time*), she recently expanded her repertoire to include erotica with *All the Wrong Places*. As Karin says, "Nice Girls Do." She fell in love with her best friend at the age of 16, and still shares her life with that same woman, and their two children, nearly 30 years later. Visit her Web site at www.kallmaker.com.

Jennifer Lawicki is a 25-year-old Administrative Assistant from Buffalo, NY. She received her B.A. in History from Canisius College in 2002, and spends lots of her time reading and writing about the supernatural. She plans to pursue her Masters in 2006.

Sue Molyneaux has been writing for far longer than she should ever admit. She is the author of *Ice Quest*, and works in an office, but not with Jeri. She is married to long-time partner Kelly, and lives in Toronto with two furry, four-legged children. This is her first erotic story.

Heather Osborne is a speculative fiction writer from Calgary, Alberta. She is a member at large of the Imaginative Fiction Writers' Association. Her work has appeared in *Legacy Magazine* and two anthologies: *In Places Between* and *Call of the Dark*.

Joy Parks writes articles, interviews, and book reviews for the *San Francisco Chronicle*, *The Advocate*, and many other GLBT and mainstream publications. "Sacred Ground," her column on lesbian books, can be found at www.gaylinkcontent.com and in a number of print and online publications. She began writing fiction as a 40th birthday present to herself and her stories appear in *Back to Basics*, *Hot & Bothered 4*, and *Call of the Dark*. She lives in Ottawa, Canada, and is (of course!) working on a novel.

Radclyffe, having practiced surgery for 30 years while writing for pleasure "on the side," established Bold Strokes Books, Inc., a lesbian publishing company in 2004, and retired from medicine to write and publish full-time in May 2005. In addition to writing, she collects lesbian pulps, enjoys photographing scenes for her book covers, and shares her life with her partner, Lee, and assorted canines.

Her lesbian romances include *Safe Harbor* and its sequels *Beyond the Breakwater and Distant Shores*, *Silent Thunder*, *Innocent Hearts*, *Love's Melody Lost*, *Love's Tender Warriors*, *Tomorrow's Promise*, *Passion's Bright Fury*, *Love's Masquerade*, *Shadowland*, and *Fated Love*; two romance/intrigue series: the Honor series (*Above All, Honor, Honor Bound, Love & Honor*, and *Honor Guards*) and the Justice series (*Shield of Justice*, the prequel *A Matter of Trust*, *In Pursuit of Justice*, *Justice in the Shadows*, and *Justice Served*; two erotica collections: *Change of Pace: Erotic Interludes* and *Stolen Moments: Erotic Interludes 2* edited with Stacia Seaman, and selections in numerous anthologies.

Nicolette Rivers is married and living in the wilds of northern Minnesota. She loves animals, *Buffy the Vampire Slayer*, long walks on frigid Midwestern beaches, and—of course—old sitcoms. Her dream is to discover a recipe for no-cal cheesecake, then she can die with a smile on her face.

Ellen Tevault lives in Indiana with her hersband of eight years, Melissa. Her short stories have been published in *Common Lives/Lesbian Lives*, *Early Embraces III*, and as Fred Towers in *Bearotica*. In addition, she has had articles published in *Reading in Indianapolis*, *AdLib*, *ISL Connection*, and the *Encyclopedia of Indianapolis*.

krysia lycette villón is a mixed-race Latina femme dyke of Peruvian and Polish descent and is married to the love of her life. She's the daughter of musicians and is the oldest of five beautiful children. Born and raised in the Boston area, she currently lives in western MA. krysia received her B.A. from Mount Holyoke College in 1996, where she began her path first as a poet and then as a writer. Her work has since been published in various literary journals, magazines, and anthologies. She enjoys performing her work and can sometimes be found rattling papers and fondling microphones in dimly lit cafés and college campuses.

Vicky 'Dylan' Wagstaff. I am a new gal to the world of writing. I only picked it up over the last 18 months or so to stretch the limits of my dirty little mind. I live in England on my own, in a semi-reclusive state due to far too many hours spent attempting to hone any skill at writing I may have by littering the world of fan fiction with my paltry attempts at erotica. This is my second published story, but hopefully not my last as I have plans for more and am some way into my first book attempt.

MJ Williamz, a true romantic who believes every day should be celebrated like Valentine's Day, lives in Portland, Oregon. The fresh northwest air and the women who enjoy it provide plenty of fodder for her imagination. MJ has had several short stories published and is working on her first novel.

Kristina Wright's fiction has appeared in more than 20 anthologies, including *Call of the Dark: Erotic Lesbian Tales of the Supernatural* (Bella Books), *Ultimate Lesbian Erotica 2005* and *2006*

(Alyson Books), and *Best Lesbian Erotica 2002, 2004,* and *2005* (Cleis Press). She lives in Virginia and is pursuing a graduate degree in Humanities. For more information about Kristina, her writing, and the real Bubba Chryst band, visit her Web site at www.kristinawright.com.

About the Editors

An incurable romantic, *Barbara Johnson* loves being wooed by starry-eyed butches bearing flowers, jewelry, and sinful selections from Victoria's Secret. But all she really wants on Valentine's Day is "a simple, heart-shaped box of chocolates." Preferably Godiva, of course.

Barbara is the best-selling author of *Stonehurst*, *The Beach Affair*, *Bad Moon Rising*, and *Strangers in the Night*. Her short stories have appeared in almost a dozen anthologies, including Bella Books' *Back to Basics: A Butch-Femme Anthology* and *Call of the Dark: Erotic Lesbian Tales of the Supernatural*. She's written two novellas for Bella: "Charlotte of Hessen" in *Once Upon a Dyke: New Exploits of Fairy Tale Lesbians* (a 2005 Lambda Literary Award finalist) and "Sea Witch" in *Bell, Book and Dyke: New Exploits of Magical Lesbians*. Her third novella, "Running with Stone Ponies," will appear in the upcoming *Stake Through the Heart: New Exploits of Noire Lesbians*.

Therese Szymanski, having been frequently accused of not being a romantic, thought editing this book might help her chances of getting a date on a Saturday night. She's written seven books in the Lammy Finalist Brett Higgins Motor City Thrillers and edited *Back to Basics: A Butch-Femme Anthology* (which made the Publishing Triangle's list of notable lesbian books for 2004) and *Call of the Dark: Erotic Lesbian Stories of the Supernatural.* She wrote "A Butch in Fairy Tale Land" for the Lammy finalist *Once Upon a Dyke: New Exploits of Fairy Tale Lesbians* and "By the Book" for *Bell, Book and Dyke: New Exploits of Magical Lesbians.* She's been shortlisted for a Spectrum Award, contributed to a few dozen anthologies, and is an award-winning playwright. She enjoys backpacking, all forms of skiing, and anything else she can hurt herself doing. Somehow, through the years and sometimes without her consent, she's started collecting swords, Zippos, and bears. She keeps herself apartmented by copywriting and designing. You can e-mail Reese at tsszymanski@worldnet.att.net—preferably not to try to sell her a new penis-enlarging device.

Publications from
BELLA BOOKS, INC.
The best in contemporary lesbian fiction

P.O. Box 10543, Tallahassee, FL 32302
Phone: 800-729-4992
www.bellabooks.com

MURDER AT RANDOM by Claire McNab. 200 pp. The Sixth Denise Cleever Thriller. Denise realizes the fate of thousands is in her hands. 1-59493-047-3 $12.95

THE TIDES OF PASSION by Diana Tremain Braund. 240 pp. Will Susan be able to hold it all together and find the one woman who touches her soul? 1-59493-048-1 $12.95

JUST LIKE THAT by Karin Kallmaker. 240 pp. Disliking each other—and everything they stand for—even before they meet, Toni and Syrah find feelings can change, just like that. 1-59493-025-2 $12.95

WHEN FIRST WE PRACTICE by Therese Szymanski. 200 pp. Brett and Allie are once again caught in the middle of murder and intrigue. 1-59493-045-7 $12.95

REUNION by Jane Frances. 240 pp. Cathy Braithwaite seems to have it all: good looks, money and a thriving accounting practice . . . 1-59493-046-5 $12.95

BELL, BOOK & DYKE: NEW EXPLOITS OF MAGICAL LESBIANS by Kallmaker, Watts, Johnson and Szymanski. 360 pp. Reluctant witches, tempting spells, and skyclad beauties—delve into the mysteries of love, lust and power in this quartet of novellas. 1-59493-023-6 $14.95

ARTIST'S DREAM by Gerri Hill. 320 pp.When Cassie meets Luke Winston, she can no longer deny her attraction to women . . . 1-59493-042-2 $12.95

NO EVIDENCE by Nancy Sanra. 240 pp. Private Investigator Tally McGinnis once again returns to the horror filled world of a serial killer. 1-59493-043-04 $12.95

WHEN LOVE FINDS A HOME by Megan Carter. 280 pp. What will it take for Anna and Rona to find their way back to each other again? 1-59493-041-4 $12.95

MEMORIES TO DIE FOR by Adrian Gold. 240 pp. Rachel attempts to avoid her attraction to the charms of Anna Sigurdson . . . 1-59493-038-4 $12.95

SILENT HEART by Claire McNab. 280 pp. Exotic lesbian romance. 1-59493-044-9 $12.95

MIDNIGHT RAIN by Peggy J. Herring. 240 pp. Bridget McBee is determined to find the woman who saved her life. 1-59493-021-X $12.95

THE MISSING PAGE A Brenda Strange Mystery by Patty G. Henderson. 240 pp. Brenda investigates her client's murder . . . 1-59493-004-X $12.95

WHISPERS ON THE WIND by Frankie J. Jones. 240 pp. Dixon thinks she and her best friend, Elizabeth Colter, would make the perfect couple . . . 1-59493-037-6 $12.95